GOODBYE SWEETHEART

GOODBYE
SWEETHEART

Lilian Harry

LONDON NEW YORK SYDNEY TORONTO

This edition published 1994
by BCA
by arrangement with Orion Books

CN 9705

Printed and bound in Great Britain by
Mackays of Chatham PLC, Chatham, Kent

'To my Mother and Father.
With all my love. Lilian Harry.'

CHAPTER ONE

THE BUDD BROTHERS, Tim and Keith, came roaring up the garden path and in through the back door of number 14 April Grove as if the devil were after them. Their faces were grimy, their shirts hung half out of their short trousers and their socks were wrinkled round their ankles. They looked as if they had just fought in some historic battle and their eyes blazed with the triumph and delight of victors.

'We won!' Tim yelled as they burst into the small back room, jostling to be the first with the news. 'We won! We beat 'em hollow.'

Jess Budd, pregnant at forty with her fourth child, put out a hand to save her teacup from being knocked over. Her sister Annie, who lived at the top of the street, tutted and grabbed at the plate of biscuits that were about to be sent flying.

'Is that the way to come bursting in on your Ma of a Saturday afternoon?' she demanded. 'Can't she get any rest? And look at your boots, covered in mud – what've you been doing, mudlarking?' She touched her newly waved dark hair, cut to ear length in the latest fashion, and drew her skirt closer around her legs. She was wearing her new rayon frock today and wanted Jess to remark on it. So far, to her annoyance, she didn't even seem to have noticed.

'Certainly not,' Jess said sharply. 'Frank and me don't allow any mudlarking.' She looked at her sons. She knew quite well where they had been – down at the newspaper offices in Stamford Street, waiting for the football results, though how anyone could get that dirty just waiting in the street only boys would know. 'Quieten down, the two of you, and tell us what you're on about.'

'We told you – we've won,' Tim said impatiently. At almost ten years old, he was the elder of the two boys, though a childhood illness had left him the smaller. His curly hair was tousled and his hazel eyes sparkled. 'We beat 'em four-one. Four-one.' Forgetting his muddy boots, he began to dance a jig around the dining-table that took up most of the room, and chanted, 'Pompey's won the Cu-up, Pompey's won the Cu-up.'

Keith, nearly two years younger but chubbier than his brother, with a round face and dark brown eyes like his mother's, took up the chant too and Jess waved her hands at them for quiet.

'The Cup? You mean that football cup? Is that what all this fuss is about?' Annie asked, knowing very well that it was, and the boys stared at her as if she had just come down from the moon.

'You must know it's the Cup Final today, Auntie,' Tim said. 'It's all people have been talking about. Portsmouth's been playing against Wolverhampton, at Wembley. The King's presenting it to the captain. You must know about it. Uncle Ted would know.'

'Well, maybe I did hear something about it,' Annie said offhandedly, and Jess smiled. It was one of Auntie's habits to ignore football completely, mainly because she didn't like the interest her husband took in it. 'Just like little boys,' she'd say scornfully when he and Jess's husband Frank came home for their tea discussing the latest match. And she didn't have much more patience with her nephews. 'You'll grow up just like your dad,' she told them now. 'Football mad.' She watched as the two boys, unable to keep still, grabbed a biscuit each and clattered out into the garden again. 'The whole town's gone crackers,' she went on, 'and for what? Twenty-two grown men chasing a ball around a field. Don't they have anything better to do?'

'It's not so much a question of have nothing better to do,' Jess said quietly. 'Seems to me too many people have got something worse to do these days.' She looked out of the window at her sons, now capering up and down the garden path pretending to be footballers, but her brown eyes were abstracted. 'And if the boys grow up to be like their dad, I'll be more than pleased. He's a good man, is my Frank, and so's your Ted.'

2

She pushed back a tendril of hair, the colour of beechnuts and almost untouched as yet by grey. She'd washed it after dinner and it wasn't properly dry yet. Perhaps Annie would do it up for her before she went.

'Oh, I know,' Annie said. 'I was just teasing them, that's all. You don't want to take any notice of me.'

She reached over and poured more tea, and Jess watched her fondly. Annie was a bit sharp sometimes but she was good-hearted enough, and a good sister. And she was right, in a way. There was more to life than football, even if Pompey had won the coveted Football Association Cup. The news everywhere else was bad – countries all over the world at each other's throats, it seemed, what with Italy invading Albania and Germany invading Czechoslovakia and now it looked as if Hitler was going to go back on his promise not to invade Poland. And only a few weeks ago, Britain and France had joined forces to protect Poland, so if he did . . .

Jess didn't want to think about what might happen if Hitler went ahead with his plan. But it was impossible to ignore, for the reminders were everywhere – trenches being dug up in the parks, talk of air raids, gas attacks, invasion . . .

For people like her and Frank, who had already been through the Great War, it was frightening. And they said this time it'd be worse.

Unconsciously, she covered her stomach with her hands and Annie's sharp eyes noticed the movement.

'How're you feeling today, Jess? Got over that heartburn?'

'Not really. The baby's riding too high – I had it right through with the others anyway.' She sighed and shifted a little in her chair. 'It's the sciatica really gets me down. Sometimes I can hardly sit comfortably, it's like toothache all down my leg. The doctor says the baby's pressing on a nerve and there's nothing he can do about it.'

'Well, I suppose you can't expect much else at your age,' Annie remarked, and Jess sighed. She knew a good many people disapproved of her having another baby at forty, but she and Frank had talked about it and agreed that they wanted one, while there was still time. Another two or three years and it could be too late.

3

And when Mr Chamberlain had come back from Munich at the end of September last year, waving a piece of paper and declaring that it was 'peace in our time' the omen had seemed too good to ignore.

Peace in our time! A phrase full of hope for a world that had, after all, averted catastrophe. Along with twenty thousand others, she and Frank had gone to the Peace Thanksgiving Service in the Guildhall Square and sung hymns to the accompaniment of the Royal Marine bands. The sound of rejoicing had filled the air, bringing tears to the eyes of almost all who stood there, and on the Guildhall steps the Lord Mayor and the Bishop of Portsmouth had given thanks with the rest.

Jess and Frank had strolled home arm in arm, Jess with eleven-year-old Rose clinging to her other arm and the two boys walking in front, quiet for once. The October air was mild, with a hint of smoke in the air from the first fires of the autumn, and that night they had lain in bed, relief drawing them close. The world which had been teetering on the brink of disaster was once again a safe place.

What better time to have a baby?

And by the time the bitter knowledge had dawned that the 'peace' was no more than an uneasy respite, that war loomed blacker and larger than ever, it was too late. Jess was pregnant and the world a dark and dangerous place to be born into.

The boys came dashing back through the door.

'Mum! Mum! Can we go down the railway station, see the team come back? Bob Shaw next door says they'll be bringing the Cup. Can we, Mum?'

'Are you going to be with Bob?' Jess asked, and they nodded vigorously. 'All right, then, but mind you're back before dark. I don't want you roaming round the streets. And no mischief, mind.'

She watched as they tore away down the garden path. 'Bob Shaw's good to them. There's not that many lads of nineteen will bother with two boys like Tim and Keith, taking them swimming and fishing when their father can't spare the time. And Peggy and Bert are good neighbours too, always ready to give a hand.'

'Hm.' Annie pursed her mouth. Like Jess, she wore no make-up save for Pond's vanishing cream and a dusting of powder. 'I don't know about the girls, though – that Diane's altogether too flighty

4

and knowing for a girl of fifteen, and Gladys thinks she's grown up now she's eighteen and been out at work a few years. And you know – ' She broke off to pick up the brush and comb and start working on Jess's hair. 'I don't know why you don't get this lot cut off. It'd look ever so much smarter, it's got a nice wave in it.'

Jess smiled. 'Frank likes it this way. Go on, what were you going to say about Gladys?'

'Oh, nothing at all. Only that she took a fancy to our Colin before he went off to sea, you knew that, didn't you?'

Jess nodded. Her own daughter Rosemary was barely twelve and inclined to look up to the girls next door, and Jess had already had a few worries about what she might be learning from them. The Shaws weren't quite so strict with their daughters as Ted and Annie.

Annie was eight years older than Jess and had married at twenty. To Jess, she had always been 'grown up', more like a mother than a sister, and it was only when Jess had had her own family that they had drawn closer as friends. But Jess had always been a welcome visitor at Annie's home, and had helped with her sister's children from the time they were born. Olive and Betty and their brother Colin, now twenty-five and the pride of Annie's heart when he came swaggering down the street in his bell-bottoms, meant almost as much to Jess as her own three did.

'How's your Olive getting on with her Derek?' she asked. 'He seems a nice enough young chap.'

'He is.' Annie's mouth was full of hair-grips. 'She's asked him to tea a few times. Got good manners and no side to him, for all his dad's her boss.'

Jess leaned away for a moment to pour more tea. 'Think anything'll come of it? It'd be a good match for her.'

Annie pursed her lips again. 'Who can tell? They seem fond enough of each other, and I suppose she's old enough to get engaged. But you know what Ted's like. He won't have either of the girls getting serious too young. He didn't even like them going out with boys till they'd turned eighteen and I must say I think he was right. You don't know what they might get up to these days, not like when we were young.'

Jess nodded. Annie had had her share of suitors as a girl, but chose to forget them now. None of them had been 'serious' she would declare. And Jess had had no other boyfriends before she met Frank. If she had, she knew their father would have been every bit as strict as Ted. Home by ten o'clock unless they'd asked permission to be out later, and no string of boys knocking at the door. One at a time was the way he and their mother had believed in, anything else made a girl look 'cheap' and 'common', and got her a bad name.

That was the trouble with Peggy Shaw's two. Gladys was always out somewhere, often not getting home till gone eleven, and Diane spent far too much time on street corners, talking to boys. Jess was surprised at Peggy for allowing it, especially when they had the example of Nancy Baxter at number 10 before them . . .

'And what about Betty?' Betty had been a tomboy, wanting nothing more than to shadow her brother Colin whenever he was home on leave from the Navy, and had usually been found playing cricket and football with the boys in the street rather than joining the girls with their dolls and skipping. It was all right when she was a child but Ted and Annie had been worried that she might be turning into a flirt.

'Betty? I don't know – she doesn't let on much. Ted reckons she's getting too saucy, but I tell him she can't get up to much mischief working in the dairy at the top of the street. She keeps talking about getting something else – something more exciting, if you please!' Annie sniffed. 'Exciting! I asked her what she meant by that and she said she didn't know. She's all mixed up, that's her trouble. Doesn't want to be a boy any more and doesn't know how to be a girl.' She put down the brush and fixed the last grip in the knot on Jess's neck.

'Still, I daresay she'll sort herself out,' Jess said. 'Most girls are a bit here and there at her age.'

Annie nodded. 'Well, I'd better be going. I promised Mum and Dad I'd slip down and see them this afternoon. And then Ted'll be in for his tea, full of this Cup Final win, I daresay. I wouldn't be surprised if they've dressed the ferryboat overall in honour of the occasion!'

Jess laughed. Ted was a skipper on one of the boats which plied between Portsmouth and Gosport and as proud of his little craft as an admiral of his fleet.

6

'It'll be all over the front page of the *Evening News* too,' Annie went on. 'Well, I suppose it's better than talking about war, which is all we seem to get these days. Gas attacks, digging trenches in the parks – it's enough to turn you cold. Trenches! What good are they going to do us if war breaks out?'

'We're supposed to be getting shelters,' Jess said. 'Anderson shelters for the garden. And they'll be digging big ones in the streets for people who haven't got gardens.'

'And do you suppose they'll be any good if a bomb hits 'em?' Annie asked scornfully. 'They're expecting hundreds, thousands, every night. What use will a few tin huts be then?'

Jess was silent. Like her sister, she could remember the air raids over London in the last war – and they said this lot would be far, far worse.

That time, the Germans had used mostly Zeppelins, huge airships that looked terrifying as they loomed overhead but didn't do very much damage. This time, they had hundreds – perhaps thousands – of aircraft, able to fly faster and farther than ever before, carrying huge loads of bombs. Their navy had ships such as had never been seen at sea before and their army had been training for years, before they'd even begun to invade the other countries of Europe.

They want to take us all over, she thought with a jab of fear. And what can we do to stop them?

She felt the baby kick inside her and clasped her fingers together, as if in prayer, over the heaving bulge. Stay there, she begged it silently, just stay there inside me where you'll be safe. Don't get born.

But she knew that if war came, nowhere in Portsmouth would be safe. With one of the naval dockyards and harbours as target, she and Frank and the children would be in the front line.

Annie was watching her with concern.

'Are you all right, our Jess? You've gone dead white.' An expression of self-annoyance creased her face. 'That's me, I suppose, opening my big mouth and putting my foot in it as usual. Look, you don't want to take no notice of me. I don't suppose there'll be a war anyway, not when it comes down to it. The King can't be expecting it, after all – he wouldn't be going to Canada

7

next week if he thought we were going to be at war.' She picked up yesterday's edition of the *Evening News*, which had been lying on a chair. 'Here – it tells you about their itinerary in Portsmouth on their way to the ship – arriving by train, they'll be, him and and the Queen, and then walking through to the Guildhall and driving down to the Southern Railway Jetty. They reckon there'll be two thousand children lining the route. And the Princesses will be with them.' Annie looked down at Jess. 'Why don't we go and see them?'

Jess puckered her face. 'I don't know, Annie. Not in all those crowds, the way I am.'

'No, you're right, better not. But I might go. I could tell you all about it, what they were wearing and that. Be something to cheer us up a bit.'

'That's right,' Jess said, 'you do that.'

She took back the paper. Annie was easily enough cheered up. But she hadn't read the rest of the news. The mention of compulsory military training for all men over twenty years old. The plans for evacuating the city's children.

It all made war seem very close.

Annie was still watching her face. She put out a hand and touched her sister's knee.

'Hitler'll back off – sure to. You don't want to worry, Jess.'

Jess smiled at her. That was Annie all over, first letting fly and then remembering that Jess was her baby sister – even at forty! – and had to be petted and soothed. But no amount of petting and soothing was going to stop this war coming, and they both knew it, even though until it was properly declared everyone had to put on a pretence of hoping.

'I'm all right,' Jess said. 'Just a bit of a twinge . . . Thanks for popping in, Annie. Give Mum and Dad my love and tell them I'll be in on Tuesday, when I've been to the doctor's . . . And I like your new frock. It suits you. And the hairdo.'

Annie looked at her for a moment, then smiled. 'And I thought you hadn't noticed.'

'Go on with you,' Jess said, rising clumsily to her feet and gathering up the cups. 'Of course I noticed, the minute you walked in. I was just teasing you – like you teased Tim and Keith. Football, new frocks – we're all the same when it comes down to it, aren't we?'

8

Olive Chapman was spending Saturday afternoon walking along Southsea seafront with her young man, Derek Harker. They had gone out in one of the vans belonging to Derek's father, who ran the building business where Olive worked. She had been in the office for six months now, having moved there from her previous office job at a garage, and had been going out with Derek for three of those months.

She still couldn't quite believe her luck. Derek was one of the best-looking boys in the Copnor area, a good six foot tall with dark gold hair carefully combed into waves and shiny with Brylcreem. He dressed well too, with a suit for weekdays and a Fair Isle pullover and grey slacks for weekends. And he had a good job with a local firm of accountants as well as helping his father with the business.

'Of course, I'll take over one of these days,' he said carelessly as they strolled along. 'The old man's bound to want to retire before too long. And he deserves a rest – he's worked hard, building it up. There's not another builder in Portsmouth can touch him, you know.'

'I know.' Olive hugged his arm. It was cool today, with a wind blowing straight up the beach from the sea and whipping her chestnut hair around her face. She was glad she'd worn her new spring jacket. It was a light green tweed with a big collar and a wide belt and she'd put on a dark green skirt to go with it. It looked unconventional but Derek had given a little whistle when he saw her, and that was enough for Olive.

They stopped for a while to look across the Solent at the Isle of Wight. It was very clear, the buildings of Ryde and Shanklin showing up sharply on the horizon, and the wind was tossing the sea into a thousand dancing white horses. Between Southsea and the island could be seen the Spithead Forts, the three grim-looking bastions that had been built there over a century ago to protect England's southern shores from invasion. Olive stared at them and shivered.

'Cold?' Derek slipped his arm round her waist and Olive felt a sudden thrill of excitement. Derek often put his arm round her, especially when he was walking her home at night, and sometimes in the pictures though she was always nervous of who might see them, but they'd had an unspoken agreement that he wouldn't do it in public in the daytime. But this afternoon, Olive felt reckless. They'd been going out together for three months, after all, and who was going to see them anyway?

'A bit. But I was just thinking about – you know. About the war. And those forts. D'you think they'd be any good, Derek? D'you think there is going to be a war?'

'Well, I reckon they'd stop most ships getting through. We've got better guns now than we had when they first built them, after all.' He frowned, remembering how his father and other men talked when they discussed the possibility of war. 'It all depends on what Hitler does next. If he goes into Poland – '

Olive shuddered and he held her more tightly. She leaned against him.

'Would you – would you go and fight, Derek?'

'If I had to. We'd all have to do our bit.'

'Even if it meant going away?'

'Well, it'd be bound to mean that, wouldn't it? We don't want Hitler coming here, do we?'

Olive pouted a little. 'You don't seem too bothered. P'raps you want to go away.'

'No, I don't.' Derek still had his arm round her. She felt his hand move a little on her waist, the fingers straying under her arm. 'I don't want to go away at all. It'd interfere with my plans.'

'Oh? What plans?' Olive felt another small tremor of excitement. She was very much aware of those fingers and glanced around, wondering if there was anyone about that she knew, but most of the other people on the beach that afternoon were children or young couples like themselves.

'Well, I want to buy a sports car. One of those little MG two-seaters. Red, if I can get hold of it. I know a bloke who's got one he's thinking of selling and he'd let me have it for fifty quid.' Derek's eyes gleamed. 'Think of it, Livvy – whizzing round the roads in a red sports car! Wouldn't it be fine? We could go anywhere – Brighton, Dover, even London.' His blue eyes gleamed and he hugged her close against him.

Olive gasped and giggled a little. At first she'd felt piqued and disappointed, but the idea of dashing about the countryside at Derek's side in a red sports car was too dazzling for her to continue to feel hurt. And Derek was obviously including her in his plans, which was the main thing.

'And have you got any other plans, Derek?' she asked coquettishly, her head on one side as she looked up at him. The sun was gleaming on his hair and his skin was already tanned. Just like a film star, she thought.

Derek looked into her eyes. His lids half-closed and he pursed his lips very slightly in the way that always made her heart turn over. Slowly, he smiled and drew her closer. He bent his head so that their lips were almost touching.

'Any other plans?' he murmured, and she could feel the warmth of his breath against her mouth. 'Well, I might have. But that'd be telling, now, wouldn't it?'

Frank and Jess Budd had lived in April Grove for nearly eight years. It was their first real house – before that, they'd lived in a couple of rooms in Frank's aunt's house, half a dozen streets away. Aunt Nell and Uncle Fred had been good to them, letting them stop while they saved up the money for a deposit on the little two-up, two-down terraced house, but it had been a relief to them all when Frank and Jess, together with Rosemary and Tim, had been able to move out at last with the few bits of furniture they'd collected, and set up in their own home.

Jess had been expecting Keith then, and Mrs Seddon, who ran the little corner shop just across the road, often said how she'd pitied the young woman moving into number 14.

'Two little ones under three and another on the way,' she would say to Jess as she weighed out sugar and biscuits, 'and only two bedrooms in that little house. I didn't know how you were going to manage.'

Well, we managed well enough, Jess thought as she moved heavily about getting tea ready, after Annie had gone. It was like a palace after living in two rooms, after all. It was the first time since Rose was born that she and Frank had had a bedroom to themselves, and the two children were still small enough to share the back bedroom. Later on, when the baby – as Keith continued to be called, even after he was long out of nappies – moved into the back bedroom, Rose was put downstairs in the front room on a camp bed. It wasn't ideal, but since they only used the front room on Sundays and when visitors came to tea, it didn't make much difference. And they'd always meant to move somewhere a bit bigger, once Frank was earning a bit more in the Dockyard.

But somehow the move never happened. Frank's wage went up a bit and they were able to afford a few more treats for the children – a bag of sweets on Saturday night, coloured ribbons for Rose's hair, a cap gun for the boys. But with war looming like a black cloud over everything, it didn't seem the right time to be thinking of moving.

Once 'peace in our time' had been declared, however, the idea cropped up again, and they began to look about for somewhere else to live.

'It needs to be near the allotments,' Frank said. 'I've just got that patch into good shape now, and there's all those vegetables and fruit coming along. I don't want to lose them.'

'Nor do I.' Jess had always liked the situation of April Grove, with the allotments running along the bottom of the narrow gardens. It was almost as good as being in the country, to be able to look out of the back window and see patches of green stretching away.

Frank's allotment wasn't actually close to the house, it was true – a good five minutes' walk, in fact – but seeing him off with his gardening tools over his shoulder made her feel good. It was satsifying, somehow, to know that he was going off to do something he really enjoyed, something out in the fresh air after the long hours spent in the boiler-shop, stoking up great furnaces and operating a huge steam-hammer.

Jess could barely imagine what Frank did all day long in the Dockyard, but when he was on the allotment she knew he was digging or raking, or hoeing. And she knew that when he came home he would be bringing a bucketful of potatoes, some carrots or a firm green cabbage.

It seemed the right thing for a man to be doing – feeding his family.

Frank grew more than vegetables on his allotment. He also grew soft fruit – currants, gooseberries, rhubarb and, as a special treat, a few strawberries.

The cupboard in the alcove beside the fireplace in the front room was filled with jars of jam and bottled fruit. There were pickles too, made from onions and the tomatoes that grew in the back garden because the allotment was full. Out in the shed were sacks filled with potatoes and root vegetables, and in summer there was always plenty of salad – lettuces, celery, cucumbers, spring onions and radishes.

He was a good provider, was Frank, and he worked hard. It didn't mean he was always easy to live with – tiredness and the frustration of his job made him short-tempered sometimes, and he'd never been one to suffer fools gladly anyway. But Jess knew he always wanted the best for her and the kids, and he was prepared to work all the hours God sent to make sure they got it.

Frank came in as she was slicing bread and spreading it with margarine. She paused for a moment to smile at him and he bent to kiss her. He was a big man, almost six feet tall and heavily built, his muscles developed by years of hard toil in the Dockyard. His hair, almost black like Rose's, was greying now he was in his mid-forties and beginning to recede a little but he didn't let it worry him. 'A high forehead's a sign of intelligence,' he would say, 'and I'm getting more intelligent every year!' Like Jess, he thought there were more important things in life than appearance, though he liked her and the children to look well cared for.

The cloth was on the table and he sat in his armchair, reading the *Evening News*, while Jess boiled the kettle on the gas stove out in the little lean-to scullery. She had made some rock cakes earlier that afternoon and she piled them on a plate and set them in the middle of the table, with a jar of home-made blackberry and apple jam and a pot of sardine and tomato fishpaste.

'Where are they all?' Frank asked as she came in with milk and sugar.

'The boys have gone down the railway station with Bob Shaw to see Pompey come back with the Cup. Goodness knows when they'll be home, but I told them to be back before dark. Rose is up at Joy Brunner's, she's stopping to tea. We might as well have ours now.'

Frank put down his paper and got up from the armchair. As always, he looked huge in the small room. He could strike terror into the hearts of guilty small boys (and in his eyes, small boys almost always were guilty) and command respect from most other men. His principles were rigid and sometimes harsh. Only Jess knew how soft his heart was in reality.

He sat down at the table. As usual, the family had eaten their dinner at one o'clock and there would be a supper later in the evening, a cooked snack of something on toast, or an egg. Tea was invariably bread and cake of some kind, usually home-made. The only cakes Jess bought were doughnuts or cream fancies, which they sometimes had on Sunday.

'So how's our Ted and Annie?' he asked, spreading his bread with fishpaste. At the sound of the jar being opened, Henry the tabby cat got up from the rag rug in front of the fireplace, stretched and came to sit beside Frank's chair. Frank cut a small triangle of bread and held it down to him, and the big cat reached up a paw and took it daintily. 'I thought Ted might walk over the allotment.'

'Ted was doing an extra shift on the ferry. Annie just popped in for a cup of tea on her own.' Jess poured him a cup of tea. 'Frank, d'you reckon there really is going to be a war?'

He shrugged. 'I don't know, Jess. Sometimes it seems as if there's no way of stopping it – sometimes it looks as if everything's going to be all right after all. How can we tell? We don't know anything, really – only what the papers and the wireless tell us. It's all up to the politicians, isn't it?'

'But why should it be?' she asked rebelliously, and her hands moved once more to protect her stomach. 'Why should they be able to mess our lives up? Nobody asks us if we want a war, and I don't suppose anyone's asked the Germans either – not the ones like you and me, who just want to live peaceful with their families.'

'I know, girl. But that's the way it's always been – them and us. People don't get any say in it, and it's no good expecting any different.'

Jess was silent. This was where she and Frank differed. He seemed to be able to accept his lot in life, unfair though she thought it had been, whereas she was always wanting something a bit better. If not for herself, for her children. She'd have liked to see the boys get on, do more in life than Frank, bless him, had had a chance to do. But he shook his head over her ideas.

14

'Doctors? Teachers? People like us don't do those sorts of things, Jess. The boys'll do well enough at a trade, or maybe in the Army or Navy. That's the best sort of life for them.'

As for not having any say in the way the country was run – what was the point in having a vote if it didn't mean anything? Sometimes, though she never admitted it to Frank, she thought there might be something in the Labour Party's ideas. But Frank was a staunch Conservative and wouldn't hear a word in favour of Socialists.

Still, surely even he must agree in that it was wrong to force people into a war they didn't want.

'Didn't we lose enough men in the last war?' she asked. 'All those young chaps, not much more than boys most of them, cut down like a field of corn. And what for? Just so it could all start again twenty years later?'

'I know,' he said again, but Jess was not to be stopped.

'And it's going to be worse this time.' She stared at Frank, her brown eyes wide. 'Thousands of aeroplanes coming over, all dropping bombs . . . And where d'you think they're going to drop them, Frank? On Portsmouth, that's where. On us. You and me. The boys. Rose. And – ' The baby kicked inside her and her voice shook with tears. 'Oh, Frank,' she whispered, 'what's going to happen to us all?'

Frank stared at her across the tea-table. Then he got up and came round to put his hands on her shoulders. She felt his big fingers kneading her flesh and turned to lay her head against him. He was so big, so solid. But he couldn't keep the might of Hitler's Germany at bay.

'I'll tell you what's going to happen, girl,' he said quietly. 'First smell of war, and you and the children are going into the country. You'll be evacuated, that's what, somewhere safe where there's green fields and trees, and nothing to bring aeroplanes dropping bombs. And then when it's all over – and it won't last long, not like the last one did – we'll find that new house and settle down together like we promised ourselves. Somewhere up Hilsea way, I reckon, don't you? You like it round there and it's not so far away from the rest of the family and our friends.'

Jess smiled shakily. 'It's a bit further for you to go to the Yard from Hilsea.'

15

'Well, I've got legs, haven't I? A nice walk never hurt anyone. Or I could go on me bike. And there's a good trolley-bus service for wet days, so no need to worry about that.' He held her close for a moment. 'I want you to have the home you've been looking forward to, Jess, even if we do have to wait a bit longer while they get this mess sorted out. So don't you go fretting that anything's going to happen to us – it isn't.'

Jess smiled again and fished for a handkerchief in the pocket of her pinafore. She dabbed at her eyes and Frank gave her a kiss and went back to sit down in his chair and go on with his tea.

It was only later that she realised that not a word had been said about the allotment. Hilsea was too far away from Copnor for Frank to be able to pop over for an hour's gardening as he did now. There were allotments at Hilsea, she was sure there were – but hadn't he always said he didn't want to leave the one he'd worked on for the past eight years?

So had he changed his mind – or did he, really and truly, think it was all no more than a dream, something that was never going to happen?

Fear jabbed her again. And the shadow of war crept a little closer.

Tim and Keith came back late that night, flushed with excitement and even dirtier than when they had gone out. The footballers had arrived at Fratton Station at 9.30, long after the boys' bedtime, but by then they were too caught up in the excitement to think of the trouble they would undoubtedly find themselves in when they got home.

Along with the thousands of other enthusiasts, cheering themselves hoarse, they followed the two coaches along Elm Grove and King's Road to the Guildhall. There they wriggled to the front of the crowd and scrambled up on the stone lions to get a good look at their heroes. They were swiftly dragged down by a policeman, but he was a football supporter too and did no more than give each boy a light cuff before allowing them to crouch down and peer between his legs.

'We saw Tinn holding the Cup over his head,' Tim reported when they finally reached home to a frantic, white-faced mother and a grim father. 'We actually saw the Cup!'

'And now you're going to see stars,' Frank promised, reaching for the thin cane he kept hung in a corner beside his razor-strop. 'Don't you realise your mother's been worrying herself sick?' He ignored the shock on his sons' faces and reached for them. 'Come here.'

'But Dad— ' Tim protested in outraged tones. 'It was the Cup.'

'Cup or no Cup, I'm not having you roam the streets till eleven o'clock at night, worrying your mother half out of her mind.'

'Were you worried, Mum?' Tim turned his large, hazel eyes on his mother. 'We never meant to worry you. We were with Bob all the time. Well – up until we got to the Guildhall. But we know our way back from there, we wouldn't have got lost.'

'It's not a question of getting lost –' Frank began, but Jess interrupted. She laid her hand on his arm.

'Let's forget it now, Frank. They're back safe and that's all that matters. Don't hit them, not at this time of night. They're just boys, and it was something special. Portmouth's never won the Cup before.'

'That's not the point,' Frank grumbled, but he was tired and thankful to see his sons and, though he'd never admit it, not nearly so angry as he made out. Looking at their faces, he'd seen an innocence, a childish excitement and absorption, that he'd missed in his own childhood. And when Jess begged him not to cane them at this time of night he was painfully reminded of Saturday nights from his own boyhood, when his father had come home the worse for drink and beaten not only him but his mother too.

Frank Budd was never the worse for drink, for he never took any. The scenes of childhood, when his father and uncles had come roaring home from the pub, had seared themselves into his mind like a brand. Ever since then, he had been afraid of violent anger – his own as much as that of others – and had fought to keep it in check. He knew all too well that his temper, once unleashed, would be formidable and that his strength was enough to do real damage. He dared not take the risk.

All the same, the boys had done wrong in staying out so late and must be punished. In Frank's view, children had to learn the difference between right and wrong, and the only way to teach them was by discipline.

17

'All right,' he said, lowering the cane. 'I'll let you off this time. But half-past seven's your time on Saturdays, and don't you forget it. And there'll be no going out to play for either of you next week, understand?'

'Yes, Dad.' The two boys went out to the scullery to wash. Their faces were downcast, but not unduly so. Not being able to go out to play would come hard during the next few days, but they were still too buoyed up by excitement to think of that now.

They had seen Pompey come home with the Cup. And nothing could take that away from them.

The Monday after the Cup Final win was also May Day, and the Portsmouth Labour Party led a demonstration which marched four miles through the city in pouring rain. Bob Shaw, who lived next door to the Budds, was still thrilling to the scenes as the footballers had returned home and enjoyed their own triumphal procession through the streets. He went along to hear Peter Paine, the Labour candidate for Parliament, speaking on conscription.

'If the government are asking young people to make sacrifices,' he declared, 'there ought to be a levy on the wealth of others.' And Bob and the rest of the crowd there in the rain, cheered and clapped.

'We lost enough youngsters last time,' a man near him said. 'Cannon-fodder, that's all they were. Send enough over the top and in the end a few got to survive. And they don't care which ones it is, so long as there's enough to keep firing at the other side.'

By 'they', Bob understood the man to mean the politicians and military top brass who ran wars from behind the scenes. The ones who went on aeroplanes to meet other politicians in other countries and came back waving pieces of paper and talking about peace; or directed events on a battlefield from hundreds of miles away, playing it out on a big table as if it were some kind of board game.

'Well, I reckon we ought to go over there, teach these Huns a lesson,' he said. 'I'd go, if they asked me. I'd join up.' His eyes burned with patriotic fervour in his thin face and he flicked back the lock of mousy hair that flopped over his forehead.

The man turned and looked at him. He looked old enough to have been in the last war and his face was scarred and pitted as if he had been burned. He shook his head.

'You wouldn't be saying that if you knew what it was all about. Months in the trenches, up to your knees in freezing mud, bullets like hail over your head. Mustard gas. Strong men breaking up with shell-shock, crying like babies. It's not pretty and it's not exciting. Most of the time it's dead boring, except that you might be killed at any moment.' He shook his head again. 'You ought to go down on your knees and pray it'll never happen, son. I do, every night.'

Bob stared and then turned away. His blood was still racing with the excitement of the Cup win on Saturday, and the speech he had just heard had filled him with frustration. The Labour Party were against war, against the government who were doing their best to avert it yet still making all the precautions they could. Of course they should bring in conscription – a country had to be ready with its army, didn't it? And there was going to be a war, make no mistake about it. The whole of Europe had been marching towards it for years.

The speeches over, the crowd dispersed and Bob roamed restlessly through the busy street. Even on a wet Monday, Commercial Road, the main shopping street of Portsmouth, was thronged with shoppers. Women mostly, crowding through the doors of the Landport Drapery Bazaar, commonly known simply as 'the Landport', or in and out of Woolworths, Marks & Spencer, Littlewoods and the British Home Stores. All much the same as one another, as far as Bob could see, apart from Woolworths, where you could at least get sensible things like tools and puncture repair outfits. He wandered in and stared at the counters for a while, bought a bar of chocolate and then wandered out again.

In the street, he encountered Graham Philpotts. The two had been at school together though not special friends, until Graham's family had moved across the harbour to Gosport. But now they fell into step and turned towards the harbour. The rain had eased and a fitful sun poked through the scudding clouds, brightening Graham's red hair. He'd always been called Ginger at school and had been the ringleader in a good many escapades. Bob wondered if he had changed much. From the look of mischief in his bright blue eyes, it didn't look as if he had.

'There's a lot of ships in,' Graham said as they walked down

Edinburgh Road towards Queen Street. 'Plenty of matelots about, too.'

There were always sailors in Queen Street. Long, straight and narrow, it led straight from the heart of Portsea to the Dockyard gate. The shops, cafés and pubs along its length were the sailors' Commercial Road, providing everything they required, from the 'worst drop of beer in Pompey' to a tattoo. There were several naval outfitters, where sailors would pay regular sums in order to be able to afford their uniforms when needed, and the two young men stopped to look at a window display.

'Look at the sword,' Bob said admiringly. 'I reckon I'd look a bit of all right with one of them slung round me waist, don't you?'

'Fat chance,' Graham sneered. 'That's a captain's sword – maybe an admiral's. Chief stoker's your limit, Bob, with a shovel to carry.'

Bob dug him in the ribs with his elbow and Graham swung a punch at his head. The two went on. A gang of matelots were coming along the road towards them, their bell-bottoms flapping round their ankles.

'First of May. They've got their whites on,' Bob said, looking at the white cap covers. 'D'you fancy their uniform, Ginge?'

'Me? Nah – when I join up, it'll be the RAF.' He spread his arms like a small boy pretending to fly an aeroplane and made a high whinnying sound. 'Bombers, that's what I'll fly. Or maybe fighters. The Spitfire they're building out at Southampton, that's what's going to win the war. I wouldn't mind flying one of those.'

'You definitely going to join up, then?'

'Well, we'll have to, won't we? All of us.'

'Not if it doesn't happen. Not then if we're in a – what do they call it? – "reserved occupation". If we get jobs.'

'What's the point?' Graham stopped to look in another shop window, where a few flyblown cardboard advertisements mysteriously extolled their range of 'rubber appliances'. 'They'll declare war the day we start and we'll have to down tools and go anyway. Here, what d'you reckon they really sell in these places, Bob? I mean, what are rubber appliances?'

Bob glanced in. The pictures on the advertisements seemed to be of male corsets. 'They're trusses, aren't they? For fat blokes with hernias, and that.'

'Yeah, I know that, but d'you think that's all they sell?' Graham nudged him and winked. 'How about going in to see, eh?'

Bob moved on quickly. He knew as well as anyone else the reputation Queen Street had. Leading from the Dockyard gate straight to the middle of town, every sailor who came ashore had to walk up here, and it was the natural haunt of prostitutes. Whether you could buy their services in a shop advertising rubber appliances, he didn't know, but he thought you probably could. There couldn't be that many sailors whose most urgent need was a corset.

He looked round nervously. As well as sailors, there were plenty of girls walking about, some respectable-looking enough, others heavily made up and wearing clothes that would have made his mother and Mrs Budd next door sniff. Were they tarts? How could you tell?

There was a woman in April Grove who was a tart, or so everyone said. Nancy Baxter, who lived at number 10 with her mother, Granny Kinch, and her son Mick, the same age as Tim Budd. Nancy Baxter was nothing to look at, thin with straight black hair and eyes like buttons, but she went out of an evening in a red coat that she wore unbuttoned, showing a blouse that revealed a lot of neck and a skirt that was always shorter than anyone else's. She wore a lot of lipstick too, bright red, the sort Bert Shaw would have gone mad over if he'd caught Gladys or Diane wearing it.

When Bob was about ten he and the rest of the boys round September Street used to snigger about Nancy Baxter. Preg-Nancy, they'd called her, and nudged each other knowingly when she'd appeared with baby Mick. There'd been no husband around, though Granny Kinch, who spent nearly all day standing at her front door watching all that went up and down April Grove and March Street, swore she was married to a soldier, just before they'd moved into number 10. 'He's away a lot,' she'd told the neighbours. 'Got posted the day after they were married. Nancy goes to meet him for weekends when he gets time, but he's a high-up and don't get much leave.'

'And the band played "Believe it if you like",' Tommy Vickers commented. He lived in the end house in April Grove and had something to say about everything, but like everyone else he was tolerant of Nancy Baxter and her mum. Granny Kinch, standing at her door with curlers in her hair, her beady black eyes missing nothing, was a good-hearted old soul and at least Nancy never brought her business home with her. The boy Mick was turning into a bit of a hooligan but what could you expect with no father to keep him in order?

Bob had wondered just where Nancy Baxter carried on her trade. Hanging round the Dockyard gates, he supposed, but perhaps she worked in Queen Street. He looked across the road. There was a girl now – not Nancy Baxter, but she was wearing a red jacket, unbuttoned over a slightly grubby white blouse. There was something about that blouse that made him feel uncomfortable, something loose and abandoned. And he knew his sister Gladys would never have walked about with her coat unbuttoned like that. Was this girl a tart? Were her unbuttoned coat and loose blouse signs?

She caught his eye and stared at him, lifting her eyebrows.

'Know me again, will you?'

Bob felt himself blush scarlet and looked away. Beside him, Graham sniggered.

'She looked a bit of all right. Reckon she's on the game?'

'I dunno,' Bob said shortly. 'She wouldn't be interested in us, anyway. They're after sailors down here.'

'Bosh. They're after money. Don't matter to them what kind of trousers a bloke wears, so long as he takes 'em off.'

'Well, I've got no money so they're out of luck. Anyway, I'm not interested. I'd rather have a proper girlfriend.'

'With the emphasis on proper? You won't find out what it's all about that way, Bob.' Graham jingled a few coins in his pocket. 'Reckon I might have a go one day. Where's the harm? It's what they're for.'

Bob said nothing. He was embarrassingly ignorant about sex and wasn't sure how much more Graham knew. Not many parents seemed to tell their children the facts of life, and the subject was never mentioned at school unless you were caught wanking in the lavatories. You were left to find out for yourself, from other boys, and how were you to know that what they said was true?

The only time Bob's dad had spoken to him about it was when they were walking down this very street on their way to the harbour a year or so ago. A couple of girls had passed them, skirts up to their knees, their frocks so tight they were almost bursting out of them, and Bob hadn't been able to help looking. Bert Shaw had given him a proper tongue-lashing and told him never to go with any of those girls. 'You'll get more than you bargained for,' he'd said grimly, and proceeded to explain in gruesome detail just what Bob might get. The graphic pictures of toes coming off in his socks and a brain rotting away in his head like putrefying meat, had kept Bob awake for a few good nights after that.

The thought of having a 'proper' girlfriend who refused sex until marriage, so could neither pass on these horrible diseases nor present him with the other nightmare, an unwanted baby, was much more attractive. Even though it didn't stop him wondering – just wondering – what it was like to go with a girl. Just once, to see . . .

But Dad hadn't minced his words. Just once was all it needed, he'd said with a glare so ferocious that he might have been suspecting Bob of having tried it already. Perhaps he did. He'd been eighteen himself once, after all, though it was hard to imagine it, so he probably knew just what kind of thoughts went through Bob's mind.

'That girl looks as if she knows you,' Graham said suddenly. 'Been having it off on the sly, have you?'

Bob glanced across the street and saw Betty Chapman, who lived at the other end of April Grove. She was coming out of a fish-and-chip shop, a newspaper packet in her hand. She came across, already unwrapping the parcel, and offered it to the two boys.

'Hullo, Bob.' Her short brown curls were tousled from the rain and her hazel eyes looked Graham up and down with interest. 'Want a chip? They're good ones, plenty of salt and vinegar.' She flicked her eyelashes saucily. 'What're you two doing down here on a Monday afternoon? Got no homes to go to?'

'Just having a walk round, Betty,' Bob said defensively, brushing back his hair with his fingers. Betty was only a year or so younger than himself and had joined him and his mates for a game of cricket or football in the street when they were younger. The boys liked her because she wasn't like most girls, never burst into tears because the ball hit her a bit hard or wanted extra turns just because she was a girl. He hadn't seen much of her since they'd all left school but just lately he'd thought once or twice of asking her to go to the pictures with him. 'Ginger says there's a lot of warships in, we thought we'd go and have a look. Anyway, I might ask you the same question – what're you doing down Queen Street? I thought you had a job in the dairy up September Street.'

'That's right. Mrs Marsh sent me down here on an errand and gave me some money for a bit of dinner.' Betty took a chip and gave Graham another bright equiring glance. 'I've seen you before, but you don't come from round our way, do you?'

'I used to,' Graham said. 'I live in Gosport now but I used to sit next to Bob at school. And I remember you – you were in the class below us.'

'Oh yes,' she said, staring at him. 'You used to pull my pigtails.'

Graham grimaced and looked at the golden brown curls. 'You don't wear pigtails now.'

'I don't want 'em pulled, that's why,' she retorted with a toss of her head. 'But maybe you've grown out of doing that to girls.'

'Maybe I have. Maybe I've found better things to do.'

There was a brief silence. Bob, standing by, felt suddenly excluded. He shifted his feet and said rather more loudly than he'd intended, 'Well, are we going to look at these ships or not?'

'Sure.' Graham half-turned to move on, then looked back at Betty. 'Why don't you come too? Or d'you have to get back to work?'

'No, this is my dinner-break.' She shrugged carelessly. 'I might as well.' She walked beside Graham along the narrow pavement, Bob slouching moodily in their wake. He felt irritated but couldn't tell why. Maybe it was because he didn't want Betty tagging along, spoiling the fun he and Graham had been having. Or maybe it was because he'd rather have been the one walking with Betty.

He made up his mind that he would ask her out to the pictures. There was a good film on at the Odeon that week. He thought of taking her there, perhaps getting one of those double seats they had in the back row. Or was the first time out too soon for that? She might think he was going too fast. He watched the way she kept glancing up at Graham and giggling. What was he saying that was so funny anyhow? Bob had never found his jokes that hilarious.

Perhaps when they got to the Hard, Graham would go back over the ferry. That would leave him free to take Betty back to Copnor on the trolley-bus. The journey took a quarter of an hour, which should give him time to ask her out. Somehow it seemed easier to do that on a bus rather than back in the street where they both lived.

'You're too cheeky for your own good, you know that?' he heard Betty say as they neared the wider end of Queen Street and he was able to walk beside them again. She looked at Bob, her face full of laughter. 'Did you hear what he said to me? Well, it's just as well – it's not something I'd want repeated.' But it was obvious that whatever it was, she'd liked it and Bob sent a glowering look at his friend. 'I don't reckon any girl'll be safe once you get into bell-bottoms,' she told Graham.

'But he's not—' Bob began, and received a sharp nudge from Graham's elbow. 'I thought you said— '

'I haven't decided yet,' Graham said airily. 'I reckon there's a lot to be said for the Navy. After all, they say every nice girl loves a sailor, don't they – and I reckon I could be the sailor every nice girl loves.'

'Ooh!' Betty squealed. 'Well, count me out! I don't want to be one of a crowd.'

'Choosy, are you?' Graham challenged, and she tossed her head.

'I can afford to be, can't I? There's as many sailors in Pompey as there are fish in the sea.' She glinted a sideways look at him, her hazel eyes almost green now. 'I'm not interested in the ones who have a wife in every port.'

'Who said anything about wives? You were talking about fish a minute ago.'

'I was talking about sailors,' she retorted, 'but there's not much difference.'

Bob listened as the banter flew back and forth between them. He felt even more left out. He looked at Graham Philpotts. He'd been a weedy sort a chap at school, nothing to look at with that ginger hair and all those freckles. Now he was taller than Bob and not so thin, and anyone could see he thought a lot of himself. He wore a good raincoat that he'd left unbuttoned, like Humphrey Bogart in a gangster film, and underneath it was a Fair Isle pullover in about

25

ten different colours. It had taken Bob all his time to persuade his sister Gladys to make him one in five colours.

By now, they were coming down to the Dockyard gate and in view of the harbour. As usual, it was thronged with craft. Alongside the Southern Railway Jetty lay the *Empress of Australia*, ready to take the King and Queen on their visit to Canada next week and, beyond that, a huge aircraft carrier, its wide deck overhanging its steep sides. A fleet of ships, grey and sombre in the shifting light, stretched into the distant recesses of the harbour, further than the eye could see. The docks, built on reclaimed land, were like a city in themselves and mostly out of sight from anywhere but the air. But it was from the air that they would be threatened.

There were plenty of other boats, large and small, crowding the harbour. At the end of the jetty, trains brought people from London to the paddle steamers that tied up there to make the journey across to the Isle of Wight. The *Whippingham* was there now, looming over one of the small launches operated by the two ferry companies which plied between Portsmouth and Gosport. They kept up a ten-minute service, from early in the morning until late at night, and when the Dockyardmen came out they were packed tightly with Gosport men going home.

They walked a short distance along the jetty and stood looking over the railings. The tide was out and although it was a school-day there were a few mudlarks wading waist-deep in the thick black mud under the long ferry ponton, lifting up their arms to those who walked above and calling for pennies to be thrown down.

'That'll stop,' remarked a man standing nearby, watching the boys scrabble in the mud for the coins and putting them in their jamjars. 'They'll be treading on bombs and mines down there in a few months. Prime target, Pompey's going to be.'

Betty shivered. 'Don't! It scares me to death to think of it. I can't imagine what it'll be like – bombs falling out of the sky and blowing everything up. Nobody's going to be safe.'

'They're going to send the kids out into the country,' Bob commented. 'Your auntie'll be going too, seeing as she's having a baby.'

'There'll be hardly any people left,' Graham said. 'It'll be all women and old men. How're they going to keep the place going?'

The man chuckled. He had a straggly moustache and a big, bulbous nose. 'The women'll do that, same as they did in the last lot. Turned into bus drivers, ambulance drivers, went into the Navy – that's when Wrens first started – went on the land to do the farming – oh, the women were everywhere and a bloody good job they made of it too. That's why they had to give 'em the vote. Couldn't have won the war without 'em, see.' He grinned, showing broken teeth. 'Wouldn't have bin worth winning anyway, without them to come back to. And it'll be the same this time.'

'You really reckon there's going to be a war, then?' Bob asked. Like a lot of young people he was both anxious and fed up with hearing about war, but at least it was better than listening to Graham and Betty flirting with each other.

The man snorted and rubbed his nose with the back of a hairy hand. 'No doubt about it! I given 'em another two months – maybe three – to stop dragging their feet and make up their minds, and then we'll be in the thick of it. You'll get all the fighting you want, lads, and then some.' He looked down at the boys scrabbling beneath the jetty, their bodies plastered with thick, evil-smelling mud. 'I wouldn't be surprised if some of those poor devils do, too.'

'Go on,' Graham said, 'if we do decide to give Hitler a licking it'll all be over by Christmas.'

'They said that last time.' The man watched the mudlarks for a few more minutes, then thrust his hand into his pocket and took out a fistful of small coins. 'Here you are, kids – fish for that lot,' he shouted, tossing them over the rail, and the boys cheered and made a dive, elbowing each other aside in their rush to retrieve the money. One of them fell and had to be dragged out. He stood upright, eyes blinking from a black face. The man chuckled but when he turned away his face was grave.

'I used to be in the Navy,' he volunteered. 'I was a chief cook.'

'Why aren't you scarred then?' Graham said cheekily, and then added, 'I suppose you were in the last war?'

'If it can be called that – the "last" one. I was, and I saw a lot of action. Got sunk twice, shelled more times than I can count. I tell you, I've seen men dying all around me, bits of bodies blown all

27

over the decks, the bulkheads running with blood. It's no joke, war, and getting into uniform might get you the girls but it'll get you a lot else besides. And the next one— '

'I know,' Graham said in bored tones, 'it'll be even worse. Everyone tells us that. But that's not going to stop it happening, so we might as well make the best of it.'

Bob could see that Graham was growing restless. He whispered something to Betty and she giggled and smothered her mouth with her hand. They moved away a little along the railing.

'There's a Copnor bus up at the stop,' Bob said before Betty could move out of earshot. 'You'll be late back from your dinner-hour if you don't catch that one.'

Betty glanced at him, then looked back at Graham. He said something Bob couldn't hear and she nodded quickly.

'Well, I'll be off back to Gosport then,' Graham said loudly. 'Good to have seen you again, Bob. We must get together again, have a pint and another walk down Queen Street, eh?' He grinned and winked, and Bob flushed and looked away. He caught Betty's eye and felt his colour deepen. She was laughing, but at what he had no idea. Me, probably, he thought miserably, and then – But at least she'll be coming back on the bus with me. And then I can ask her out.

The man was still leaning on the railings. Graham was grinning, as if he could hardly wait to say something funny about him. But Bob wasn't in a mood to hear it. The expression on the man's face was one he didn't properly understand. But he knew somehow that when the stranger looked over the side of the jetty at the boys wading in the mud below, he was seeing something different.

Perhaps he was seeing other boys, from a distant past, who had found themselves scrabbling in a different kind of mud, who had been floundering not for pennies but for their lives. Or perhaps these boys in a future that no one could quite imagine, when the black, stinking mud of Portsmouth Harbour was no more than a nostalgic memory.

Bob remembered the words of the man he had met in the Guildhall Square. 'Cannon-fodder. Bullets over your head like hail. Men crying like babies . . .'

He looked up at the sky. If war came, it would be black with enemy aircraft, raining bombs instead of bullets.

28

Graham had turned away and was sauntering down the pontoon, on the way to catch the ferry back to Gosport. Betty, her face quivering with secret smiles, was waiting for Bob to go and catch the trolley-bus back to Copnor.

A quarter of an hour in her company, with no one else to interfere. They'd go up top, see if they could get the seat at the front. And he'd ask her to go to the pictures with him on Saturday.

Bob quickened his step. He forgot about the man at the railings and the man in the Guildhall Square. He forgot the mudlarks, lifting their doomed, mud-blackened faces and their arms in appeal. He forgot the glimpse he'd been given of the past and the vision of the future and thought only of Betty, snuggled beside him in a double seat in the back row of the Odeon on Saturday night.

Betty was ten minutes late back for work in the dairy that afternoon but Mrs Marsh said nothing beyond asking whether the trolley-buses had stopped running and giving her the job of cleaning out the big refrigerator, which was the task Betty disliked most. It was pleasantly cool in the back room of the dairy on hot days, but the stone-flagged floor was cold to her feet and the air from the fridge chilly even when it had been turned off. And she didn't like being shut away from the front of the shop. Serving was what Betty enjoyed most, chatting with the customers and hearing all the latest gossip.

But she had plenty to occupy her mind today as she sponged round the inside of the fridge with a paste made from water and bicarbonate of soda. And the secret smile Bob had observed as Graham strolled away down the pontoon was permitted to tug harder at her mouth and even escape now and then as a small, hastily smothered giggle.

Two boys had asked her out, within half an hour of each other! Betty, at seventeen, had begun to despair of ever getting a boyfriend. All her friends had been talking about boys from the age of fourteen or fifteen and a lot of them were going steady by now. Whereas Betty, who had played with the boys more than the girls, had suddenly found herself out in the cold. Boys who had encouraged her to play football, climb trees and run races with them were no longer interested, and she didn't know how to make the transition from tomboy to girlfriend. She had given herself no practice in being a woman and the boys didn't seem to see her as a girl at all.

But this afternoon had restored her confidence. That boy Graham she'd met with Bob Shaw, was a smasher. Good-looking, with curly red hair and bright blue eyes, and cheeky with it – he'd made her laugh, and Betty liked anyone who made her laugh. And he'd seemed to like her too – enough to make a date with her for Saturday night. The Troxy, with Fred Astaire and Ginger Rogers in *Carefree*, that's what he was taking her to see. And Betty wouldn't mind betting he'd get seats in the back row – he was that sort, the sort who always did get what he wanted.

Not that he'd get too much of what he wanted, she thought as she stacked eggs in the clean refrigerator. Holding hands and perhaps a kiss at the end of the evening, that was all – none of this cuddling and necking a lot of boys seemed to want to do. Betty hadn't yet had any experience of that and wasn't at all sure she'd like it. Just for a start, it was good enough to be simply going out with a boy. Other things could come later.

Betty and her sister Olive had been told often enough not to bring 'trouble' home and she wasn't going to let any boy mess up her life. And he wasn't the only fish in the sea by any means. Hadn't Bob Shaw asked her out too, not fifteen minutes after Graham?

If Bob had asked first, she'd have accepted. He was one of the boys she'd played football and cricket with, but he seemed different now. More grown-up. He had a nice smile too – really, he was quite good-looking. But not as much as Graham. And because she'd known him all her life, not as exciting.

Betty finished restocking the fridge and went to the little back scullery to wash her hands. It was nearly four o'clock and time for the cup of tea Mrs Marsh allowed in the afternoons. She put the kettle on and stood gazing out of the window at the small backyard, thinking of Graham.

On Monday afternoon, in number 14, Jess Budd and her family were having tea. Tim and Keith were still bubbling over Portsmouth's win, but Rosemary wasn't interested. She was telling her mother about her friend, Joy Brunner.

'People are saying she's German. She's not really, is she?'

'Course she is,' Keith said. 'Brunner's a German name. It means Brown.'

'Why aren't they called Brown, then?' Keith asked, spreading his bread thickly with blackberry and apple jam.

'Because Mr Brunner is German,' Jess told him. 'He came from Germany a long time ago and married Mrs Brunner and they opened the shop.'

'You can hardly tell he's German now,' Rose said. 'And Joy doesn't sound a bit like a German.'

'She's not,' Tim said, eyeing the doughnuts.

'She is,' Keith contradicted him. He was looking at the doughnuts too. There was one which had jam already oozing out of one side and he wondered if anyone else had noticed it.

'She's not.'

'She is.'

'Stop it, you two,' Jess said. 'Joy isn't German because she was born in England. And Mrs Brunner isn't German either. She's lived in Portsmouth all her life. She went to Copnor School.' She looked at Rose. 'Are people being unkind to Joy?'

Rose shrugged. 'They're just saying she's German. It makes her cry sometimes.'

Jess tightened her lips. What did you say to children when this sort of thing happened? Mr and Mrs Brunner had run the newspaper shop at the top of the street for years. He knew everyone in the district, always had a friendly word and worked hard, as newsagents had to do. He was part of the little community of this network of streets. Most people had forgotten he wasn't English.

But there were always a few who were ready with spiteful gossip and now, with war looming, they were finding readier ears. Talk of spies and 'Fifth Column' was rife. There had been German spies in Portsmouth just before the last war started and it was only common sense to suppose that there would be more about now. An important naval dockyard, with a Marine barracks close by and who knew what secrets hidden in the great forts that lined the top of Portsmouth Hill and even stood out to sea in the Solent, between the mainland and the Isle of Wight – why, it stood to reason there would be spies about.

And who was more obvious than an actual German, even if he had lived amongst them for twenty years? Didn't that make him an even better choice? Didn't he have friends, even relatives, in the city who trusted him? Wasn't he a newsagent, handling papers every day, with all kinds of people coming in for a gossip and a chat? Wasn't it a newsagent that one of the German spies in the last war had enrolled as an accomplice?

The fact that the newsagent involved then had immediately reported his suspicions to the authorities was forgotten. The memory of the story was hazy in most people's minds, for it had never been officially told and no doubt there had been distortion over the years. But enough detail had survived to add fuel to the suspicions about the Brunners.

Jess had heard the gossip herself. *He was probably sent over specially, all those years ago, to worm his way in and make friends. And, worse still – she must have known. She's in it as much as he is. Look at the way they go over there every year, to see his mum. Mum! A likely story!*

Jess had known Alice Brunner all her life. They had attended the same schools, been in the same class. They had played hopscotch and five-stones on the pavements, walked out to Hilsea Lines to gather blackberries, learned to swim in Langstone Harbour. They had given birth to their daughters within weeks of each other and now those daughters were growing up together in the same way.

Jess and Alice had never been close friends. They were simply part of the crowd of children who lived in the little network of streets, who knew each other more or less casually, more or less intimately. They were on the same terms now – friendly, stopping for a chat whenever they met, interested in each other's families, but not close enough to pop in for a cup of tea or to go to the pictures together of an afternoon.

All the same, Jess would have been ready to go into court and swear on oath that Alice Brunner was no Fifth Columnist. Nor her husband, who was a gentle, kindly man with pale brown eyes peering short-sightedly through round glasses. He could be seen every Sunday evening at the little church at the top of Deniston Road, praying earnestly, and it was almost impossible to believe he could be a spy.

She felt sorry for him and Alice, and even more sorry for their daughter Joy, who was a nice girl with pigtails and her father's mild brown eyes and shy smile.

'Well, I hope you stand up for her,' she said to Rose. 'Joy hasn't done anything wrong and I don't believe her father has either. It doesn't help anyone to spread nasty stories like that about.' She looked sternly at the two boys. 'That goes for you two as well.'

'We don't tell stories about her,' Tim said indignantly.

'Well, see that you don't, then. All right, you can have a doughnut.'

She went out to the scullery to put more hot water into the teapot and stood for a moment gazing out of the window. There was no view to be seen, only the wall of Ethel Glaister's scullery next door, but she watched it and suddenly shivered.

It didn't matter where you went or who you talked to, it was war, war, war. She was still trying desperately to believe that it wouldn't happen, that her baby would be born into a peaceful world, that her boys would grow up without ever having to fight.

But the world wasn't peaceful. The whole of Europe was getting dragged into this horrible mess. And not just Europe – as far away as Russia, people's lives were being disrupted by the mania of one man.

Adolf Hitler.

He's mad, Jess thought. He's making a hell on earth for everyone else. And we're letting him.

And now it's spreading to our own doorsteps. A madness and a hell that can't be stopped, except by making it worse.

The baby kicked inside her and she put her hands over the bulge. What was going to happen to them all?

CHAPTER TWO

PORTSMOUTH had been preparing for war for the past four years. Jess's uncle, John Bellinger, was on the City Council, and he had often told the family that when war came – if it came – Portsmouth meant to be ready for it. And Tommy Vickers, along the street, who worked for the council and seemed to have a finger in most pies, had nosed out a good deal more than Uncle John would reveal.

'Latest idea's doing a dustcart up as a fire engine,' he told Frank. 'Those big ones, used for squashing rubbish down small so they can shift huge amounts. They're watertight, see, so you can fill 'em with water and pump it out just like from a proper fire engine. What's more, they can be used to decontaminate gas.'

Everyone was afraid of gas attacks. Those who could remember the last war recalled the sufferings of soldiers returning home, not only their skin but their lungs as well, burned away by mustard gas. They never recovered. Some of them still survived, but they were coughing shells of the men they had once been, and those whose faces had been eaten away by the corrosive fumes were forced to become accustomed to looks of pity, shock and even repugnance.

In the 1914–18 war, only soldiers had suffered gas attacks. But now everybody was at risk, and before Jess's baby was born gas masks were issued to everyone in the country.

'They're horrible,' Rose exclaimed when she received hers. She took it out of its brown cardboard box and stared at the black rubber snout. 'Have we got to wear these?'

'If there's a gas warning, yes.' Frank was unravelling the straps on his own mask. He fitted it over his head and fastened them. The rubber clung to his face and he peered out through the transparent face-piece.

Rose gave a little scream.

'Oh, you look awful! Like some sort of monster.'

'A monster from outer space,' Tim said. He dragged his on and began to caper about the room, thrusting his black snout at his sister. 'Yaah! I'm a monster from outer space. Yaargh!'

'Stop it! Stop it! You're a horrible little boy.'

'Stop it, Tim,' Jess said, and Frank caught his son by the back of his collar and jerked him to a standstill. Tim stood turning his muzzle from one person to another like a dog wondering why it has been chastised.

Keith giggled and Jess felt a smile twitch at her lips. But Rose was looking sulky and Frank annoyed.

'It's not a toy,' he said severely. 'That mask is meant to save your life, not play with. Take it off – carefully – and put it back in its box. Rose, Keith, you'd better make sure you know how to put yours on. And then we'll have a practice every Saturday night. Apart from that, I don't want to see them out of their boxes.'

'Not even if there's a warning?' Tim murmured, and backed hastily out of his father's reach. Jess gave him a look which was intended to be reproving but, from the wink her son gave her when his father's back was turned, seemed to have failed. That was the trouble with Tim. Cheeky he might be, and forever up to mischief, but he could always win you over with that grin and those hazel eyes. And he was never rude or deliberately naughty.

'Dinner's ready,' she said, going out to the scullery. 'Put the masks away now. Rose, you lay the table.'

Later, she voiced her own fear to Frank. 'The children can put their masks on all right. But what happens to the baby, Frank? There's no masks for them. You couldn't get them to stay on.' She looked at him, her eyes full of fear. 'I couldn't sit and watch my baby die like that.'

'I know.' He laid his hand on her shoulder. 'They'll think of something, girl, don't you worry. They won't have forgotten about the babies.'

35

'I hope not.' She could feel the baby moving now, energetic little arms and legs pounding at the wall of her abdomen. If only she could keep it there, safe inside her. If only it didn't have to be born.

Children shouldn't have to suffer war, she thought with a sudden passion. Little babies, who can't understand – they shouldn't have to be born into a world of gas masks and bombs and air-raid shelters. It isn't fair, and they – the 'they' who sent troops marching on other countries, who signed pieces of paper with pledges they had no intention of keeping, who decided that young men should have to set aside their own lives and become soldiers when all they wanted was to live peacefully at home – they had no right to force it on them.

But there was nothing people like she and Frank could do about it. Like millions of others, they must just go where they were pushed.

'Air-Raid Precautions' became a familiar phrase, quickly abbreviated to ARP. The first appeals for volunteers for this part of Civil Defence were largely ignored; when several thousand men were requested in May, only seven hundred put themselves forward. But gradually more men and women offered their services, though they were still liable to be the butt of sneers from their neighbours, or – worse still – accused of warmongering.

'Never mind warmongering,' said Frank, whose working hours were too long to allow him to become a warden, but who agreed to be a fire-watcher should the need arise. 'It isn't people like us who do the warmongering. We just have to take the consequences of those who do.'

Once formed, the ARP personnel were trained. Most weeks found them engaged in various exercises simulating what the authorities expected to happen in war. Mock explosions were staged and emergencies of all kinds set up. The whole city was blacked out on several occasions and mock 'bomb damage', with craters, fractured gas and water mains and sewage pipes, and burning houses, prepared for air wardens, repair gangs and first-aid parties to deal with.

At first, a good many people preferred to turn a blind eye to these preparations. Others sneered. The ARP wardens, strutting about the streets in their uniforms and tin hats, looked faintly ridiculous. There wasn't going to be a war, was there? Not after the last lot. And who were folk like these wardens to set themselves up as something special anyway? They weren't nothing but greengrocers or coalmen, no better than the rest of us. Don't want 'em telling us what to do.

Their rebellion turned to glee when one of the newly appointed wardens was detailed to give a demonstration of fire-fighting in the local recreation ground, known generally as the 'rec'.

A small platform was set up as a stage on the grass and the warden, looking self-conscious in his new dark-blue uniform, placed a bucket of sand, a stirrup-pump and what looked like a replica of a bomb in the middle. As he did so, a desultory crowd gathered to watch, a sarcastic comment ready on everyone's lips.

'Fight fires!' one man murmured. 'Old Fred Stokes couldn't fight a fly.'

'What're you putting your mac on for, Fred?' someone else called out. 'Don't you want to get yer nice new uniform dirty, then?'

'Can't you see it's raining? What'll his mum say if he gets his feet wet?'

There was a roar of laughter. Old Mrs Stokes wasn't far off eighty but she was one of the characters of the September Street area, known for speaking her very tough mind, and it was generally agreed that she'd never allowed Fred to grow up.

'Leave the bloke alone,' Frank said sharply as more jeers rose around him. 'He's doing his best.' But he watched in embarrassment as Fred tried in the drizzle to set fire to the bomb, which sat sullenly refusing to ignite. Why didn't the man give up, for goodness sake, and put the demonstrations off till another day?

'What a farce!' someone snorted, and another sniggered and made some remark about Guy Fawkes Day. Frank glanced round in irritation and moved, intending to go and help Fred.

But before he could do so, his embarrassment turned to dismay as Fred, getting desperate, threw some paraffin over the weakly flickering flames. Instantly, fire leapt up, almost enveloping him, and he sprang back with a shout of fear. The watchers began to laugh harder than ever, but Frank saw that the sudden flare had actually set light to the warden's mackintosh and he dived forwards, shouting for help.

'He's burning! For God's sake, some of you – can't you see he's afire?' He pushed Fred to the ground and rolled him over and over. 'Stop that stupid jeering and help.' His own hands were stinging, but the flames were out now and he glowered up at the slightly shamefaced men who were coming to give him aid. 'Think it's funny to watch a man burn to death, do you?' he demanded savagely.

'Take it easy, mate. He ain't going to burn to death. He's just scorched hisself a bit.' Hands turned Fred over, examining him for damage. 'Look, all he's done is singe that posh mac of his. And get his face dirty. His mum'll soon wash that for him.'

'She'll want to know where his eyebrows have gone, though,' someone said, and the crowd laughed again. Fred, released from their ministrations, scrambled to his feet and brushed himself down. He looked miserably at his burned coat.

'Never you mind, mate,' one of the men advised him. 'Council'll buy you a new one. They got plenty of money for the ARP. Shelters, sandbags, posh uniforms, funny faces – you ask for it, they'll pay for it. And none of it a blind bloody bit o' good, if you ask me. If the Jerries come over here we'll all cop it, the whole bloody lot of us, and a few holes in the ground and rubber masks ain't going to help us, that's for sure.'

'Rubbish! There ain't going to be no war. It's all a waste of money.' The speaker was a thin, sandy-haired man who lived a few streets away. 'Didn't Chamberlain promise us peace in our time? Didn't he say? Well, then.'

'That's right,' someone else agreed. 'All this fire-fighting and stuff, it's all play-acting. It's to take our minds off the depression, that's what it is. Give people summat to do when there's no real jobs. Keep us in our place. War! What good 'ud all this be if the Jerries come over with their bombs? Old Fred Stokes and a bucket of sand ain't going to save us.'

There was a chorus of agreement. 'Government be better off giving us proper jobs, that's what.' 'Stop all this arsing about and get down to some real work.' 'Never mind what's happening in Czechoslovakia and them places – it's what's happening here we're

38

interested in.' And, finally, 'You go back home to your mum, Fred, and tell her you fell down playing in the rec. She'll look after you when the Red revolution comes.'

The crowd dispersed, still making disjointed comments. Frank helped Fred Stokes gather up his bits and pieces and dismantle the platform. They stood for a moment looking at the faintly smoking remnants of the bomb, now smothered with sand.

'They're right, Fred,' Frank said at last, heavily. 'A bucket and a stirrup-pump aren't going to be much use if what they say about thousands of bombs is true.'

'It's all we've got, all the same.' Fred lifted the bucket. He had painted it red and scrawled 'SAND' on its side. 'And we've got to do what we can, haven't we, Frank? We can't just sit and let the city burn down around us without even trying.'

'Most people don't think it's going to, though. They're like ostriches – burying their heads in the sand.' He glanced again at the bucket and its smouldering contents. 'In fact, there's so many heads buried in the sand there won't be room for bombs as well.'

'Well, maybe they're right. I hope to God they are,' Fred said soberly. 'I've got a feeling we're all going to know soon enough, whichever way it goes.'

Olive told Derek about Fred Stokes and the bomb as they drove down the coast to Brighton. It was their first trip out in Derek's new car – the red MG he'd told her about. His father had given him the rest of the money he needed as a birthday present, and he'd come straight round to collect Olive.

The whole family had come out to admire the new acquisition, though Ted had looked down his nose a bit and asked Derek a lot of questions about his driving experience while Olive stood by squirming with embarrassment. But Derek hadn't seemed to mind. He'd answered politely enough, reminded Ted that he'd been driving his father's vehicles around ever since he was old enough to have a licence and some of them were vans and lorries, a lot bigger than this little red beauty. He stroked the gleaming bonnet as he spoke and Olive could see her father was secretly envious and would have jumped at the chance of a ride.

Annie made no secret of her admiration. 'It's lovely. But you won't go too fast, will you, Derek? Not while you've got our Olive with you.'

'Oh, *Mum*,' Olive protested, tying a bright green scarf round her chestnut hair. 'Derek's been driving for years. He's not going to have an accident.'

'Never you mind, *oh, Mum*,' Ted told her sharply. 'She's right to worry about you. Anyone can have an accident, specially when they get a bit too cocky.' He stood in the road, a short, stocky man with rough brown hair, glowering at the car. He still hadn't got used to his daughters going out with men – even young men like Derek, who lived only a few streets away – and to think of them going out in a car, out of Portsmouth, where he could have no control over them, had him in a state close to panic.

'Well, Derek isn't too cocky.' Olive put her hand on the door. 'Can we go now, if everyone's finished having their say? Or d'you want to have tea out here in the street, staring at it?'

'And there's no call to be cheeky either,' Ted began, but Annie touched his arm.

'Don't grouse at the girl, Ted. She's only going out for an afternoon with her young man – there's no harm in that, is there?' She gave Olive a smile. 'You go and enjoy yourselves. I know Derek'll be careful.'

They watched as the car roared away up the street – not that it could work up much of a roar just going up March Street, towards September, where it had to stop again for traffic. But she knew Derek was bound to let it out a bit when they got to the open road over Portsdown Hill, and she knew it wasn't a bit of use worrying about it.

'We've got to let them go their own way,' she said to Ted as they went indoors. 'Olive is old enough to make her own decisions now. And she's fond of young Derek, you can see that.'

'She's smitten by him, you mean,' he said. 'I just hope he's not going to take advantage of her. I don't like it, this jaunting round the countryside in a car. It's not our style, Annie. He could get up to anything, taking her miles away from home like that.'

'He could get up to anything anytime,' Annie said, but she knew what Ted meant. Out in the country, miles from Portsmouth, where no one they knew was likely to see them, it would be much more difficult for Olive to keep control. But there was nothing to be done about it. There came a time when you just had to trust your kids. Trouble with Ted was, he just didn't want them to grow up.

Olive, meanwhile, was apologising to Derek for her parents. 'They don't seem to realise I'm grown up,' she grumbled. 'Dad's the worst – treats me like a kid. D'you know he wouldn't even let me wear make-up till I was nearly seventeen!' She giggled. 'Not that I let that stop me! I used to put it on when I was in the bus on the way to work and wipe it off again on the way home. In the end, I got Mum to persuade him.'

'Shame,' Derek said, only half listening. He was nursing the car along the main road out of Portsmouth. Soon they would be on the coast road and then he could let her rip. He listened to the engine purring beneath the bonnet and looked forward to the moment when he'd hear it give that throaty snarl that meant it was gathering speed.

Olive sat close against his side. She too was looking forward to the moment when they'd be out on the open road. She pulled the green scarf more securely over her hair and wished she had sunglasses, like a film star. Turning her head, she looked at the passers-by, wondering if anyone she knew had seen her. Well, the whole of April Grove and March Street must have known Derek had a new car, and if they didn't old Granny Kinch would tell them – she'd been standing at her front door as usual and her little black eyes had nearly popped out of her head when the sleek red motor had purred to a stop outside the Chapmans' house.

The drive to Brighton was exhilarating. The road was almost empty, all the way through Emsworth, Chichester and Arundel. Olive's scarf slipped off and her hair streamed back in the wind. She laughed up at Derek, her dark eyes sparkling, and he grinned back, excited by the speed and the sense of freedom. 'No more buses for us, eh?' he shouted above the roar of the wind. 'We'll go where we like now, Livvy – Brighton, London, the New Forest. You name it!'

'I don't care where it is so long as I'm with you,' she answered recklessly, and he took his hand from the wheel and caught hold of hers, pressing it down firmly on his thigh.

Olive gasped. She'd never touched him so intimately and

immediately experienced the sense of guilt that was her warning signal. Over years of delicate hints and oblique references her mother had, without ever making a direct comment, given her a full manual of instructions on how a 'nice girl' behaved when out with her young man. The main criterion, it seemed, was to avoid 'cheapness'. A kiss was permitted, but prolonged kissing was cheap. So was allowing any touching other than on the places where anyone at all might be permitted to touch – on the arm, for instance, or the shoulder, or the back provided the touch did not stray below the waist. Indeed, any touching below the waist was strictly taboo.

These strictures had the unintended effect of making any touch at all highly exciting. Derek might have been surprised to know that his casual stroking of Olive's dark hair, when his fingers brushed her neck, or the absent-minded movement of his fingers on hers as they sat holding hands in the cinema, were enough to have her melting with desire. But he did not know – at least, Olive hoped he didn't know – for she had also been schooled not to show her emotions, and her own fear of what might happen if she 'led him on' kept her cool and still in his arms when her body longed to respond with heat and vigour.

It was getting more difficult to remain cool lately, though. Derek's goodnight kisses were becoming more lingering and she'd found herself snuggling into his arms and wanting more. Why was it 'cheap' to let your chap kiss you more than once? Kissing was good – she liked the feel of his lips on hers, moving gently but purposefully. And she liked it when he hugged her close against him, so that she could feel the hard muscles of his body, so different from hers. Sometimes she felt a bit more than she'd expected and when that happened she gasped and tried to wriggle free, but Derek only grunted and held her closer. And really, she hadn't wanted to get away at all.

Afterwards, Olive would lie in bed thinking over every moment of their goodnight kisses, reminding herself of the feel of Derek's arms about her, the feel of his hands on her body. He'd never gone any further than she wanted him to, never tried to touch those forbidden zones. But she knew that each time he kissed her, he got a little nearer, and she had doubts about whether she would be able to stop him when he did try to go further. Or even whether she wanted to.

They spent the afternoon in Brighton, strolling along the front. Derek brought Olive a huge pink cloud of candy-floss and she buried her face in it, laughing. They watched some jugglers and a Punch and Judy show and played some of the machines on the pier, coming away with a fluffy white toy kitten and a watch that had stopped before they were back at the car. They bought some rock to take home to the family and had tea in a café on the front. They went down to the beach and chased the waves, regretting that they hadn't brought swimming costumes with them.

'We've never been swimming together,' Derek said. 'I bet you look smashing in a bathing suit.'

Olive blushed. 'I don't know. I look all right, I suppose.'

'All right? With a figure like yours?' Derek slipped his arm around her waist and squeezed her. 'You'd look gorgeous, I know you would.'

'Well,' she said breathlessly, 'p'rhaps you'll see sometime.'

'I'll take that as a promise.' He nuzzled her neck. 'It's been a good day, hasn't it?'

'Mm.' She glanced anxiously up and down the beach and then reminded herself that they were in Brighton. Nobody they knew was likely to see them here. She relaxed and let herself lean against him. 'Mm, it's been lovely. Thanks for bringing me, Derek.'

'It wouldn't have been any fun without you,' he murmured, and nuzzled closer. Olive felt her heartbeat quicken. 'So what d'you fancy doing now?' he went on. 'I reckon we've seen most of what there is to see in Brighton, don't you?'

'Well – go home, I suppose.'

'Just go home? Seems a bit tame.'

Olive looked at her watch. It was a small chromium-plated one, a present from her parents for her twentieth birthday.

'It's nearly six. It'll be getting on for eight o'clock by the time we get back to Portsmouth.'

'That's too early to be going home,' Derek said decisively. 'I mean, most Saturdays we'd be going to a dance at Kimball's, or to the flicks. They won't be expecting you back that early, will they?'

'I don't know. I've never been out like this before – in a car, for

43

the afternoon. Mum probably thought we'd be back for tea. I wouldn't like to worry her.'

'But she knew we were coming to Brighton.' Derek squeezed her again. 'Stop worrying, Olive. Let's go and have a drink and a sandwich in a pub somewhere on the way back, have a walk on the Downs perhaps. I'll get you back by ten, I promise.'

Olive laughed and gave in. Of course it didn't make any difference that they were in Brighton and not Portsmouth. And a snack on the way home in a pub would be fun. Dad didn't approve of girls going into pubs, though he wasn't as strict about that as Uncle Frank, but country pubs were different. Charabanc outings always stopped at pubs on the way back and all the women went into them and had a drink. Anyway, wasn't she old enough to decide for herself now?

What was even more important was that she didn't want Derek getting fed up with her. Derek, with his good looks, his dark gold hair and his sports car, wouldn't have any trouble at all in finding a new girl to go around with, one who wouldn't fuss about her parents or have to be home by ten.

'All right,' she said, 'let's do that. Mum and Dad'll just have to get used to it. It's time they stopped treating me like a kid anyway.'

'That's the stuff,' Derek laughed. 'Mind you, we don't want them to take against me, do we? So we won't take any chances – we'll be home by ten, like I said. This time, anyway.' He bent his head and gave her a quick kiss. 'I don't promise I'll always be so good,' he murmured wickedly. 'Not now we've got the car and can go just where we like.'

Olive giggled and gave him a push. 'Get away with you! Just because you've got a car, Derek Harker, doesn't mean to say you can do just what you want. I'm a respectable girl, remember? I don't want to go jaunting around dark country lanes late at night.'

'Why not?' he asked. 'Afraid I'll run out of petrol?' And when Olive squealed and giggled again, he drew her close, his face suddenly sober. 'Don't you worry, Livvy, and tell your mum and dad not to worry either. I think too much of you to do anything you wouldn't want. But just for now – let's have a bit of fun, shall we? We might not get many more chances if this war starts.'

Olive stared at him. His voice was as serious as his face and she

44

felt a tremor of half excitement, half fear. He'd said he thought a lot of her, and said it as if he meant it. That was more than he'd ever said before. But then, even before she could begin to analyse what he had meant, he'd brought the war into it. And it was clear he wasn't joking.

War! she thought in disgust. Everlasting war – it gets into everything. She'd thought for once they could forget it, but here it was again, rearing its ugly head like some monster from the deep.

She looked out at the rippling sea and shivered. The bright afternoon was suddenly dulled, the glittering waves heavy and sinister. A few swimmers splashed in the water and a fleet of sailing dinghies swooped by like butterflies, their sails blue and white and brown wings of freedom against a wide and cloudless sky.

Over there was France, and beyond that Germany, where jackbooted troops were preparing to march on yet another helpless country. And if they did, men like Derek who wanted nothing but to sit on a beach with their girls, or take them driving in sports cars with the wind in their hair, would have to go and fight.

It's not fair, she thought with bitter anger. Just when our lives are starting. It just isn't *fair*.

'D'you think you'll ever have a car, Graham?' Betty asked wistfully. They were walking along the beach at Stokes Bay, over in Gosport, and she glanced about her with dissatisfaction, thinking of Olive on the way to Brighton for the afternoon.

'Course I will. Soon as I've got the money. But I'll have to get a better job first – working for old man Surrey won't make me rich.'

Andrew Surrey was a chemist and Graham had worked for him on and off ever since leaving school. He'd started as an errand and delivery boy and now served in the shop and sometimes mixed ingredients for Mr Surrey's potions and ointments. But he was restless, always looking for something better, and had tried several other jobs.

'Can you drive?' Betty asked, and he nodded.

'Been driving for old Surrey the past three years. He took me out in his van a couple of times and then I taught myself. He says I can drive it better than him now.' He glanced at her. 'Here – I could borrow it of a weekend, take you out somewhere. That'd be a bit of all right, now, wouldn't it?'

'Oh, yes.' Her eyes lit up. It might not be an MG sports car but at least they'd be able to get away from Portsmouth. 'We could go down the New Forest, see the wild ponies.'

'That's right.' They turned away from the beach and began to walk along Jellicoe Avenue, back towards the town. Betty had come over to have tea with Graham and his parents. They lived in one of the streets off Carnarvon Road, barely fifteen minutes' walk from the bay.

Betty had not yet met Graham's mother and father. So far, Graham had come over to Portsmouth to meet her and they had gone to the pictures together or for a walk. But he'd been to tea twice with the Chapmans and Betty had made it clear she expected a return invitation.

After five or six weeks, Betty considered herself settled now as Graham's girlfriend. She was still thrilled to be going out with him and enjoyed boasting to her friends about her 'young man' but like her sister she drew very definite lines as to Graham's behaviour. Kissing had turned out to be pleasurable, and she enjoyed snuggling up to him in one of the shelters out along Southsea seafront, but she would quickly slap Graham's hand away if it roamed too far, and there was never any danger of her being 'carried away', as Olive sometimes feared she might with Derek. There were, as she had told Graham when she first met him, plenty of other fish in the sea, and one of them not a hundred yards from her own doorstep.

But although she knew now that Bob Shaw would ask her out any time she cared to give him the hint, Betty had no desire to break with Graham. He was cheeky and fun to be with; he made her giggle, and when she pushed his hand away he just laughed and kissed her, as if he'd known she would do that and had only been trying it on to tease her.

'You'll let me one of these days, Bet,' he said. 'You're no different from the other girls really. You'll like it just as much as anyone else.'

'Oh, and how would you know that?' If anyone else had talked to her like that she'd have sent them packing, but Graham had a way of saying things you couldn't take offence at. 'I suppose you've had more girlfriends than I've had hot dinners,' she challenged him, wanting him to deny it.

46

'That's right,' he agreed equably. 'One every night of the week and two on Sundays. How else d'you think I know so much?'

'Oh, Graham! You're awful – I don't know why I go out with you.'

'Because you like me, that's why,' he said, and kissed her again, one of the lingering kisses that Betty liked in a queer, tingling way and remembered afterwards as she lay in bed, listening to Olive breathing a few feet away from her.

They were at Graham's gate now and he opened it and led her inside. The small front garden was rough and overgrown with weeds – Betty could imagine what her Dad or Uncle Frank would have had to say about that. The house itself looked neat enough on the outside, with a green front door and green-painted window-frames, but the step wasn't white and shining like her mother's – in April Grove it was almost like a competition to see whose step could be the whitest. It didn't look as if Graham's mother bothered about such competition.

Inside there was a passage, papered with dark red Anaglypta. The floor was covered with brown linoleum and a man's bicycle stood leaning against one wall. Graham and Betty squeezed past it. Graham tinkled the bell as he did so and a door at the end of the passage suddenly opened.

'Is that you, our Gray?' A big blowsy woman with unruly ginger hair appeared, filling the doorway with her bulk. She was wearing a flowery apron that stretched across a massive bosom and almost covered the blouse and skirt beneath. 'And is this Betty, then? Betty Chapman? Come here, love, let's have a look at you.'

'Well, move yourself out of the way so we can get through,' Graham said cheerfully, and pushed his way into the back room. 'Here she is. This is my mum, Betty, and you don't need to take any notice of what she tells you about me, it's all lies.'

'Hark at him!' his mother exclaimed. 'Lies, indeed! What a way to talk about your own mother, eh? I hope you don't stand no nonsense from him, Betty.'

Betty laughed and shook her head. Already she was feeling at home in this untidy household. It was plain to see where Graham got his cheeky, easygoing ways, she thought, and then noticed the man in the armchair by the fireplace.

'This is Dad,' Graham said as the man got up. He was smaller and thinner than his wife, with cautious blue eyes, but he smiled welcomingly enough and held out his hand.

'I remember your dad from when we lived up September Street. Ted Chapman, that's right, innit? Ferryboat captain.'

'That's right.' Betty could just remember Mr and Mrs Philpotts, though she wouldn't have known them in the street. They had moved to Gosport when she was about eight years old. Moving to Gosport was, to most Portsmouth people, rather on a par with emigrating to Australia. Once over the water they were liable never to be seen again. Of course, she knew other people who lived there – Uncle Frank had a brother there and she'd met him and his wife at family parties. But nobody went to Gosport unless it was to visit.

'Oh, I remember Ted Chapam,' Elsie Philpotts said, rolling her eyes. 'All us girls fancied him! He was a real bit of all right, I can tell you.' She laughed and dug Betty in the ribs with her elbow. 'Still, better not go telling tales out of school, had I? I don't want to cause no trouble.'

'Go on,' Graham said affectionately, 'you cause trouble wherever you go, can't help it.'

'Like mother, like son,' she retorted, and fixed her eye on Betty again. 'I hope you don't allow him no liberties. He needs a bit of keeping in order.'

'Oh – no. No, I don't,' Betty said, blushing scarlet as she remembered those moments when she'd pushed away Graham's straying hands. 'I mean, he doesn't – we don't— ' She broke off in confusion as Elsie Philpotts roared with laughter.

'Don't tell me he never tries it on! Well, he doesn't take after his father then.' And she turned and dug her elbow this time into her husband's ribs. 'Does he, Charlie? My, we could tell 'em a thing or two, couldn't we? Maybe our Graham needs a few lessons!'

'Give over, Else,' Charlie said. His voice was mild and dry, like fine worn sandpaper on wood. 'You're embarrassing the girl.'

'Course I'm not. Am I, Betty?' Without waiting for an answer, she bellowed with laughter again, then hurried on. 'Well, it's time for a cuppa. I bet you two could do with one, couldn't you? I'll go and see if the kettle's boiled. Come and give me a hand, Charlie.'

Her husband looked startled. 'But I was just— '

48

'Never mind that. You come and give us a hand in the kitchen.'
Elsie went through an elaborate pantomime of significant glances
and jerking of the head. 'Come on. Don't stand there like a stuffed
dummy. Can't you remember what it was to be young?'

Graham watched as his mother hustled his father out of the
room, then turned to Betty and grinned. 'That's so we can do this,'
he said, putting his arms round her. He gave her a smacking kiss
then leaned back and grinned again. 'So we'd better do it, hadn't
we? Wouldn't like to disappoint the old girl.'

'Graham! That's no way to talk about your mum. Old girl!
Don't you have any respect?'

'Oh, she's all right. She wouldn't mind. She'd just laugh.
There's not much that doesn't make my mum laugh, come to think
of it.' He cocked an eye at Betty. 'She likes you.'

'Does she? How can you tell?'

'Easy. She wouldn't have left me in here with you if she hadn't.
So that I could do this.' He kissed her again and Betty responded a
little nervously, half afraid that Mrs Philpotts would come
unexpectedly back into the room and catch them. But perhaps she
wouldn't have minded if she had. Not like Betty's mother, who
would have been embarrassed and probably disapproving.

That Elsie Philpotts was unlikely to come back unexpectedly was
made clear by a rattle of teacups and an overloud voice outside the
door a few seconds before it opened to admit her bulk. She carried a
large tray set with cups and saucers and a big fruit cake, while
Charlie followed with the pot and a jug of milk. Graham swept
aside a pile of papers on the dining-table and his mother set the tray
down and stood panting slightly.

'There. The cup that cheers. How d'you like it, love, as it comes?
We like it strong in this house, strong enough to stand a spoon in as
my old dad used to say, but I can easy put some more milk in if you
want it a bit weaker.'

'No, that's just right.' Betty sat down in one of the armchairs and
accepted a cup of tea and a slice of fruit cake. She looked around
with interest. Her first impression had been of a large airy room,
comfortably cluttered, and now she saw that this was true.

The room was bigger than the living-room in her own home,
with french windows that opened on to the back garden. There

49

were four armchairs – two by the fireside, two in the opposite corners. The dining-table stood against the wall opposite the fireside, piled with papers and bits of needlework, while beside one of the fireside chairs stood a sagging wicker basket filled with socks presumably awaiting mending. There was a big mirror over the mantelpiece, which was piled with letters, boxes of matches, pipecleaners and packets of cigarettes. In the middle of it was a large clock and on each end an alabaster figurine of a scantily dressed girl holding a torch above her head. Around the walls were gaudy pictures of seaside resorts or mountain scenes with shaggy cattle standing up to their knees in bogs under threatening skies.

'Now then,' Elsie Philpotts said, settling herself comfortably in the chair by the socks, 'tell us all about good old September Street and what's been going on there. How's your mum? I remember her from school, though we wasn't in the same class. I was more her sister's age – Jessie, wasn't it? She married Frank Budd.'

Betty nodded. 'That's right. Auntie Jess is having another baby soon.'

'No! She's not, is she?' Elsie leaned forwards. 'But how old's the youngest – what was his name, Kenny? Surely he's getting on for ten years old now?'

'Keith. He's nearly nine. The baby's due next month.'

'Well!' Elsie looked across the hearth at her husband. 'Did you hear that, Charlie? Jess Budd having another baby! Why, she's the same age as me.' She reached across and, being unable to dig him in the ribs, poked him sharply on the knee instead, so that his foot kicked upwards and he almost dropped his cup. 'Here, there's hope for us yet! How would you like a baby sister for Christmas, Gray?'

'Give over, Ma,' Graham said, turning red, and she squawked with laughter.

'Now I've embarrassed you! Well, I never thought I'd live to see the day.' She gave Betty a conspiratorial wink. 'Come out in the kitchen with me and we'll talk women's talk. It's no good with men around, they only want to talk about football and fishing. Here, pour yourself another cup of tea and bring it with you.'

Betty did as she was told. It struck her that probably most people did as they were told when Elsie Philpotts was around. Not doing so would be like arguing with a large, soft but very noisy bolster.

Anyway, she didn't mind. Graham's mum might be loud and even what Annie Chapman called 'common' but she was kind and good-hearted, and her house felt comfortable to be in. Already, Betty felt one of the family.

One of the family . . . The thought startled her. As she followed Elsie Philpotts into her cheerfully untidy kitchen, she wondered if she could be getting serious about Graham. No, she told herself decisively. It's too soon yet. Anyway, I don't want to settle down. I just want a bit of fun.

And to have fun, you needed a boy to go around with. But it needn't be any more than that.

To Jess, the winning of the FA Cup that summer seemed to be the last sign of peace. After that, there was talk of nothing but war. Trenches to be dug in public spaces. Shelters in your own garden or at the end of the street. Air defence. Evacuation tests – did they really mean to take the children away, to make them live with strangers far from everything they knew? She watched and listened with dread, and her thoughts were as much with the coming baby as with her living children. What had she and Frank been about, to bring another child into the world as it was today?

May passed into June and June into July. The news grew more serious daily. Frank bought a big map of Europe and pinned it up on the living-room wall, over the piano. He marked the advance of the Germans with pins and it was horrifying to see how they were spreading over the whole continent. How could anyone believe that they really meant to stop their ruthless invasions, when so many countries had already succumbed? How could they be trusted to let Poland stay free?

'We'll have to step in if they don't,' Frank said, frowning. 'We've signed a pledge. It's getting close, Jess.'

'I know.' She had been feeling unwell all day, her back aching and the baby squirming inside her. The midwife had come last night and said the birth was imminent; she was coming back this evening. 'I don't know what you've got in here, Mrs Budd,' she'd said, feeling the collection of knees and elbows that made protruding lumps on Jess's stretched abdomen. 'Feels more like a spider than a baby!' She'd laughed but Jess knew it meant a difficult birth. Not that she'd ever expected any different. They'd all been difficult and she was nine years older now than when Keith had been born.

'They're bringing Anderson shelters round now,' she said. 'Backbury Road got them today and I could hear the clatter from the garden. There was talk about builders coming to install them but they never will, not that many. Only for old people and them that can't manage. You'll have to do ours.'

'That's no problem.' It just meant a few hours when he wouldn't be able to work on the allotment. Or sit and read the *Daily Express*, his one relaxation at the end of a long day. 'I'll do it at the weekend.'

'Perhaps the boys will be able to help you.' She sat quietly for a few moments, then put a hand to the small of her back. 'Frank – '

'Is it the baby?' He was at her side at once. 'The nurse said it'd be soon, didn't she?'

'Yes. I've been feeling a bit queer all day.' She looked up at him, her face distorted by sudden pain. 'Frank, the children – '

'It's all right. I'll see to them.' It had all been arranged weeks ago, that the children were to go to Annie and Ted, at the top of the street, for the night. None of them, not even Rose, knew that a baby was expected; like most of their generation, Frank and Jess didn't approve of children knowing too much about the 'facts of life' and avoided difficult questions. They'd find out soon enough, and they'd all been taught not to make personal remarks so had not even commented on their mother's size. Jess thought that probably the boys hadn't even noticed it.

Rose was up at her friend Joy's for tea and the boys had bolted theirs down and then rushed out to play again. When they came back, they'd be sent up to their aunt's. Meanwhile, Frank went next door to ask Peggy Shaw to come and sit with Jess while he hurried to the telephone box at the top of the street to call the midwife.

'I always have a bad time,' Jess said when the two women were alone. She was in bed now, everything put ready for the birth. 'I can't bear down properly, you see. The baby just has to manage by itself. I can't help at all.'

Downstairs, Frank waited to let in first the midwife, then the doctor. He had been through this three times already but the anxiety was never any less and now, with this one, Jess was so much older. Forty – a couple of weeks off forty-one – was old to have a baby, however you looked at it. And Jess had been so worried lately, so frightened by the threat of war. He knew she believed that the things she thought and felt could affect the baby, and her own fears had worried her twice as much on that score. Was she right? Would it make any difference to how things went tonight?

The children were up at Jess's sister's house now. They'd been surprised and a bit querulous to find themselves shoved off up there at a moment's notice, and Rose had wanted to know what was wrong with Jess, but he hadn't the time or patience to answer their questions. And Annie had taken them in cheerfully enough and put the two boys to sleep up in Colin's room, which was a treat for them. Frank had left them there, knowing they were in good hands, and hurried home again.

He could hear sounds from the room above. The nurse had told him as soon as she came that the doctor would be needed. It meant extra expense but he'd put the money by a few weeks ago – there were some things that had to be afforded. There was enough there for all the things the baby would need – a few clothes, for Jess had got rid of most of Keith's baby clothes years ago, a cot and a pram. Luckily someone in September Street had a toddler just growing out of both, so it had been arranged that they could be fetched as soon as Jess's baby was born.

Everything was ready. And by the grunts and groans now coming from upstairs, it sounded as if the baby was ready too.

Frank switched on the wireless. At times like this, he almost wished that he smoked or drank. A cigarette or a stiff whisky, wasn't that what helped men through these anxious hours? But he'd never been able to afford to smoke and he'd turned his face steadfastly against drink ever since he was a boy. He'd seen too much of it . . . But he wouldn't let thoughts of those times get into his mind now. He'd shut them away long ago, told only Jess what had happened when he was a boy, and never referred to it again.

The nurse came down for more hot water. It was the only thing Frank could do to help, keep the kettle boiling. He stared at her in mute misery and she gave him a cheery smile.

53

'No need to look so worried, Mr Budd. She's doing fine. The baby'll be born in good time for you to go to work, see if it isn't.'

Go to work! That was hours away. He looked at the clock that ticked on the mantelpiece, the clock he wound every Sunday morning. It was just past midnight and Jess was having a hard time of it up there. If only he could go and see her, hold her hand.

But the midwife was shocked when he suggested it. 'No place for a father, Mr Budd,' she said firmly. 'You're better off down here. Anyway, what with me and the doctor there'll be no room for you. We're bumping into each other as it is.' She gave him another professional beam and went upstairs with the bowl of hot water.

Frank sighed and filled the kettle again. No doubt she'd be back for more in a minute, and if not he'd make a cup of tea. He was sure they could all do with one. He set out cups, fetched milk from the meatsafe outside and got the sugar bowl from the cupboard.

The wireless had finished for the night. He'd barely heard it anyway – just gramophone records on the Light Programme and some sort of play on the Home Service. He could have done with something light and cheerful – *Band Waggon*, perhaps, with Arthur Askey and Stinker Murdoch. But it might have seemed a bit callous to sit down here laughing at their antics, with poor Jess going through the mill upstairs.

He sat down and picked up the *Daily Express*, stood up again, stared at the map on the wall. Things were looking bad, there was no doubt about it. The pins he had stuck in showed a steady, inexorable march across Europe. Czechoslovakia gone – what chance had Poland? Hitler had already denounced the 1934 pact of non-aggression. In May he had signed the Pact of Steel with Mussolini, agreeing on mutual support in any future war. He'd be sucking up to Stalin next, and the great Powers would be lined up, facing each other.

The great Powers . . . Could Britain really take on the might of Europe alone? The Dominions were there, of course – Canada, South Africa, Australia and the rest. But would they give their support? Or would they keep out of it, preferring to see it as Europe's battle? And what about America?

It was all of Europe. Turkey, Greece, Denmark – everyone was getting involved. But it's not just our fight, Frank thought. The situation's grim all over the world. Russia and Japan at each other's throats, Japan blockading the British at the Chinese port of Tientsin, it seems as if every country's got some quarrel, some score to settle. As if the whole world is a great festering boil waiting to swell and burst with its own poison.

And as if all that wasn't enough, there were the troubles that went on all the time. The IRA, who set off no less than thirty pillar-box bombs one day last month. And the loss of the submarine *Thetis* on the first of June.

Fourteen Portsmouth men had been aboard the *Thetis* when she dived during her acceptance trials in Liverpool Bay that day. She hadn't even been at sea – that was what seemed so cruel about it. She went down in one hundred and thirty feet of water and stayed there, her stern on the surface. And none of the desperate efforts with salvage equipment was enough to save the men trapped inside.

Only four escaped. Of the rest, all hope was given up until tapping heard from inside the hull threw everyone into a frenzy of excitement and renewed bids to raise the stern. The country had held its breath, listening to the news on the wireless, scanning the front pages of newspapers . . . but in the end hope had died with the men who were even yet still trapped in their grim coffin. And only a week later, a memorial service had been held in the little church of St Ann in Portsmouth Dockyard, and Frank had seen the weeping mourners as he walked through the Yard and had felt a premonition of the future.

If war came – when war came – there would be many more ships sunk, many more men sent to a grim, choking death beneath the waves. And there would be others too. Soldiers, fighting a bloody battle in the mud and gore of the trenches, such as Frank himself remembered from the last Great War. Airmen, spinning from the skies in flames. And old people, women and children, blasted to death in their own homes, or huddled like animals in holes in their own back yards.

Babies, like the one Jess was struggling to bring into the world at this very moment, their lives smashed before they even knew what life was.

Footsteps sounded heavily on the stairs. He turned quickly as the scullery door opened and the doctor appeared, tired and grey. At the same moment he heard – and knew that he had been hearing for some minutes without even realising it – the cry of a newborn baby.

When Jess and her sister Annie were fourteen they left school and went out to work. Annie went into service and learned how posh people lived, with jugs of water on the dinner-table and forks as well as spoons for 'afters' – which she called dessert or sweet. Jess, who had always been handy with a needle, was apprenticed to a dressmaker and learned a craft that would be useful throughout her life.

Most of her afternoons were spent in dressmaking, either for herself and Rose or for neighbours who would pay her to run up a frock or a blouse and skirt from a paper pattern. The children were accustomed to the floor of the front room being spread with tissue paper marked with strange hieroglyphics and fabric being cut into odd shapes. They were used to the rattle of the treadle sewing machine, which stood in a corner and could be employed to do duty as a horse when it had its wooden cover on. And Rose was delighted to be able to have clothes that were different from those of her friends.

During the fortnight after baby Maureen's birth, however, there was no dressmaking in number 14 April Grove, for Jess stayed in bed the whole time, not even allowed to put a foot to the floor. And with the children at school and Frank, after that first day, back at work, she had time for her other main spare-time occupation, reading.

Jess had always been a great reader. As a child, she read all of Dickens's novels – Dickens being a son of Portsmouth, this was almost obligatory, but Jess enjoyed them anyway. She read Jane Austen and Charlotte Brontë and when she went to the library she seemed to seek out the thickest, heaviest novels to bring home. Every evening, from eight until nine, she read. It was sometimes the only hour of relaxation of her day.

But for once, the library books lay on the bedside table, largely untouched.

'Look at these leaflets,' she said to Annie when her sister came in to bring her a bit of lunch. That was another thing about Annie –

she always called the midday meal 'lunch', whereas to most of the other residents of April Grove and its neighbouring streets, lunch meant the sandwich or couple of biscuits you had halfway through the morning. Sometime between noon and one o'clock, depending on when men or children were home from work and school, you had dinner, and that was the main cooked meal of the day. Tea was bread and jam and cake at five o'clock, and most women, like Jess, turned to again at about nine in the evening and cooked supper – eggs and chips or something on toast, washed down with mugs of cocoa. During the week, for Frank and many other men who couldn't get home at noon, supper was the only freshly cooked hot meal they had.

Jess cooked for herself and all three children, for the school was near enough for them to walk home in less than ten minutes. She always saved a good plateful for Frank and covered it up in the meatsafe just outside the back door for the afternoon. At supper-time she would take out yesterday's empty plate from the box he carried to work, and put in today's, and he would heat it up to eat the next day. Where he heated it up, she wasn't quite sure, but there would be plenty of places in a boiler-shop.

But for this fortnight, meals were something she didn't have to worry about. Annie gave the children their 'lunch' every day and got dinner cooking ready for Frank when he got home. He was back before six, having arranged to do no overtime, and finished off the meal and served it. Jess imagined him downstairs, sitting at the head of the dining-table, keeping a stern eye on every plate. Every scrap had to be eaten and he was never soft like she was sometimes, going out to the scullery when Tim wouldn't eat his cabbage so that he got the chance to throw it on the fire. Otherwise he'd sit there for hours, staring miserably at it and refusing to eat, and neither of them would win.

Jess smiled, remembering the battles she and Tim had had over that cabbage. Once, he'd hidden it down the side of his father's armchair and it had been found several days later, black, soggy and stinking. Tim had been given a hiding for that and only narrowly escaped being forced to eat it anyway, after Jess had pointed out to Frank that it would probably make him really ill. Another time, caught halfways towards the fire with it in his hand when she had

57

come unexpectedly into the room, he'd jumped and let it fly so it came to rest draped over a photograph of Frank's mother on the mantelpiece. She'd been hard put to it not to laugh outright that time and had gone hastily back out to the scullery, which had given him the chance to climb up on a chair and rescue it.

'He can't be allowed to get away with it,' Frank said sternly, but he wasn't the one who had to cope with Tim's next trick, which was to force himself to be sick whenever cabbage was put on the table. She'd kept him at home from afternoon school several times before she realised what was going on, and even took him to see the doctor, who examined Tim and pronounced him perfectly healthy. It was only later that she realised he was doing it deliberately, and she'd never told Frank. But, seeing that Tim really did hate cabbage, she'd decided not to force him any more. Instead, she gave him the opportunity to get rid of it in his own way – except on Saturdays and Sundays when, under his father's eagle eye, he dared not refuse and somehow swallowed the tiny portion she put on his plate.

'These leaflets,' she said. 'They're pouring through the letter-box every day now.' She picked them up and flicked through them. ' "Things You Should Know if War Should Come." "Your Gas Mask and Masking Your Windows." "Evacuation. Why and How?" "Your Food in Wartime." They must know it's coming, Annie. Otherwise why go to all this trouble?'

Annie shrugged. 'They have to, I suppose. I mean, we'd all look a bit silly if it came and we weren't ready for it. And I reckon it is coming, don't you?'

Jess shuddered. 'I've been trying not to think about it, with the baby on the way. But now – looking at all this . . . There doesn't seem any way of stopping it. It's as if it was some huge animal, getting closer and closer all the time. Or like a big cloud in the sky that's going to blot out everything.' She looked at her elder sister. 'Why is it happening, Annie? What started it all?'

'You mean who started it all,' her sister said grimly. 'And we all know the answer to that. It's that man – Hitler. He's mad and he's sending everyone else mad. That's what Ted says and I reckon he's right.'

' "Most of the injuries in an air raid are caused by flying

fragments of debris or bits of shells," ' Jess read aloud. 'That's from bombs hitting buildings, Annie. And who are the people who are going to get injured? You and me – the children – old Mrs Seddon over the road. We never wanted a war, none of us. Why should we have to be treated like that? And what about the youngsters – your Olive, and boys like Derek Harker who're going to have to go and fight? All they want to do is get on with their own lives.'

'I know. It's unsettling them. I can see our Olive getting hurt whatever happens. Either they'll want to get engaged and she'll be miserable when he does go, or she'll want to and he won't.' Annie shook her head. 'It's pushing them too fast, Jess. Without the war they'd have been happy just to go out together and get to know each other properly. And there's our Betty with a young man too now, and only just turned eighteen.'

She sighed and got up to go. 'Well, don't upset yourself, Jess. It's bad for the baby. You don't want to lose your milk, do you?' She picked up Jess's empty plate and passed her a bowl of rice pudding, left over from yesterday with a bit of jam on top of it. 'I'll have to go now, the children'll be home any minute. You leave those leaflets alone and get a bit of rest. Forget it for a while.'

She went downstairs and Jess heard the front door open and close and her sister's footsteps hurry up the street. She ate the rice pudding slowly and then lay back on her pillows. Beside her, in a drawer pulled out from the dressing-table, Maureen lay fast asleep.

But Jess could not forget the war that loomed ever closer. She had not been allowed to. On 4 July, the very morning that the baby was born, the Anderson shelters had been delivered to April Grove and she had lain in bed, exhausted and wanting nothing but sleep, listening to the clatter of corrugated iron being dumped outside every house, to the shouts of the men and the exclamations of the neighbours as they peered at their new acquisitions. Then there had been the noise of the building – a deafening cacophony that echoed the worst of all from the gardens of October Street. For the first time, Jess had regretted the position of number 14, looking up the length of October Street's back gardens as it did. It seemed that she shared in every hammer-blow, in every yelled instruction, in every oath and curse, every blackened thumb. And now, after only a brief respite, came the leaflets. And she could not ignore them. They had to be read.

She picked them up, scanning through them again although she already knew most of them by heart.

There were going to be special anti-gas helmets for babies. That was something, anyway, though they weren't to be distributed before an emergency arose. That would be a bit late, surely? Perhaps they meant 'if war was declared'. And what sort of helmet could a tiny baby wear anyway?

Blackouts. There were to be no lights shining at night. No street-lights, no lights from cars or buses or trains, no lights from windows. Everyone had to make sure not the slightest gleam of light escaped, either by having specially thick curtains or by making blinds. Frank had already started. He'd been down to Bulpitt's at North End and bought several yards of blackout material – Italian cloth at tenpence-threefarthings a yard. This had been fixed to wooden frames which could be fitted into the windows as soon as it got dark. He'd tested it and reported that not a glimmer showed through.

The children were to be evacuated, she and Frank were agreed on that. The thought of Rose or one of the boys getting hurt in a raid was more than she could bear. But for herself . . .

'I'd rather stay here with you. How are you going to manage? You can't work long hours over the Dockyard and then come home and have to turn round and start cooking your own dinner. And what about your washing and ironing?'

'I'll manage,' he told her. 'I can cook my own dinner – haven't I been doing it while you've been laid up? And I can take my washing up to Mrs Brown's if I have to, she don't charge much. Your place is with the baby.'

The baby. Jess looked at the makeshift cot beside the bed. Maureen was fast asleep, one tiny fist curled under her chin, her downy hair a sheen of gold over her head. She was a good baby, never crying much, and the other children, after their first astonishment, adored her – although Jess had thought she detected, at first, a touch of resentment in both Rose and Keith. It had quickly faded, however, and now Rose was a real little mother to her baby sister while Keith would sit for half an hour at a time cradling her in his arms.

Tim took her, as he took everything else, in his stride. His first pleasure had been entirely unforced, but since then he accepted her very much as a natural development of the family. It was as if she had slipped into a place he had already prepared for her, as if they were friends from the start, so right that it barely warranted a mention.

But even though Jess now felt her family to be complete, she still couldn't help thinking it was a bad time to be bringing a baby into the world. Or a bad world to be bringing a baby into. And if it weren't for Maureen, she could stay at home with Frank when war came.

As if aware of the thought, Maureen stirred and began to whimper. And Jess, washed with guilt, reached down to pick her up. She cradled the baby close to her, whispering against the downy head, then bared her breast.

Frank was right. If war came, this precious little life must be protected. And she was the only person who could do it.

Once up and about again, Jess began her own preparations for war.

One of the leaflets dropped through the letter-box concerned food in wartime. It told how, during the past eighteen months, the government had been buying large reserves of essential foodstuffs – so they had been expecting it! What about that trip to Munich? she thought indignantly. What about that 'piece of paper'?

She resumed her reading. All ordinary householders were advised to lay in their own stocks – the quantity normally used in one week – to keep by them in case local shops ran out. Things like canned meat and fish. Flour. Suet. Dried milk. Sugar, tea, cocoa. Biscuits. And once having built up this reserve, to use and replace the items regularly, so they were always fresh.

It was something Jess did anyway. She had never had much housekeeping money and there had been times when the cupboard was almost as bare as Mother Hubbard's, but since Frank had been earning a little more she'd taken advantage of cheap offers in the shops and now kept a modest but complete little store-cupboard. And there were always the jars of home-made jam and the Kilner bottles of fruit from the allotment. And potatoes, carrots and turnips stored out in the shed all through the winter.

All the same, she didn't look forward to rationing. And Frank would need plenty of meat, doing the hard, strenuous work he did. It might be as well to lay in a few more tins of that, as well as make as much jam and bottle as much fruit as she could.

The family's clothes too needed attention. If the children were going to be evacuated, Jess was determined that they should look respectable. She wasn't going to have some countrywoman pursing her lips over torn trousers or frayed shirts. So there was a lot of sorting out to do, a pile of mending and darning, collars to be turned and buttons to be sewn on.

She discussed it over the fence with Ethel Glaister at number 15. She wasn't as friendly with Ethel as she was with Peggy, on the other side, but you had to be neighbourly and pass the time of day and they'd always managed to keep on reasonably good terms.

'Rose needs two new winter skirts. She's grown so much this past year, the ones she's got are up past her knees. And I'd better knit her a new cardigan for school.'

'How do you know she'll be going to school?' Ethel said, patting her hair. She had just had it permed by the new hairdresser at North End and Jess was certain she'd had it dyed too. It surely hadn't been that shade of yellow yesterday. 'Once they're evacuated their schooling'll go right down the drain.'

'Oh, I'm sure it won't,' Jess said. 'The teachers are going too. They had a rehearsal on Monday – we had to pack their cases just as if they were really going. All the teachers will be going with them.'

'But they won't have no schooling,' Ethel persisted. 'Look, it stands to reason. Country schools are only big enough for the children what are already there. How're they going to fit ours in? You only have to think about it.'

Jess stared at her. As well as newly permed hair, Ethel had a new blouse with a frilly neck. And she was wearing lipstick. Lipstick at her age! thought Jess, who never wore any make-up at all.

'But how'll they get on, then?' she asked. 'Some of them will be leaving school before long. And the infants – how'll they learn to read and do their sums?'

Ethel shrugged. 'Don't ask me. Ask them as is getting us into this bloody war. Anyway, when it comes I don't reckon as that'll be our biggest worry. Staying alive'll be all we're interested in then.'

Jess was silent for a moment.

'What are you going to do about yours, then?'

'Well, what can I do? Joe and Carol are out at work now, they won't get evacuated. They can just get bombed, along with the rest of us, don't matter that there's rich people's kids the same age as them still at school, getting pampered out in the country. And I suppose I'll have to stay here to look after George, he's useless on his own.'

Jess listened to the whining self-pity in Ethel's voice and felt a twinge of irritation. 'What about your Shirley?' she asked. 'She's only seven – will you let her go?'

Ethel shrugged again. 'S'pose so. Can't say I've thought about it that much. I mean, we don't know it's going to happen for certain, do we? And I've had our holiday to think about.'

She had been talking about their holiday since Easter, Jess reflected, lording it over her neighbours who couldn't afford family holidays, even though she was only going to stay with relatives. But the relatives lived in Devonshire, which made it more special, and the way Ethel talked about them you'd think they owned half the county.

'You're still going, then?'

Ethel stared. 'Of course we are. Why shouldn't we be going?'

'Well, I thought with all that's happening – I mean, suppose you got stuck down there and couldn't get back home?'

'Stuck?' Ethel said. 'Why should we get stuck? D'you think the Germans are going to invade Pompey the first day, or something?' She laughed, a shrill, whinnying laugh that set Jess's teeth on edge. 'If they do, I won't be trying to come back anyway!' She tossed her permed hair and bridled a little. 'Oh, we're going all right. No German's going to stop me going on holiday, I can tell you that.'

Jess looked at the Anderson shelter, hidden now beneath a hump of freshly dug earth. In some places, there'd been a lot of complaints about flooding but April Grove was lucky and the shelters remained dry. So far, anyway – nobody yet knew just what would happen when winter came and there was a lot of rain or snow. But Frank was going to concrete the floor to keep it dry and clean, and he'd said he'd build bunks against the walls. He'd got a hurricane lamp too and made a stout door from old planking.

63

'I can't imagine sleeping down there,' she said. 'I can't imagine what it'll be like – all of us huddled in a hole in the ground, listening to the German aeroplanes. It's like being in a cave.'

'Better get evacuated, then,' Ethel advised her. 'You're lucky – you can go.' She nodded towards the pram where baby Maureen lay fast asleep. 'I must say, you've bin clever about it. It's not often I've thought kids could come in useful but I wish I'd thought of having one.'

Jess stared at her. A sudden fury welled up inside her and she turned abruptly and wheeled the pram up the path towards the house. How could Ethel Glaister suggest – how could she even *think* – such a thing? That she and Frank had foreseen all this and deliberately set out to manufacture a baby – that *anyone* could even think of bringing a baby into the world as it was today, just for the sake of saving their own skins – why, it was disgusting!

Did other people think that too? Did those who thought she was too old to have a baby think that she'd had little Maureen just so that she could get special treatment if there should be a war?

If there should be a war . . . Jess looked up at the sky and thought, if there's a God up there, please, please stop it now. Please don't let it happen.

But as she walked on up the path, past the tomato plants and the flower patch where she grew peonies and pansies and dahlias, past the coal shed and in at the back door, she knew that it could happen. And – failing a miracle – almost certainly would.

CHAPTER THREE

'TOMORROW,' JESS SAID, staring at the front page of the *Evening News*. 'They're going to start it tomorrow. September the first.' She raised her eyes to Peggy Shaw's face. 'It's really going to happen, isn't it?'

Peggy looked at her pityingly. She was a thin, wiry little woman about the same age as Jess, full of bustling energy, always the first to volunteer to run a street party or jumble sale for some good cause. Her hair had been fair once, like Ethel Glaister's, but it had faded now to pepper and salt and her skin had faded with it to a papery pallor. She looked, Frank said, as if a puff of wind would blow her away, but there was a stalwartness about Peggy that had earned her the gratitude of many a neighbour with troubles to be shared.

She had no children of evacuation age – not that that made things any better, she thought with a clench of her heart. They were calling up twenty-year-olds now. Bob would be for the Navy within the year, if he had his way, and sailing off to God knew what. But still, you couldn't expect Jess Budd to be thinking of that just at the present.

'It's only a precaution,' she pointed out. 'Look, the headline says "War not regarded as inevitable". You'll just go off for a bit of a holiday in the countryside and be back before you know it.'

Jess looked at the newspaper again, and shook her head. Her face was white. She put out her hand and touched the handle of the pram that stood on the pavement outside the front door, where the two women were standing.

'I don't know what to do. If I go, who's to look after Frank? He's working all the hours there are, he can't come home and have to start cooking his own dinner.'

'There's canteen dinners,' Peggy said, but Jess snorted.

'Canteen dinners! You know what they're like. Anyway, he needs a meal when he comes in, he needs a bit of comfort to come home to. How can I go off to the country and leave him on his own? I know Annie'll do her best – but there's Mum and Dad too, she'll have to keep an eye on them. I feel awful, going off and leaving her to do everything.' She looked again at the pram, where baby Maureen, now two months old, slept peacefully. 'But I can't keep her here, poor litte mite, if we do get bombed . . .'

They stood silent for a moment, contemplating a future neither could really imagine. Both had memories of the last great war, the war of 1914–18. There had been bombing then, of London and the east coast. But now it was expected to happen over the whole country. Every city was a target, but especially those which were important to the war. Places where aeroplanes or munitions were made, and military or naval centres like Portsmouth.

Already the serene blue August sky was full of barrage balloons, floating like silver cigars above the city. What would it be like when it was dark with enemy aircraft, when death rained from the clouds?

'The school had another rehearsal on Monday,' Jess said. 'Our boys were full of it. They think it's all some big game. Can't wait to see the fighting.'

'That's boys all over. Our Bob's as bad. Talking about joining up, never mind waiting to be called. Down at the harbour every day watching the ships. They don't seem to realise.'

'If it was women ran the world,' Jess said, 'there wouldn't be any wars.' She put both hands on the pram handle. 'Well, I haven't got time to stand here. I've got to get the boys' clothes washed and ironed.'

'There'll be plenty as don't,' Peggy said. 'I bet old Granny Kinch wouldn't bother.'

'Is Micky going, then?' Jess was diverted momentarily. 'I thought Nancy wouldn't let him. Mind, she could go herself –she's got that baby, only four months old.'

Peggy laughed. 'And how's she going to earn a living, with no Dockyard nearby and no sailors? They might send Micky, but I wouldn't want the billeting of him, would you?' She looked at Jess. 'D'you want me to give Frank his dinner in the evenings?'

'That's good of you, but I daresay our Annie'll offer. She mentioned it the other day but I changed the subject. Daft, I know, but I just didn't want to think about it.' She looked at the newspaper again and sighed. 'Can't avoid it now, can I?'

'I see her Olive's young man's got a smart new car,' Peggy observed. 'How does your Annie feel about her going out with him?'

Jess smiled. 'Well, you know our Annie. She's always wanted to go up in the world. It suits her to have a nice red sports car standing at the door! I don't think Ted's quite so keen though, between you and me. He's like Frank, thinks people like us ought to know their place.'

'Go on!' Peggy said. 'There's nothing special about the Harkers. I knew old man Harker when I was a girl – his dad started the business from nothing. Jobbing brickie, that's all he was.'

'Well, they're something better than that now. Did you hear young Betty's got a boy, as well? Graham Philpotts. Elsie and Charlie's boy – used to live in September Street before they went over the water.'

Peggy sighed. 'All growing up, aren't they? Our Gladys is off with a different chap every week and young Diane looks like going the same way. I can't make up my mind if it's better that way or the other. At least they don't get too serious, but you can't help worrying about them, can you?' A piercing whistle sounded from inside the house and she tilted her head. 'That's my kettle boiling, I'd better go and get on with it.'

She went back indoors and Jess eased the pram through her own front door. There was scarcely room for it in the narrow passage but there was nowhere else for it to go. Maureen was still asleep, thank goodness. She went through the back room and out into the scullery to start the washing.

Luckily, there wasn't much. She'd done a good big wash on Monday and it was all dry and ironed now. There were just the things the boys had been wearing during the week – she'd have to do today's as soon as they went to bed and hope to goodness she could get them dry by morning.

There was plenty to do to have the three children ready and at school for seven next morning. But Rose would be a help. And the boys could be trusted to behave properly when they had to – not like Micky Baxter, up the road, who was always in mischief. Jess hoped that if he did go he wouldn't be billeted with Tim and Keith. He was a bad influence.

For the next couple of hours she was too busy to worry much about the future. Washing on a Thursday afternoon meant getting the copper heated up, something she normally only did on Mondays, and turning to with the washboard to scrub the boys' shirts. It wasn't only their things, either. If she was going too, Frank must be left with as many clean shirts as possible. And there were those trousers of his to be mended, and a pile of socks to be darned, and she'd better make some cakes to start him off with.

But what was going to happen to him when the sheets wanted changing again? And he'd worn more holes in his socks? And run out of cakes?

Jess stood at the sink, the washboard held in her left hand while she scrubbed with the right, and the tears came into her eyes and dripped on Keith's school shirt.

What was going to happen to her boys, sent to live with strangers? To herself and Rose and the baby? What was going to happen to the family she and Frank had made?

She thought of their Sunday walks together. She and Frank, walking side by side with the pram in front of them, Maureen's downy head on the pillow. Rose, a new ribbon in her shining hair, one hand on the pram as if it were her baby that chuckled at the clouds. The two boys running ahead – Tim's fair curls glinting in the sun, Keith's darker hair cut short and smooth. For Jess, it was one of the best times of the week, when she could look at her family with pride and satisfaction.

When would they be able to walk together again?

For weeks the papers and the wireless had been talking about evacuation. The children had been rehearsing at school, lining up with their gas masks and parading round the streets. War was 'not inevitable' but nobody could doubt that it was on the way. And now, surely, it must be close. Evacuation was no longer just a word. It was real and happening this morning.

By seven o'clock the school playgrounds were filled with children, some excited, some bewildered, some crying, others with set faces. Each one had a cardboard box containing a gas mask and a small case or satchel packed with clothes. Each had a packet of sandwiches and to this was added a large bar of chocolate and a bag of biscuits.

'Don't eat them now,' Tim's teacher admonished him as his eyes widened in delight at this unexpected treat. 'It's for later on.' She fastened a brown luggage label to his coat.

'Here, I'm not a parcel,' he protested, but when he tried to remove it she stopped him.

'It's so that we know who you are.'

'But you already know who I am. *I* know am who I am.' He was indignant at being treated like a small child. But Miss Langrish took no notice. She went round all the children, fastening labels, straightening coats, wiping eyes and noses and getting them to stand in lines. Small children were allowed to stay with their older brothers and sisters, and clung tightly to their hands. Friends huddled together, anxious not to be parted. Necks craned and eyes peered for a last glimpse of the parents who stood on the pavement outside the playground, watching helplessly as their children were taken out of their lives for who knew how long.

Most of the children wore their winter coats, even though it was only the first of September. It was cool enough at this hour of the morning, for it had rained in the night and large puddles lay on the ground. But as Jess had said to Frank that morning as he stood looking at their sleeping faces before setting off for work, you didn't know how long the kids were going to be away and they'd need warm clothes before they needed light ones.

'We don't even know where they're going,' Jess heard one woman say. 'How am I going to sleep tonight, not knowing where my little Alan is? How do I know they'll look after him?'

Jess was almost too exhausted to answer. She had been up all night getting things ready, and the baby had been fretful, needing several feeds. Dawn had come too soon and she didn't feel ready to face the day and its partings. The first of so many partings.

69

'He's only four,' the woman was saying. Tears were running down her face and her hands were bunching her pinafore up in front of her. 'It can't be right, sending away little ones like that. They're just babies.'

'His sister'll look after him,' Jess comforted. She knew the woman. Her name was Molly Atkinson and she lived in September Street; her husband and father-in-law ran the greengrocer's shop. 'Wendy'll take care of him.'

'But she's only eight herself. And what if they split them up?' Molly Atkinson's voice was rising. 'What if he loses his label and nobody knows who he is?' She stepped forward, thrusting herself through the crowd. 'I've changed my mind. I don't want him to go – not my little Alan – he's too young – '

'So's Martin.' Another woman was joining in, as if the panic were infectious. 'It's not right, sending them off like this.'

'They'll be safer in the country.' Jess wished she could believe it. Who was to say that bombs and gas attacks wouldn't happen everywhere? 'The teachers will look after them.'

'They need their mothers.' Martin Baker's mother turned and stared at her with angry misery. 'It's all right for you, Jess Budd, you're going too. You'll be out there with your kids, you'll know what's happening to them. You don't know what it's going to be like for us.'

I do, Jess wanted to cry, but she knew that Mary Baker wouldn't believe her. How *could* she know? How could anyone know, before it had happened? But she could see the pain in these mothers' faces, she could feel her own distress at watching her children leave, and she could imagine very well what the separation was going to mean to them.

Outside the playground were the buses which were going to take the children to the railway station. Their arrival seemed to make it all the more real. There had been rehearsals before, with the children lined up just as they were now, but never buses.

Jess looked at them miserably. She could understand Molly Atkinson's distress all too well. In a few minutes, her own three children would be on those buses, being whisked out of her sight.

For her, it was only a day or two and then she'd be evacuated to the same place herself. But for most of the women here, there was no knowing when they would see their children again.

'Where d'you think they'll go?' someone else asked. 'It said in the paper they'd be going to the Island.'

'Some of 'em will. Some are going to the New Forest, or Salisbury or Winchester way. We'll find out soon enough. Once they're there they can send postcards home, see, then we'll know.'

'But my Alan can't write!' Molly Atkinson had been turned back from the school gates. 'How can he send a postcard?'

'Wendy will,' Jess said. 'Wendy'll look after him, you'll see. She's a sensible girl.'

She watched the crowd of children in the playground. They were growing restless and beginning to break out of the lines into which the teachers had formed them, shouting to make themselves heard over the hubbub. It would be better if they could just go now, she thought. This waiting was awful for everyone.

The crowd outside was constantly shifting as mothers tried to push nearer the railings for a last shouted message. Molly Atkinson was standing by one of the horse-chestnut trees that grew at the edge of the pavement. One hand clenched against the bark, the other pressed against her mouth.

Jess found herself next to a man. She recognised him as a milkman who would normally have been trundling his electric milk-cart around the streets at this time. She looked for his wife, then remembered she'd heard she was ill.

'Is your little girl going this morning?' she asked, and he nodded. His eyes were fixed on the crowd beyond the railings. Jess noticed his face looked puffy.

She racked her brains for his wife's name. She'd known her slightly at school, but she'd been several years younger. Margaret, was it? Maggie?

'How's Madge?' she asked as the name slipped back into her mind. 'I heard she was ill.'

He looked at her for a brief moment and she read the message a split second before he answered her. There was just time to wish she hadn't asked, to hope he wouldn't answer, but it was too late.

'She died on Monday,' he said flatly. 'The funeral's today.'

'*Today?* But – ' She stared at the playground full of children,

71

then looked back at the man's face. There was no expression there; it was as if he had been carved from stone. 'But – ' And there was nothing to say. No words to express her feelings.

'She's better off out of it,' he said drearily. 'No mother to look after her. And I'm no good. Better out of it.'

His eyes were red with tears. Jess reached out and laid her hand on his arm. She wanted to offer comfort but felt totally helpless. What could you say to a man who had just lost his wife and was about to lose his child? What comfort was there for him?

She saw him peer again into the milling crowd of children, now being formed yet again into their ranks. Could he see his own daughter there? Or had she disappeared into the throng? Jess looked into his face, seeing the pain behind the stony mask, in the reddened eyes. From here he must go to bury his wife. How could he bear it?

A little girl broke free from her line and ran to the railing. She clutched one iron bar in each hand and peered through the gap. Her plaits, clumsily tied with inexperienced hands, were already coming undone and her face streamed with tears.

'Daddy! Daddy!' She saw the milkman and stretched both hands through in entreaty. 'Daddy, I want to come home. I don't want to go. *I want my Mummy!*'

The milkman stared at her. He took a step towards the railings. But before he could reach them a harassed teacher scooped up the child and carried her none too gently back to her place in the line.

'You just stand there, Susan Cullen, and don't dare move again. We're starting now and I don't want any more nonsense from any of you.'

The milkman stopped in his tracks. He stared, baffled, at the lines of children, at his weeping daughter. And then a whistle blew and the children began to move.

Suddenly silent, they filed out of the school yard and on to the pavement. The crowd of parents fell back to give them room. Led by their teachers, the children climbed aboard the buses and could be seen finding seats, arguing over them, squashing together and pressing their faces to the windows.

Susan Cullen had disappeared. So had little Alan and his sister Wendy. Jess saw Rose shepherd a group of smaller girls aboard, while Tim and Keith scampered up the stairs to the top deck. She found that her own hands were pressed against her mouth, just like Molly Atkinson's, and she felt her teeth dig into her knuckles.

Molly Atkinson suddenly let go of her tree and ran after the bus, screaming for her baby, her Alan, to be let off, he was too young to be sent away, too young to leave home. A few other mothers, crying themselves, caught her arms and held her back, huddling together to share their grief. Their weeping released the tears of others and there were few mothers in the crowd who did not have wet faces as they watched the buses move away down the road.

But Sam Cullen, the milkman, said nothing. His face grim, he turned away and marched from the school without glancing back, on his way to bury his wife.

Some of the mothers went to the station to see the children off on the trains, but Jess had no heart for it. The baby was due for a feed and in any case the buses were all being used to transport the children and blind people who were being evacuated that day. She could not walk with the pram all the way down to the Town station and she didn't think most of the mothers would get there before the trains left. Besides, as Frank had said, the more people there were milling about, the more difficult it was for those who were organising it all.

She went back to April Grove. The streets seemed unnaturally quiet now that the children were gone. It was eight o'clock and most of them would have been at home anyway, getting ready for school – but still you could tell somehow that they weren't there any more. It was like that old story of the Pied Piper of Hamelin, she thought. This is what it must have been like then. A town with no children in it. Dead.

She felt a sudden surge of bitterness towards the man who had made this necessary, the small, commonplace house-painter who wanted to take over Europe. What right had he to do this? How had he ever been allowed to grasp the power to ruin so many people's lives? Even if they come back tomorrow, she thought, the damage will have been done. Those tiny children, torn away from their mums and dads, without any idea why. The milkman's little girl crying for her dead mummy. Molly Atkinson's Alan,

73

frightened and alone but for his sister – and she only eight years old herself.

There must be thousands like them. Little children, the first victims of a war they're still saying isn't inevitable. Their little minds and hearts have been hurt already and nobody will ever be able to make them better.

As she walked down October Street, she could see old Mrs Kinch standing at her doorway. Mrs Kinch wasn't really that old – probably in her early sixties – but she was known to most of the people along the street as Granny Kinch. Her house was number 10, looking straight up October Street, and she spent hours either sitting on a chair or standing in the doorway, watching all that went on.

'Gone off, have they?' she asked as Jess came nearer. 'I saw you going, not long after your Frank went to work.'

My God, Jess thought, does she stand there all night as well? 'Yes,' she said, 'the whole school's evacuated. I don't think many people have kept their children at home.'

'I suppose you'll be going too, seeing as you've got a baby,' the old woman said, looking at the pram. She was wearing a pinafore with a faded pattern of flowers, over a skirt and blouse of indeterminate brown, and her thin grey hair was as usual tightly wound in curlers. To Jess's knowledge, nobody had ever seen her without these curlers.

'She's saving her beauty for Nancy's wedding,' Tommy Vickers had once said and everyone had laughed, though the women tried to look disapproving.

'Will your Nancy be going?' she asked. Nancy's baby Vera had been born two months before Maureen, just after Portsmouth's famous football triumph. Nobody had asked who the father was, though it was known that Nancy had registered her in the name of Baxter. That was the name of the husband no one in the street had ever seen. He was supposed to be in the Navy, his ship based in Plymouth, and when Nancy went off for the occasional weekend Mrs Kinch let it be known that they were together.

'And the band played, "Believe it if you like",' Tommy Vickers commented sarcastically.

Once again the women tutted and tittered, but they all knew he

74

was right. Where Nancy had got the name Baxter was a mystery – perhaps she had once been married and perhaps ten-year-old Micky really was legitimate – but where she got baby Vera was all too easy to see.

As Peggy said, how would she earn her living far away from the Dockyard gate?

'My Nancy?' Granny Kinch said. 'No – she wouldn't go and leave her old ma. She's not letting our Micky go either. No, we sticks together. We've got our shelter down the garden if the bombs come. We'll be snug enough down there.'

Jess looked at Granny Kinch, standing there in her old flowered apron and curlers. Some of the children called her a witch, but the old woman was good-hearted enough. She would bring out a bag of toffees sometimes and get the children to gather round before scattering them over their heads. It was a shame Nancy had gone the way she had, and that Micky was growing up a bad lot.

All the same, Jess envied her. War might come to Portsmouth but Granny Kinch wasn't going to be separated from her loved ones. She would have them with her in the house or in the shelter, day and night. She would know what was happening to them.

'You look done up,' the old woman said suddenly. 'Why don't you go and have a cuppa with your sister?'

'I was going to,' Jess said. 'But it's not long gone eight. I can't knock on her door at this hour. They'll all be getting ready to go to work.'

'Course you can,' Granny Kinch said. 'What's a family for? And she'll have a pot on the go, bound to. You go along and see.'

Jess thought of her own house, empty and too quiet. The old woman was right. Annie would welcome her and it didn't matter that the house would be in turmoil with the girls tripping over each other to get out.

'Well, if you don't want to go into your sister's yet,' Mrs Kinch said, 'why not come in and have a cup with me? Our Nancy's not back from work yet and I've had the kettle on this past half-hour, waiting for her. It's brewed and I reckon you could do with it.'

Jess hesitated. What would people say if they saw her going into Granny Kinch's house? What would Frank say? And suddenly she didn't care. She didn't want to go back to the empty house, with all

75

its reminders that her children had left it. And neither did she want to go to Annie's — not just yet, with everyone scrambling to get ready for work. She needed somewhere to sit and catch her breath, with someone sympathetic, and as she looked up at Granny Kinch in her faded apron and curlers, she knew that this was her unlikely haven.

'All right, I will,' she said, and parked the pram outside the door. Maureen would be all right there, fast asleep. She followed the old woman into the house.

Jess had never been in number 10 before. The residents of April Grove weren't given to popping in and out of each other's homes, unless they were friends or had some reason to call. And nobody called on Granny Kinch and Nancy. You didn't need to, after all — the old woman was always at her door.

The passage was dark and musty. The sun came up at the back of April Grove, filling the back rooms with light but leaving the fronts dim. In number 14 it would be pouring through a shining window, making the mirror and the polished wood of the piano gleam. But here in number 10 the sunlight was dusty, filled with drifting motes, and the room wasn't comfortably, if shabbily, furnished like her own, but almost bare, with no rug on the floor and only a couple of old armchairs with sagging seats, and four kitchen chairs round a table covered with American cloth.

An old pram stood in the corner and Vera, Nancy's baby, lay snuffling in her sleep. Jess stopped to peep in and was disturbed by the baby's appearance. She wasn't plump-cheeked and rosy like her own Maureen, but pale and wizened, as if she had been born old.

'Beautiful, ain't she?' Granny Kinch said proudly. 'And good as gold. Never keeps me awake at night while our Nancy's at work.' She busied herself in the little scullery, bringing the kettle to the boil again and making tea in a brown pot.

'Nancy's job's still all right, then?' Jess hardly knew how to put it, but she had to keep up the fiction that Nancy had a proper job. The story was that she worked in a posh hotel at night, cleaning the shoes left outside rooms by the guests and polishing silver, but nobody believed it. Nancy Baxter had been seen too many times hanging around the Dockyard gates or walking up Queen Street on the arm of some sailor.

76

'Oh yes. She might be getting promotion soon. Reception work.'
Mrs Kinch set out two cups and saucers. One of the cups was
cracked and the saucers didn't match. She fetched a bottle of milk
from outside and poured some into the cups, then filled them with
strong tea. 'Here you are, duck, this'll make you feel better.'

Jess sipped the brew. It was hot and sweet and although she
didn't normally take sugar she found it heartening. She smiled at
Granny Kinch. Maybe they were all wrong about Nancy after all.
Maybe she really did work nights in a hotel. She heard Tommy
Vickers' voice inside her head. 'And the band played . . .' and
stifled a sudden giggle.

Perhaps the truth was that it didn't really matter what Nancy did,
so long as she wasn't hurting anyone else. After all, what was she
doing other than giving a few poor lonely sailors a bit of comfort? Was
that really so bad, when you thought of what other people were doing
– marching into other countries, persecuting and killing people who'd
never done any harm, sending little children away from their parents
without even time to say goodbye . . . ?

Jess's face crumpled. She put her cup on the table and bent
forwards, covering her face with her hands, and burst into tears.

Granny Kinch sat quietly beside her. She didn't tell Jess not to
cry, she didn't tell her it was all for the best, she didn't say the
children would be better off where they were going. She simply
waited for the storm to subside, offering no comfort other than a
touch on Jess's shoulder. Perhaps, thought Jess as she found a
hanky and wiped her eyes, she knew that there was no comfort, for
the wounds were too deep. And it wasn't only her own wounds she
was crying for, but the wounds of the children, of little Susan
Cullen with her clumsy plaits, motherless and now fatherless, of
Alan Atkinson, still little more than a baby and his sister Wendy
carrying responsibilities too heavy for an eight-year-old to bear.

Haltingly, she tried to explain some of this to the old woman, and
the grey head with its tight steel curlers nodded.

'You're right. It shouldn't be happening. It ain't natural,
sending little 'uns away from their mums. They oughter be in their
own 'omes. 'Ow do they know they're ever going to come 'ome
again? 'Ow does any of us know? Families oughter stick together,
that's what I say.'

77

'I think so too,' Jess said, grateful to have found someone at last who understood and agreed with her. 'But my Frank says they'll be better off in the country and I must say I don't want them here if we're bound to get bombed.'

'But you're going too, ain't you? You've got a baby.'

'Yes. I'll be with Rose and the boys won't be far away. But it isn't the same as being at home. And Frank's got to stay here.' She looked at Mrs Kinch and her eyes filled with tears again. 'I don't want to leave him any more than I want to be parted from the children.'

'Well, it ain't going to be easy for none of us,' the old woman said. 'And we all has to decide for ourselves.' She lifted her head. 'Is that our Nancy coming? I'd better get the kettle on again.'

Jess wiped her eyes again and blew her nose. She felt suddenly embarrassed to be sitting here. Like most women in the street, Jess didn't have much to do with Nancy. She passed the time of day with her, of course, but she could never forget the younger woman's reputation, and the thought of the way she earned her living nagged at the back of her mind. It was as if she knew more than she wanted to know about Nancy's private life. And the arrival of baby Vera, with no father, confirmed her guilty knowledge.

Granny Kinch didn't seem bothered, however. Whatever she said to Nancy in private, she had outwardly accepted the baby as her legitimate granddaughter, the child of that mysterious, high-ranking naval officer, and even thought the wizened little creature beautiful.

She bustled about, making fresh tea and frying bacon and eggs. Jess's eyes opened wide. Bacon and eggs on a weekday! It was more than Frank and she could afford. But perhaps that was where Nancy's money went, instead of on furniture. And even if it wasn't Jess's way, who was to say it was wrong?

The door from the passage opened and Nancy came in. She grinned at Jess and shrugged out of her red jacket. She wore a bright yellow frock underneath, too skimpy for September and with half its buttons undone to show a lot of chest. She had no stockings on and there was still a smudge of lipstick on her thin lips.

'Hullo, Jess,' she said. 'I knew you were here, saw Maureen in her pram outside. She looks as if she's thriving.'

'So does your Vera,' Jess said politely, though privately she thought Nancy's baby a skinny little thing. But maybe she just took after her mother, for no one could call Nancy voluptuous. She was a thin, angular woman, who looked older than her thirty-odd years, with gaunt features and sharp bones. Not at all the sort you'd expect to find luring sailors up the primrose path. But as Tommy Vickers had once remarked, all cats were grey in the dark.

Nancy dropped her jacket on a chair and flung herself down in another. As her mother placed a cup of tea and a plate of bacon and eggs before her, she dragged a crumpled packet of Woodbines from her pocket and lit one. She smoked, ate and drank alternately, talking through whatever happened to be in her mouth at the time.

'Thought I'd never get home this morning, Ma. There's not a bus to be had anywhere. They're taking all the children off on this evacuation lark. Droves of 'em, full of kids, going to the railway stations.' She looked at Jess. 'Your lot gone?'

Jess nodded. She wanted to cry again but Nancy's casual talk wasn't like her mother's sympathy.

'I won't let Micky go. You don't know what'll happen to 'em, out there in the country. Farmers treating 'em like slaves, posh lah-di-dah women turning the girls into servants. I'd rather have him with me, where I know what's happening to him.'

'But what about school?' Jess asked. 'Is there anywhere for him to go? All the teachers have gone away.'

Nancy shrugged. 'School!' she said scornfully. 'What good's school ever been to my Micky? They've never liked him, they're always picking on him – anything goes wrong and it's my Mick gets the blame. He's well out of it. He knows as much as he's ever likely to learn from teachers and he'll be old enough in a few years to leave and start earning a living. Till then, he might as well make himself useful at home. He can always do odd jobs, run errands and that.'

'There's a couple of teachers left anyway,' Mrs Kinch put in. 'They're 'aving classes at someone's house. Coming once a week and giving the kids 'omework, for what good that'll do.'

Nancy finished her breakfast and leaned back, lighting another cigarette. She looked at Jess through the smoke and spoke again, her voice softened.

'I bet you're not feeling so good, sending your kids off?'

Jess was too surprised to prevaricate. 'No, I'm not. It's silly because I'll be seeing them tomorrow, but – well, it seems as if everything's crumbling away. I don't feel as if I can get hold of things any more.'

Nancy nodded. 'I know. It's a bad business.' She smoked for a minute or two in silence and then said, 'Look, if there's anything you want done while you're gone – I mean, for your Frank – ' And before Jess could speak, she went on quickly, 'And I don't mean the obvious! I'm not after your man, that's not my style. I've got my work and it's just a job to me, and when I come home I don't want more of the same, no more'n anyone else. But I don't mind doing a bit of cooking or washing and I've got time to go in and clean up a bit if you like. But I won't do it if you don't. I'm not going behind your back.'

Jess was touched. It was clear that Nancy's offer was genuine and that she had no ulterior motive. Come to think of it, it made sense that she wouldn't have. As she had just said, she got enough of that sort of thing on her nightly excursions to the 'hotel', she wasn't likely to want to start all over again when she got home, and for nothing too!

'That's nice of you,' she said. 'I expect Annie will be keeping an eye on Frank. But I'll tell him you offered.'

Nancy nodded. 'We got to stick together in this lot,' she said. 'But I don't want no trouble. People writing letters to you and that sort of thing. It's got to be above board.'

She saw Jess to the door, then came back to her mother and poured another cup of tea.

'Jess Budd looks worn out.' She lifted the baby from her pram and rocked her for a few minutes. A half-empty bottle stood on the table and she stuck the teat in Vera's mouth, then picked up the Woodbine packet. 'Only one left! I'll have to go up the street, get some more.' She found the box of matches and lit up again. 'Mind, I reckon everyone is this morning. I've never seen anything like it – all them kids going off to God knows where. Half of 'em crying their eyes out, the rest looking as if they don't know what's happening to 'em. Don't reckon they do, either, poor little sods. I mean, how d'you tell a kiddy of four about the war? They must wonder what on earth it's all about.'

80

'You 'aven't changed your mind, then?' her mother asked. 'About our Micky, I mean?'

'Nah. Don't see no point. Anyway, he'd hate it in the country.' Nancy glanced around the room. 'Where is the little tyke, anyway?'

'Got up and went out early. Down to the station, I expect, to say goodbye to his pals. He might get a bit fed up 'ere on 'is own, Nance.'

'We'll find him plenty to do. And he can run errands for people – there'll be plenty who miss their own kids to send to the shops. Our Mick will earn hisself a bit of pocket-money.' Vera finished the milk and whimpered, a thin little cry. Nancy held her against her shoulder, rubbing the baby's back. 'Anyway, he's not the only one stopping. Young Joy Brunner from up the road, she ain't going either.'

'Well, I'm not surprised. Her dad must be worried stiff, and Alice too. I'm surprised he ain't bin took away already. Ain't they supposed to be putting all them whatjercallits, aliens, inside?'

'That's what I thought but he's still around. Still, war ain't bin declared yet, has it, and maybe it still won't be.' Nancy finished her cigarette and laid the baby back in the pram. She stood up, stretching her thin body. 'I'm just going up for some more fags, Ma, and then I'll get a couple of hours' kip. I feel proper done up. It upset me a bit, seeing all them kids being took off.'

Granny Kinch nodded. She found her brown coat and put it on to accompany her daughter to the door. It was well after breakfast-time now and the street would be coming to life. All the other women who had seen their children off on evacuation would be coming out again, their tears dried, ready to compare notes and share each other's troubles, and Granny Kinch didn't want to miss it.

'You go on,' she said. 'You needs your sleep. I'll take care of the baby and keep Micky quiet when he comes home.'

She stood at the door, watching her daughter walk up October Street. There were plenty of women about, standing in little groups, but none of them did more than give a brief nod of good morning. But Nancy's back was straight and she walked past them all like a queen, her head held high in the air.

That's right, Granny Kinch thought, you keep your head up,

my girl. You're as good as them any day. And there's not a bloody one of them would do any different, if they'd been handed your plate of luck.

It was a pity they wouldn't be more friendly, though. They were, she knew, good enough at heart. It was just that they couldn't forget what Nancy did to earn her living.

Still, maybe this war would bring people together a bit more. Maybe it had already started, with Jess Budd coming in for a cup of tea this morning. Maybe number 10 would be what Granny Kinch had always wanted it to be – a place where people came for a talk, to get things sorted out in their minds, to let off steam and have a bit of a cry and a bit of a laugh.

That was what everyone needed, after all. It was as simple as that.

Meanwhile, Jess pushed Maureen's pram thoughtfully up the road to Annie's house. Once again, she wondered if they were right to look down on Nancy. She might not be much to look at and her way of life not what Jess would want but, like her mother, she was good-hearted. And who knew why she'd started to live the way she did? It hadn't been easy these past few years to get jobs and earn a living, especially for a woman on her own with a baby.

Annie and Ted's address was really March Street, but their house was separated from the terrace. It was detached and had its own small garden all around it. It faced down April Grove and the side windows looked out over the allotments. But most interesting of all, it had a small tower at one side with a top just like a castle. The rooms inside this turret were not much more than cupboards but Annie's eldest, Colin, had had the upstairs one as his bedroom ever since they'd moved there, and had been the envy of all his friends. Jess could remember him as a small boy, spending hours on the top with a home-made bow and arrow, until he'd knocked a neighbour's cat off a wall. The neighbour had been furious, Ted had given Colin a good hiding and after that bows and arrows were banned from the turret.

Jess wheeled the pram along the side passage and parked it beside the back door. She could hear voices inside. The girls hadn't yet left for work.

'If I've told you once, I've told you a dozen times, our Betty,' Annie was saying, 'you've got to wash your stockings out yourself. I'm not doing them for you, a great girl of eighteen like you. And if you haven't got any clean, it's your own lookout. Who's that at the door?' She looked round, her morning face shiny under curlers and hair-net, as Jess knocked and pushed the door open. 'Here, it's our Jess. Come in, love, and sit down. Push the cat off that chair. Olive, get your auntie a cup.'

Her own cares were forgotten at once. She dropped the stockings she was holding and came over to her sister, enveloping her in a hug. Jess quivered for a moment. She'd thought she'd got over this at Granny Kinch's but the emotions she was feeling that morning were too strong to be dealt with so quickly, and once again she burst into tears.

'That's it, that's right,' Annie crooned, rocking her gently. 'You have a good cry, love. Let it all out. It'll do you good. Better out than in, that's what I always say. You'll feel better soon.'

Jess wept against her sister's breast. Annie hadn't held her like this since she was a little girl. But she was glad enough now to rest in the comforting warmth of her sister's arms and be a little girl again for a while.

'I don't know why I'm being so silly,' she said at last, sitting up a little straighter and finding her hanky again. It was still wet from the tears she'd shed in Granny Kinch's back room. 'I'm going myself tomorrow. I'll see them then. Some people don't know when they're going to see their children again. But – I don't know, watching them go off like that – '

'It's made it all seem real, all of a sudden,' Annie said. 'That's what it is. I mean, we've got used to all the talk – it's been going on for years. But lately, what with the Andersons coming and the shelters in the street, and the blackout – '

'The blackout!' Jess said. 'It took Frank and me hours to get the back bedroom one right. He's made wooden frames with blackout material on them, to fit in the windows, and try as we would there was a tiny chink of light showing through the back one. I didn't think it'd matter, being at the back, I mean, who's going to see it there, but no, it had got to be right. Germans might see it from aeroplanes, he said, and he had to take it all to pieces and start

83

again.' She looked at her sister. 'D'you think he's right, Annie? Can they see little bits of light like that from aeroplanes?'

Annie shrugged. 'If they say so, I s'pose it must be right. Anyway, if everyone had a little bit of light showing – '

'That's what Frank says. There'd be no point in a blackout at all. We've all got to do our bit, same as everything else.' She sighed and sipped at the cup of tea Olive had put in front of her. 'I don't know, Annie. I don't know what the world's coming to. And when I think we've just had a baby – I mean, what a time to bring a baby into the world. What a time!' Her face puckered again. Olive and Betty, ready to go to work, hovered uncertainly by the table and their mother nodded at them.

'You two go off or you'll be late.' She watched them go and sighed. 'I know, Jess. It don't seem any time for young people now. You just wonder what they've got in front of them, don't you? Babies or girls like our Olive and Betty. And as for the boys – ' She shuddered.

Jess was immediately filled with guilt. 'Annie, I'm sorry. Here I am, thinking only of myself and you must be worried sick. Where's Colin now?'

'Somewhere at sea, that's all we know. They don't tell you now and we don't get many letters. Thank God he's not on submarines like Cliff Barker round June Close, that's what I keep telling myself. When I think of those poor devils on the *Thetis* . . .'

The two women sat in silence for a few minutes. The sinking of the *Thetis* had been like a shadow from the future. In wartime there would be not one but many ships and submarines sent to the bottom. And what efforts could be made to save their crews while battle raged overhead?

'I'd better go,' Jess said at last. 'The baby's due for a feed and I've still got a lot to do if I'm going tomorrow.'

'You haven't changed your mind?' Annie looked at her anxiously. 'You ought to be out of it, Jess, with the baby.'

'I know – but I hate leaving Frank. He's got so much to do, and I'm afraid he won't feed himself properly or do his washing – '

'Well, that's no problem,' Annie said briskly. 'He can come here for his supper and I'll do his bits of washing along with ours. After all, I've got two great girls to help me and only Ted to look after now. You don't need to go worrying about Frank, Jess.'

'Oh, Annie.' Jess's eyes filled with tears. 'That takes a real weight off my mind. I didn't like to ask, what with Mum and Dad to look after as well, but – '

'You didn't have to,' her sister said. 'We're family, aren't we? Well, then, we help out. Frank'll be all right, you see. Now you go back and get yourself ready. A bit of country air'll do you good. You still haven't got over having the baby, you know.'

Jess smiled and went out to the pram. Maureen was beginning to stir and the two women bent over the pram.

'Look at her,' Annie said. 'Don't know a thing about it all. Best time of their lives, if they only knew it. Well, I'd better get on, I'm all behind like a donkey's tail and it's my day for cleaning the windows today.'

She went back indoors and Jess wondered just what it would take to persuade Annie to deviate from her routine. Washing on Monday, ironing on Tuesday, windows Friday . . . even Hitler would have his work cut out to stop Annie from keeping her house as she thought it should be kept.

She wheeled the pram down the back alley and up the narrow garden path. The tomatoes were ripening and spiders' webs shimmered between the rows. The few dahlias she liked to grow at the top of the garden glowed like jewels in the morning sun.

She parked the pram outside the scullery door and glanced into the little shed where they kept coal and the bits and pieces there was no room for indoors.

Keith's scooter was leaning against the wall. And beside it, looking rather soft, lay the football Tim had been given for his last birthday.

Without warning, the tears began to flow again. And as Jess fed the baby they dripped salt on to her breast and on to the baby's face, like a rain that would not stop.

For Tim and Keith, evacuation began like a holiday.

Their experience of travel was limited to a few day trips to London, where Jess had relatives. But even that was more than many of the children had. Some had never been on a train at all. And the reality of being suddenly taken away from home was beginning to sink in now that they had actually said goodbye to their parents. All at once, it was no longer a rehearsal.

85

They filed down the platform in subdued silence. A few mothers had managed to get to the station in time to wave goodbye, but the children were half-dazed by the suddenness of it all, by the early hour and the tears that had already been shed. They looked around uncertainly and those who did spot their mothers in the small crowd by the gates began to cry. The teachers ushered them through the gates and on to the trains. There was no time now for farewells.

Tim and Keith kept together. Rose, in the top class, had been told to look after some of the younger children. In any case, she wasn't likely to be put in the same billet as them. It had already been arranged that, if possible, she would be placed with someone prepared to take Jess and the baby as well. Nobody was likely to have room for the whole family.

'Why not?' Keith asked again as they stood on the platform. 'People have big houses in the country. Farms are big. We could sleep in a barn. I'd like that.'

Tim shrugged. 'I don't care where we sleep. It's going to be fun – milking cows, helping with the chickens and all. Like that day Dad took us over the hill and we met that farmer and helped make hay. We'll be farmers' boys.'

A red-haired boy standing nearby sneered.

'Farmers' boys! You couldn't milk a cow!'

Tim turned at once. Brian Collins was in his class, though nearly a year older, and never missed a chance to get at the Budd brothers.

'Bet I could, then.'

'Couldn't.'

'Could.'

The two boys scowled at each other and fists were being raised when Mr Wain, the headmaster, came along and separated them with a firm hand on their shoulders. 'Now then, boys, there's enough fighting already without you two starting your own private war. Get on the train and behave yourselves. Is that your gas mask, Tim?'

Tim looked at the cardboard box lying perilously near the edge of the platform and grabbed it quickly. The knot must have come undone – or been untied. He glared at Brian Collins but the red-haired boy was already on the train, and by the time Tim and Keith had scrambled aboard they found themselves crammed into a separate compartment. It was full of heaving bodies, but by dint of much pushing and shoving they managed to secure two window seats and sat back, well pleased with themselves.

The train pulled out of the station. The children stared out of the windows as the streets and houses of Portsmouth passed slowly by, looking oddly unfamiliar. Fratton. Copnor. Farlington . . . Somewhere was their own house, over the allotments, but it was gone before they could pinpoint it. They stared out, disappointed, and Tim realised that he had been hoping for a last glimpse of Mum, perhaps waving from the back bedroom window. His eyes blurred and he blinked rapidly and brushed his sleeve across his face, hoping no one had noticed.

They were in real countryside now, passing fields with cows in and small villages. His brief misery passing, Tim leaned forward for a better look.

'Where d'you think we're going?' Keith asked. He had already asked a dozen times, but no one had known, not even his parents. It seemed queer to think of going away somewhere, in a train, with all his clothes packed in a case and not even Mum and Dad knowing where he would sleep that night. How would they find out? he wondered. Would someone remember to tell them? Suppose they didn't? Suppose he and Tim got lost somewhere and nobody knew? Panic caught his breath and he looked wide-eyed at his brother.

'The teachers'll know,' Tim said. 'They'll tell us when to get off. And then people will come and choose us to go and live with them. Farmers and people like that.'

But his voice didn't sound quite so confident as it had before and Keith saw him look quickly out of the window again. His mouth looked tight, as if he didn't want to talk any more, and although Keith was longing to ask yet again where Tim thought they might be going, he bit the question back and stared out of the window too. His chubby face was pale and he wondered if he was going to have one of his tummy-aches.

The train was gathering speed now. It raced on through an endless succession of fields and woods. All at once, the country seemed to be a very big place.

Nobody was quiet for long, however. The first parting over, the children began to recover. Paper bags were opened and sandwiches, intended for dinner, quickly eaten. The bags of biscuits and bars of chocolate, which someone had told them were to give to their new families, were also broken into. Wrappers lay on the floor or were tossed out of the window, and scuffles broke out. Smaller children began to snivel and one was sick. Fortunately, one of the bigger girls realised in time and held the child up at the window, but the view was spoiled for Tim for the rest of the journey.

Shrugging, he took a crumpled copy of *Dandy* from his pocket and began to read. He was soon engrossed in a story of Desperate Dan, and oblivious of the noise going on around him.

Keith sat staring at the countryside. Most of the trees were still green but a few were beginning to show touches of gold and brown. He still felt peculiar in his stomach, half excited, half frightened. The vomit on the window made him want to be sick himself and he looked away from it. He wondered what Mum was doing now, and how the baby was.

Maureen's arrival had come as a complete surprise to all three of the Budd children. Nobody had even hinted to them that there was a new baby on the way. It wasn't the kind of thing that was discussed in front of children and although they'd noticed that their mother had grown rather fat, they had no idea what it meant.

The night before Maureen had arrived, they had all been sent up to Auntie Annie's to stay. Mummy was feeling poorly, they'd been told, and sure enough as they set off along the pavement carrying their pyjamas and toothbrushes, they'd seen the doctor's car come down the road. Rose had been frightened and wanted to go back home, but Auntie Annie had told them there was nothing to worry about. And Uncle Ted had taken them up on to the roof of the turret and let them play at castles.

Next morning, when they'd gone home and found Mum in bed with the new baby beside her, they'd been totally bewildered.

'But where did she come from?' Keith kept asking, but no one could tell him. Rose blushed and looked embarrassed and Tim was thoughtful for the rest of the day, as if trying to work out some difficult sum, but Keith could see they didn't really know. And the story that she'd been found under a gooseberry bush on the allotment sounded much too far-fetched. He'd gone to look and found the Dinky car he'd lost a fortnight before, still there, and the ground obviously not disturbed.

Having a new baby in the house was strange and exciting but he wasn't sure he really liked it that much. It was quite fun to see her being bathed but none of them, not even Rose who seemed to think the baby was hers as much as Mum's, liked the nappy-changing business. He liked cuddling her, especially now she'd started to smile, but he didn't like the way Mum kept disappearing upstairs to feed her. What was so secret about a baby being fed? Again, Rose looked embarrassed when he asked, but Keith was more concerned about himself than about actual information. Until now, he'd always been the 'baby' of the family and now he was supposed suddenly to be grown up. And Mum just didn't have so much time for him any more. Babies, it seemed, needed a lot of attention.

And now Mum was home alone with Maureen. He knew she was supposed to be coming next day, but suppose she didn't? Nothing seemed as safe now as it had once been, and he felt as if he was treading on the cakewalk he and Tim had once been on in a fairground, where the floor had shifted under their feet. It had been funny then but now all he wanted was to be on firm ground again, where you knew what was going to happen next, where babies didn't arrive overnight and families could stay at home together.

The train slowed down. It was running alongside a platform and after a moment it came to a halt. Teachers began to walk along the corridor, poking their heads into the compartments to tell the children to get their things ready, and there was a general scramble to collect up belongings.

'Keep hold of my coat,' Tim ordered his brother as they pushed their way off the train. 'Mum said we'd got to stay together. And try to get near Rose.'

It was only afternoon but the children were tired, hungry and thirsty. They had all been up early, most had eaten their sandwiches long before dinner-time, and they were grubby from the sooty smoke that had poured in through the open windows. They stood dispiritedly on the platform, waiting to be told what to do.

'Form up into twos,' Miss Langrish told them. 'We're going to the village hall. You'll be given your billets there.' She came along the platform, urging the children to line up. Some of the smallest were crying again but she had no time to comfort them. With the other teachers, she got them into some kind of order and they trailed out of the little station and down the lane.

Already, everything was strange. Tim and Keith had seen the countryside before, for Frank Budd was a countryman at heart and had taken his children out at weekends, but some of them had never even walked along a country lane. Two or three fell into the ditch before they had even turned the corner and they stared doubtfully at the hedges and even more uncertainly through the gates into fields full of cows.

Before they could comment, however, they were at the village hall and they found a gathering awaiting them. It seemed the whole village had turned out to welcome the newcomers, but the welcome was a variable one.

'They don't look too clean, do they,' one woman sniffed, giving Tim and Keith a disparaging glance.

'Well, they've come a long way, and you know what trains are.' Her friend was obviously more disposed to make allowances. 'The little fair-haired one's got a nice face.'

'Looks cheeky to me. Bet he's into everything,' Which Tim had to admit was true. He was insatiably curious and forever getting his fingers slapped for poking them into things that didn't concern him. But it was interesting to know how things worked, he argued when his father found him with the alarm clock strewn in bits over the dining-table. And he was still quite sure he'd have been able to put it together again, if he'd only been allowed.

The hall was set out with long tables on which stood big jugs of lemonade and plates of buns. The children's eyes brightened. Some of them made a dash for the tables and began cramming food into their mouths. Others, like Tim and Keith, held back a bit and then realised that if they didn't look out for themselves, no one else would, and joined in the rush.

'Manners!' A big woman in a tweed suit was standing arms akimbo at the head of the tables. 'There's no need to grab. There's enough for everyone.'

The children evidently didn't believe her and, from the way some were tearing at the food, it seemed they had justification. Brian Collins had already filled his pockets, and two thin, ragged little girls from Newbury Street who probably hadn't had any breakfast and no lunch other than the packet of biscuits and bar of chocolate that had been issued to each child, were fighting with a bigger boy over a whole plate of buns. The plate crashed to the floor as the tweedy woman spoke. Shards of broken crockery sprayed themselves about the children's feet and some of the buns were trampled on before they could be picked up.

'Children! Children!' Miss Langrish was amongst them, her face weary and harassed. 'How dare you behave like this. You're no better than a pack of wild animals. What would your mothers and fathers say? Now, calm down at once and get into your lines. At *once*.'

Mr Wain was there too, his face thunderous, twitching his cane against his thigh. The boys saw and understood at once, and all but the most rebellious fell back. There were not many boys in the hall who did not know the sting of that cane, and they knew from the headmaster's expression that any boy who came within its range this afternoon would feel more than a sting. Swiftly, they formed the lines they had rehearsed so often, and stood waiting. The girls joined them, subdued and suppressing nervous giggles.

After that, matters progressed in a more or less orderly fashion. Each child who had not already obtained one was given a bun and a glass of lemonade. The villagers, more reluctant than ever, it seemed, after the exhibition given by the evacuees, stepped up to the tweedy woman to be allocated the children who were being billeted with them. They went off together, giving each other cautious glances, and Miss Langrish heaved a sigh of relief.

The atmosphere in the village hall was now one of barely repressed anxiety. Children who had hardly spoken to each other in the streets and playgrounds of Portsmouth now felt an urgent desire to cling together. They stood in little huddles, feeling like slaves in a market as strangers looked them over, assessing, passing on, choosing. What was wrong with me? Rose thought, half hurt, half indignant. Don't I look clean enough? Aren't I pretty enough? But Miss Langrish, turning just in time to catch the expression on her face, slipped a comforting arm around her shoulders.

'We're waiting for someone who can take your mother and baby sister too,' she said, and Rose remembered that this request had been made right from the beginning. She had refused to be evacuated at all if she couldn't stay with Mum. She nodded and relaxed, confident that it would be all right.

Tim and Keith stood nearby, holding hands. They too wanted to be together. Tim watched the faces, trying to decide which one he liked best. There was a stout, comfortable-looking woman with rosy cheeks and a smiling face. She might be the sort who would be forever baking, producing cakes and scones and home-made bread from the oven at all times of day. Farmers' wives were like that, he'd heard. He gazed hopefully at her, but to his astonishment she chose Brian Collins.

'My husband said to be sure to pick a good strong-looking lad who'd be able to give him a hand on the farm.' She ran her smiling blue eyes over Brian's sturdy limbs. 'This one looks as if he could be useful.'

Brian looked cocky and flexed his arm. 'See them muscles?' he said proudly. 'Biggest in the school, they are.' He went off with the plump woman, looking pleased with himself.

Two elderly sisters were gazing along the lines of children. They wore identical dark-blue coats and hats, and their faces were pale. One wore tortoiseshell spectacles and had whiskers sprouting from a mole on her chin, while the other was small and timid with nervously blinking eyes. She reminded Tim of a white mouse.

'We'd like a nice little girl. We could take two, if they were sisters.' They looked at Rose, still shepherding the younger children. 'She looks quiet and clean.'

'Rose needs a place where she can be with her mother, who's coming tomorrow.' Miss Langrish looked at the children. 'Could you manage a brother and a sister? Wendy Atkinson and her little brother Alan want to stay together.'

'A boy?' They gazed doubtfully at him. 'Oh, we didn't really want a boy . . .'

'He's a very nice little one. He's only four years old,' Miss

Langrish said coaxingly, as if at that age it would be difficult to tell the difference. 'And Wendy looks after him very well.'

'Yes, but she's very small too, isn't she.' Their eyes strayed again to Rose. 'That one looks much more capable.'

'Could you take her mother too? And a baby?'

'Oh no!' They recoiled at the very idea. 'No, we couldn't manage all that. Very well, we'll take the little girl and her brother.' They continued to gaze at little Alan with some doubt, as if he were of an alien species. 'Only four years old?'

'Almost five,' Miss Langrish said. 'His birthday is in October.'

'Will he be able to . . . see to himself?'

'He can dress himself, certainly, and I'm sure Wendy will be able to help with anything he can't quite manage.' Miss Langrish was beginning to look less sure of the wisdom of sending little Alan to live with two elderly spinsters. But there was no time to quibble. Other villagers were pressing forward, the billeting officer was growing impatient and Alan himself looked as if he might be about to cry. Hastily, she picked up his little case and handed it to one of the ladies. 'Here are his things. We'll be calling tomorrow to make sure everything's all right.' And before they could answer, she turned away to deal with the next child.

Tim scanned the faces of the remaining villagers, trying to pick out which he favoured. The two women who had first commented on the children's appearance caught his eye again. The one who had thought they looked dirty – and you try keeping clean on a train! he thought indignantly – was talking to Mr Wain about a tall girl with plaits, who had somehow managed to remain fairly tidy. It looked as if she was choosing her. And I hope you like her, he thought, knowing Penelope Tyson, who lived in October Street, for one of the most spiteful girls in the school.

He regarded the second woman and made up his mind she looked nice. She had yellow hair rolled up over her ears and a friendly smile. He grinned at her and she smiled back and went up to the billeting officer.

'I'd like to take that little boy. The one with fair curly hair.'

The billeting lady looked at Miss Langrish.

'That's Tim Budd. He's with his brother, Keith, they want to stay together.'

The woman looked at Tim and then at Keith. Keith gazed back at her, his brown eyes large in his round face. He rubbed his cheeks with his sleeve, hoping to make them cleaner.

'Well, that's all right. We've got room for two. We can easily make up another bed in the room.' Her voice was warmed by a soft burr. She held out both her hands. 'Would you like to come and live along with me?'

Suddenly shy, the two boys went forward. Keith reached out a grimy paw and laid it in her hand. Rather more awkwardly, Tim did the same. The young woman laughed and squeezed their fingers.

'So you're Tim and Keith. How old are you?'

Tim found his voice.

'I'm nearly ten. My birthday's in October. Keith's eight.'

'My birthday's in May,' Keith added.

'Are you the youngest, then? I'd have thought it was the other way, around, you being bigger.'

'No, I'm older than Keith. I had measles when I was five and they stopped me growing.'

'Oh, I see.' Her smile was sympathetic. 'Well, I daresay you'll start again before long. Anyway, I should say you're just about the right size for now. Well – ' she squeezed their hands again ' – let's go home, shall we? There's nothing else we have to do here, is there, Mrs Tupper?'

'No,' the billeting officer said. 'Just leave your name and address and the names of the children. Someone will be round to see you in the next few days to see how you're getting along. Oh, and the teacher said something about the boy's mother – she's being evacuated herself. I expect she'll want to come and see them too.'

'Bound to,' the young woman said comfortably. 'Well, we'll be pleased to see her, won't we? Have to make a cake specially. Come on, now.' She led them out of the hall. 'My name's Mrs Corner, by the way – Edna Corner. My husband's name is Reg and he works on a farm. Anything you want to know, you just ask. There's no need to be shy with Reg and me.'

The two boys trotted along beside her, still carrying their cases. Their gas masks, hung over their shoulders, bumped against their backs. There were tired, hungry in spite of the buns and a bit

94

apprehensive. It was the first time they had ever been away from home without their mother and the excitement of the train journey and the new sights and sounds were overlaid by apprehension. Mrs Corner seemed nice – but what was it going to be like, living with her? And with Mum just around the corner, too?

Tim stifled a nervous giggle. Fancy living round the corner from Mrs Corner. And there was a Mr Corner too. He wondered if they had any children. Would four Corners make a square? Or three a triangle? He looked at Keith, wanting to share the joke with him, but remembered Mum telling him it was rude to make fun of people's names and decided to keep quiet. Perhaps it wasn't so funny anyway. It couldn't be really, or why would he suddenly feel like crying?

The village street was straggly, hardly a street at all, just a few houses and cottages scattered beside the road. They passed two or three large ones, then came to one standing on its own. By Tim and Keith's standards it was big, with its front door set in the middle and windows on either side. That made it twice the size of number 14 to start with. And its front garden was as long as their back one, with the path going up the middle, a bit of lawn on one side and neat rows of vegetables on the other. Tim had been over to his father's allotment often enough to be able to recognise most of them. Runner beans, carrots, cabbages, Brussels sprouts, and a good patch of potatoes. Someone had already started to dig them. He wondered if Mrs Corner would be as strict as his own mother over eating things he didn't like, and felt the sudden ache of tears in his throat again.

'Here we are,' Mrs Corner said cheerfully, opening the front door. 'Home in time for tea. I expect you're hungry, aren't you?'

The two boys nodded dutifully but Tim wondered if he would be able to get anything past the lump in his throat. The day which had started out so exciting had suddenly changed. This morning, it had all seemed to be a big adventure, getting on the train to go somewhere so secret that not even his parents or the teachers knew, looking forward to weeks with no school, spent roaming the fields and woods and having adventures like those he'd read about in books. He'd imagined himself and Keith, leaders of a club, solving mysteries, catching criminals, perhaps even spies. That's what children did in books and everything that had happened just lately had seemed more like a book than real life.

But now it seemed very real. Frighteningly real. Here they were, he and Keith, miles away from home, with no one they knew close at hand. The other children and the teachers were in the village somewhere, but he had no idea where. If he went out into the street now he wouldn't know how to find them. And kind though Mrs Corner seemed to be, she was still a stranger. She wasn't Mum.

Suddenly, Tim wanted his mum very badly indeed. And when he looked at Keith, he saw in his brother's face the same desperate longing and knew that there was no comfort to be had there; nor had he any to give.

Rose found herself following a neat, motherly looking person in a brown coat through the lanes. She walked quietly, still wearing her best red coat and carrying the small new suitcase Mum had bought, her brown eyes noticing the bright red of the rose-hips in the hedgerows, the pink and golden fronds of honeysuckle that trailed through the leaves. There was no traffic other than an occasional horse and when they passed a gateway she could see cows and sheep grazing.

This was real country. Mum and Dad had brought them out for picnics to places like this sometimes. They'd caught a bus from the main road and gone up over Portsdown Hill and out to some quiet spot where they'd got off and gone walking, Dad carrying a bag with their tea in it. Sometimes Mum would take a big basket and they'd pick blackberries, and occasionally they'd found mushrooms gleaming like pearls in the dewy grass.

They hadn't done it this summer. Mum had started to get fat and didn't seem to want to go walking far any more. Rose knew now that this was because she'd been expecting a baby, but nobody had told her that and she hadn't even suspected it until that morning when Maureen was born. When she'd gone to school, full of the news, some of the bigger girls had stared at her and laughed. Hadn't she known! Didn't she know that's what happened when mothers were having babies? And Rose had felt angry and upset. She'd felt left out. She would have liked to know what was happening. She would have liked to be able to help get things ready, choose a name, speculate whether it might be a boy or a girl. Instead, all this had been denied her, everything done in secret, as if it were something to be ashamed of.

'We thought you were too young to know,' Mum had said when Rose had tried to tell her this. 'Little girls don't have to know about these things.' But Rose had gone on feeling angry. And to compensate and bury her feelings, she had almost taken over the baby for herself, dressing her, bathing her, playing with her, taking her for walks in the pram. The only thing she refused to do was change her nappeis. If Mum wanted to have a baby without telling her, she could do that too.

The neat woman, whose name was Mrs Greenberry, opened a gate in the hedge at the side of the road and went in. Rose followed her into a garden that ran all the way round the house. A red brick path led to the door. On the left was a shady part, overshadowed by a tall tree, but the garden to the right was filled with afternoon sunlight. The brilliant colours of dahlias and chrysanthemums gave way to rows of vegetables very similar to those which, had Rose known it, her brother Tim was looking at not a quarter of a mile away across the fields. And close to the back door of the house, as Mrs Greenberry led the way up the red-brick path, was the raised circular wall and winding handle of a well.

Rose stared at it. Did they really get their water from a well? Hadn't they got taps in the house? But she had no time to ask questions, for Mrs Greenberry was already indoors, waiting for Rose to follow.

The room they were in was a kitchen, larger than any kitchen Rose had ever seen – as large, she thought bemusedly, as all their downstairs at number 14 knocked into one. There was a big table in the middle of the room and a tall dresser taking up nearly all of one wall, its shelves bright with plates and bowls and cups. Under the window which looked out into the garden was a low earthenware sink – with no taps, she noticed at once – and in the opposite wall was a big alcove with a range in it.

Rose knew what a range was. Auntie Nell had one in the house where she and Tim had lived before Keith was born. She still liked going round there, to sit in front of its glowing coals in winter and listen to the kettle purring gently on the hob. Great-aunt Alice

97

would be there too, as often as not, and she would hold her palms out towards the fire and then take Rose's hands between hers and rub them gently to warm them.

The sight of the range in this kitchen brought a rush of homesickness. But at the same time, it held a promise of the same warmth, the same comfort that Rose always found in front of Aunt Nell's range. Almost involuntarily, she went towards it, holding out her hands.

'That's right,' Mrs Greenberry said approvingly. 'You just sit yourself down on that stool and get warm. There's a proper nip in the air today – be a frost tonight, I wouldn't wonder. Now, what do you say to a cup of tea, love, and then we'll get you settled in your room and you can help me get things ready for your mum when she comes tomorrow. And a new baby too, they tell me? Well, that'll be nice, won't it, having you all here together.'

Her voice murmured on as she bustled about the kitchen, taking cups off the hooks on the dresser, fetching milk from a cool pantry, pouring water from the kettle into a big brown teapot. But Rose hardly heard her. She was sitting close to the bars of the range, staring at the hot coals. Like her brothers, like every other child in the village, she was feeling the sudden immensity of what had happened. Like all the rest, she had been brought face to face with reality.

If war came, she might be living here for months – years. She might never go back to live in number 14. She might never live again with her brothers, her father, never see her family she had left behind.

Nobody really knew what the war would be like. They talked about bombs, about gas, about air raids and invasions . . . but nobody knew. Whole cities might be flattened, even villages like this one poisoned by a creeping fog of burning fumes. They might be starved, burned or shot to pieces. Nobody knew.

There might still, of course, not be a war. Every day they said it still wasn't inevitable. But if it wasn't, why were they here? Why had Rose and her brothers been torn from their homes, why had Wendy and Alan Atkinson been wrenched away from their mother, why little Susan Cullen taken from her father on the very day of her mother's funeral?

In any case, for Rose and her friends it was too late. Even if there was no war, if they were all simply given a holiday in the country and then sent home again, to go back to the lives they had lived until yesterday – nothing would ever be the same again. They would never be the same again. The shock had been too great, the impact too severe. The damage had been done.

All this, Rose sensed rather than thought as she stared at the burning coals in Mrs Greenberry's range. Her mind was too bemused to make shapes of the bewildered emotions that circled in her head. But she knew, without doubt, that something vital had happened to her and to all the others in the past few hours. Something vital and irrevocable.

As night fell over the village, the evacuees lay down in their unfamiliar beds and tried to sleep.

Wendy Atkinson helped her brother Alan to undress and made him say his prayers. The little ritual comforted them both, but when he was in his bed he turned large blue eyes on her and she saw the hopelessness in them and felt tears in her own eyes. He wants Mummy, she thought. He doesn't understand. And why should he, for she barely understood herself why they should find themselves in this dark mausoleum of a house with its furniture that mustn't be touched for fear of sticky fingerprints, its rugs that mustn't be trodden on, its delicate china that must be handled so carefully in case it broke.

The sisters, both confusingly called Miss Woddis, hadn't seemed to know what to do with them. They had given them tea – thin sandwiches and a slice of dry seed-cake which Wendy disliked and Alan had refused to eat – and then sat gazing helplessly at them. Finally, they had suggested that the children might like to go out into the garden – but had laid down so many strictures about flowerbeds and grass that Wendy and Alan had been afraid to do anything other than crouch on the path, staring at the grass and looking into an endless future of tiny sandwiches and seed-cake that couldn't be swallowed, and no mother to brush their hair or wash their faces or cuddle them to sleep at night.

All had been relieved when it was bedtime. But Wendy, lying uncomfortably in her own bed, missing the busy sound of night in

Portsmouth and anxious about the strange noises and even stranger silence of the countryside, wanted morning to come. She wanted to see her friends, to reassure herself that there was still someone familiar nearby. She wanted her teacher. Most of all, she wanted to be at home.

A soft sound made her turn. Alan was sobbing under his breath, little heart-broken sobs. Wendy felt her own tears begin to flow.

She climbed out of bed and crept over the little strip of mat to Alan's. She slipped into bed beside him and felt his body shaking against hers. They wrapped their arms around each other and clung tightly, weeping out their fear and loneliness and terror. And as the darkness swept through the swaying trees outside and the owls called through the last few hours of peace, they fell asleep.

Tim and Keith fell asleep too, reaching out to clutch each other's hands. Their sister Rose, delighted as she was with her little bedroom under the eaves of Mrs Greenberry's cottage, warmed though she might be by the kindness of the neat, motherly woman and her big, cheerful husband, lay longing for tomorrow, when her mother would come with baby Maureen.

Even the biggest children, like Penelope Tyson and Brian Collins, felt their confidence ebb as they went to bed for the first time in their billets. And the little ones alone, without brother or sister to cling to, shed many tears that night. Some shed them quietly, unheard by foster-mothers and fathers; others wept noisily and refused to be comforted. Martin Baker, appalled by the privy at the end of the dark, tangled garden, lay clutching himself in the desperate hope that he could wait until morning. And Susan Cullen, to whom so many bewildering things had happened in the past few weeks, spent the greater part of the night on her knees beside her bed, praying to a God who seemed to have abandoned her, begging forgiveness for the sins she felt she must have committed to bring such retribution on her head, until she fell asleep where she knelt and woke in the morning, stiff and freezing, on the cold linoleum floor.

It was a night of anxiety and bewilderment for every child in the village, far away from home, and a night of anxiety too for those who had taken them in. How long would they have to look after these children, no kin to them and from a strange background? For how long must their homes be invaded, their lives thus disrupted?

And back in Portsmouth and the other cities from which children had been taken, mothers like Jess and fathers like Frank lay equally wakeful, wondering where their children were that night and who had seen them to bed. Had they been received grudgingly, or with kindness? Would they be cared for or neglected? Were they at this moment crying for a mother who had never been out of reach? Did they feel abandoned and betrayed?

'You'll be with them tomorrow,' Frank murmured to Jess, reaching out for her in the big feather-bed. But as she turned into his arms he felt the wet heat of tears on his shoulder and knew that she was crying.

'And I'll be away from you,' she wept, quivering against him. 'Oh, Frank, it's so cruel. Just when we were getting along so well. And where's it all going to end?'

He held her close, his big hands moving slowly over her back. It was a question that must have been asked in millions of homes that night, a question that neither he nor anyone else on earth could answer.

If war should come . . . Could anyone, now, doubt that it would?

CHAPTER FOUR

'EVERYTHING I BELIEVED IN *has crashed into ruins this morning.*'
The words that Neville Chamberlain, Prime Minister of Great
Britain, spoke in the House of Commons at noon on 3 September
1939, echoed the feeling in the hearts of millions. For as they had
listened to his wireless broadcast an hour earlier, their world too
had crumbled and shattered about them. The lives they knew, the
ordinary lives they had lived and expected to go on living, had come
to an end. Their future was uncertain; for some of them, yet
unknowing, there was no future.

Jess sat in the Greenberrys' kitchen and listened to the wireless.
In her arms, she cradled baby Maureen, while Rose sat on a low
stool at her knee. Harold Greenberry was in his accustomed chair
at the head of the big kitchen table, while his wife sat at his elbow.
Nobody spoke as the solemn notes of Big Ben filled the kitchen,
and they listened with dread as the Prime Minister began to
speak.

'*This morning the British Ambassador in Berlin communicated to
the German Government that unless we heard from them by eleven
o'clock that they were prepared at once to withdraw their troops
from Poland, a state of war would exist between us.*

'*I have to tell you that no such undertaking has been received
and that consequently this country is at war with Germany.*'

Rose heard the sharply indrawn breath of the adults. She looked
up into her mother's face, then at the Greenberrys. Their fear
struck at her breast and she felt the tears spring to her eyes.

'You can imagine what a bitter blow it is to me that my long struggle to win peace has ended.'

'He tried,' Mrs Greenberry said. 'Nobody can say he didn't try.'

Her husband shushed her with a hand, lifted only a few inches from the table. The Prime Minister continued to speak. His voice was trembling slightly. He talked of his belief that, even to the last, an honourable and peaceful settlement could have been bought, but Hitler would not have it. He talked of joining together with France to go to the aid of Poland, even now bravely resisting a wicked attack upon her people. He talked of a clear conscience, of a situation which had become intolerable and must now be finished.

'May God bless you,' he concluded in a voice that sounded itself not far from tears, 'and may he defend the right, for it is evil that we are fighting against – brute force, bad faith, injustice, oppression and persecution, and against them, I am certain, right will prevail.'

The broadcast was over. Another voice began to speak, giving details of the plans that had been made and asking all engaged with the fighting force and in Civil Defence to report for duty. Mr Greenberry moved suddenly, making everyone jump. He stood up, scraping his chair back on the quarry tiles of the kitchen floor, and went to a cupboard. He took out a tin hat and his gas mask.

'I'm going down to the hall,' he said, and his voice sounded strange and creaky, as if it had not been used for a long time, and loud in the quiet kitchen, drowning the voice of the BBC announcer. 'They'll be wanting us down there.' He stood awkwardly for a few seconds, looking at the two women as if he felt that this moment should be marked in some way, by more than a few words. If he had been alone with his wife, Jess thought, he might have kissed her. But the presence of strangers held him back. Instead, he laid his hand on her shoulder and gave it a brief squeeze. Then he ducked his head at Jess, turned away and, as if he could no longer clearly see his way, blundered out of the kitchen door.

The two women looked at each other.

'That's dreadful,' Jess said at last, in a low voice. 'They've declared war.' She reached out an arm and drew Rose against her. 'What's going to happen now? What's going to happen to us all? What's going to happen to the children?'

Mrs Greenberry shook her head. 'I don't know, dear. I just don't know.' She stood up, resting her hands on the table as if she had suddenly grown old. Together, the three of them went out into the garden. They stared up at the September sky, so blue and innocent, the sky from which death would come. How soon would it arrive, the evil black rain they had been told about? Was it already on its way? Were Hitler's forces already unleashed, the bombers already in the air, their droning yet unheard but inexorably approaching?

'We're not ready,' Jess said in a sudden panic. 'We're not ready. I can't face it – not yet. Not with the baby and Rose, and the boys not even here. And my Frank, back there in Portsmouth, all by himself. It's wrong – all wrong. We can't . . .'

'We don't have no choice.' Mrs Greenberry's country voice was warm and her hand on Jess's arm intended to give comfort, but there was little comfort to be had. 'They don't ask us, do they? If it was left to us, there wouldn't be no wars. And I don't mean just us – I mean everyone like us, all over the world. There must be people like us in Poland and France, even in Germany, who just want to go on living their own lives, not interfering with nobody else. But we don't get the choice.'

'I know – and that's what's so wrong.' Jess's voice was passionate now. 'We don't get any choice at all. We just have to go where we're pushed. We have to leave our homes, that we've worked for and built up. You have to take strangers into yours. They take our children away from us just when they need their mothers and fathers most, and they take our boys away and make them fight, when half of them don't even know what they're fighting for. And they put hate into their souls. My sister's boy Colin – Bob Shaw next door – who've never hated anyone in their lives, nor ever would – they make them hate the Germans so that when they go to war they'll kill without even caring about it. Our Colin, killing people – it doesn't bear thinking of. But he will – he'll have to – if he lives long enough.'

'He'll have to if he wants to live,' Mrs Greenberry pointed out. 'But you don't want to go talking like that too much, my dear. People won't understand. And if it turns out to be a long war, like the last one – '

'I hope to God it doesn't! Four years, that was. Four years. We'd never stand four years of bombing, not the sort of bombing they've been talking about.'

'Well, let's hope we don't have to. Let's hope it'll be a short one – over by Christmas.' Mrs Greenberry touched her arm again. 'Let's go inside now, dear, and have a cup of tea. And then you walk over to Edna Corner's and see those boys of yours. Why don't you ask them over to tea this afternoon, eh? You didn't see much of them yesterday, what with being worn out after your journey and everything.'

Jess nodded. Suddenly, she fet overwhelmingly tired. It had indeed been an exhausting day yesterday, from the moment when she'd clung to Frank for their final goodbye as he set off for work at six, all through the struggle down to the school carrying Maureen and as much luggage as she could manage – thank goodness for Annie's help as she joined the other overburdened mothers, trailing along the streets in the sad exodus – and through the slow, dusty train journey with its many unexplained stops and their final arrival at the village hall.

It all seemed more like a dream now. Tim and Keith had been there with their foster-mother, who seemed a nice enough woman, and Rose with Mrs Greenberry. But Jess, after the first relief at being with them again, had been more concerned with the baby than anything else. Maureen had been fretful all day and was now crying a weary, hopeless cry that splintered Jess's heart. She must be hungry, yet seemed uninterested in the breast, and Jess felt its slackness and knew that there was little milk there. Fear stabbed her. It didn't take long for a baby as young as Maureen to lose weight and cease to thrive. And if she lost her milk . . .

'It'll come back,' Mrs Greenberry said reassuringly. 'It's only natural, after what you've been through. You'll be all right in a day or two, see if you're not. And there's always the bottle.'

Jess nodded. But she hated the idea of putting Maureen on to the bottle so early. She'd fed the others for at least six months each, and she'd wanted to do the same with this baby, the last she would bear. Feeding the baby yourself, with your own milk, was the right, the natural thing to do. It was finishing the job you'd started.

To put Maureen on the bottle would seem like failure. And another grievance to lay at Hitler's door.

Rose stayed out in the garden by herself while the two women went into the house. The big kitchen was too dim after the brightness outside. She wandered down narrow paths between the rows of vegetables and stared out over the rolling fields and woods.

It was hard to understand what was happening. She knew about the war, of course, had shared the anxiety as it approached. But now it was here. The Prime Minister had said so, on the wireless. She'd heard his words herself, seen the effect they had on the grown-ups.

Nothing would ever be the same again. And yet – nothing was any different.

She looked up at the sky. It was still blue, overlaid with the faint haze of early autumn. The trees were still green, just a few birches and horse-chestnuts beginning to turn with golden colour. The hedges were bright with hips and haws, and rich with glistening purple blackberries. At the bottom of the garden she found a gnarled, twisted tree with apples hanging like orange lanterns from its branches, and another that bore a few late plums.

The air was quiet, with no threatening drone of approaching death. Instead, she could hear the whisper of a breeze touching the long grass. A robin sang from a nearby bush and a flight of tiny birds with pink breasts and long tails skimmed past her head and settled in the apple tree. Mrs Greenberry's black cat, Tibby, emerged from the grass and came to rub himself round her legs, and she wondered suddenly how Henry would get along at home, with no one there all day.

Thinking of Henry made her think of her father, also alone at home. How was he spending this Sunday? Had he gone over to the allotment this morning? Had he heard the wireless? Did he know there was a war on?

She supposed he'd be going up to Auntie Annie's. What would they talk about, as Uncle Ted carved the joint? Were they worrying about Colin, away on his ship?

Rose sat down on the grass. She drew her knees up and rested her chin on them, her head bent so that her dark fringe fell forwards and made a little cave of darkness. She shut her eyes tightly and tried to imagine it all, feeling the fear, sensing the dark shadow of ominous clouds looming above. Her skin grew cold.

And yet when she opened her eyes again, the sky was still blue, the hips red, the trees green with a touch of gold. The robin sang from his bush and the breeze rustled the leaves. And Tibby rubbed his head against her legs with a mew, asking to be picked up.

It doesn't matter what they do, she thought, they can't stop this. Even Hitler can't stop the apples getting ripe or the birds singing. And no one can stop a cat from getting on your lap.

Frank listened to the King's broadcast in the afternoon and then went down to the *Evening News* offices in Stanhope Road to buy the special edition of the paper. With a crowd of other men and women, he stood in the street, scanning the front page with its dramatic headline.

'This Country Is At War.'

Frank stared at the words, his heart sinking. He already knew it was true. The Prime Minister had said so. The King had said so. But to see it, printed in black and white in Portsmouth's own evening paper . . .

He looked at the rest of the page. As well as a full account of the Prime Minister's speech on the wireless, there was a report of his words to Parliament immediately afterwards. *'This is a sad day for all of us,'* he had said. *'For none is it sadder than for me.'* And then, striking the table with his hand, *'There is only one thing left for me, and that is to devote what strength and powers I have to forwarding the victory of the cause for which we have to sacrifice ourselves. I trust I may live to see the day when Hitlerism has been destroyed, and a restored and liberated Europe has been re-established.'*

Will he? Frank thought, folding the newspaper and pushing it into his pocket. Will any of us? That man has marched all over Europe, smashing and destroying wherever he's gone. What's to stop him doing the same in Poland, as he's already begun to do? What's to stop him doing the same in France? And then – with only a narrow strip of water to hold him at bay – what chance do we have against such might?

He wheeled his bicycle out into the road and swung his leg over the saddle. The street was full of people, standing in groups discussing the news. A few women were crying, while men were looking anxious, angry and, in some cases, even elated. 'Now we'll show the bastard,' one declared, waving his fists in the air. 'We can stop all the shilly-shallying about and do something about him. Get our boys over there, that'll wipe the silly smirk off his face. He'll find out he's bitten off more than he can chew.'

There was a murmur of agreement. Nobody was happy about the war, but at least, it was felt, they now knew where they stood. The suspense was over and the worst known. And, once known, could be faced.

'We showed Kaiser Bill what we thought of him in the last lot. We'll show this twerp too. A house-painter! Who does he think he is, trying to take over the world? A bloody maniac, that's what he is.'

'That's right. Well, he might be able to overrun some of those tinpot little countries in Europe but he won't be able to do it to Britain. He'll find we're a different kettle of fish.'

Frank cycled home. It had been a queer day right from the start. For the first time in their married life he had woken up without Jess beside him. He had lain for a while trying to pretend she'd just got up early and was downstairs getting breakfast ready, but it was no use. The house was silent without her and the kids, and he felt almost as if they had never existed, as if the past fourteen years were all a dream.

He'd got up eventually and got his own breakfast, then pottered about in the garden, waiting for the Prime Minister's broadcast at eleven o'clock. He'd listened to it by himself, sitting at the table – it didn't seem right to sit in his armchair while such an important announcement was made – and as soon as the grave voice had finished speaking he'd heard the doleful wail of an air-raid siren.

'My God – they haven't started already!' He'd run outside, and there were all the neighbours, staring up at the sky. There were no planes to be seen, only the glint of barrage balloons floating like huge silver fish above their heads. And after a few minutes the 'Raiders Passed' signal had sounded and they'd all sighed with relief. A false alarm. But they hadn't gone back indoors. They'd stayed outside for a while, talking across the garden fences to each other and wondering what was going to happen next.

Frank couldn't settle to anything. In the end, he'd got his tools and walked over to the allotment. He didn't know who was going to eat all the vegetables he'd grown, now that Jess and the children were away, but he couldn't let them go to waste. He'd take a few down to Jess's parents at North End.

After a couple of hours' digging, he felt better and went back to Annie's to have a bit of dinner, listen to the King's broadcast and then cycle down to the newspaper offices to get the special edition. Arthur and Mary were glad of the vegetables and he stopped to talk about the news for a while and have a cup of tea in their stuffy, overcrowded little back room.

'It's a bad job,' Arthur kept saying in his thin reedy voice. 'A proper bad job.' And Mary had nodded, her fingers plucking at a trembling lip. 'I don't know what the world's coming to, I really don't.'

It's not fair, Frank thought, cycling home again. They've been through too much already, old folk like them. They shouldn't have to face this, not at their time of life.

He entered the silent house and Henry, the cat, came to meet him, miaowing as if to ask where everyone was. Frank bent to stroke him.

'There, old chap, it's all right. We haven't deserted you. I'm still here. You'll still get your cods' heads for supper.'

But would he? When would Frank have time to buy them? Out in the mornings soon after six to walk down to the Dockyard, not home till seven or eight at night . . . It was another thing he'd have to ask Annie to do. And Annie had enough on her plate already, without Henry's cods' heads.

His mouth twitched, thinking how Jess would have laughed if he'd said such a thing. It was just the kind of inadvertent joke that amused her. And then he felt pain sweep over him, for Jess wasn't here to laugh and he didn't know when she would be here again. This war, that was supposed to be 'over by Christmas'. They'd heard that before, hadn't they? And last time, it had been four long years . . .

Four years in an empty house? Four years without Jess and the kids?

He looked at the newspaper again. Winston Churchill had made a speech in Parliament too. As always, he had spoken with force, using words in the way that was so inimitably his. *He* ought to be leading us, Frank thought. He's the man we need in this mess, not Chamberlain with his mealy mouthed talk of appeasement.

He read the words again, letting them roll around in his mind.

'Outside the storm of war may blow and the lands may be lashed with the furies of its gales, but in our hearts this Sunday morning there is peace.'

Yes, Churchill certainly knew how to use words. Frank could imagine him, speaking in slow, measured tones as he delivered his rousing message.

'Our hands may be active but our consciences are at rest . . . There is another note which may be present at this moment, and that is a feeling of thankfulness that if these great trials were to come upon our Island there is a generation of Britons here now ready to prove itself not unworthy of the days of yore, and not unworthy of those great men, the fathers of our land, who have laid the foundations of our laws and shaped the greatness of our country.

'This is no war for domination of imperial aggrandisement, for material gain – no war to shut any country out of its sunlight and means of progress. It is a war to establish and revive the stature of man.'

Frank laid down the paper. The stature of man. That was what they all had to hold on to. Forget some whippersnapper of an Austrian house-painter, snatching other countries for his own greed. Forget the lust for power which had brought them to this brink on which the world now stood. Remember instead that people – men, women, children – were being persecuted, tormented, driven from their homes and treated like animals. It didn't matter what country they lived in, they should be free to walk with heads held high. It didn't matter what race they were, they were human beings.

The stature of man.

Henry jumped up on to his lap and began to knead Frank's thighs. Frank laid his hand on the furry head, grateful for the contact, for the warmth of another living being. He stroked the cat's back.

The war was, as Parliament had agreed, a right war, a just war. It must be fought for the sake of humanity.

To those who had thought that the war would start slowly, the sinking of the *Athenia* on its first day came as a shock.

The liner had left Liverpool on Saturday, bound for Montreal and carrying fourteen hundred passengers and crew. She had travelled two hundred miles west of the Hebrides when, without warning, the German torpedos struck. The captain told reporters later that the missile had gone right through the ship to the engine room. Most of those aboard were saved by nearby ships, who raced to the rescue, but a hundred and twelve died.

'The only good German's a dead German.' The phrase was on everyone's lips. Killing had suddenly become a part of the national mood. Even the games of the few children who had not been evacuated suddenly took on a new and sinister aspect. Instead of cowboys and Indians, the boys played at war. But nobody wanted to be the Germans, so the part of the enemy was given to the least popular boys.

'They said I was a dirty Jerry,' a small boy wept as he was taken home, bruised and grazed from a tumble in the road. 'They pushed me over . . . I didn't *want* to be a Jerry.'

'Don't know why they have to pretend anyway,' someone said to Frank. 'Not when there's real live Huns living in September Street.'

'The Brunners aren't Huns,' Frank said sharply. He made a point now of going in to buy his *Daily Express* at the little newsagent's shop instead of from the kiosk on the Hard, as he'd been accustomed to do. Custom had fallen off badly, Alice Brunner told him as he handed over his penny. People just didn't come in any more. It was as if they were ashamed to be seen coming through the door.

'They ought to be ashamed of walking past,' Frank said. 'They've known you and Heinrich long enough to know what sort of people you are. You're as good as anyone else round here. Better than a lot I could name.'

Alice shook her head. 'That's not what most of them think. They're saying Heinrich should be taken away.'

Frank stared at her.

'Taken away?'

'You know. Interned. Put into prison.'

'Prison?' Frank said. 'But he's done nothing wrong.'

Alice shrugged. 'He's a German. Isn't that enough?'

The papers were full of war news now. In the edition that reported the sinking of the *Athenia*, Frank read that Egypt had broken off diplomatic relations with Germany, Australia had declared itself at war and France had gone into action with all three forces. Anthony Eden had been made Dominions Secretary and Mr Churchill was back in the Cabinet as First Lord of the Admiralty. In Portsmouth, the offices at the Guildhall were being removed to the Northern Secondary School and the chimes of the Guildhall clock were stopped 'for the duration'.

That was another phrase that was on everyone's lips now. The children had been evacuated 'for the duration', and cinemas, theatres and dance-halls were closed 'for the duration', a move that was as unpopular with the younger members of the community as evacuation had been with others.

'It's not fair,' Olive said as she, Betty and Gladys Shaw walked home from work. 'Derek and me were going to see *Idiot's Delight* at the Ambassador. It's Norma Shearer and Clark Gable.'

'Clark Gable!' Gladys said, rolling her eyes. 'I think he's smashing. And Norma Shearer's gorgeous. I wouldn't mind looking like her.' She swaggered a little in her tight-waisted blue frock and passed a hand over her yellow hair, as if imagining herself as a film star. 'I'm thinking of doing my hair the way she does hers, I reckon it'd suit me.'

'Robb Wilton's supposed to be on at the King's,' Betty grumbled. 'Graham was going to take me.'

'Is that the chap I saw you with at Kimball's?' Gladys asked. 'Tall, with ginger hair?'

'It's not ginger,' Betty said at once. 'It's auburn.'

Gladys grinned. 'Thought it looked a bit carroty, myself. Why don't you go out with our Bob? He's been mooning about over you for weeks.'

Betty flushed scarlet. 'Don't be daft!' But she felt a quiver of secret delight. A boy – even if it was just Bob Shaw that she'd

112

known since she was in her pram – mooning over her! 'How d'you know, anyway?' she couldn't help asking.

Gladys laughed. 'He's my brother, ain't he? We live in the same house. I can tell. Anyway, he's got your picture pinned up in the bedroom.'

Betty stared at her. 'My picture? Where'd he get that from?'

'Oh, sometime when we all went swimming last summer, I should think. You've got that striped bathing costume of yours on, anyway. He's cut off the other people in the snap and just left you – proper pin-up girl, you are.'

Betty tossed her head, the brown curls bouncing. 'What a cheek! I shall just tell him to take it down, next time I see him.'

'Don't do that. He's not doing any harm. I mean, it's not as if he was sticking any pins in it or using it for a dartboard, is it!' Gladys dug her in the ribs. 'He'll get over it.'

This, for some reason, irritated Betty even more. The idea of Bob Shaw keeping her photo on his bedroom wall was rather flattering, much as she might pretend otherwise, but the insinuation that it was no more than a passing fancy was an injury to her pride.

'Oh, I don't care whether he gets over it or not,' she said offhandedly. 'Come to that, I don't care if he sticks life-sized posters of me on his wall. If he can't find anything better to do with his time—'

'Or his wall,' Olive interposed.

' – well, I'm sorry for him, that's all,' Betty finished with a scathing look at her sister.

'Well, don't be too hard on him, Betty,' Gladys said. 'He might be called up before long and have to go away. It's good for them to have someone at home to think about, someone to come back to. And he's never had a proper girlfriend, you know. He's too shy.'

'Well, going in the Forces would soon change that,' Betty remarked. 'Our Colin was shy before he went into the Navy but to hear him now you'd think the women were queuing up for him.'

Gladys looked at her. The fun had died from her face and she looked suddenly unhappy.

'There's no one special, is there?'

'No, of course not,' Olive said with a scowl at Betty. Honestly, wasn't she ever going to learn to mind her tongue? Had she forgotten that Gladys Shaw and Colin had started going out together just before he went off on the *Exeter*? It wasn't much more than that as far as Olive knew – Colin didn't even seem to be writing to her – but it was obvious that Gladys was carrying a torch for him. She was always asking if they'd heard from him. 'It's just talk. You know what sailors are.'

But that didn't seem to be the right thing to say either. Everyone in Pompey knew what sailors were. There were enough of them about, roistering around the Guildhall Square on a Saturday night. Only last week, on the way home from the pictures with Derek, she'd heard a couple arguing drunkenly in the darkness of the blackout. *'I'm looking after you.' 'No . . . I'm looking after you . . .'* And neither of them fit to stand, by the look of their stumbling bodies in the dim light of a quarter moon.

But Olive didn't have too much energy to spare for Gladys and Bob Shaw, nor even for her sister. She was meeting Derek that night and, as usual, she didn't know whether she felt excited or scared.

Since their afternoon in Brighton, Derek had taken her out several times in his red MG. They had been down to the New Forest, where the wild ponies roamed freely through the trees and even into the little villages of Brockenhurst and Lyndhurst, and Olive had laughed to see one nose its way into the greengrocer's shop and steal an apple from the rack. The following Saturday they'd gone to Guildford and explored the Hog's Back and the Devil's Punchbowl, and last weekend they'd gone to Salisbury and wandered in the cathedral close, under the shadow of the tall, slender spire.

But wherever they went, there was no escape from the talk of war. Last Saturday, especially, the atmosphere had been particularly tense. Salisbury and its surrounding villages were filled with newly evacuated children and their schoolteachers, with a few mothers who, like Jess Budd, had small babies. Olive and Derek had seen them, wandering aimless and disconsolate, along the lanes, and it had taken the shine off the afternoon. They'd come home sobered, wondering like everyone else what Mr Chamberlain was going to have to say the next day.

Now, like everyone else, they knew. The country was at war and, as if to prove it, life was already beginning to change.

I couldn't bear it if Derek had to go away and fight, Olive thought miserably, hardly hearing her sister and Gladys Shaw sparring and giggling. I just couldn't bear it.

'I suppose Kimball's will be closing too,' Gladys said. She screwed up her mouth in disgust. 'What are we going to do with ourselves?'

The other two girls shrugged and shook their heads. The future looked bleak and grey. No pictures, no dancing. No lights at night, so you couldn't even go for a walk without fear of being run down by a car or bus. And the wireless seemed to play nothing but 'Sandy McPherson at the Theatre Organ' on the Light Programme or else talk endlessly about the war on the Home Service.

'Well, at least you've got your chaps at home,' Gladys said. 'I keep thinking about your Colin. I mean, they haven't dropped any bombs yet like everyone reckoned they would, but they're already fighting at sea. That liner that went down . . . And they don't tell us everything. My dad reckons it'll all be kept secret in case spies get to hear what's happening.'

'That's daft,' Olive said. 'People are going to know when their boys write home.'

'No, they won't be allowed to say where they are. D'you know where Colin is?'

'Well, not exactly. Going down the South Atlantic was the last we heard. He'll be safe enough there, anyway.'

'We hope,' Gladys said. 'What about your Derek? Is he going to be called up?'

Olive sighed. She'd been trying for the past few minutes to push her fears to the back of her mind. 'I don't know. He hasn't heard anything yet.'

'What'll you do if he is? Get married before he goes?'

'Fat chance of that! I'm not even twenty-one till next October.'

'Surely your mum and dad would stretch a point,' Gladys said. 'What's a few months?'

'Dad always said none of us would get married till we were twenty-one. Anyway, we're not even engaged. I don't know that Derek wants to get married.'

'They wouldn't let you get married quick anyway,' Betty said. 'Think what people would say!'

Olive blushed and dug her sister in the ribs. 'You shouldn't talk like that.'

'Why not? It's true. Look at Sheila Brown, round Carlisle Crescent. She got married in a hurry at the end of July and the old gossips haven't taken their eyes off her belly since.'

'Betty! If our Dad heard you say things like that!'

'Well, he won't. Anyway, it's better to know what's what. I'd hate to be like young Rose, no idea her mum was expecting till she saw the baby in its cot. I think children should be told the facts of life, not left to find out for themselves.'

'How did you find out, Betty?' Gladys asked curiously. 'Did your mum and dad tell you?'

'Them? Not likely! I heard about it from other kids, same as the rest of us. And then I found a book in the library.'

'What, in the children's library?'

'Don't be daft. In the big library, in the medical section. Diagrams and all. Mind, it puts you off a bit. I don't really fancy it myself. I mean, kissing's all right, but I don't think I'll bother with all that other stuff.'

'I bet that's not what Graham thinks!' Gladys said with a hoot of laughter. They had reached the Chapmans' gate now and she turned to walk down the back alley of April Grove to her own house. 'I daresay he's got a few ideas about what to do in the blackout.'

Olive and Betty went indoors. Their mother was out but Ted was there, reading his paper with Suky the cat on his lap. He looked tired and in need of a shave.

'Hullo, Dad. Had a good day?'

'Same as usual.' Ted's job as skipper of a ferryboat kept him plying back and forth across the harbour for the whole of his shift. The journey took a little over five minutes, with five to unload and load passengers at each side. It was never tedious, with the tides and currents changing all the time and ships coming in and out of harbour, but it was exhausting. You had to be continually on the watch, standing up on the bridge the whole time. And since the blackout, it was worse.

'You can't see a thing out there at night when there's no moon,' he grumbled. 'The other night I was halfway up to Whale Island before I realised it. And I'd got a boatload of Dockyardmen going home. I thought I was going to get lynched, they were that fed up.'

Betty giggled but her father gave her a glare. 'It's not funny, my girl. We could have run into anything. What it's going to be like with bombs dropping all round us, God only knows.'

'Anything from our Colin?' Olive asked, scanning the mantelpiece where letters were always put.

'No, there's not. Your mother's worried sick. I keep telling her no news is good news but she won't listen.'

The girls looked solemn. Olive went out into the kitchen and filled the kettle. There was a tin full of freshly made rock cakes and she set a few on a plate and carried it through to the living-room.

'Is Uncle Frank coming in for his dinner?'

'Supposed to be.' Ted reached out for a cake. 'I saw him on the boat this morning.'

'Must seem funny, with no one else in the house. Have the Glaisters come back yet?'

'Dunno.' The family in number 15 had been away on holiday, somewhere down in Devonshire it was believed, when war was declared. The two oldest children, Joe and Carol, were sixteen and fourteen, and both out at work. Shirley, the 'afterthought', was seven and presumably would have been evacuated if they had come back in time.

'Perhaps they'll stay down in Devon. They've got family there, haven't they?'

'So Jess was saying. But George Glaister's an Army reservist, he'll probably be called up.' Ted looked at the clock. Annie ought to be back by now. He was starving for his tea, in spite of the two rock cakes he'd eaten. 'Can't you start getting a meal on, Olive?' he asked irritably.

Olive sighed and got up from her chair. She was tired after her day's work, but although her father had almost certainly been sitting in his armchair for the past hour, it did not occur to her to suggest that he might help.

'I'll do the potatoes, Bet,' she said. 'You do some carrots. I don't know what meat there is.'

Betty looked in the larder. 'Just some beef, left over from yesterday. And there's some veg too. We'll have bubble and squeak, shall we?'

The two girls prepared the meal. Both were feeling depressed. Nobody had been able to talk about anything but the war all day and although some voiced relief that a decision had been made at last, most were still clearly feeling the dread that had greeted the Prime Minister's announcement on Sunday. And the touch of excitement that many of the younger people, who had no memories of war, had felt, was soon dissipated as the sheer dreariness of their new life began to come home to them.

'No pictures, no dances, no nothing,' Betty groaned as she chopped leftover vegetables. 'What's the point of it all? People have got to do something. And what about the men, home on leave, aren't they supposed to have a bit of fun?'

'I suppose they think it's dangerous to have a lot of people crowded together. If a bomb dropped on a cinema – '

'It could just as easy drop on a church,' Betty argued. 'Or a bus or a train. Or an office. Know what I think? I think they're a lot of killjoys. Anything people like doing, they'll stop. Life just isn't going to be worth living.'

Olive went silent. Her brother was at sea, perhaps already fighting German ships, and Derek was likely to be called up any time. Would they think life was worth living when they came home, even if they couldn't go to the pictures for a while?

And Auntie Jess. She'd been really upset when she came in the other morning, after she'd seen Rose and the boys off. All she wanted was to be at home and have her family together again. She wouldn't care if the cinemas were open or not.

'Don't be selfish, Bet,' she said sharply, cutting in on her sister's moans. 'There's plenty would think they were well off to be where we are now. At least we've got a warm house and enough to eat and a wireless to listen to. You want to think about others for a change.'

Betty stared at her sister in astonishment. The two rarely quarrelled and Olive's angry retort took her completely by surprise. Defensively, she began, 'I only—' but Olive broke in again.

'I know what *you only*. You only think about yourself and what you want. Well, there's a lot of people worse off than you, and there's going to be more and more if this war goes on. You don't have any idea what it's going to be like, Bet. Mr Harker and some of the men at work were talking about it today. It's going to be horrible. People being killed, soldiers and sailors coming home without arms or legs, houses being bombed and smashed, little babies – ' Her voice broke and she stopped and bit her lips hard. Then she said more quietly, 'It's going to be horrible, that's all.'

Betty mixed the chopped vegetables with beaten egg and tipped it into the frying pan. She could think of nothing to say. Olive was right, she knew, but did she need to bite her head off like that? And then she thought of Colin, somewhere at sea. Would he ever come down the street again?

And Graham, the first boyfriend she'd ever had. Would he be called up? Would he be taken away from her?

The chill of fear touched her heart and slid like a snake deep into her stomach, where it seemed to coil itself like some lurking monster. She looked at her sister and reached out a tentative hand. 'Livvy . . . ?'

The elder girl turned her head and their eyes met. But there was no anger in Olive's expression now, only a terrible, dark misery. And Betty, staring at her, felt the snake of fear lift its head and hiss.

Was this misery only the beginning? By the time all was over, would its blackness seem like a pale shadow beside what suffering lay waiting for them?

'Dont look so miserable, Livvy,' Derek said. 'It might never happen.'

She turned to look at him. They were sitting in the front room of Derek's parents' house, close together on the sofa. From the room next door came the sound of the wireless and the occasional murmur of voices.

Derek's open face was cheerful but there was concern in his eyes. She laid her head on his shoulder. She had brushed her hair loose this evening, with a bang over her forehead, and when he stroked it, it lay like a tawny web over his fingers.

'I can't help it, Derek. Ever since this war was declared I keep thinking about you having to go away.'

'Well, nobody's said I do have to go away yet, have they?' He squeezed her against him. 'Maybe it won't come to that. If it's over quick – '

'Dad says it won't be. He says they said that about the last war – that it'd be over by Christmas. And look how long that lasted. Years.'

'Well, this one's not going to,' he said. 'We've learned a lot since then. We can beat the Germans with one hand tied behind our backs.' His voice quickened with sudden enthusiasm. 'Tell you what I'd like – I'd like to fly a Spitfire. That's real fighting, that is, up there in a plane, dodging round the sky and— '

'*Derek!*' Olive lifted her head and stared at him. 'You see, you *do* want to go – oh, you're as bad as all the rest.'

He looked shamefaced but defensive. 'I'm sorry, Livvy. I don't really want to. But when I hear other blokes on about it – and see them in their uniforms . . . And when I think what's happening and how they really do need us . . . Well, it's natural for a chap to want to do his bit, isn't it?'

'I suppose so,' she said drearily. 'And what are we women supposed to do? Sit and wait?'

'You can do your bit too,' he said. 'Look, Olive, it's no good ducking it. All right, so maybe it isn't going to be over by Christmas. So we've got to face it, haven't we? We've got to think what we can do. For us blokes, it's the Forces. For you girls, it's – '

'Factory work,' she said. 'Munitions. The Dockyard. Driving buses. Milking cows. All the jobs the men don't really want to do anyway. I reckon you're all pleased to be able to go off and play soldiers and sailors.'

'Some might be,' Derek said quietly. 'But not all of us, Livvy. I bet there's a hell of a lot like me who'd rather be staying home, taking their favourite girl out for a spin in their car. Specially when it's a little red MG sports like mine, and the girl's called Olive Chapman and has long chestnut hair and big brown eyes and a figure like Betty Grable's.'

Olive laughed and gave him a push. 'Oh, you! You'd talk anyone round, you would.'

'Well, it's too nice here to worry about me going away. Let's talk about staying instead. We don't really want to go out, do we?'

Olive hesitated. They had arranged to go for a drive and then a walk but the evening had turned dull and wet, and there was a spiteful breeze in the air. The idea of staying here in Derek's front room, cuddled together on the sofa, was much more attractive. 'But aren't your mum and dad going out?' she asked.

'Mm, they're going over to Southampton to see Uncle Percy. But that doesn't matter.' He pulled her close again. 'In fact, it's all the better,' he whispered. 'It gives us the house to ourselves.'

Olive quivered. 'Derek – ' she began nervously, and he hugged her.

'Don't worry, Livvy. You know I wouldn't hurt you.'

It's not hurting I'm worried about, she thought, but said nothing. She was more and more aware lately that Derek wanted more than their goodnight kisses and their cuddles in the car or on the sofa, and she was aware too that her own body was urging her towards the same goal. She wanted to relax against him, to open her mouth to his kiss, to let him fondle her breasts and undo her blouse and her bra. Sometimes, her head swimming as they pressed close in the little MG, she had allowed him to touch her trembling body, to kiss her tingling bare skin, but the sensation of spinning and falling, the growing desire that throbbed through her, were too powerful and she'd been afraid and drawn back. And then, when they had parted and she'd gone to her own lonely bed, she'd lain in the darkness reliving every precious moment, excitement spiralling through her body, half thankful that she'd managed to resist and half regretful.

And each time Derek had taken his love-making just a little further; and each time she had let him, telling herself that she could keep control, that she could always stop, that she could always stop him.

Until now, time had always been on her side. There was always the need to go home by ten or risk her father's wrath. There was always haste.

But if they were alone for a whole evening in Derek's house . . . ?

'Will they mind us being in when they're out?' she asked doubtfully, knowing her own mother would never have allowed it.

'They don't have to know, do they? We can go out for a while – then come back. There's no harm in that, is there?' He grinned at her, then pulled himself out of her arms and went to the door, opening it to poke his head through to the other room. 'Olive and me are off now,' he said cheerfully. 'You're going up to Uncle Percy's, are you?'

Olive heard their voices reply and felt herself blush, even though there was no one to see. She looked at him with uncertainty as he came back and pulled her to her feet.

'Derek, I feel awful. It's – it's like telling lies.'

'No, it's not. We haven't told any lies. All I said was we're going now – and we are.' He picked her jacket up from a chair and wrapped it round her shoulders. 'Now, stop worrying and we'll have a spin along the front. And if we feel like having a drink, we'll stop and have a drink – and if we don't, we won't.' He gave her a quick kiss. 'There. Now d'you feel better?'

'I suppose so.' She gave him a wavering smile. But already the treacherous excitement was coiling and tingling in her stomach and she knew quite well that they would not stop for any drink and that within half an hour they would be back and ensconced once more on the big, comfortable sofa in Derek's front room.

Betty too was feeling the stirring of excitement as she and Graham said goodnight at the front door later that evening. She had been over to have tea at his house again and spent most of the time sitting beside his mother, going through an old family photograph album. Snaps of Graham as a baby, lying stark-naked on a rug, had made her giggle and his mother had said, 'Go on, there's nothing to laugh at – he was a fine little boy. Wasn't he, Charlie? All his bits and pieces present and correct –that was the first thing I asked the midwife when he was born, are all his bits and pieces there, and she said you don't have to worry about that, Mrs Philpotts, this little chap's going to break hearts wherever he goes!' She gave a squawk of laughter. 'Not that he has, not my Graham, he wouldn't hurt a fly, would you, love? You don't have to worry about my Graham, Betty, he won't lead you astray. Well, not if he hasn't already!' And she'd gone off into another peal of laughter and gone out to the kitchen to make a pot of tea.

Betty blushed and giggled again, giving Graham a sideways look with her hazel eyes. He wrinkled his freckled face at her.

'Don't take any notice of Mum. She shows all my girlfriends that album. Dunno whether she's trying to encourage them or put 'em off!'

'Go on,' Betty said, 'you're as bad as she is. Worse.' She got up to help Elsie Philpotts with the tea. 'We'll have to go after this. I want to get home before it's dark. I hate being out in the blackout.'

'Oh, I know,' Elsie said, piling sugar into her husband's cup. 'There you are, Charlie, love . . . It's awful trying to find your way round the streets with no lights. And the cars, I know they're only supposed to go at twenty miles an hour but some of them dash about just as if it's broad daylight.'

'Twenty miles an hour's too fast anyway,' Mr Philpotts said, making one of his rare remarks. 'You can still get killed by half a ton of metal moving at twenty miles an hour. They ought to be banned altogether.'

'That wouldn't please our Olive,' Betty said. 'She'd practically live in Derek's car if she could. They're always out in it.'

'They won't be,' Charlie Philpotts said, 'when petrol's rationed.'

Olive and Derek were still out somewhere when Betty and Graham reached home. They stood in the shadow of the front door, watching the last of the twilight fade from the sky. Earlier on it had been raining but now the shower had passed and the cloud was thin and high, veiling the moon. The dark shadows of barrage balloons loomed like drifting monsters beneath the stars.

'D'you want to come in for a cup of cocoa?' Betty asked. 'Mum won't mind.' They had already seen Ted on the ferryboat. He'd given them a brief nod and told Graham to make sure he got Betty home before blackout time. Then, his face set with concentration, he'd mounted his little bridge and stayed there throughout the five-minute journey across the harbour. 'As if he was skipper of the *Queen Mary*,' Betty whispered with a giggle.

'All right,' Graham said, and Betty led him along the side passage to the back door.

They were drinking their cocoa when Olive and Derek came in. Olive looked flushed and bright-eyed and she avoided her mother's eyes. She showed Derek in and then went quickly back to the kitchen to make more cocoa. Derek lounged in Ted's chair and talked about his car, but Betty thought he looked as if he was

123

thinking of something else, and a small grin kept pulling at the corners of his mouth.

'They've been up to something, those two,' she said to Graham as he kissed her goodnight. 'What d'you think it is?'

Graham sniggered. 'What do *you* think? Derek looks like the cat that's had the cream and your Olive is just as bad. I saw your mum looking at her once or twice as if she wanted to ask a few questions.'

'Oh no,' Betty said. 'Our Olive wouldn't do that.'

'Why not? She's human, isn't she? Like you and me?'

'Course she's human. But – '

'Well, then.' He held her closer and kissed her ear. 'Don't say you wouldn't like to do it, Bet. You and me. You know you would.'

Betty pulled sharply away. 'I don't know anything of the sort, Graham Philpotts, and neither do you. And I don't believe our Olive has been doing anything she shouldn't, either. Why, our dad would kill us if he thought – '

'Your dad doesn't have to know.' He put his hands against the wall, one on each side of her, and moved closer so that their bodies touched. Then he moved himself against her, slowly and sinuously. 'That's nice, isn't it. Go on, Bet, admit you like it. Go on.'

'Well, maybe I do,' she said, 'but that doesn't mean – '

'And this.' He took his hands away from the wall and ran them down her body from shoulder to hip. 'That's nice too. It feels nice to me – does it feel nice to you? Say yes.' His mouth was close to hers, his lips brushing her skin as he whispered the words. 'Tell me you like it, Bet.'

Betty shivered. Graham's hands were moving lightly over her body, tracing the contours of her shoulders, her breasts, her thighs. His palms cupped her buttocks and he lifted her towards him so that their bodies pressed together, hip to hip. Holding her there, he kissed her open mouth and she felt his tongue push against hers. He moved against her and she felt the shape of him and heard his breath quicken.

'Graham, don't. Suppose my mum came out and found you behaving like this? She'd never let you in the door again.'

'Well, we'll have to make sure we do it where she can't see, won't we,' he murmured, not letting go. He bent to kiss her again.

Betty wound her arms around his neck and closed her eyes. Her body felt as if it were melting. Graham's hands were splayed over her buttocks, his fingers moving in tiny circles on the softness. She quivered and Graham slid his mouth down her neck, into the hollow of her throat. He nuzzled there for a moment and she felt one hand slide up to cover her breast. Her head felt as if it were spinning. She wrapped her arms tightly around his shoulders, holding him firmly against her.

'You still out here, our Bet?' The front door had opened so suddenly they almost fell into the blacked-out hallway. Olive stood there, no more than a deeper shadow in the darkness and Betty sensed that Derek was close behind her. 'I thought you'd gone to bed.'

'Just saying goodnight,' Betty said defensively, but she hardly knew whether to be annoyed with her sister or grateful for her interruption. 'You can't get any privacy around here!'

'Strikes me you've had more than enough.' Olive stared through the darkness at her sister. 'What've you been doing?'

'I might ask you that,' Betty retorted. 'You came in tonight looking like you'd been dragged through a hedge backwards.'

'So would you if you'd been driving along the front in an open-topped car.' Olive gave her a push. 'Go on, you two've had long enough to say goodbye. Go in and give someone else a turn.'

'I'll have to be going now anyway, Bet,' Graham said. 'It takes a long time getting home in the blackout and I've got to be up early tomorrow morning.'

'All right.' Betty reached up and gave Graham a quick kiss. Maybe it was a good thing Olive had come out just then. Things had been moving a bit faster tonight than she'd meant them to. Another few minutes of Graham's kisses and the way he had of moving his hands, and she might not have been able to call a halt.

She went indoors, said goodnight to her mother and climbed the stairs to bed. Was that really what had happened to Olive tonight? Had things gone further than she'd meant, so that she'd been unable to stop them?

If so, she looked pretty pleased about it, Betty thought. And felt, mixed with her feelings of relief and half regret, a nagging curiosity.

What was it *like*? If only she could try it just once, just to find out, just to know . . .

The children who had been evacuated knew now where they were. It was Bridge End, a small village near Romsey, with a village hall and a school that had only two rooms. It was there that they had been marshalled on the first Monday and told what would be happening to them.

'School in the afternoons!' Tim crowed when his mother and Rose came over to see the boys at the Corners' cottage. 'We don't have to go in the mornings, that's when the village kids go. We can do what we like!'

'You'll do some extra schoolwork, that's what you'll do,' Jess said sharply. 'And help Mr and Mrs Corner. It makes a lot of extra work, having two boys to look after.'

Tim pushed out his lips. Now that his family was – except for Dad – with him again, he'd got over his homesickness and almost forgotten what it had felt like. Now he wondered whether it was so good having Mum nearby.

Some of the other boys had already begun to make plans about what to do with their spare time. Carts made from old pram-wheels, rafts to sail on the river, trees to climb, dens to be built –all this sounded far more interesting to Tim and Keith than doing extra schoolwork or helping Mrs Corner. What could they help her do anyway? There was only housework and cooking, and those were girls' jobs.

'You're lucky,' Rose said later, when Mum had gone indoors to feed the baby. 'You've got a good place here. So've we. Some of the others don't like where they are at all.'

Wendy and Alan Atkinson were among those who weren't happy. The two elderly sisters who had taken them in seemed to think that because the children were small they would also be both invisible and inaudible. It had not dawned on them that they would also need more care, nor that they might have problems older children had outgrown.

'Eleanor! The boy's wet his bed!' the younger of the sisters exclaimed that first morning, in tones of shock and outrage. And Alan, crying with misery and humiliation, had been made to have a

126

bath while Wendy found herself faced with a pile of sheets to be washed.

'He's your brother, you must take care of him yourself. And the mattress will have to be scrubbed too.' She was given a brush and a large bar of yellow soap, both almost too big to close her small hands round. 'They didn't tell us we'd have to put up with this sort of thing,' Miss Millicent went on, going downstairs to her sister, and the two children, up in the bathroom, could hear the indignant voices in the kitchen below.

The bathroom was large and cavernous, its walls distempered a muddy green, and the bath stood in the middle of it on huge legs with clawed feet. It was more like an animal than a bath. At any other time it might have been fun, but now, in an atmosphere of disgust and disapproval, it loomed menacingly in the sludgy green cave.

At the head of the bath, fixed to the wall above it, was a large geyser. Wendy, whose home, in common with most of the others she knew, had no bathroom, eyed it dubiously. Miss Millicent had turned it on and started the hot tap, but there had been many strictures about not using too much hot water. It was gushing out now and clouds of steam were rising from the bath. Perhaps there was already too much.

'Have I got to get in there?' Alan asked fearfully. 'Won't I drown?' He was still sobbing.

'Of course you won't drown.' She spoke briskly, but the bath looked immense. Alan would need to stand on a stool to climb in. She peered over the top, wondering how deep the water was, but could see little through the steam.

'We'd better have some cold in as well.'

She twisted the big brass tap with both hands, but it wouldn't move. She struggled with it, wondering if she dared send Alan down to fetch one of the sisters up. But Alan was sitting shivering on a small, cork-topped stool, and he had nothing on. Wendy had already noticed how the sisters averted their eyes when confronted with naked bodies.

'I can't do it – *oh*!'

The tap suddenly loosened and cold water burst out as if a dam had been breached. The bath was filling rapidly. Wendy tried to turn the hot tap off, but now this one was too stiff.

'Oh dear. Oh, it won't shut. Oh, Alan . . .' Her voice rose in panic. 'I can't turn either of them off. You'll have to go and get one of the ladies.'

'I don't want to.' Alan had almost stopped crying but now his voice quivered and his face began to redden. Wendy gave him a despairing glance. She knew that he wasn't far off losing control, and if he did that he was capable of crying for hours.

But someone had to turn these horrible taps off, and if she couldn't do it herself . . .

'I'll go then. You stay here.'

She ran downstairs to the kitchen. The table was neatly laid, with a packet of cornflakes, a jug of milk, toast in a rack, butter and marmalade. The two sisters were eating.

'Please – ' she panted, and they turned and stared at her. The hair sprouting from Miss Eleanor's mole quivered alarmingly.

'What is it, child? What are you doing down here? Have you washed those sheets yet?'

Wendy shook her head. 'I can't. The— '

'What do you mean, you can't?' Miss Eleanor demanded ominously. 'Of course you can. It might help you to see that your brother learns to behave himself. Has he had his bath yet?'

'No. You see— '

'Why not?' Eleanor Woddis rose from her seat. She was tall, thin and angular, and in her black frock with a heavy silver cross hung round her neck she looked like some vengeful being from one of the stories Wendy had heard and only half understood at Sunday School. 'What are you doing up there?' She looked at her sister. 'I thought I told you to see that they cleaned themselves and the bedding properly.'

'I did, Eleanor. I took them into the bathroom and gave them everything they needed.' Miss Millicent spoke quickly, as if afraid of being blamed for the children's misdemeanours. Her pale lips trembled a little and her nose twitched like a rabbit's.

'Then why is the child down here?'

'I don't know, I'm sure.' The younger sister turned to Wendy. 'Go back at once and don't come down until you've finished.' Her voice was stronger when she addressed Wendy.

'But I can't— '

'And don't answer back, miss! The impertinence of it!'

'But— '

'Go upstairs at once!'

Wendy turned and fled to the door. But once there, the hopelessness of the situation overcame her. In the distance, she could hear the relentless gushing of water and knew that it must be near the top of the bath now, if not actually overflowing. Desperate, she turned and faced the two accusing women.

'I can't turn off the taps!' she yelled. 'It's not my fault – they're too big. And Alan's crying, he's frightened of that great big bath, he's frightened he'll drown. Oh, I wish we'd never come here, I wish we could go back home, I hate it here, I *hate* it!'

Without waiting to see the effect of her outburst, she dashed back upstairs. Her one thought now was to get her brother out of the bathroom before the bath overflowed and swept him away. Her mother had told her to look after him, and she would do her best – but she hadn't realised it would mean bathing him in that horrible room all by herself and washing the sheets.

Behind her, she could hear the feet of the two sisters, but Wendy was past caring now. She burst into the bathroom and grabbed her brother from where he was still sitting, naked and crying, on the stool.

The room was full of steam. The damp sheets were in a pile on the floor. Miss Eleanor Woddis entered behind her and gave a scream of horror.

'Whatever have you been doing, you naughty, naughty children? Look at this, Millicent. They've got both taps full on and the plug out. Have you ever seen anything so wilfully naughty in your life?'

With a rapid twist, she turned off both taps. Relief swept over Wendy as she saw that the bath had not overflowed. And, looking in, she realised that it probably would not have done, for Alan must have pulled out the plug and the water was running away almost as fast as it came in.

'Such a waste,' Miss Eleanor went on, rolling up her sleeve and plunging in her arm to replace the plug. 'I don't know what you can have been thinking of. No, don't answer me back again. I don't wish to hear your excuses.' She straightened up and looked at the two children in disgust. 'Now, perhaps, you'll do as you were told.

And I don't want to see either of you downstairs until you have. Is that understood?'

Wendy nodded. Inside, she was seething with anger and misery. If Mummy was here, she thought, she wouldn't let them treat us like this.

But Mummy wasn't here. She was far away at home, where everything was comfortable and known, where the bath was made of tin and hung on a nail outside the back door, to be brought in and filled with buckets of hot water from the Ascot on Saturday nights. She was having her own breakfast of Weetabix and hot milk and sugar. Perhaps she was thinking about Wendy and Alan, wondering where they were and hoping they were all right.

Tears filled Wendy's eyes again. She helped Alan into the bath and soaped him all over. Then she got him out and wrapped him in a towel before heaving the sheets into the water.

How did you wash sheets? She swilled them about a bit, then pulled out the plug. Her small hands gathered the sheets in a bit at a time, squeezing them ineffectually. Vaguely, she knew that they ought to be rinsed, but she dared not turn the taps on again. She looked at the sodden heap lying in the bath and wondered what she was supposed to do with them now. Through all this, the tears had not stopped streaming down her cheeks. Alan, too, was still sobbing. The two children got dressed and then stared at each other.

'I don't like it here,' Alan whispered. 'I want to go home. I want my Mummy.'

'I do, too. But we can't.'

'Why can't we?' Alan asked, looking into her face. 'Why can't we go home? Doesn't Mummy want us any more?'

'Of course she does. It's because – ' But Wendy could not answer him. Instead, she sat on the stripped bed, forgetting that she was supposed to scrub it, and cuddled him against her.

Why had they been sent here, to live in this strange house? Had they done something wrong? And why could they not go back home?

Wendy had heard little about the war. It had not been talked about in her presence at home and she'd only half understood the talk of other children. Just as children take for granted the world they find themselves in, accepting each new development as part of normal living, so she had taken for granted the digging of trenches in the parks, the arrival of the Anderson shelters, the blackouts and the sky full of barrage balloons. Evacuation had been just one more event, and it wasn't until it actually happened that she'd realised her mother's distress and connected it with herself.

Now, she felt totally bewildered. The only rock in this world that had suddenly turned upside down around her was the responsibility her mother had laid on her in those final moments of goodbye. Look after Alan. Take care of your little brother.

CHAPTER FIVE

SINCE THE DAY when he and Graham had met Betty Chapman down near the harbour, Bob had thought more and more about the girl who lived at the top of the street.

He'd always liked Betty Chapman. She was more fun than her sister – Olive was a bit toffee-nosed at times, as if living in a detached house made her better than everyone else. Her mum was a bit like that too, putting on airs because she'd worked in posh houses and talking about doilies and antimacassars, whatever they were. But Betty had always been ready, with a sparkle in her eye, for a game of cricket with stumps drawn in chalk on the side of the end house, or football in the wide bit where the road bordered the allotments. She wasn't forever fussing about with dolls or bits of ribbon and she could fight as well as any boy.

These attributes hadn't seemed so important when Bob was first beginning to take an interest in girls and, having seen Betty as a kind of surrogate boy, he found it difficult to think of her as female. But that day down at the Hard, hearing her voice with that new, flirtatious note in it, and seeing the saucy look she was giving Graham, he'd suddenly realised that she could be fun in a different kind of way. And since then, his days had been built around the chance of seeing and speaking to Betty.

'Our Bob's smartened himself up a bit lately,' Gladys Shaw remarked, coming across him as he smoothed Brylcreem into his hair at the kitchen mirror. 'Must be in love – nothing else'd make him clean his fingernails twice in the same week!' And she'd ducked and giggled as Bob rounded on her.

Peggy Shaw found her son suddenly keen to go shopping in September Street, especially if it meant a visit to the dairy. He would be gone for longer than she thought necessary, coming back sometimes depressed and taciturn, at others with a secret grin on his thin face. She sighed, knowing quite well what was happening, for she too had seen that photograph on the bedroom wall, and she knew from Jess Budd and Annie that Betty was going steady now with Graham Philpotts.

'You ought to look for some other girl,' she told Bob. 'Betty Chapman's not for you.' But he'd closed his lips firmly and buried himself in a copy of *Hotspur*.

'A job wouldn't be a bad idea,' Bert Shaw said caustically, but he knew as well as anyone else that jobs had been hard to come by in the past few years, and didn't pursue the matter. It wasn't Bob's fault he was unemployed, and with this war coming he'd be in demand soon enough, along with all the other youngsters.

Meanwhile, Bob lived for his snatched meetings with Betty. Sometimes days would go by without a word. The dairy would be full of women when he went in, or she'd be working at the back and Mrs Marsh would serve him instead. Sometimes she'd be on her own and he could linger, but although she was friendly enough she would never agree to go out with him.

'Sorry, Bob. I'm going out with Graham that night.' And when he suggested another evening, 'I can't. Graham wouldn't like it.' And she shook her head so that the soft brown curls danced around her face.

'You're not engaged to him, are you?' Bob said once and she blushed.

'I don't have to be engaged to be loyal. You wouldn't like it if your girl two-timed you, would you?'

'Not if she was you,' he said. 'I'd want you all to myself.'

And Betty had blushed a bit more and looked almost as if she liked that idea, but she'd only shaken her head again and said, 'Well, there you are, then.' And the door had opened to admit an old woman wanting a pint of milk, and at the same moment Mrs Marsh had come out from the back of the shop and glared at Bob, and he'd had to go.

After that, Betty hadn't been so ready to talk to him and the next time she's seen him in the street she'd told him quite sharply to stop asking her out.

'If I've told you once, I've told you a dozen times, I'm going out with Graham. I don't want anyone else. And you're getting me into trouble with Mrs Marsh. She says I'm encouraging you and it looks bad. The other customers don't like coming in and finding you always hanging about.'

Bob stared at her. 'You mean you don't want me coming in any more?'

Betty avoided his eye. 'Can't stop you, can I? Not if you're doing your mum's shopping. Only don't make a meal of it, see? And don't keep on at me to go out with you.'

He bit his lip. He hadn't realised just how much his days depended on seeing Betty, having a laugh with her in the shop, and on the hope that one day she would relent and agree to go out with him. He felt cold inside, as if she'd driven a spear of ice deep into his heart. He didn't know how to deal with it. He clenched his jaw and turned away.

'Well, if that's the way you want it . . .'

'It is.'

'I won't bother you any more. I'm sorry I've been such a nuisance.' His voice was tight with misery. He scuffed with his toe at the loose gravel at the side of the road.

Betty looked at him. She put out her hand, then drew it back again. Her voice awkwardly gentle, she said, 'I'm sorry, Bob. It's just – '

'Oh, I know. It's just that I don't match up to Ginger Philpotts. Well, I wouldn't, would I? I'm not like him, I don't know how to talk to girls, I don't have money to flash around. Well, you go out with him, Betty, and good luck to you. I just hope you don't find you've bitten off more than you can chew, that's all.'

Betty stared at him. 'What d'you mean?'

'Oh, nothing,' Bob said. 'Nothing you won't find out for yourself. And when you do, when Graham Philpotts chucks you like he chucks all his girls, you'll know where to come, won't you? Except that I might not be here by then.'

He turned on his heel and walked away, back towards his

own house. And Betty, left standing in the street, stared after him.

Bob had been really hurt, she thought in surprise. I didn't know he'd take it that way. I didn't know it mattered that much.

But there was nothing she could do about it. She was Graham's girl and that was that. And if Graham had chucked girls in the past, what did it matter? He'd just been waiting for the right one. And the right one for Graham was Betty Chapman.

On the other side of the Budds' house, silent and empty during the day now that all the family had gone, the Glaisters were returning after their holiday in Devon.

'I knew we shouldn't have gone,' Ethel said, pulling clothes out of suitcases and dropping them in piles ready for the wash. 'I knew it. It's as if we're fated. Our first holiday in years and they declare war in the middle of it. I said we shouldn't have gone.'

'It wouldn't have made any difference,' George said. He was a thin, lanky man with a mournful face. He was several inches taller than his petite blonde wife but had developed a stoop, as if he were trying to hide the fact. 'I don't suppose us staying home would have stopped them declaring war.'

Ethel glared at him. 'You know what I mean. We should have stopped home. Suppose we'd got stuck, down there in Devon? Suppose we hadn't been able to get back?'

'But we did get back,' he pointed out.

'We might not have done. And then what would we have done? Our Joe and Carol with jobs to go to, you supposed to report for Service . . . You could have had the Military Police after you for desertion.'

George sighed. Pointing out that they had managed to return home with very little trouble and that the trip had given them a chance to see his relatives for the first (and possibly the last) time in several years, as well as having enjoyed several days' holiday, seemed of little use. He performed the trick he had learned during the early years of his marriage to Ethel and closed his ears to her tirade, while still retaining enough awareness to be able to nod, shake his head and murmur 'yes' or 'no' at appropriate intervals.

'. . . now our Shirley's missed the evacuation,' Ethel was saying when he next tuned in. 'All the other children have gone to the country, you realise that? They're safe. I wonder if you'll ever be able to forgive yourself, George Glaister, if she gets killed by a bomb simply because you insisted on having a holiday in Devon.'

George's recollection was that it was Ethel who had insisted that they should have a holiday. His only stipulation was that it should be at the end of August, when he could take his annual leave. But that wasn't important now.

'I did suggest we should leave Shirley in Devon,' he reminded his wife. 'My sister would have been only too pleased – '

'Your sister's got enough to do, with that farm and all those hulking great boys to look after.'

'One more wouldn't have made much difference. She'll probably have to take an evacuee anyway. And the boys love Shirl, you know they do. They made a real pet of her.'

'I don't think it's suitable. Shirley's not used to boys.'

'Not used to boys? What about our Joe?'

'He's her brother.' Ethel picked up the washing and pushed past him to the scullery, which she dignified by the name of kitchen. Some time ago, she had bullied George into roofing over the area between their scullery wall and that of number 12. This was known as the conservatory and was the envy of the street, forming as it did another room, as well as making it possible to go to the lavatory without having to put on outdoor shoes. Ethel also kept the copper out there and did her mangling, another job that needed to be done under cover.

'So what are you going to do about Shirley?' George asked, when she came in again.

'What, are you still here? I thought you'd have gone over the allotment or down to the shed. There's plenty to be done, even if you are still on holiday.'

'I just wanted to know what you want to do about Shirl,' he repeated patiently. 'Now there's no school – '

'Well, you don't need to tell me there's no school! That's what I've been telling you all day. All the other children have gone and so have the teachers. There's nothing for her to do now and she'll be under my feet all day, not that you'll care when you're back at work – '

'I don't suppose I'll be going back to work,' George said, raising his voice slightly to make himself heard. Ethel stopped and stared at him. Her mouth hung open and he could almost fancy that he saw her unspoken words, teetering just inside.

'What do you mean, you won't be going back?'

'I'm a Territorial, aren't I? I'll have to report for duty. Didn't you hear what they said on the wireless on Sunday, what they've been saying ever since? Reservists and people like that, they all have to report at their centre for duty. Didn't you listen?'

'Of course I listened,' she said sulkily. 'I heard what they said. But it doesn't affect us – '

'Of course it affects us. I'm in the TA. I'll have to go.'

'Well, I know that,' she said impatiently. 'But you've only got to report – you won't be going away.'

'I might. I expect I will. That's what they were saying.'

Ethel stared at him. 'But what about us? Me and our Shirley? Joe and Carol? How're we supposed to manage?'

'Same as everyone else, I should think. There'll be plenty of families left on their own, Ethel.'

'Yes, but . . . What about your job? What about your pay? What are we supposed to live on?'

'I'll get paid by the Army.'

'And will they keep your job for you?' Her voice was rising. 'What are you going to do when you come out of the Army and your job's gone? Have you thought of that?'

'Of course I've thought about it. Mr Browning says my job'll be kept open for me. But even if it isn't . . . Look, we knew this might happen. God knows they've talked about it enough. Why did you think I joined the TA in the first place? What did you expect?'

Ethel did not answer. She turned away and began to fill the copper with water. She heard George go upstairs. When he came down again in his Territorial uniform she was standing at the sink, scrubbing his shirt collars. He stood behind her for a moment but she did not turn round, and she did not reply when he said awkwardly, 'Well, I'll be off then.'

Out of the corner of her eye, she saw him hesitate by the back door. Then he sighed, shrugged and took himself off down the garden path. She heard him get his bike out from the shed and close the gate behind him.

Ethel scrubbed furiously. Her eyes were blurred with angry tears. Just as if I don't have enough to put up with, she thought. Three children to look after, and all he can think of is getting away to play soldiers. That's all it is in the Territorials, just playing soldiers. A night a week out with his mates and weekend camps when he ought to be doing the garden – what good will all that be in a war? Why, he can't even swat a fly, let alone fire a gun. And never mind how I'm going to manage, left stuck here on my own. Never mind our Shirley, left behind when all the other children have been taken somewhere safe. The selfish beast!

She hadn't really minded when he'd suggested joining the TA, when they'd appealed for volunteers last year. It got him out of the house one night a week, out from under her feet. And she hadn't really minded him going off on the camps either, not at first. It meant she could get the house looking nice and keep it that way for the weekend, without his books and papers scattered all over the place. She could have Mum and Auntie Ellen over for tea for a good old natter. You couldn't do that with a man around. They always put a damper on that sort of thing, men did.

Still, she hadn't banked on him going quite so often as he did. And she wasn't too keen on the way he was when he came home, either. He'd looked really red in the face the last time or two, as if he'd been out in the sun too much – or in the pub. She was certain there'd been beer on his breath. And he'd had a silly grin, and kept grabbing hold of her and making – well, suggestions. She'd stopped that straight away. 'We're not a couple of newly-weds now, George Glaister,' she'd said sharply. 'There's time enough for that sort of thing at the weekend.'

'This is the weekend,' he'd said, fondling her, and she'd pushed his hand away quickly.

'It's Sunday evening. You've got to go to work tomorrow. And I'll have all the housework to do, so if you don't mind . . .'

She didn't really care whether he minded or not but she wasn't going to change their routine now, not after all these years, just because he'd been with a lot of men for a couple of days and got ideas.

But it wasn't just that, she thought, rinsing out the washing before putting it through the mangle. Men were all the same as far as that was concerned. What she didn't like was the way the TA was changing George in other ways, and not for the better in her opinion. He wasn't so easy to manage these days. Too inclined to argue when she wanted him to do something, and really snappy at times. And too set on having his own way – like today, going off to the hall in spite of what she said. As if he didn't care any more . . .

Ethel took the washing out and hung it on the line. Next door, Frank Budd had hung out a few bits and pieces. He must have done them last night, after getting home from work. They flapped dolefully on the line, looking rather pathetic. Jess's line was usually so full, with all the children's clothes and a row of white sheets.

Ethel looked at Frank's line thoughtfully. He was a fine figure of a man, Frank Budd, and it was a shame he had to do his own washing. He must be lonely too, there in that house all on his own in the evenings.

Suppose George did go away. It wouldn't hurt her to offer to do Frank's washing for him. Maybe a bit of cooking, too. And it'd be handy to have someone next door who could help with the odd job in return.

They'd always got on well enough, her and Frank, though she'd not had a lot to do with him, just the odd word over the fence. All the same, she'd often thought what a big, strong chap he was, and wondered what he saw in little Jess. And now Jess was away. For 'the duration'. Whatever that might mean . . .

Feeling suddenly more cheerful, Ethel picked up her basket and went back indoors.

Heinrich Brunner was having supper with his wife and daughter. They always ate together at six o'clock, after the shop was shut. Alice worked in the shop too, and spent the last hour or so dashing out to see to the cooking, but as Joy grew more capable she was able to leave more and more of it to her.

'She did all the supper tonight, didn't you, love?' she said tonight. 'She's getting to be a real little help, I don't know what we'd do without her.'

Heinrich looked across the table at his daughter. She was like him, quiet and anxious to please, with brown eyes and straight hair, but luckily she hadn't inherited his weak sight. He took off his glasses and polished the thick lenses on his handkerchief.

'Are you feeling lonely without the other children to play with?' he asked. His German accent had almost gone and sometimes people who came into the shop didn't realise he wasn't English. They thought he came from the north of England. 'If you would still like to be evacuated –'

Joy shook her head. 'I don't want to go away from home.'

Her parents looked at her doubtfully.

'But all your friends have gone,' Heinrich said. 'That nice little girl from April Grove – Rosemary Budd, Rosebud – has she gone away?'

'They've nearly all gone,' Alice said. 'There are only a few children left around here.' She pushed back her mousy hair. Since all the talk of war had begun, she had grown thin and pale. Her eyes were tired from waking in the night, worrying about what would happen to them all – about what would happen to Heinrich.

'It would be safer for you when the aeroplanes come,' Heinrich said.

But Joy shook her head again. 'I'd rather stay here.'

Heinrich sighed and looked troubled. Most parents, he knew, didn't give their children the option. But he and Alice had always treated their daughter almost as if she were grown up, as if she could make her own choices. And Joy was a thoughtful child, who would consider carefully before she made any decision. If she wanted to stay at home, she had good reasons.

'I wonder if we should tell her she must go,' he said to Alice as they went to bed that night. 'It's bad for her to be here, with so few children about. And when the bombs come . . . Why do you suppose she doesn't want to go?'

'I don't think many of the children did,' Alice said. 'They just didn't have the choice. But there's more to it than that, with Joy.' She hesitated, then said, 'I think it might be because of you.'

'Me?' Heinrich looked at her, then sighed and nodded. 'Yes. I wondered if it might be that.' He took off his trousers and folded them neatly over the back of a chair. 'Have the other children been making her unhappy?'

'Only some of them. She hasn't said much to me – you know Joy. But I think some of them have been teasing her.'

'Not little Rosebud?'

'Oh no – none of the Budds would do that. And Rose is a good friend of Joy. I've heard her standing up for her.'

Heinrich frowned. He struggled for a moment with his collar-stud, than said, 'But wouldn't it be better for Joy to be away? The othe children would soon forget. And if there is any unpleasant-ness . . .'

'What sort of unpleasantness?'

Heinrich didn't answer. He had talked with his family during his visits to Berlin and knew what sort of unpleasantness there could be when a country turned against its inhabitants who were different in any way. Heinrich was not a Jew, but he'd heard what was happening to them there. Forced to wear yellow stars, to brand them as the butt of any lout who wanted a bit of sport . . . turned out of their homes, dismissed from their jobs . . . herded together into camps. Stoned in the streets, attacked for no reason, arrested on trumped-up charges. And if it were not these things, there were others. Dogs' excreta pushed through the letter-box, or even rags soaked in paraffin and set alight.

He'd seen the hate already in people's eyes. He'd noted the sharp fall in customers coming to buy their newspapers and cigarettes. And the war was not yet a week old.

'Joy would be better out of it,' he said, getting into his striped pyjamas.

'I don't think she'll go, all the same.' Alice was already in bed, her shoulders covered with the pink lace of the nightdress he liked best. 'She's afraid you'll be interned.'

'Interned? Oh, I don't think that's likely. I've lived here so long. Anyway, there's nothing for Joy to fear in that. It only means I'd go away for a while.'

'Does it?' Alice looked up at him. 'I think Joy's afraid that if you go away we'll never see you again.' Her voice quivered suddenly and she held out her arms. 'I'm afraid of it too, Heinrich. I dream about it at night. I don't want our family to be parted.'

Heinrich pulled back the sheets and climbed into bed beside her. She wound her arms around his neck and he drew her close. She could feel the warmth of his skin through the cotton and the lace that separated them, and the beating of his heart against her breast.

'We won't be parted,' he said softly. 'We'll stay together. If Joy wants to stay at home, she shall. And they won't take me away. What good would it do? Everyone knows Heinrich.'

Alice clung to him. Ever since she had known him, Heinrich had always been able to calm her fears and chase away the shadows that lurked cold and dark at the edges of her mind. Here in this small bedroom over the shop he had soothed her when her demons had grown too insistent, here he had given her love and reassurance.

Now the world was full of demons, and the shadows enveloped the whole of Europe. Heinrich was her only rock of sanity in the madness that was sweeping over them all. If she lost him, she would lose her rock.

Gladys Shaw went down the alley, between the gardens of April Grove and the allotments. Each garden had its hump of Anderson shelter down near the back gate, covered with earth. One or two people, who had lawns, had dug up turfs and laid them over the top, and others had put in a few stones or bricks in an attempt to make the shelter look like a rockery. But most of them had left the earth bare and weeds like groundsel and dandelions were already starting to grow.

Gladys hated the shelter. It was cold, damp and full of spiders. But her mother had tried to make it look homely, with a few magazine pictures stuck on the walls and a bit of old carpet on the floor, and Dad had made a couple of benches with planks laid over boxes and more carpet tacked on to them. All the same, the idea of spending hours down there – maybe whole nights – made Gladys shiver and she made up her mind that if the bombs did come she'd take her chance indoors. She'd heard people say you were as safe under the stairs as anywhere.

Bob was the only one home when she let herself in the back door. He was lounging back in his father's armchair, his feet up on the mantelpiece, reading *Hotspur*. As she opened the door, he lowered his feet guiltily and then grinned.

'You needn't look like that,' Gladys said, standing in the doorway between the back room and the scullery. 'I saw you through the window. Haven't you got anything better to do?' She looked at the sink, piled high with dirty dishes. 'Couldn't you even have done the washing-up?'

'That's women's work,' Bob said, returning to his reading.

'Oh yes? And I suppose you've been hard at it all day, slaving away to earn your keep.' Gladys marched in and snatched the comic from his hands. 'You're turning into nothing but a lazy slob, Bob Shaw. Why should you sit around all day doing nothing while Diane and me work fifty-two hours a week to keep you in fags? And Mum could do with a bit of help too. Women's work! You helped make those dishes dirty – you damned well make them clean again.'

Bob stared at her. 'Now look here—'

'No. You look here.' Gladys stood with arms akimbo, glaring down at him. 'I've just walked home with Olive and Betty Chapman. Olive's worried sick because her Derek's likely to be called up soon and *he's* got a job – '

'He works for his dad!'

'That's a job, isn't it? Anyway, he doesn't just work for his dad, he's an accountant. He works bloody hard – '

'You'd better not let our dad hear you talk like that – '

'I'll talk how I like to you. I'm telling you, Derek's got a job, he works morning till night doing something worth doing, and he's going to have to go and fight. While you sit here on your backside reading kids' comics and letting our mum run round after you and our dad pay for your fags. Don't you ever feel ashamed of yourself, Bob Shaw? Don't you ever wonder what it is makes you so special you don't even have to lift a finger to do anything for yourself? Why, you'll be calling out to have your bottom wiped soon!'

Bob leaped to his feet. 'Look here, our Glad – '

'Yes?' Gladys stared up at him. He was a good eight inches taller than she and, although thin, he was strong, but her eyes challenged him to use his strength against her. She pushed back her yellow hair. 'What are you going to do, then? Hit me? Go on, and see if it makes you feel better.'

Bob hesitated, then shrugged.

'You're not worth hitting,' he muttered, turning away. 'You're getting like all the rest of them, nagging a bloke just because he puts his feet up for a few minutes – '

143

'I bet you've had your feet up all afternoon.'

'I haven't.'

'So what else have you done? What time did Mum go out?'

'Just after two,' he mumbled.

'And where's she gone?'

'I dunno. Said something about the First-Aid Post up the school. They're getting it kitted out for when the raids start.'

'And she didn't have time to wash up. And when she comes home, she'll have to run round and start getting a meal ready. Dad'll be in at six and you know what he's like – expects it on the table. And you've been sitting here ever since.' Gladys turned on the tap and rolled up her sleeves. 'Just tell me this, Bob Shaw, when and if you finally do get a job – just supposing anyone's daft enough or desperate enough to give you one – how're you going to know what work is? 'Cause I don't think you'll recognise it when it hits you in the face.' She took a piece of washing soda from the jamjar that stood on the windowsill and dropped it in the water.

Bob scowled. 'And what would you know about it, Miss Clever? For all you know, I've already got a job. There'll be plenty going now, you know, with men being called up. That Derek bloody Harker with his posh car and his fancy clothes – '

Gladys whirled. 'You'll never get Derek Harker's job! His dad's not going to give you his job while he goes off and fights to save your yellow skin.'

'Yellow? Who are you calling yellow?' Bob was as angry as she. He stared at her, his face white. 'You'll take that back, Gladys Shaw.'

'I won't.'

'You will.'

'I—' But Gladys was cut short by the sound of the front door opening. She closed her mouth abruptly, gave Bob a furious look, and turned back to the sink. Almost at random, she snatched a plate from the pile and plunged it into the water.

Bob grabbed a tea-towel. He took the plate from his sister and when Peggy Shaw walked through from the front room they were standing, apparently amicably, sharing the washing-up.

Peggy dropped her shopping bag on a chair and sat down, giving a sigh of relief.

144

'I thought I'd never get home. The things we had to do! And I've got to go for training two nights a week. I don't know what your father's going to say about that. They're looking for more volunteers too. I wondered if you might think about it, Bob.'

'Shan't be able to,' he muttered, avoiding his sister's eye.

'Oh? Why not?'

'Because I'll have other things to do.' He spoke reluctantly, still not looking at Gladys.

Gladys said sarcastically, 'He's got three months' worth of back *Hotspur*s to catch up on. Little Keith next door wants them back.'

Bob flung down his tea-towel.

'Oh, you think you're so ruddy clever, don't you, you and your posh job in British Home Stores and your posh friends with their flashy cars, and Olive Chapman with her Derek who's got a job and getting called up soon. I suppose you think he'll win the war single-handed? Well, he won't – he'll need a few other poor buggers to help him and shall I tell you who one of them's going to be? Well, shall I?' He stood glowering at her, his head lowered slightly and his chin pushed out.

'Bob!' his mother exclaimed. 'Watch your tongue – I won't have language like that in this house.'

But her words went unheeded. Brother and sister stared at each other. Then Gladys shrugged and turned away.

'Tell me if you like. Why should I care?' She swished a plate about in the water.

'No, you don't care,' Bob said bitterly. 'All you care about is your fancy friends. Well, you might be sorry for that one day –when it's your own brother marching out of here in uniform and getting blown up by a Ger—'

'Bob!'

Peggy was on her feet, staring at him, her face suddenly pale. Bob stopped abruptly and looked shamefaced. He glanced sidelong at Gladys, who was as scarlet as her mother was white.

'Now look what you've done, you idiot,' she muttered.

'What have you done, our Bob?' Peggy whispered. She grabbed him by the arms, shaking him so that he was forced to meet her eyes. 'What have you done?'

Bob looked down at her. He licked his lips and lifted his

shoulders slightly. His glance shifted away and then back to his mother's face.

'I've joined up,' he said at last. 'I've been down the recruiting office and joined up. Well, isn't it what you wanted me to do?' he demanded, his voice suddenly loud. 'Don't you think I know what you're all getting at with your remarks about jobs and sitting on my backside all day? D'you think I want to have to ask for fag money and see other blokes getting all the kudos because they're in uniform? Well, I did something about it, that's all. I went and joined up, and on Monday I have to report to Hilsea Barracks and I hope you're all satisfied!'

He wrenched himself away and stared out of the window. Peggy and Gladys looked at his back, then at each other.

'What've you been saying to him, our Glad?' Peggy asked, her voice quivering.

'Me? I haven't said nothing. You're not blaming me for what he does.' Gladys's voice trembled. 'All I said was he ought to do a hand's turn about the place, that's all, give you a bit of help. I just came in to find him sitting here reading a comic, with all this washing-up staring him in the face. I never said he had to go and join up.'

'I'd already done it then,' Bob retorted. 'I just thought I was entitled to a bit of comfort, my last weekend in civvy street.'

'So why didn't you say?'

'Why didn't you ask?' he countered.

Gladys turned away with an exasperated sigh. She started to swish plates in the water again, but it was cooling now and the soda did little to remove the grease.

'I'll have to run off some more hot water now,' she said impatiently. 'That's waste, that is.'

'I never told you to—' Bob began, but Peggy shook him again and then sat down as if it were all too much for her. Her thin body sagged.

'Can't you two ever stop squabbling? There's a war on – and here's our Bob going off to fight in it. Don't that mean nothing to you, Glad?'

'It's only her stuck-up friends she cares about. She said so.'

'Stop it!' Peggy slapped her hand on the table and glared at them both. 'Stop it, the pair of you. You're behaving like a couple of kids.' She watched as they both bit their lips and glanced sideways at each other. It was just the same as when they'd been little. They used to get themselves into a squabble then and you could tell they really wanted to make it up, only neither of them wanted to be first to say so. They were too alike, that was their trouble.

'Say sorry,' she commanded, as she'd so often done before, and saw the unwilling grins pull at their mouths. They knew, then. They remembered the old formula. But would they comply with it, now they both reckoned they were so grown up?

To her relief, they turned to each other, still with those rueful grins on their faces, and said simultaneously, 'Sorry.' And then burst out laughing.

'Honestly,' she said, smiling in spite of herself, 'you two won't never grow up,' And then, the smile fading, 'But d'you really mean it, Bob? Have you really joined up?'

'Yes, I have. I've gone in the Army. Gunners.'

'But why?'

'Why d'you think? There's a war on. They're crying out for volunteers. And the pay's regular.'

'Oh, Bob.' Peggy shook her head. 'Why didn't you talk about it first?'

'What was the point? I've been all this time, since I left Mumby's, without a job. I'm not going to get one now – who's going to take on a chap my age, knowing he's likely to be called up any minute? So I thought I might as well just go and do it.'

'You mean you really did go and do it off your own bat?' Gladys said.

'Look, I'm not a little kid, I can make up me own mind – '

'All right,' Peggy said, 'don't start again. If this really is your last weekend, Bob, let's make the most of it. Get that washing-up finished, Glad, and let's have tea on the table ready for when your father and Diane come home.' She sighed. 'I'm proud of you, Bob, though I wish you hadn't done it. You could have waited . . . And I don't know what your father's going to say.'

'He'll say I did the right thing,' Bob said, but he didn't sound too sure and he picked up the tea-towel again and started to wipe the plates Gladys had dumped on the draining-board. Peggy went out to the shed and came back with the potatoes and carrots. It was too late to go and buy anything special for Bob's last meals at home, but she had a large tin of ham in the cupboard and she went to fetch that, and a can of peaches and Ideal milk for afters.

Gladys ran some hot water into the bowl. That was the third lot, and they were supposed to be saving fuel, but it wasn't every day your brother announced he was going to go for a soldier. She felt proud and upset and ashamed, all at the same time, and guessed that Bob probably felt much the same way, so that made them equal.

They'd always squabbled a lot, her and Bob, but they'd always been close, too. With only thirteen months between them, and Diane four years younger, they'd been more like twins. And they'd generally made their fights up quickly enough.

It was just that, coming in today and finding him there with his feet up as if he was lord of the manor – well, it had touched her on the raw. Especially after hearing that Derek was likely to be going away soon and seeing how upset Olive had been. If Bob had only said – but she supposed she hadn't really given him much chance. And now he was going too.

She wondered how much Betty Chapman had had to do with it. She'd been leading Bob on a bit, Gladys reckoned, for all she'd pretended she'd not known he fancied her. Girls always knew when a chap fancied them. Maybe she'd given him the cold shoulder and that was why he'd gone off and done it so sudden.

Gladys put the last plate on the draining-board and swilled the water round in the bowl before pouring it down the sink. What with that liner being torpedoed, all the kids sent away and the queues at the recruitment offices, this war seemed to have started with a vengeance. And they reckoned the air raids would start any day now.

She looked up at the bit of sky she could see through the scullery window. The tail of a barrage balloon drifted into view. They said the balloons would stop any low-flying aircraft. But that wasn't going to prevent others coming in higher up, and dropping their bombs, was it?

Betty Chapman didn't see Robb Wilton at the King's Theatre that

148

week, but she did hear *Band Waggon* on the wireless on Saturday night, with Arthur Askey and Richard Murdoch. She was sitting in the front room with Graham, and they had switched the speaker on and now sat on the settee holding hands and laughing at the antics of the two comedians.

'That's a good idea, having speakers through from the other room,' Graham said when the programme finished. 'Did your brother do it?'

'No, it was Dad's idea. There's one up in the front bedroom too, so Mum could listen when she was poorly last winter. We wanted them put through to our rooms too but he wouldn't let us.'

'There's a new programme starting next week,' Graham said. 'On Tuesday night. It's Tommy Handley.'

'Oh, I heard about that. *It's That Man Again.*' Betty laughed. 'Everyone's been saying that about Hitler. Whatever goes wrong now, he gets the blame. Even when Mum spilt tea all over her new tablecloth and Mrs Marsh dropped a bottle of milk, we all said *it's that man again.*'

'Well, he's come in handy for something, then. It's useful to have someone to blame.' He sat stroking her fingers for a while. 'I'm glad I met you, Bet,' he said quietly. 'With all this going on – nobody knowing what's going to happen next – it's good to have someone special to think about.'

Betty leaned her head on his shoulder.

'Bob Shaw down the road's joined up,' she said. 'He's going Monday. Mum met Mrs Shaw in Mrs Seddon's shop. She'd gone in for a few rashers of bacon for Bob's last breakfast at home.'

She was silent for a moment. She had received the news with mixed feelings. One part of her was proud that Bob had volunteered. Even though she'd refused to go out with him, she still felt as if, in some way, he half belonged to her. But another part of her felt guilty – had he really joined up because of her? –and afraid that something might happen to him. Would his family think it was her fault? Would Diane and Gladys blame her?

'Old Bob joined up?' Graham said. 'What did he want to do that for? He could've hung on a bit, surely. I suppose he's gone into the Navy – he was talking about it the day we met you down Queen Street.'

'That's what surprised Mrs Shaw. They didn't know he was even thinking about it till today. And they thought he wanted to go into the Navy too, but he's gone for the Army. Gunners.'

'The Navy are a bit more choosy,' Graham remarked. 'Not that there's anything wrong with Bob Shaw, I don't mean that, but they just take longer to get around to taking people. If you go into the Army Recruiting Office you're lucky to be allowed home to fetch your toothbrush.'

Betty giggled. 'Fancy thinking about toothbrushes, when you're going off to war.'

'Well, you know what I mean. Mind, they're fussy about that sort of thing. I bet Bob'll spend the next six weeks learning to blanco his belt, before they even let him get near a gun.'

'D'you think you'll join up?' Betty asked.

Graham shrugged. 'Don't have any choice. I'm twenty-one in January.' He hesitated, then said casually, 'Matter of fact, my call-up papers came through today.'

Betty sat up straight. 'Oh, Graham! You never said anything.'

'I was waiting for the right moment,' he said with a grin on his freckled face. 'And then *Band Waggon* was on and you wanted to listen to that.'

'But not when you were thinking about your papers!'

'Well, I wanted to hear it too. And half an hour hasn't made any difference to my call-up. We all need a good laugh these days, Bet.'

'I know, but . . .' She turned suddenly and buried her face against his chest. 'Oh, Graham, I shall miss you.'

'I'll miss you too.' He stroked her hair, twining his fingers in the curls.

They were silent for a few minutes and then he said, 'Look, Bet . . . I know we've only been going out together for a few weeks, but – well, you're different, somehow. Different from other girls, I mean. You're special.'

'Am I, Graham?' she whispered.

'Yes.' He held her closer, his fingers moving gently on her waist. 'You're so special I think all the other blokes must want to go out with you.'

Betty laughed. 'Well, if they do, they haven't said so!'

'Bet they do, all the same.' He bent his head and kissed her ear.

'Will you say yes if I go away, Betty? Will you go out with other boys?'

Betty turned her face up to his and looked up into his eyes. 'Course I won't. Well, not unless – '

'Unless what?'

'Unless you don't want me any more,' she whispered.

Graham bent his head. She felt his lips touch hers. She stayed quite still as he let go of her hand and slipped his arm around her shoulders, drawing her closer. His lips moved against her mouth and she felt the strange excitement spiral in her stomach. His hand touch her breast and she quivered.

'Oh, Graham,' she murmured as he lifted his head again. 'Graham, I do love you. I don't want you to go away.'

'I love you too, Bet. I wish – '

'Wish what?'

'I wish there was something we could do before I go. So I could know you'd still be here, waiting for me.'

'Of course I'll be here,' she said, her eyes shining. 'You know that.'

'Well, we haven't known each other all that long. You might not feel the same way after a while. You might get fed up with waiting and want to go out with other blokes.'

'I shan't,' she declared. 'I shan't want to go out with anyone else.'

'I don't know,' he said. 'Girls say that when a feller goes away. But after a while . . . I don't blame 'em, mind. It's as bad for them as it is for the blokes. Being apart and not having anything to remember, to sort of hold on to.'

Betty said nothing for a moment. Graham's hands were becoming more persistent, more exploratory, and she was finding it difficult to think. She wanted him to go on, but she knew she ought to tell him to stop. It had never been difficult before – he'd been cheeky, knowing she'd pull his hands away when they went too far, and he'd just laughed and told her that one day she'd let him. But tonight was different. Tonight, she had the feeling he'd be really upset if she stopped him.

'If I could just be sure,' he whispered in her ear. 'If I could just know we really loved each other. If you could just *make* me sure, Betty . . .'

151

Betty's mind whirled. She knew what he meant. He wanted to make love to her – perhaps here, this very minute, in her mother's front room. Panic blotted out her other feelings. Suppose they did and Mum came in – or, worse still, Dad. And suppose something went wrong – suppose she got caught and fell for a baby. She remembered her parents' warnings, the tight-lipped disapproval of other girls who had found themselves in such a position.

Graham was kissing her neck, his lips nipping and tugging at the soft skin. Betty heard him make a sound deep in his throat. His hands were on both her breasts now, stroking and squeezing. If she didn't stop him soon, she wouldn't be able to.

'We could get engaged,' she said. 'Then you'd know. I'd belong to you then, Graham, and you'd belong to me and everyone would know it.'

'Get engaged?' He stopped kissing her and sat up a bit. 'But I thought you said your dad wouldn't let you get married till you were twenty-one.'

'That's what he's always said. But things are different now, aren't they? There's a war on. Anyway, I didn't say married, I said engaged.' She gazed at him, her eyes shining. 'Oh, Graham, wouldn't it be wonderful? Knowing we belonged to each other, that wherever you went I'd be waiting for you to come back. And when it's all over we'd be able to get married – '

Graham looked dazed. 'But suppose it's all over by Christmas, like people are saying?'

'Oh, well, then we'd just go on being engaged, I suppose. Two or three years isn't that long.' She looked at him. 'So are you going to ask him? Mind, he might take a while to come round to it.'

Graham was silent for a moment. Then he said, 'Course, if you don't think he'd let us . . . Well, we could be secretly engaged.'

'Oh, yes!' Betty sat up straight. 'We could, couldn't we? Nobody could stop that, could they?'

'And I'd still know you'd be waiting for me.'

'Yes. And when Dad sees I'm not interested in anyone else – well, maybe about Christmas, we could get engaged then. I'd like to get engaged at Christmas.'

'That's settled, then.' He pulled her back into his arms. 'We'll be secretly engaged now and then ask your dad at Christmas. He should be used to the idea by then. I wouldn't mind betting your Olive'll be wanting to get engaged too. Or even married – she's not far off twenty-one, is she?'

'No. And if Derek goes into the Army – ' She stopped and looked up at him again. 'Graham! You've never told me what you're going into. And when do you have to go? Is it soon?'

'Next week,' he said, his face suddenly serious. 'I'm going into the Navy. I'm going to be a writer.'

'A writer? What, books and things?'

'No, silly – it just means a clerk. Doing the office work and that sort of thing, like I do now.'

'Oh.' She gazed at him, relieved yet at the same time vaguely disappointed. 'So you won't be actually fighting, then. You won't be going to sea.'

'I expect I will. They still have office work to do, even on ships. Anyway, I'm reporting to the Naval Barracks next week so we'll know then. Once I'm in, I might be able to get transferred. I wouldn't mind being a gunner.' He felt obscurely irritated about Bob Shaw. He'd come tonight full of his own news, ready to be treated as a hero, only to find that Bob had got in first. And as a gunner too! You had to admit, it sounded a lot more exciting than a writer. But if the ship went down, it wouldn't make any difference what he was, he'd drown just the same.

'Oh, Graham.' Betty gazed at him. She felt a mixture of emotions. Fear, excitement, anxiety and pride, all surging together inside. And over all, the realisation that she was engaged.

Engaged! She'd actually had a proposal – and she was only eighteen! Betty felt a thrill of excitement. Of course, it was a secret engagement and she wouldn't have a ring to flash around – unless she could persuade Graham to buy her one to wear on a chain round her neck, under her blouse – but she could drop the odd hint, couldn't she? And although she didn't want Graham to go away, there'd be his letters to look forward to.

'When will you get your uniform?' she asked. 'Will it be bell-bottoms, like Colin's?'

'Yes. I'll have to learn how to do up all those lanyards and things.' He grinned at her a bit self-consciously.

'Oh, you'll have to come round here – we had to practically dress

153

our Colin every time he went out at first. We're experts!' Betty realised suddenly how her words might have sounded and blushed. 'I mean – '

Graham laughed and hugged her. 'I know what you mean! At least, I think I do.' His smile faded and he held her tightly. 'Oh, Bet, it makes me feel good to know you feel the same way about me as I do about you. It'll make all the difference when I'm at sea, to know you're here waiting for me.'

Betty slid her arms around his neck. 'I'll wait, Graham,' she promised. 'It doesn't matter how long it is, I'll be here. And when it's all over . . .'

'We'll have a proper engagement,' he said.

'And a proper white wedding. And our own little home.'

'Yes.' But to Graham, these seemed too far into the future to be considered just yet. They were dreams, no more – dreams that he felt sure would come true, but much too distant to be real now. What was real now was his last week at work, reporting to the Barracks next week and starting a new life.

At the thought of going into the Navy, he felt both excited and scared. Service life had never appealed to him much, but when it looked as if war was coming he'd begun to feel differently. Like a lot of his friends, he wanted to 'have a crack at Hitler'. And the glamour of the uniform was undeniable. It was the boys in blue who got all the girls, no mistake about that. Go to a dance on a Saturday night and you could see them there, helping themselves to all the best lookers.

Of course, he wouldn't be interested in that sort of thing, not with Betty at home waiting for him. But a chap had to have a bit of fun when he was away from home, didn't he? Couldn't just sit in the mess, aboard ship all the time.

All the same, the idea of joining the Navy and going to sea was a bit overwhelming. What would it be like? He'd seen films, of course, and he knew a few blokes from school who'd joined up, but he still couldn't quite imagine it. Living with a lot of men, for a start – that would be different. It would be queer not to have his own room, to have a bunk in a mess below decks with everyone else. And he knew that there were cooks but did you have to do your own washing? How did you get it dry? And what about ironing? He'd never ironed so much as a handkerchief. And the Services were sticklers for being smart, at least the Army and Navy were – the Air Force didn't seem to bother quite so much.

Still, at least he'd have Betty to think about. He'd get her to give him a photo to stick inside his locker. And he could spend his time writing to her and reading her letters.

He just hoped he wouldn't be seasick. The only sea trip he'd ever had was on the Isle of Wight ferry, in one of the paddleboats. He'd been all right then, but it hadn't really been rough.

He glanced at Betty. She had a dreamy look on her face. She was really pretty, he thought, with that curly brown hair and those big hazel eyes. She didn't wear a lot of make-up but she had nice red lips and her face wasn't shiny. And she had a good figure, slim but not thin, with enough on her to make her nice and cuddly.

His arm was still round her and he tightened it a little. Perhaps now they were engaged, she'd be a bit more willing to let him make love to her. He was willing to bet she wanted it as much as he did – she was just scared. Girls usually were. But things were different now, weren't they?

He bent his head again and nuzzled his face against her neck. Betty made a little sound, half squeal, half giggle, and twisted slightly so that he could kiss her lips.

'Oh, Graham,' she whispered, and he felt a surge of excitement. He pulled her a little closer. Everyone knew that being engaged meant you could do more than just kiss, didn't they? And Betty hadn't really protested that much when he'd kissed her at the door the other night. Surely now she'd let him go a bit further.

There was a rattle at the door and Graham and Betty snapped apart. By the time the door opened, they were sitting side by side about six inches apart, staring straight ahead.

'Supper's on the table,' Annie said, putting her head round the door. 'Are you going to have a bit with us, Graham? I've made plenty of cocoa.'

The Shaws were up early on Monday to see Bob off to Hilsea Barracks. Gladys and Diane sat at the table, watching him eat his

155

breakfast of bacon, eggs and fried bread. Gladys thought about the squabble they had had and the way she'd shouted at her brother, and the tears came into her eyes.

'Don't worry, sis,' Bob said. 'I'll be back before you know it, with a row of medals on me chest.' He winked at her and she gave him a scornful look.

'I wasn't worrying about you. I was thinking about something quite different.'

'Someone, you mean,' Diane said. 'That boy I saw you talking to down Charlotte Street the other day. I know him, his sister works in the laundry.'

'For goodness sake!' Gladys said, blushing. 'I was only talking to him. You don't have to make something of it.'

'Now then, you two,' Peggy said automatically, but her voice was subdued. 'It's time you were going, anyway. You don't want to be late for work.'

Diane made a face. 'I wish I could be joining up. Fancy having to work in a laundry. What sort of a job is that in a war?'

'People still have to keep clean,' Peggy said sharply. 'And if you don't get a move on, you won't have a job at all.'

Diane got up reluctantly and went to the door at the bottom of the stairs to fetch her coat. She looked at Bob and hesitated.

'Cheerio, little 'un,' he said, and stood up to give her a clumsy kiss. 'Mind what you get up to down Charlotte Street, now.'

'And you mind what you get up to,' she retorted. 'Just because you're getting a uniform won't mean you're God's gift to women.'

'Whoo! Hark at her,' he mocked. 'You'd better mind what you say to me from now on. Play your cards right and I might bring you home a nice soldier-boy for Christmas.'

'Bob!' his mother exclaimed. 'I've told you before, that's enough of that kind of talk. She's getting quite forward enough as it is. I sometimes wonder whether we did right, letting her go to work at that laundry,' she went on as Diane hurried out, still pushing one arm into her coat-sleeve as she went. 'They're a real common lot down there. I don't want her getting flighty.'

'Oh, our Di's all right,' Bob said. 'She's just lively. Better'n some of the girls I know, hardly got a word to say for themselves.' He drained his teacup. 'Well, it's me for the off now. I don't know if I'll get time to come in and say goodbye later on – well, I don't know where they're going to send me. So give us a smacker now, Glad, there's a good girl.' He held his sister for a moment, then turned to his mother. His face was suddenly serious. 'Bye, Mum.'

Peggy's eyes misted with tears. Bob's face swam before her eyes and for a moment she saw him again as he had been. A baby, her firstborn, asleep in her arms or suckling at her breast. A toddler, taking his first steps with a grin of delight on his round face. A small boy walking away from her on his first day at school. And now tall and straight, a man, leaving home for the first time on a journey whose destination nobody could know.

She put her arms round him and held him close. It was a long time since she'd touched his body like this. The Shaws were not a demonstrative family and hugs and kisses were reserved for going away, or coming back. Bob had not been away since he went to Scout camp four years ago, and he would not have welcomed such effusion then. It must be years longer than that since she had been so close to this body that had come from hers, which she had once known more intimately than her own.

'Bye, son,' she said, her voice creaky with tears. 'Look after yourself, now.'

'I will.'

'Don't let your feet get wet. You know how easy you catch cold.'

'I won't.'

'And make sure you eat your greens. Sailors used to get scurvy from not eating greens.'

'I'm not going in the Navy, Mum.'

'That doesn't make any difference,' she said, recovering herself a little. 'I don't want to see you come home with all your teeth dropping out.'

'I won't,' he said quietly. 'Don't worry, Mum.'

She gave his shoulders a pat and stepped away briskly. 'Well, off you go then. You don't want to be late, your first day.'

They went to the front door together. Bob hesitated, glancing up the street towards the Chapmans' house, and Gladys saw the look and understood what was going through his mind. She felt a sudden surge of bitterness towards Betty Chapman. Did she know she was responsible for Bob going off like this? If he gets killed, Gladys thought, it'll be her fault.

'Don't you worry,' she said to her brother. 'You'll find someone else a lot better than her. There's plenty of other fish in the sea.'

Plenty of other fish in the sea . . . Betty had said that to Graham, that first day. Bob remembered her, standing there on the Hard with the wind tossing her curls round her face, a paper of chips in her hand and her eyes laughing. It was the first time he'd seen that saucy look and it had turned his heart over. That's when it happened, he thought. That's when I knew I wanted her to be my girl.

But she'd chosen Graham. And now he was going away, to God knows what, leaving Graham a clear field because he just couldn't bear to see her any more.

'Cheerio then, Mum,' he said with a sudden gulp. 'Cheerio, sis. Write to me, won't you.'

They nodded, but neither could answer. Gladys stared at him for a moment and then threw her arms around him, holding him close. Peggy held them both, her face working with the tears she was trying so hard to hold back. And then he drew himself out of their arms and walked away. He crossed over to the corner where Mrs Seddon had her shop and then turned to wave before disappearing up October Street.

'That's it, then,' Peggy said with half a sigh, turning to go back indoors. Her face was closed and grim. 'And you'd better get off too, our Glad. You've got your job to think about.'

Gladys looked at her mother. She saw the taut mouth, the reddened eyes. She thought of all the other young men, walking away from mothers and sisters, sweethearts and wives, the way Bob had just walked away, and saw a disturbed muddle of pictures of just what they might be walking into.

'I can go in late for once,' she said. 'They can manage without me for an hour. I'll help you clear up and have a cup of tea with you first.'

Peggy opened her mouth to protest and then closed it again. She went back indoors and sat down heavily at the table while Gladys filled the kettle and set it on the gas stove.

'He looked as if he'd turned into a man overnight,' Peggy said, looking at the tablecloth. There was a brown ring on it where Bob had stood his teacup. She was always nagging him about not putting it back in his saucer, but this morning she hadn't said a word. 'Yesterday, sitting here reading that comic, he was still a boy. But this morning . . .'

'I know,' Gladys said. 'And when we see him in uniform he'll look completely different. Not like our Bob any more.' Her eyes filled with tears and she stared at her mother. 'Is it going to change them all, Mum? Won't they ever be the same again?'

Peggy looked up and saw the fear in her daughter's eyes. Poor kid, she thought, this is hitting her real hard. It's hitting them all. All the young ones, the boys who've got to go and fight, the girls who've got to give up their boys, the wives who are going to end up as widows. And none of 'em have done anything to deserve it. All those lives ruined, just because of one crazy madman.

She reached across and touched Gladys's hand. It was easier to do than it had been with Bob, and maybe it was something they should do more often.

'Of course they won't change, ' she said stoutly. 'They'll still be the same person inside. Bob'll still be our Bob. Nothing'll make any difference to that.'

But as they sat and drank their tea, both remembered Bob walking away up the street. He had looked different. Taller, bigger, more of a man. And if that was what one night could do . . .

It's going to change us all, Peggy thought. Every one of us. And how will we ever get back to normal once it's over?

159

CHAPTER SIX

'GOODNESS KNOWS what sort of home they came from,' Miss Eleanor Woddis said disdainfully. 'The boy's not even house-trained. He – well, he relieves himself wherever he happens to be. And the girl's rude and sulky. I really don't know how we can be expected to put up with it.'

Mrs Tupper, the billeting officer, sighed. This was the twelfth house she had visited that morning and only three had been happy with their evacuee children. Bed-wetting was the most common cause of complaint, with refusal to eat a close second. In many homes, she knew the food offered was fresh and wholesome, but the children behaved as if they had never seen it before.

'Can't you use a rubber sheet on the bed?' she asked without much hope. The two spinsters really didn't look the type likely to welcome strange children into their immaculate home. But they had the room, and everyone who had room was expected to take in someone. 'Perhaps you'd prefer adult evacuees. Some of the male teachers – '

'Oh no!' Miss Eleanor said at once. 'We couldn't take men.' The hair on her chin quivered as if with indignation at the very thought.

'They're perfectly respectable.' But it was clear that the sisters would not entertain such a suggestion. It would have to be rubber sheets then.

'Of course we've put rubber sheets on the beds,' Miss Millicent said impatiently. 'We went out on the first morning and bought them from the chemist. And not a moment too soon,' she added. 'It seemed half the village was buying them. But it was extra expense. Are we supposed to pay for that? And all the other damage?'

'Has there been other damage?' Mrs Tupper tried to remember what the Atkinson children were like. Surely they were the two small, quiet-looking scraps that Miss Langrish had said were well-behaved and nicely brought up, just the kind that the Woddis sisters would be able to manage. Had there been some mistake?

Miss Eleanor held up her hands and counted on her fingers.

'Taps left running on the first morning and a whole tankful of hot water wasted. Water spilled all over the bathroom floor by sheets not properly wrung out – the floor's only just dry now. A broken milk jug. A stain on the carpet – that was the boy. I've already told you about his disgusting habits. And I've had to clean up after him myself. The girl seems quite incapable.'

'But surely – ' Mrs Tupper referred to her papers ' – she's only eight years old.'

'At eight years old,' Miss Eleanor said coldly, 'children used to work in factories. Or down the mines.'

'All we're asking,' her sister chimed in, 'is that she should help a little around the house. It's not much, surely? It would show a little gratitude for all we're doing for them.'

Mrs Tupper gathered up her papers. She still had a dozen families to see that day and had already spent too long with the Woddis sisters.

'Why don't you give them another chance?' she suggested. 'It's early days, after all. It's bound to take them time to settle in. They're very young, and they must be missing their mother.'

The spinsters glanced at each other. They knew that everyone with spare rooms was expected to take in evacuees. If it wasn't the Atkinson children, it would be someone else. Perhaps bigger children, even more difficult to manage. Or perhaps, as Mrs Tupper had suggested, a man.

And the billeting money was useful. Ten shillings a week for the two children was a sum that could make quite a difference to them provided they were careful with it. Two small children didn't need much to eat, after all – older ones might want much more. And men had dreadfully large appetites.

The little girl could probably be trained to be quite useful about the house, and once the boy had been properly disciplined . . .

'Very well,' Miss Eleanor said at last. 'We'll give them one more chance. But they must improve if they want to stay here. I hope someone can make that plain to them.'

'I'll ask their teacher to have a word,' Mrs Tupper said, and escaped. She walked down the village street, scanning her papers for the next address. Each child was supposed to be visited within the first few days of evacuation, but it was a slow job. Almost every home had a tale to tell and the billeting officer was expected to listen and do something to put the situation right.

'They don't ever seem to have seen proper food before,' one woman complained. 'I go to all the trouble to cook them a nice meal – lamb chops we had yesterday, and potatoes and carrots and cabbage – and what do they do? They turn up their noses and ask for fish and chips. Fish and chips! Well, there's nothing wrong with that but they want it every day. And not a nice piece of coley cooked at home and my own chips, oh no, they're not good enough. It's soggy chips in newspaper they want, and cod in batter from the shop.'

'But there's no fish and chip shop in the village,' Mrs Tupper said unwarily.

'Of course there's not! And even if there was, I wouldn't be popping round there every five minutes. Good home cooking's always been good enough for me, and if these little whatnames won't eat it, they'll just have to do the other thing.'

'I expect they're just missing their mother,' Mrs Tupper said, as she'd already said a dozen times. 'I'm sure they'll settle down.'

But as she went on her rounds and heard complaint after complaint, she began to doubt whether either the evacuees or their hosts would ever settle down. She heard of children who refused a good cooked breakfast and demanded bread and dripping instead; of others who wanted beer to drink rather than milk or tea; of some who had never seen stewed fruit or any other kind of pudding, and others who didn't know what to do with a bowl of soup.

'And if they've never seen it before, they won't even try it,' she was told. 'It makes you wonder what sort of homes they come from. Don't people eat proper meals in towns?'

Food was not the only source of complaint. Manners and 'dirty habits' brought problems too. Bed-wetting was the worst offence but apparently it didn't stop there. Like little Alan Atkinson, some children hardly seemed to know what the lavatory was for.

'I found him going in the cabbage patch the other night,' a cottager said indignantly. 'Said he was scared of the privy! I gave him a right walloping, I'll tell you!'

Mrs Tupper looked down at the little boy who was being held in front of her. Martin Baker, she thought consulting her notes. Six years old. No brothers or sisters here. He stared back at her and she saw the tears in his large blue eyes and felt suddenly sorry for him.

'Why are you afraid of the privy?'

He shook his head and his hostess snorted. She was a widow in her late fifties, her own children long since grown up and departed. Mrs Tupper could not recall their having visited her for several years.

'He's not afraid! It's just a way of getting attention. I know what children are.'

Martin's mouth trembled. Mrs Tupper bent to hear what he was whispering.

'Tell me. What is it you don't like?'

'There's nothing – ' Mrs Hutchins began, but the boy was whispering and Mrs Tupper lifted her hand for quiet.

'Spiders? You don't like the spiders?'

'Spiders!' Widow Hutchins almost spat her indignation. 'Afraid of a few spiders? Don't tell me they don't have spiders in Portsmouth!'

'Perhaps there are more than he's accustomed to,' Mrs Tupper said mildly. 'He's only six, after all. If you could just sweep them out . . .'

'I see. So my house isn't clean enough for him, is that it? He can spread his filth in my cabbages but I have to clean the house to make it fit for him to live in. Well, I didn't realise I was having royalty to stay with me. Perhaps you should have said. I would have bought some satin sheets, specially.'

Mrs Tupper sighed. She opened her mouth to utter the words that were fast becoming a platitude – 'he's probably just missing his mother' – but she could see from the look on Mrs Hutchins's face that nothing she could say would improve matters. She could only mark Martin off on her sheet of paper as being in his billet and 'satisfactory', before moving on to the next.

Susan Cullen. Now here was a child who really was missing her mother. Mrs Tupper was aware that Madge Cullen had died only a few days before evacuation and she looked at the pale, red-eyed little girl with pity. Poor little mite, she thought, what can she be thinking in her little head? But there was no allowance made in the war for children who had lost their parents, and there'd be a good many more before it was over.

Susan's foster-parents were doing all they could, but it obviously wasn't easy for them, having to cope with a child who refused to talk or eat and did nothing but cry. Mrs Long looked almost as weary as Susan, and her husband just looked fed up. There'd be trouble there too, soon, Mrs Tupper thought, but what can we do? The child can't go back home to a father who's out at work from four in the morning.

'She'll get over it soon,' she said to the Longs, hoping it was true. 'Children are very resilient.' And she left the house, trying not to be haunted by the memory of Susan's stricken white face and the feeling that she'd somehow let the child down.

Not all children were unhappy in their new homes. Tim and Keith Budd had settled down without any trouble at all and were clearly as delighted with the Corners as Edna and Reg were with them. The four of them were playing Ludo when Mrs Tupper called and she felt heartened by the sight of them sitting round the kitchen table, mugs of lemonade and a plate of home-made biscuits at their sides.

'No need to ask if you've got any complaints,' she said, accepting Edna's offer of a cup of tea.

'Oh no, we're fine. These two scamps have really livened us up. I feel quite guilty, taking them away from their mother.'

'But she's in the village too, isn't she?'

'Yes, she and the girl and the baby are with the Greenberrys. They come over quite often, of course, or the boys go to see her, but I think she feels a bit awkward about it. You know, taking up our room, or all four of them being over there. It's not like being in your own home, is it?' Edna poured milk and tea into a cup and

164

gave it to Mrs Tupper. 'She's a nice woman though. And Rose is a good girl. Always willing to lend a hand.'

'Well, it's good to hear of someone happy.' Mrs Tupper drank her tea. It was the first she'd been offered all morning. 'Not everyone's taken this as well as you.'

'How else can we take it?' Reg asked. He was a big young man with a thatch of yellow hair, straight and stiff as straw. 'We all have to do our bit.'

'That's not what everyone thinks, all the same. Some people don't seem to realise yet there's a war on.' Mrs Tupper nibbled a home-made biscuit. 'Mind, I don't blame some of them for complaining – they've got a lot to put up with. It's not easy taking strange children into your home, and when they wet the beds and break your things and won't eat – well – '

'The poor little mites are just missing their mothers,' Edna said, as Mrs Tupper herself had said over and over again.

'But what sort of mothers are they? Some of these children arrived dressed in nothing more than rags. Filthy dirty – not just from the train, either. At least six of the ones I've seen so far had nits and several have got impetigo. And they seem to live on the most peculiar food. One little boy said his mother gave him a penny every day to buy his own dinner. He bought a bag of chips or Oxo cubes. What kind of mothers have they got?'

Edna shook her head. 'You can't always believe what little children say. But I agree it's a shame when they're not properly looked after. Still, it gives us a chance, doesn't it? Show them what life can be like.' She sat down beside Keith and cuddled him against her. 'You only have to give them a bit of love. It doesn't matter about the rest.'

Mrs Tupper departed looking more cheerful and the Corners finished their game of Ludo. Then Edna sent Reg out with the two boys for a walk while she got dinner ready.

'Take them over Hanger Wood,' she said, handing them each an old biscuit tin. 'See if you can find any blackberries.'

They set off along the lane, then went through a gate and began to cross the fields.

'Look out for mushrooms too,' Reg said, scanning the grass. 'Know what they look like?'

'Yes, we've collected them before. But Mum always tells us whether they're really mushrooms or not. Some of them are poisonous.'

'It's easy enough to tell the difference. There's others you can eat as well as mushrooms, but it's best not to pick them unless you're sure.' Reg suddenly dived across to a patch of dark-green grass. 'Look, here's some.'

The two boys followed him and helped pick the creamy cluster. Reg showed them how to recognise a mushroom by its pinky-brown gills and the collar of skin around its stem. Some of them were small and round, the collar not yet broken away, but you could still see that they were mushrooms. 'They'll make a nice breakfast,' he said, 'with a bit of bacon and an egg or two.'

They wandered on across the fields. Tim's biscuit tin was soon full of mushrooms and in the hedges they found blackberries, rich and sweet.

'Mum used to pick these to make jam,' Tim remarked, and this led to a discussion about fruit and vegetables generally and a discussion about Frank's allotment and what he grew there. And, from there, to the question of babies which had been puzzling the boys ever since Maureen was born.

'She was just there,' Keith said. 'Nobody seemed to know she was coming. And why did Mum have to stay in bed? If she came in the doctor's bag or they found her over the allotments—'

'I don't believe either of those things,' Tim interrupted. 'I think it had something to do with Mum getting fat. And our Rose knows something about it, I'm sure she does.'

Reg stopped and looked at them. 'Don't you know? Don't you know where babies come from?'

'Well, nobody will tell us.' Tim looked annoyed. 'They just say "Wait until you're older" and "don't ask questions". What's all the secret about?'

Reg laughed. 'It's no secret. Look, you know about flowers and vegetables, don't you? You know how they grow.'

'They grow from seeds,' Tim said. 'But – '

'And so do babies.'

The boys stared at him.

'Babies grow from seeds?'

'That's right. But the seeds aren't planted in the ground. They're planted in their mother's tummy. That's why your mum got fat. The baby was growing inside her from a tiny seed.'

Keith looked suspicious and Tim disbelieving. 'How did it get there, then?'

'Your dad put it there.'

'Dad did? But – '

'Where did he get the seed from?' Keith asked practically. 'Did he get it from a shop?'

'No, not a shop. He'd got the seed in his body. He keeps it in his willie.'

'In his *willie*?' Tim said, outraged.

'Yes. That's the right place for it, that's where it's always kept. And then, one day when he's feeling very happy and kissing your mum because they love each other, he puts his willie inside her and lets the seed out. And that turns into a baby.'

The two boys gazed at him.

'But where does he put it?' Keith pulled up his shirt and examined his stomach. 'Does it go in her tummy-button?'

'No, not there. That's where you were joined on to your mum when you were born.'

'So where does it go?'

'Well, you know girls don't have willies. They have a little hole instead. That's where he puts it.'

'But that's dirty!' Tim said. 'Our teacher said so. Ann Jenkins said she'd show me hers if I showed her mine and the teacher saw us and said we were being dirty. And Brian Collins told me – '

'Never you mind what Brian Collins told you. Or what your teacher said. There's nothing dirty about it, it's natural. But you don't need to do it until you're grown up. It doesn't work till then.'

'I wouldn't want to do it anyway,' Tim observed. 'Perhaps by then they'll have found some better way.'

Reg grinned. 'Perhaps.' He looked at the woods on the far side of the field. 'Let's see if we can find some chestnuts. Edna likes sweet chestnuts.'

The subject of babies was forgotten. The two boys, enchanted with their new life, wandered amongst the trees, filling their tins with nuts and berries until at last Reg told them it was time to go home. They returned with stained fingers and faces to find their mother in the kitchen, talking to Edna, and Rose sitting under a tree out in the garden. She was rocking Maureen in a pram borrowed from the Greenberrys' eldest daughter. Tim and Keith stopped and peered in at their baby sister. Her eyes were open and she was gazing up at the leaves that rustled above her. At the sight of their faces, she smiled and laughed, reaching out small hands to touch them.

'I still don't believe it,' Keith muttered. 'It's just another story, like the gooseberry bush.'

But Tim was looking thoughtful. He put his finger into the baby's hand and she clutched it, giving a gurgle of pleasure.

So far, he thought, everything Reg had told them was true. But seeds in willies? Babies planted like cabbages in mothers' tummies?

Maybe it's different in the country, he thought, and, satisfied, went indoors to have dinner.

In Portsmouth, the cinemas and dance-halls reopened after only twelve days and people began to think that the war wasn't so bad after all. No bombs had yet been dropped, most of the people had been saved from the *Athena* and the city seemed to be getting organised. There were First-Aid Posts in schools and hospitals, more wardens appointed and a Citizens Advice Bureau set up in the Girls' Southern Secondary School. The Northern Secondary School was converted into an office and over a hundred voluntary workers went there each day to fill in innumerable forms and prepare for the control of food and rationing that was expected to start soon.

'Everyone's going to have a ration book,' Annie, who was one of the volunteers, said as the family ate their dinner together. 'Even babies. There's meat on them, and butter, and sugar – everything.'

'How's it going to work, then?' Frank asked. He was still coming to Annie for his meals, though he missed Jess's cooking. Annie's tastes were too fancy for him. Tonight she'd done meat with rice. Rice! That was for puddings, in Frank's opinion. He'd rather have a few potatoes to fill him up.

'Well, there's pages for meat and other pages for the fats and things. They're all marked off into little squares with numbers on –

coupons, they're called – and when you have your ration the shopkeeper cuts off one of the squares. And when you run out, that's it, you don't get no more.'

'But that's daft,' Ted said. 'Some people are going to eat it all in the first week.'

'No, they can't do that. The coupons can only be used in the right week. And you have to be registered with grocers and butchers, you can't go just anywhere. It'll depend what they've got in.'

'But how much are we going to get?' Olive asked.

'Some of it'll be done by weight and some'll be by price. So if your ration was a shillingsworth of meat a week, you could either have something cheap like sausages or liver and get a lot of it or something expensive like beef and only have a little bit. As long as the butcher's got it, that is.'

'Sounds complicated to me,' Ted said. 'It's going to take the poor buggers half the day to cut out all these little squares. They won't bother.'

'They'll have to,' Annie said. 'They'll get into trouble if they don't.'

Betty said nothing. Today was the day Graham was due to report to the barracks and she didn't know whether she was going to see him again before he went to sea. He'd promised to come and tell her what was happening if he could, and she was sitting with her ears pricked up for a knock at the door. The conversation passed her by.

'Anyway,' Annie went on, 'it doesn't matter about all that. Did Ted tell you, we've had a letter from our Colin?'

'No. That's good news.' Frank held his plate out for more rice and mince. Might as well eat the stuff if that's all there was, but he'd cook a few spuds as soon as he got back home, to take to work tomorrow. 'Where is he?'

Annie shrugged. 'Somewhere down South America way, that's all we know. Round the Falklands. That's where they've been lately. At least they're out of the way of the war there.'

'That won't last long,' Frank said. 'It's going to spread. The Jerries are sending their ships all over the oceans, trying to stop our merchant ships getting through. It's like putting us under

169

siege. If they can stop us importing food and things, they reckon they can bring us to our knees. Some hope!'

'I've heard the *Graf Spee*'s on its way down to the South Atlantic,' Ted remarked. 'Remember seeing her at the Coronation Review at Spithead? Pocket battleship, they call her. More guns than a cruiser and armour a foot thick. She can do twenty-six knots and go nineteen thousand miles without refuelling.'

'I thought the Germans weren't allowed to have ships like that,' Annie said. 'Wasn't there some sort of rule about it?'

'That's right,' Frank said. 'They weren't allowed to build ships of over ten thousand tons. Battleships were always bigger than that, so they got round it by building these small ones. The *Graf Spee*'s loaded with guns. And now she's prowling round disguised as a French warship, ready to start picking off our merchantmen the minute Hitler gives the word.'

'But that's piracy!' Annie exclaimed.

'It's war,' Ted said grimly.

There was a knock on the door and Betty jumped to her feet. 'That'll be Graham!'

She ran through to the front door and flung it open. 'Oh, Graham – I was afraid you wouldn't be able to come.' She threw herself into his arms. 'You should have come to the back door and just walked in.'

'I wanted you to see me first.' He stepped back, a self-conscious grin on his face, and struck a pose. 'How d'you like my new uniform, then?'

Betty gazed at him. He was resplendent in new dark-blue serge, the tunic tight on his body and the trousers flaring widely about his ankles. His square rig collar was banded with white ribbon and his cap perched rakishly on his red hair.

'You look smashing. All these white lanyards. Come in and show the others.'

'In a minute.' He pulled her close again and kissed her. 'Bet, I've got to go away.'

'When?' She looked up into his face, suddenly afraid.

'Well – tomorrow. Not far,' he added hastily. 'I'm starting training on Whale Island. But I won't be able to get shore leave for the first couple of weeks. And then I expect I'll get a ship.'

'You won't be able to get leave from Whale Island? But that's just down the road.'

'I know. But nobody gets any leave at first, not even if they live near. It's the same for us all, Bet.'

'I suppose so.' She fingered his collar disconsolately. 'So when will I see you again?'

'I don't know. After I finish my training, I hope. It depends where I get drafted.'

'Are you going to shut the front door, Bet?' Ted shouted from the back room. 'Or are you going to stand out there all night?'

'All right, Dad.' She took Graham's hand and pulled him with her. 'Look at Graham. He's starting tomorrow.'

'My, you do look smart!' Olive said. 'Spanking new. D'you think you'll be able to undo yourself to go to bed tonight?'

Betty giggled. 'I told him, it took our Colin ages to learn what order to do it in.'

'That's what the training's for,' Frank said. 'Teach you to dress and undress. Once you can do that they reckon you're fit to handle a gun.'

There was a brief silence. Jokes that had seemed funny a few weeks ago were no longer so amusing. While the country was still at peace, it had been possible to pretend that even regular Servicemen would never fire a shot in anger. Now, a fortnight into the war, it was different.

'Well, I'd better be going,' Frank said after a moment. 'Got a lot to do this evening. It's still light enough to put in an hour's digging in the allotment.'

'You're never going over there now,' Annie said. 'You've been every night since our Jess went. You must have dug the whole patch twice over.'

'Wish I had. It could do with it. An hour a night's not much, Annie.' He pushed back his chair and stood up. 'Anyway, it gives me something to do. And they're telling us to Dig for Victory, aren't they? Thanks for the meal, Annie.'

He took his jacket off the hook on the back of the kitchen door and went out. Annie watched him go, her face soft.

'Poor Frank. He misses our Jess something awful. He's like a spare part without her, isn't he, Ted.'

Ted grunted. 'Wouldn't be surprised if she don't come back before long. There's already people saying the evacuation wasn't necessary. I mean, nothing's happening, is it. All that talk, all those preparations, and nothing's happening.'

'It is at sea,' Graham said. 'There's ships everywhere. And the Army's on the move too, going off to France and Belgium.'

Annie shuddered. 'Well, you can say what you like, I don't reckon we've seen anything yet. That man's going to come at us like a firestorm one of these days. What do they call it? The way he makes a rush on a country, attacking them from every side so they don't have time to look round, let alone defend themselves.'

'*Blitzkrieg*,' Ted said. 'The lightning war.'

'That's it. Well, that's what we'll get here soon enough, you see if we don't. *Blitzkrieg*.' She shivered again. 'It's a horrible word and it's going to be a horrible war.'

Frank collected a few potatoes from the shed and went into the house. He scrubbed them and put them in a saucepan, ready to cook when he came back from the allotment. Then he went down the garden path again to collect his spade.

Ethel Glaister from next door was out in the garden, looking at her runner beans. The Glaisters didn't have an allotment but grew a few vegetables in the back garden. Ethel had grumbled loudly when some had had to be dug up to make room for the Anderson shelter, but she was the first in the street to put stones over the top and start calling it a rockery.

She looked up as Frank came down the path and gave him a smile. As usual, she looked as if she was dressed up to go visiting rather than just for a walk down the garden.

'Hullo, Frank.'

'Hullo, Ethel. Got plenty of beans, then?'

'Some. They won't be as good as yours, of course. George doesn't put in the time you do. I'm always telling him, if you only put in the time and effort that Frank does, we'd eat a lot better than we do.'

Poor George, Frank thought. It's a wonder he doesn't hate me.

'Well, not everyone takes to it.'

'No, but you can turn your hand to anything, can't you. Not just

172

the gardening. All the decorating and repairs about the place, making furniture, mending shoes . . . I hope Jess appreciates you, Frank.'

'Oh, I think she does.' Frank felt himself grow embarrassed. There was a funny look on Ethel's face, a sort of arch coyness. And surely she'd got lipstick on. 'And I appreciate her,' he added firmly.

'Oh, I'm sure you do.' Ethel had come a bit closer to the fence. She laid her hand on the top of it and gazed up at him. A waft of scent caught in his throat. 'You must feel really lonely in that empty house all by yourself. How are you managing, Frank?'

'Oh, pretty well, considering.' He took a step back. 'Annie gives me my supper most nights and does my washing. I get along all right.'

'Still, it can't be the same, can it.' She smiled. 'If there's anything else you want done, Frank – anything I can do . . . You don't want to impose on Annie too much, I'm sure. And it's not everything you feel you can ask family to do, is it?' She paused for a moment. 'I see Nancy Baxter's started calling.'

Frank flushed.

'She brought me in a bit of cake her mother had baked. I thought it was very good of her.'

'Oh, I'm sure it was. She's a very kind person, Nancy is. I mean, we all know that, don't we – how kind Nancy and her ma can be. Specially to a man who might be missing his home comforts.' She smiled at him and patted her hair, set in its golden waves. 'But you don't have to go to Nancy Baxter for home comforts, Frank. Not when I'm just next door, handy like.'

Frank stared at her. Didn't the woman realise what she was saying – how her words might be construed? And he a man on his own . . .

'I'd better be going,' he said abruptly, with a glance at the sky. 'Light's fading – I want to get a bit of digging in. Won't get the chance later on.'

'No, that's right. You go on.' Ethel was still smiling at him. 'We'll be getting long dark evenings soon. Have to find other things to do.' He was aware of her watching as he moved away down the path. 'Don't forget what I said, Frank,' she called after him.

173

'Anything you want done – anything – you've only got to say the word.'

Frank nodded and mumbled something. He unlatched the gate and went out into the alley. He was feeling hot and uncomfortable, and he looked back at the house and wished fervently that Jess was inside it, that he could see a light come on as he watched and know that she and the kids were there, that the warmth of his family would follow him over to the allotment and wrap itself about him on his return.

He looked up. The sun was throwing a faint glow of apricot high across the sky. It turned the barrage balloons, floating serenely above their moorings, to a shimmering russet. They looked strange and unearthly up there, but you couldn't deny they had a sort of beauty about them. And yet their purpose was anything but beautiful.

He shook his head and walked on. This war was a queer thing. All the preparations, all the expectations and fear, and yet what had happened so far? A few reports of ships caught up in pointless battle somewhere out at sea, an air strike here and there. The Army getting busy, spreading itself all over Salisbury Plain and places like that. People round the coast all staring out to sea in case Hitler decided to invade that way. And then – nothing.

Well, it was early days yet. Everyone had expected it to start at once, with aircraft screaming over, bombs dropping everywhere and maybe even gas attacks. But just because it was quiet so far didn't mean it was going to go on that way.

All the same, he couldn't help wondering if Jess and the kids had really needed to go away like that, so soon. And as he drove his spade into the earth, he felt a sudden hopeless misery.

Somehow, it all seemed so pointless.

Jess had finally decided to put Maureen on the bottle.

'She's not thriving,' she said to Mrs Greenberry. 'It's as if my milk's not good enough. Too thin. Perhaps it's because I'm too old, I can't make it so well.'

'That can't be true, my dear. You've made a lovely healthy baby, you ought to be able to make good milk. But you've had a lot of upset since she was born, what with the worry over the war and then the evacuation.' The countrywoman's voice was warm and sympathetic. 'You don't want to go blaming yourself. It's the sort of thing can happen to anyone. I daresay there's a lot of mothers having the same trouble.'

Jess sighed and went to write to Frank. She wished he were here, so she could talk these things over with him. He'd say it was up to her, of course – decisions like that were women's decisions – but it always made her feel better to talk to him. Writing letters wasn't the same. And she didn't want to worry him.

Jess was missing Frank badly. She was missing home too, and the family – even though they were all around her. It didn't seem right, Tim and Keith living with the Corners, nice though they were, and she didn't like being in someone else's house. Mr and Mrs Greenberry were kindness itself and had soon become real friends but you couldn't do things your own way when you weren't in your own home. She felt uncomfortable when the baby cried at night and she was sure that all the washing was a nuisance. And what with feeding them all, the billeting money could hardly make up for what the extra food cost the Greenberrys.

'Don't you be silly,' Mrs Greenberry told her. 'Most of the veg come out of the garden, so don't cost nothing, and young Rose don't eat enough to keep a sparrow alive. Not like those two boys of yours – I'd rather feed them for a week than a fortnight!'

Jess smiled, but felt a fresh wave of guilt sweep over her. Were Tim and Keith eating the Corners out of house and home? Were they behaving themselves? Edna and Reg said they were, but were they just being polite?

'If they are, they're the only ones in the village,' Mrs Greenberry remarked. 'I've heard some real tales about some of the evacuees and how they're going on. I hear the Woddis sisters are having a dreadful time with the two they've got.'

'What, Alan and Wendy Atkinson? But they're like little mice.'

'Not accordng to Miss Woddis. I met her in the shop this morning and she was saying what trouble they've had. Mind, I don't think they're used to children.'

Jess thought of Molly Atkinson on the morning of the evacuation. She remembered the distress on the mother's face, the way she had clung to a tree and then almost run after the bus, weeping for her little boy to be kept back. How would she feel if she heard that the people who had taken him were finding him a problem?

'But Alan's a dear little boy,' she said. 'I know the family quite well – they live just at the top of our street. His mother keeps them really nice.'

'Maybe she's done too much for them. Miss Woddis says they don't seem to have any idea how to look after themselves. I've seen them myself – hair all tangled and it doesn't look as if the boy's washed his neck since he arrived here.'

'But he's not five years old yet!' Jess exclaimed. 'He should be having his neck washed for him.'

Mrs Greenberry pursed her lips. 'Well, I daresay it's six of one and half a dozen of the other. It can't be easy for two sisters their age to have strange children to look after. I expect they'll shake down together after a while.'

Alan and Wendy had no such hopes. To them, life had changed not only for the worse but for ever. Why they had not been allowed to go on living at home with their own mother, they did not understand, for they had been protected from talk of war at home and nobody bothered to explain it to them now. As far as Alan knew, this might be what happened to all children at their age. And Wendy knew only, from listening to the talk of other children, that they'd been sent away because the Germans – whoever they were – were going to send bombs and gas and kill everyone in the cities.

She lay for hours in her lumpy bed, staring into the darkness and worrying about her parents. Were they going to be killed? Were bombs going to fall on them and blow them to pieces? Her vivid imagination showed her what this would look like, with arms and legs scattered over the streets. If so, why hadn't they come to the country with them? Why had they stayed at home?

These were not questions she could ask the Woddis sisters. Questions of any sort were discouraged, as was any conversation at all from the two Atkinsons. They were expected to be seen and not heard – and seen as little as possible. They understood very quickly that their presence was not welcome in the thin Victorian house with its dark, polished furniture.

'Fingermarks!' Miss Eleanor would exclaim. 'Have you been touching again, Alan?'

He shook his head at once, but Miss Eleanor grasped him by the ear, her fingers pinching painfully, and led him to the big mahogany sideboard with its carved drawers. 'Look at this! Fingermarks all over it. Do you know how long it takes to polish this?'

Again, he shook his head. In fact, neither sister polished the sideboard – Mrs Cherry, who came in every morning to clean and dust, did that. But her time had to be paid for, Miss Eleanor told Alan and Wendy, so it amounted to the same thing. 'I don't intend to pay her simply to clear up after you, you dirty little monkey.'

She produced a tin of polish and a cloth and handed them to the children. 'Now I don't want to see any fingermarks when you've finished, and perhaps it will teach you to keep your hands off the furniture.'

Wendy dabbed the cloth in the polish and rubbed it on the wood. It looked smeary and dull and she stared at it anxiously.

'Well, you'll have to do better than that,' Miss Millicent said sharply, coming into the room. 'It won't polish itself. Put some elbow-grease into it, child.'

Elbow-grease? Wendy looked doubtfully at the tin of polish. It said Mansion House on the lid. Miss Eleanor hadn't said anything about elbow-grease.

'I don't think we've got any,' she said timidly. 'Won't the polish be enough?'

Miss Millicent stared at her. Her nose twitched and two little spots of red appeared on her pale cheekbones.

'Don't be impertinent!' she said angrily. 'Just rub hard and then use the soft cloth. And see that your brother keeps his hands clean.'

Wendy sighed and went back to work. It seemed that everything she did was wrong and everything she said was impertinent. Cheeky, her mother would have said, but it meant the same thing. But what was so cheeky about asking questions? How else were you to find out things?

She couldn't even ask her teacher now. With only about two hours a day in the village school there just wasn't time for any more than a few lessons. The school only had two classrooms too, so they were all herded in together, the infants and lower classes in one and the two top classes in the other. The wall between was only a partition, so you could hear the other classes chanting their times tables when Miss Langrish was trying to explain proper sums, and it was very confusing.

It would have helped if they'd been able to bring books home, but that wasn't allowed. The books had to be used for the village children too. And there was enough bad feeling already over the sharing of desks, rubbers that disappeared and pencils that were left with newly sharpened points and were found next day broken.

The sideboard drawer was beginning to look more shiny now. She dabbed the cloth in the polish again and set to work on another bit.

It seemed quiet in number 13 now, without Bob. Gladys missed him more than she cared to admit, while Diane found tea-time dull without his teasing. And Peggy waited for the postman each morning, hoping there would be a letter or at least a card. 'We don't even know for sure where he is now,' she said to Alice Brunner when she went into the shop for the *Daily Mirror*. 'He went off that morning and just disappeared. I don't see why they can't tell us where they're going, do you? I mean, who's going to tell Hitler? Daft, I call it.'

'Why not ask one of the spiteful gossips around here?' Alice asked. She was looking tired, her thin face drawn and pale. 'They'll tell you who the spies are.'

'Oh, Alice! They're not still pointing fingers at your Heinrich, are they?'

'Of course they are. And me and my Joy too. I don't care for myself, but what's she ever done to deserve it? Downright cruel, I call it.' Peggy saw her face crumple as she said, 'Someone threw a stone at her yesterday.'

'Alice!'

'It was that Micky Baxter, from down your street,' Alice said, sniffing. 'As if he had anything to crow about, when you think what sort of family he comes from.'

'You don't want to take any notice,' Peggy said firmly, handing over the money for the paper. 'People like that aren't worth bothering about.'

'Maybe not,' Alice said, 'but the stones hurt just as much.'

178

Peggy went out of the shop. She called in at the dairy to buy some eggs. Betty Chapman served her. There was something a bit awkward in the girl's manner, Peggy thought, and it wasn't until she was at the door that Betty said, 'Have you heard from Bob at all? I hope he's all right.'

Peggy repeated what she had said to Alice Brunner. She wondered if what Gladys had said was true, and that Bob had only joined up because Betty had refused to go out with him. Well, if she had it was her right to do so, and Peggy wasn't going to take against her because of that. Any other time, he'd have just moped about for a while and then found someone else. But she had an idea that Betty was feeling guilty over it, all the same.

'Don't you worry,' she said. 'You've got your own troubles to think about. Your brother's at sea and your young man's gone too, hasn't he?'

'Yes, but he's only training on Whale Island, he hasn't gone away yet.' Betty hesitated. 'I think quite a lot of Bob,' she said at last. 'I wouldn't want anything to happen to him.'

Peggy's face softened. The girl really was upset. She gave her a smile, her mouth twisting with the tears that still caught her by surprise at times.

'I know, love. It's a hard time for us all.'

She left the dairy and walked back down October Street. The residents of these houses always thought themselves a bit posher than those in April Grove because they had a third bedroom built over the sculleries as well as a tiny front garden with a low wall topped with iron railings. The third bedroom wasn't all that much to write home about, Peggy thought, though she wouldn't have minded it herself. Like Jess and Frank next door, and the Glaisters, they had to shuffle about a bit to fit more than two children into the house. Her Bob had to sleep downstairs in the front room, on a camp bed, and the Budds had bought a Put-u-Up settee bed for Rose. It wasn't so bad when they were small, but it got difficult when they were older.

Granny Kinch was at her front door when she reached April Grove. She was wearing a brown herringbone coat, buttoned almost to her chin, with an inch of pinafore showing beneath the hem. It was only in the coldest weather that she didn't venture on

179

to her doorstep, and then she sat in the window, still keeping an eye on everything. But she really liked to be outside, where she could talk to anyone who passed.

Like everyone else, she asked about Bob.

'We don't know,' Peggy said. 'We just had one postcard, from a place called Caterham. He didn't know whether they'd be staying there or going somewhere else.'

'How'd he sound?' The old woman seemed really interested. But I suppose she is, Peggy thought. Interested in everyone. Otherwise, why should she stand there? I suppose we always called it nosiness before.

'Well, he sounded cheerful enough. Talking about square-bashing and khaki and all that. But underneath – well, you can tell he's lonely really.'

'He must be homesick,' Granny Kinch said. 'He's never been away from home before, has he?'

'Well, only to Scout camp.' Peggy gazed along the street. 'I keep wondering what'll happen to him when he's finished his training. I mean, will he really have to go and fight?' She looked back at the wrinkled, none too clean face under the steel curlers. 'It don't seem possible, our Bob actually shooting at people –trying to kill them.'

'No, it don't. It's different when it's other people – but when it's your own boy, being made to kill other boys – lads he'd probably have played football with if they'd lived next door – '

'That's it,' Peggy said, grateful for the woman's understanding. 'I mean, Germans can't all be bad. Look at Heinrich Brunner. You couldn't wish to meet a nicer man. There must be others like him.' She shook her head. 'And he's still got family over there too. What must he feel like, watching boys like our Bob and Colin Chapman going off to fight. They might be killing his relations, for all we know.'

The old woman nodded. She had left her false teeth out this morning and her mouth was drawn in like a purse, lips folded back over the gums. 'It's wicked. Is your Gladys still carrying a torch for that young man?'

'What young man? Colin Chapman?' Peggy shrugged. 'Don't ask me, she don't confide in her mother. But I wouldn't be surprised. But our Bob's still hankering after young Betty, that I do know. Mind, it's his own fault she wouldn't go out with him. He never even noticed her till she started to knock about with that Ginger Philpotts boy. He had his chance and wasted it, and it's no use blaming anyone but himself. But it's the war again – it's made 'em all think if they don't get what they want straight away, they'll never get it.'

'Everything's bin turned upside down,' Mrs Kinch said. 'Bits of boys going off to the Services, the kiddies away in the country. Schools turned into First-Aid Posts, shelters in the gardens, the blackout . . .'

'Barrage balloons in the sky,' Peggy joined in. 'Air-raid sirens, gas masks . . . And when's it all going to end? When are they going to do what Mr Chamberlain said and bring Hitler to his knees?'

'I don't reckon they know what they're doing,' Granny Kinch said. 'Look at it. They've never run a war, not like this one's going to be. They don't know how to do it, no more than me and old Mrs Seddon over the road would know. They've got us into this mess, the whole lot of them from Hitler to Chamberlain, and now they don't bloody know how to get us out. And that's the truth of it.'

Peggy stared at her. It's true, she thought. It's all true. And it's people like us, ordinary people with sons who have to go off and get killed, and daughters who have to watch their sweethearts go away when they ought to have their lives before them, we're the ones who suffer.

Olive was late home that night. But for once, as she told Derek, her dad was going to have to put up with it. 'It's wartime now,' she said. 'Things are different. And I'm tired of being treated like a kid.'

They had walked out past the allotments and the brickworks, down to the shore of Langstone Harbour. It was a popular spot for courting couples and the grassy banks were dotted with young men and girls, sitting in pairs.

The tide was half out, leaving the mud rippled and shiny. Boats of all sizes and descriptions lay slumped on their sides, their masts teetering at acute angles. Gulls and wading birds tiptoed between them, probing for cockles and worms, and about fifty yards away a group of men were digging for bait.

'It all looks so peaceful,' Olive said. 'I can't believe there's a war on.'

'It doesn't seem to be going the way they thought it would,' Derek agreed. 'And now that they've opened the cinemas and that, you'd hardly know the difference except for the shelters and sandbags everywhere.'

'Which we don't need to use. Mind you, we do get a lot of things to read.'

Derek laughed. 'Those leaflets! They drive my old man barmy. He says he wonders how they think we've managed to get by all these years without being told what to do every five minutes. It's "do this, don't do that" wherever you look. We had one this morning that told us not to lie on our backs in the shelters in case we snored!'

Olive giggled. 'Perhaps they think it would help guide the Germans in. We'll hear the wardens shout "Stop that snoring" like they shout "Put that light out". But the worst one was the one that told us what to do with our pets. Did you see that one?'

Derek shook his head. 'Dad doesn't even bother looking at them now. He just chucks 'em in the bin. What did it say?'

'Oh, it's awful. It says to try to find a home for your pets – and if you can't, take them to the vet! Well, we know what that means. And what sort of home are you going to find that's any safer than your own? You can't evacuate cats and dogs to the country.'

'Aren't you supposed to take them in the shelter with you?'

'No. Not the public ones, anyway. I suppose they can't stop you taking them in your own.' She shook her head. 'Our Betty would go mad if we had Suky put to sleep. We've had her six years, ever since she was a kitten.'

'I don't believe most people will have their pets put to sleep,' Derek said. 'Not cats, anyway. They can look after themselves.'

They sat quietly for a few moments. The sun was going down behind them, casting long shadows over the drying mud. On the far side of the harbour a few windows reflected golden light.

'I can't bear to think of you going away,' Olive said at last in a small voice.

Derek tightened his arm about her waist. 'I know. I'm not looking forward to it much myself.'

'If only we were – ' She hesitated, her fingers playing with a blade of grass. Her head was bent, the hair as brown and shiny as a conker falling across her face.

'Were what?'

'Well – engaged or something. I know it doesn't make any difference really – but people take a bit more notice. I mean, if they think we're just going out together they don't realise – they think –'

'They think it's not serious – you'll go out with someone else.'

'Well, yes.' She still wasn't looking at him. 'I don't want to go out with anyone else, Derek.'

'Nor do I. Only I wasn't thinking of getting engaged.'

'Oh.' She sounded deflated and he laughed and squeezed her more tightly.

'Don't sound so miserable. I was thinking of getting married.'

Olive's head flew round. Her brown eyes widened. *Married?*

'Why not?' He grinned at her.

'But – before you go away, you mean?'

'Well, it wouldn't be very easy afterwards, would it.'

'Oh, don't be so daft! You know what I mean.' Olive stared at him. 'My dad'd never let us.'

'Wouldn't he? Are you sure?'

'Yes, I am.' Her excitement disappeared abruptly. 'He doesn't believe in girls getting married too young. He's always saying so.'

'Well, what's too young? I don't reckon you're too young, Livvy.' He moved his hand caressingly on her waist.

'Dad would. And he wouldn't like you doing that, either.'

'Well, I'm not asking him.' Derek moved a little closer and nuzzled his lips into her neck. 'It's whether you like it that I'm concerned about,' he murmured, and let his fingertips stray over her breast.

Olive wriggled a little. 'Derek – don't.'

'Why not? You let me do more than that on our sofa the other night – remember?' He kissed her mouth, then her neck, nuzzling into the hollow of her throat. 'We're practically engaged now, anyway, whatever your dad says. We want to get married, don't we?'

'Yes, but – ' Olive gave up and leant against him. 'Oh, Derek, if only we could.'

'Well, I don't see why we shouldn't. We've been going out for nearly a year now. He knows me, knows my dad. What's the problem?'

'He'll just say I'm too young. I know he will.' She sighed and turned her head towards him, offering her mouth for his kiss. 'Oh, Derek . . .'

'Look,' he said firmly after a moment, 'you're not too young. If I'm old enough to go off to fight and get killed – you're old enough to get married. And that's all there is to it.'

'It's not, though. We can't get married without Dad's say-so. And he can be very obstinate.'

'Well, then,' Derek said, 'we'll just have to persuade him, won't we? Show him we mean it.'

The sun had gone now, leaving the harbour in a deepening twilight. It was almost too dark to see the other couples along the banks, but Olive knew that they were mostly lying down together, kissing – perhaps more. She felt nervous and excited. What did Derek mean?

She remembered every detail of the evening they'd spent alone at his house. They hadn't gone all the way, but they'd got pretty near it. She knew that if they hadn't been expecting Mr and Mrs Harker back at any time, they might easily have got completely carried away. She'd wanted it and she knew Derek had wanted it even more. But nervousness and the fear of getting 'caught' had held her back, as it held her back now.

'Derek – you won't – '

'I won't do anything you don't want me to, Olive,' he promised, and drew her down close. She felt his fingers at the buttons of her blouse and trembled. Then he kissed her again and the darkening sky spun above her head.

'I love you, Livvy,' he whispered against her hair. 'I want to marry you. I want to go away knowing I've got a wife. I want to know what it's like to really love you. What's so wrong about that?'

'I love you too. But I'm scared.'

'It's all right,' he promised again. 'Nothing's going to go wrong. I'll take care of that.' He was stroking her breasts now. She felt his fingertips, cool against her flushed skin. His body was hard against hers and he was breathing quickly.

184

'No, Derek. Not until we're married. I can't.'

'You can. We can. Olive – '

'No.' She wriggled away and sat up, brushing her hair back from her face. 'You know what could happen. I can't take the chance.'

'I'll be careful – '

'I'm too scared. Dad would throw me out. And then what would I do?'

'You could go and live with my mum and dad, if we were married.'

'So let's get married first.' She looked down at him and put out her hand to touch his face. 'Please, Derek. I'd rather it was all above board.'

He sighed and sat up beside her. She could barely see his face in the darkness and wondered if he was angry, but when she touched him he turned and moved closer, taking her hand.

'All right, Livvy. We'll wait. But I want to get married before I go away. I want to know you're going to be safe at home, waiting for me.'

'I'll talk to Mum,' she promised. 'I'll get her round and then she can talk to Dad. That's the best way.'

'All right,' he said, and then turned and pulled her roughly into his arms. 'Only don't take too long about it. I don't think I can wait much longer.'

Jess wheeled Maureen's pram along the lanes. It was a fine afternoon and if Frank had been with her she would have enjoyed the warmth of the sun, the bright red of the hawthorn berries and rosehips in the hedges and the changing of the leaves. But Frank was in Portsmouth, sweating in a boiler-shop, and Jess was missing him badly.

All the same, she couldn't sit and brood. There were other people who were missing their homes, children who scarcely understood why they'd had to leave them, and this afternoon she had made up her mind to go round and see a few of them, just to make sure they were well and happy.

'I'll come too,' Rose said, and now she walked by Jess's side, her bright brown eyes observing everything. The boys were off with their friends, collecting nuts and blackberries, but although Rose had plenty of friends she seemed to prefer to be with her mother. It was as if she was afraid Jess would disappear if she took her eyes off her.

Jess had already met little Martin Baker in the village street. He had been tagging along behind Mrs Hutchins, his foster-mother, but she hadn't had time to stop for a chat. Jess had looked down at Martin and asked him how he was, and he'd stared mutely back, his eyes large and round.

'He don't talk much, I'll say that for him,' Mrs Hutchins said. 'Eats plenty, though. He knows what his mouth's for!' She was in her fifties, Jess guessed, and having to cope with a six-year-old boy must have come as a bit of a shock. She had a grudging face and small, pebble-like eyes, but she looked tidy enough and the basket she carried was full of vegetables and bread. It looked as if Martin would eat well.

All the same, Jess looked at him doubtfully. He *was* a quiet child, she knew that, but he looked paler than usual and a bit scared.

I suppose they all must feel a bit frightened still, she thought. It'll take time for them to settle down. And he looks clean enough, as if she's taking care of him.

Mrs Hutchins and Martin disappeared up the narrow track leading to her cottage and Jess watched them, still feeling vaguely uneasy but trying to stifle her doubts. What could she do, after all? The billeting officer, Mrs Tupper, seemed efficient enough and called regularly on all the children. It wasn't up to Jess to tell her her job.

She walked on. Susan Cullen was living with a couple near the church. When Jess knocked on the door, it was answered by a tired-looking woman of about thirty-five, with a baby in her arms and a toddler dragging at her skirt.

'Susan? Oh, she's all right, I suppose, all things considered.' The woman looked faded, as if she'd been left out in the sun too long. She pushed back lank, stringy hair and pulled the toddler's fingers away from Jess's coat. 'No, Billy, don't put your sticky fingers all over the lady's coat. Susan's out, if you wanted to see her. She's having tea with one of her friends.'

'It's all right,' Jess said, feeling embarrassed. It was as if she were checking up on these people – as, indeed, she supposed she was.

'It's just that I promised her father I'd keep an eye on her. She lost her mother just before she came away, you know.'

'You don't have to tell me that! She's hardly stopped crying since she got here.' The woman really did look exhausted, Jess thought, and no wonder. 'Mike and me, we've done our best, but there's no pacifying her sometimes. If you ask me, it was wrong to send her. She should've stayed at home.'

'But her father's a milkman, you see,' Jess explained. 'He has to go to work at four in the morning.'

'So Mrs Tupper said. Well, I can see there was no help for it, but you can see how we're placed. I'm sorry for the child, of course I am, but I can't keep on giving her all the attention. I've got my own kids to see to as well.'

'I know.' Jess looked at her helplessly. She really did look worn out. It must be very difficult, she thought, having to take in strange children and try to cope with their problems as well as your own. 'Well, if there's anything I can do to give a hand.'

'Ta, but I don't think there's anything much. You might get your two little boys to give an eye to her at school. But I don't really see what anyone can do. She's just got to get over it as best she can.' There was a sudden crash and a wail from inside the house and the woman threw a harassed glance over her shoulder. 'Oh lor', that'll be our Freddy pulled something over, I'll have to go,' and she disappeared indoors.

'Good heavens,' Jess said as she and Rose walked away. 'However many children has she got? I didn't realise there was another one indoors.'

Rose shook her head. It was difficult to get to know the village children when you were at school at different times of the day from them. And those below school age seemed to inhabit a different world anyway.

'Where are we going now?' she asked.

Jess consulted the scrap of paper on which she had written down the names and addresses.

'The Woddises. That's where the little Atkinsons are.' She looked up and a smile broke over her face. 'Look, there's Tim and Keith. They can come along with us, they know Wendy and Alan.'

187

The two boys ran up to their mother and gave her exuberant kisses. She hugged them tightly, feeling a sudden ache of tears in her throat. How lucky she was to have them so close, even though another woman was looking after them. At least she could see for herself how happy and well-cared-for they were. And if they were being looked after properly, didn't it make sense that so were most of the other children? It was natural enough, after all, that they were missing their parents – Tim and Keith, with their mother close by, didn't have that problem. They'd settle down soon enough.

Still, she'd promised Molly Atkinson that she'd keep an eye on the two little ones and although she felt rather intimidated by the tall, Victorian house that stood alone a little way from the village, she knew she must keep that promise.

With the pram and three children clustered around her, she marched up the path and pulled the old-fashioned bell.

There was a long silence. The door, painted a dull brown, stared forbiddingly back at her. Perhaps there's no one in, she thought, and was just turning away when it opened and a thin, elderly lady with a pale face and twitching nose stood gazing out at her.

'Yes? What is it?'

'Oh – hello.' Jess hesitated under the gaze. She fumbled for words. 'I'm Jess Budd. I've been evacuated from Portsmouth – '

'We can't take any more.' The gaze slid past to the children. 'We certainly can't take any more. We've got enough on our hands already.'

'I don't want – we've already got somewhere – I haven't come to ask you – '

'Then why have you come?' The voice was peremptory. 'Hurry up and tell me, please, the door's letting all the heat out.'

Jess could feel no heat. The passage stretching away behind the elderly woman looked cold, dark and uninviting. She wondered how Alan and Wendy were faring here. It looked so different from the warm, untidy greengrocer's shop.

'I just came to see how the children are. Wendy and Alan. I know their mother, you see, and – '

'Who is it, Millicent?' a voice called from inside, and Miss Woddis turned her head.

188

'It's a person, Eleanor. A person asking about the children. She says she knows their mother at home.' The twitching nose poked sharply at Jess. 'Did their mother send you? Is she not satisfied?'

'Oh, I'm sure she's satisfied,' Jess said hurriedly, though she couldn't help remembering Molly Atkinson's face as she'd stood with one hand pressed against a tree and the other at her mouth. 'I just thought I'd look in and make sure – I mean – '

'The children are perfectly all right.' The elder sister was at the door now, even taller than the first. Jess knew at once that the boys would be staring at the mole on her chin and prayed they would say nothing about it, at least until they were safely out of earshot. 'They're having their tea now. I imagine you'll take my word for that?'

'Yes – yes, of course,' Jess stammered. 'I don't want to be a nuisance. As long as they're well and happy – '

'Oh, yes. *They're* well and happy enough. Why shouldn't they be? Do you have some cause to doubt it?'

'No – none at all.' Jess wished she hadn't come. She began to turn the pram around. 'I'm sorry to have bothered you. Perhaps I could see Alan and Wendy another time. They could come and have tea with us – '

'I don't think so, thank you.' There was a smile, but it was so frigid that it could have been made of ice. 'We don't mix with the village people.'

Jess stared at her. She felt indignation creep red-hot through her body. She saw the woman's eyes move over the children, saw the distaste in the expression. Abruptly, forgetting the Atkinsons, she wheeled the pram around.

'I'm sorry,' she said again, but now her voice was as cold as Miss Woddis's. 'Perhaps I shouldn't have come. But Molly Atkinson and I are friends and I knew she would want me to see where Alan and Wendy were living – '

'And now you have seen. The children are perfectly happy and being cared for as if they were our own.'

Jess hesitated. Angry though she was, she couldn't let her temper rule her. And she had come to see Alan and Wendy – to see for herself that they were all right.

'If I could just see them for a moment – ' she began, but already the two sisters were closing the door.

'Naturally, if their mother comes to visit, she'll be permitted to see her children. I don't think we're under any obligation to admit a procession of casual sightseers to our home. Now, if you don't mind – ' And the door was closed firmly in Jess's face.

Jess stood absolutely still. She felt as if she had been slapped. Her cheeks burned and her breath, knocked momentarily from her body, came in a quick gasp. Abruptly, she began to march back down the path, her head up to prevent the angry tears from falling to her cheeks.

The children followed, subdued. Then Tim said loudly, 'I don't like that lady, Mum.'

Jess gave a quick glance back towards the windows. But what did it matter if they heard? They'd been just as rude. Ruder.

'No, Tim,' she said, 'neither do I.'

As they walked back to the Corners' house, to leave Tim and Keith for the night, she thought over her afternoon's expedition. Had it been any use? Martin Baker seemed all right, though even quieter than usual, and Jess hadn't much liked Mrs Hutchins. Susan Cullen was obviously miserable but the woman looking after her seemed sympathetic even though she was clearly worn out by her own family – and who was to say that Susan would be any less unhappy anywhere else? And the house where Alan and Wendy were living was a lot posher than that flat over the greengrocer's shop, even if the spinster sisters did think themselves better than anyone else.

What could you do? You couldn't choose different billets just like that. There just weren't any other places for the children to go. And as long as they were being fed and kept clean, what more could anyone ask?

Jess was uncomfortably aware that children needed a good deal more. But this was wartime, and nobody was getting what they needed. And it was better than being bombed, back home in Portsmouth.

CHAPTER SEVEN

'THE PHONEY WAR,' people were beginning to call it. A war of grinding dreariness that Tommy Vickers said Hitler would win simply by boring everyone to death. 'Not that he needs to lift a finger anyway,' he added. 'We're making a pretty good job of killing ourselves, without his help.'

By the third week in September, road accidents had trebled. More people had been killed by being run over or in collision with other cars than by enemy action. The blackout became more than an irritation and people were forced to stay at home, or make visits to only their nearest neighbours. With the evenings drawing in there was little social life and those families that had stayed together huddled round their own fires, listening to the wireless.

'If it wasn't for people like Tommy Handley and Arthur Askey we'd all go mad,' Annie Chapman commented to Peggy Shaw one afternoon. 'They're the only ones as give us a laugh these days.'

'Oh, I like *ITMA*,' Peggy agreed. 'Ministry of Aggravation and Mysteries! And that Mrs Mopp – "Can I do you now, sir?" Mind, we always listen to the News as well. There's something about hearing Big Ben at nine o'clock. You need to know what's going on, don't you?'

Annie nodded. Everyone listened to the Nine O'clock News on the Home Service. The BBC had recently taken to letting the readers say their own names too – *Here is the Nine O'clock News and this is Alvar Liddel reading it*. 'It makes you feel you know them,' she said. 'As if they were your own friends, just come in for a chat.'

'Mind, it's never very good news, is it,' Peggy continued. 'Petrol rationed – not that that affects us! – income tax up to seven-and-six in the pound – and now they've got anti-aircraft batteries out on Southsea Common. And did you hear about that boy hit by a cartridge over Fratton way? Standing watching a dogfight he was, and next thing he knew he was unconscious.'

'A dogfight?' Annie said, puzzled.

'It's what they call aeroplanes scrapping,' Peggy said. 'So the Germans are getting here, you see. Our lads soon chased them off, though.'

Annie sighed. The three months since the war began seemed more like three years. Still no bombs had dropped, the Andersons and street shelters stood empty and people had begun to be careless about their gas masks. Someone had reported a spot check done on the train from Portsmouth to Waterloo one day, and two out of three people had sandwiches in their carriers instead. The air-raid warnings sounded occasionally, but most people knew it was only practice and didn't even bother to look up.

There were, however, plenty of signs that the war was being waged elsewhere. Everyone in Portsmouth was shocked when the aircraft carrier *Courageous* was torpedoed and sunk off the Hebrides, the first naval casualty of the war. That ship had been moored in Portsmouth harbour, its sailors roistered about Portsmouth streets. Some, indeed, were Portsmouth men and there were grieving mothers and widows in the city at this moment.

On 14 October another ship had gone down – the *Royal Oak*, sunk in Scapa Flow. Again, there was shock in the city that had seen so many ships go to war and still sheltered Nelson's *Victory*, the most famous of them all, in its dockyard. The war came closer, touching everyone.

Olive and Betty Chapman were as restless as everyone else. With many of their entertainments denied them, they felt frustrated and anxious for something to do. For Olive, that something was marriage and she tackled Annie about it one evening as they washed up after supper.

'Derek'll be called up soon, bound to be,' she said. 'And then he'll go away and God knows when I'll see him again. What are we supposed to do, wait the rest of our lives?'

'Don't talk daft,' Annie said, holding a plate up to inspect. 'This lot's going to be over by Christmas, everyone says so. Hitler knows he's bitten off more than he can chew this time. He'll back down soon, see if he doesn't.'

'He's not backing down at the moment. Look at the ships he's sinking. Anyway, even if it is all over by Christmas, there's still going to be men killed – and my Derek could be one of them.' Olive stopped what she was doing, a tea-towel held in one hand, and stared at her mother. 'How would I feel if he got killed and I'd never – we'd never – ' She stopped, feeling the blush creeping up her cheeks, aware of her mother's eyes. 'Well, we just want to get married before he goes, that's all,' she muttered.

Annie pursed her mouth. 'You don't know what you're saying. Getting married's for ever – not just a few months. There's plenty of people did that in the last war, and lived to regret it.'

'We wouldn't,' Olive said stubbornly. 'We love each other, Mum.'

Annie sighed. It was hard not to weaken when the girl gazed at her with those big eyes, just as it had been hard not to weaken when she was little and begging for another sweet or a new doll. And she wasn't far off twenty-one, after all. What was the point of refusing her?

'I'll talk to your father,' she promised. 'But I'm afraid he'll say the same as me, Livvy. He doesn't approve of girls getting married too young. Why don't you just get engaged?'

'Because we want to be *married*,' Olive exclaimed in exasperation, and Annie knew that there was no more to be said.

I think they really do love each other, she thought as she wiped the sink. I think they'd be all right, if they could only start off properly. But a man going off to war and his wife still living at home with her parents – that's not right. And what if it isn't over by Christmas? What if they start a baby?

And what's going to happen if Ted does agree to let them get married? What's our Betty going to say? It'll be her and Graham next, and that I *wouldn't* be happy about. They're not properly in love with each other, they're just in love with love.

But Betty had no thoughts of getting married. An engagement, even a secret engagement, was enough for her. In fact, she

193

preferred it that way – she liked the feeling of hugging a romantic secret to herself, the feeling that she knew more than other people. And she didn't want to be tied down, anyway. Life was too interesting to be shackled to a kitchen sink and a pramful of squalling babies.

'They're asking for girls to join the Land Army,' she announced at supper one evening. 'I thought I'd go along.'

Annie paused in the middle of serving out helpings of shepherd's pie. 'You thought *what*?'

'I thought I'd join the Land Army. You know. Work on a farm. Milk cows and all that. It'll be fun.'

'*Fun?*' Ted stared at her. 'Look here, our Bet, this war isn't being fought for *fun*. It's serious, that's what it is. Not to give flibbertigibbet girls like you a bit of a holiday.'

'I'm not a flibbertigibbet! And I know it won't be a holiday –but I don't see why I shouldn't enjoy it, all the same.' Betty glared at her father. 'We don't all have to go around with long faces all the time. I don't see as that helps anyone.'

'And don't give me any of your cheek!' Ted was due to go on duty soon, for the last shift of the day and his least favourite. He still found it hard, taking his ferryboat across the harbour in pitch darkness, and was always more short-tempered when working this shift. 'You're not going in the Land Army, and that's that.'

Betty's face reddened and her eyes flashed. She and her father were always rubbing each other up the wrong way these days. It was as if she couldn't do a thing right, almost as if he was determined to object to everything about her. Wearing make-up – 'making yourself look cheap' – going out with Graham – 'that ginger boy from over the water', as if Graham were some kind of foreigner – and now decent war work being called 'a bit of a holiday'. It wasn't fair!

'And how are you going to stop me?' she demanded. 'The government wants girls like me – they're crying out for them. In fact, we'll probably *have* to go, like it or not, so I might as well volunteer.'

'If you've got to go, that's different. Conscription's conscription. But until then, you stay here, under my eye – '

'Why? What d'you think I'm going to do? What sort of girl d'you think I am?' Tears of anger threatened Betty's voice. Gulping them back, she faced her father, realising that for the first time in her life she wasn't afraid of his anger. 'All I want is to go and do some useful work, something I think I'll enjoy – '

'Yes, and that's just it!' He was as furious as she. How dare she answer back like this, his daughter, who ought to be meek and submissive and do as her father told her. 'It's *enjoyment* you're after. Fun. And I know just what sort of fun you've got in mind.'

'Oh yes?' Betty challenged him. 'What sort's that, then? Just tell me. It might be something I'd never have thought of for myself!'

'Betty!' Annie interposed. 'Stop it at once. You mustn't talk to your father like that – '

But Betty rounded on her. 'Why mustn't I? He can say what he likes to me – he can make out I'm some sort of tart – '

'*Betty!* I won't have that sort of talk in this house.'

'Well, it's what he meant, isn't it? It's what he was getting at.' She looked at Ted again and this time the tears overflowed and ran down her cheeks. 'You don't trust me at all, do you,' she accused him, her voice trembling. 'You never have. You've always treated me like dirt – as if I just didn't matter. I mustn't wear lipstick, I mustn't go out dancing, I mustn't have a boyfriend . . . You hate me, that's what it is, you always have, and shall I tell you something?' She was on her feet, her eyes wild and red, her face scarlet and wet with tears. 'I hate you too! I do – I *hate* you – and I'll tell you something else – I *am* going to join the Land Army and nothing any of you can do will stop me!'

'Betty – ' Annie began, but Betty turned and rushed out of the room and they heard her feet pounding up the stairs to her bedroom.

Annie and Ted looked at each other.

'Now see what you've done,' Annie said heavily.

'What *I've* done? Annie, that girl's getting completely out of hand. She's been allowed too much freedom, that's what it is – been allowed to run wild. And this is the result.'

'Ted, all she wants is to do some war work. There's nothing wrong in that, is there?'

'Not if that's *all* she wants to do, no. But I'm not so sure it is. She's always been one for the boys, you know that.'

195

'For goodness sake! That was when she was a child. She was a tomboy, that's all. It didn't mean anything. And if it was men she was after she wouldn't be talking about farm work – she'd be wanting to join the Wrens or something.'

Ted said nothing. He had to admit that Annie was probably right about that, but he wasn't ready yet to admit it out loud. Already, his temper was subsiding and he felt guilty at the sound of Betty sobbing just above their heads. He sighed and picked up his knife and fork.

'Well, I'm not going to let her spoil my supper,' he said, and looked at his elder daughter. 'And I hope you've been taking notice, Olive. Just because there's a war on don't mean I'm going to forget all the things I've said about you girls. You're still under twenty-one, both of you, and still under my authority, and don't you forget it.'

Olive looked at him. She had sat silent throughout the whole row, knowing that any contribution from her was likely only to make it worse and hoping that her father might forget she was there. But now all she could do was shake her head.

'No, Dad. I won't.'

Ted started to eat his shepherd's pie. Annie and Olive picked at theirs and Betty's lay untouched and cooling on the place. An uneasy silence hung over the house.

He'll never let me and Derek get married now, Olive thought miserably. He'll never back down, now our Betty's riled him so bad. She's ruined everything.

But she couldn't really blame her sister for what had happened. What was wrong with the Land Army after all? And why shouldn't people do as they wanted with their own lives?

He's just another Hitler, she thought rebelliously, pushing meat and potatoes about on her plate. He just wants to be in charge all the time. Captain of a ferryboat – huh! You'd think he was Admiral Nelson, the way he carries on.

It seemed strange in the street without Jess living in number 14. There were other families whose children had been evacuated too, of course, but it was Jess that Annie missed most. The sisters had lived near each other for nearly ten years now and Annie had to remind herself every morning that Jess was no longer there.

196

Instead, she found herself chatting more to Peggy Shaw, who lived next door to Jess. The two women had always been friendly, but it was Jess who had been Peggy's particular crony, and she missed her too. So it was natural that she and Annie should turn to each other for company instead.

Annie was still brooding over Betty's outburst when they met next afternoon, outside the newsagent's.

'Don't it seem quiet,' Peggy remarked. 'No kids about, not much traffic. It's hard to believe there's a war on, isn't it.'

'It is when you look round you,' Annie agreed. 'But there's plenty going on, all the same. It's these shortages that get you down most. Onions – they're like gold now. I've seen hardly any oranges this winter, and bananas seem to have disappeared altogether. My Ted likes a banana to take for his lunch, but they don't seem to have any anywhere. I tried Shepherds' and Atkinsons', neither of them had any.'

'They'll have to start rationing soon. I thought it would have started before this.'

'So did I.' Annie had seen the ration books at the school, stacked in bundles ready for distribution. She went back to the subject that had been on her mind all morning. 'Our Betty's on about joining the Land Army.'

'What! Going to work on a farm? D'you think she'd like it?'

'She seems to think so. Her dad doesn't like the idea, neither do I much. She's too young to be going away from home, to my mind, but she says she's going to volunteer and there's not much we can do about it.'

'It's daft, isn't it,' Peggy said. 'We can stop them getting married but we can't stop them going off to join the Services. I mean, they're just bits of boys, going off heaven knows where to fight and they don't have any idea what it's all about. They think it's just a game.'

'They'll find out different soon enough. How's your Bob?'

Peggy shook her head. 'I don't know, Annie. He writes home but he don't say much really. It seems as though it's as dreary for them as it is for us. Just sitting there, they are, waiting for something to happen. I mean, what's it all about? If no one wants to fight, why don't they bring them all home and forget it? Seems to me it'd make more sense.'

197

'Where is he now?'

'Somewhere in France, that's all we know. What about your Olive's young man?'

'He'll be out there too, soon, by the look of it. He's waiting for his papers now. And that's another funny thing. He was in the TA, should have been one of the first to go, but he's still here, yet your Bob goes along to join up and he's in training before you can say Jack Robinson. It makes you wonder, doesn't it.' She paused. 'You've heard our Olive wants to get married, I suppose.'

'What does your Ted say about it?'

'Well, what d'you think? He's always said he wouldn't let either of the girls get married before they were twenty-one. Not that it's been mentioned outright, mind – though Olive had a word with me about it and Derek's all for asking him straight. But I know Ted'll just say no if they do that, and once he's said no he won't back down, he never does. No, I've told Olive, if they want to get round him they've got to do it slow and careful.'

'So you're in favour of it yourself, then,' Peggy said.

'Well, I'd rather they got engaged, but . . . you know how it is. They've known each other nearly a year. And if we don't let 'em get married – well – '

Peggy nodded. 'Well, we all know what it is to be young – and with a war on and never knowing when they're going to see each other again – '

'It's not easy for them,' Annie said. 'It's different from when we were young, Peg. But it's getting the men to see it that's the hard part.'

'You'd think they'd see it more than we do – they're the ones who push, after all. But it's funny about men, they seem to forget what they were like when it's their own daughters.'

'Maybe it's because they don't forget what they were like,' Annie said shrewdly, and both women laughed.

Ethel Glaister, walking past at that moment, stopped and looked at them. She was wearing a pale blue costume neither of them had seen before, and a hat with a small veil. Annie stared at it jealously and Peggy was immediately conscious of her old coat and the scarf she had wound like a turban round her head.

'Well, it's nice to see someone's got something to laugh at,' Ethel

198

said in her sharp voice. 'I suppose you've been in there.' She jerked her head at the newsagent's shop.

'And why not?' Annie demanded at once. 'It wouldn't do you any harm to go in and give Alice Brunner time of day, either.'

'Me? I don't go in there any more. I'd rather go down to the corner for my paper.'

'Well, it's the same paper, as far as I can see,' Peggy said, holding up her *Evening News*. 'I don't suppose it's got any better news in it for walking another quarter of a mile.'

'No, but it hasn't been handled by spies and traitors,' Ethel said sharply, and the other two women gasped.

'Alice Brunner could have you up in court for that.'

'Why? I never mentioned no names.' Ethel looked at them defiantly. 'There's spies everywhere, you know there are. Look at all the posters about it. Idle Talk Costs Lives. And pictures of Hitler hiding under railway seats. That sort of thing. You don't know what's getting reported back.'

'Well, nothing I say's likely to get reported back, wherever I say it,' Peggy said with a short laugh. 'And I don't believe either Alice or Heinrich's a spy. He's been here twenty years, for goodness sake.'

'And still goes back every year,' Ethel said darkly. 'Well, if I were you, Peggy Shaw, I'd be careful going in there. You don't want people thinking you're a sympathiser.'

'A sympathiser with what?'

'You know what I mean. A Fifth Columnist.' She stopped suddenly as Peggy lunged forward, waving her shopping bag.

'You'll take that back this minute, Ethel Glaister! Nobody calls me a traitor to my country.'

'I didn't. All I said was—'

'You as good as did. Calling me a sympathiser! Why don't you come straight out and say I'm a spy? Eh? Why not say what you think?'

'I never said you were a spy.' Ethel took a step back. 'All I said was you ought to be careful. You don't know who's listening. I'm only saying what we're all being told, only I don't go gossiping in the streets, that's all. I'd rather be doing something for my country.'

'And I suppose I'm not? Not with my Bob in the Army and likely to get killed any minute. Nor Annie here, her Colin's thousands of miles away on the *Exeter* and she doesn't know when she'll see him again. I suppose that doesn't count as doing something for your country. You'd better watch what you say, you spiteful little—'

'Peggy!' Annie grabbed her arm and dragged her back. 'Just ignore her – she's not worth getting upset over.' She gave Ethel a scornful look. 'When you've got someone serving like Peggy and me have, you might have call to talk, but until then you'd better keep a civil tongue in your head, see?'

'Well, pardon me for breathing,' Ethel said, putting her nose in the air. 'I didn't say anything about your Colin, nor about Bob Shaw. As for having someone serving, I suppose my George doesn't count? He's off next week, you might be interested to hear, leaving me all alone to manage with three children, so put that in your pipe and smoke it!'

She marched off, indignation in every line of her body, and the two women stared after her.

'George Glaister joining up! Well, did you ever?'

'Mind, you can't blame him, can you? I reckon any man'd be glad to go off and serve his country after a few years serving Ethel.' Annie giggled suddenly. 'I can't see him firing a machine-gun though, can you? I mean, if that's what we're depending on to win us the war – '

'It's going to be a long job,' Peggy finished. 'Well, I reckon I'd better get home and start cooking Bert's tea. He's a stickler for having it on the table the minute he gets in and our Diane won't have thought of doing the potatoes.'

They said goodbye and Annie walked back to her own house. Every time you went out, she thought, you heard of someone else going off to the war. George Glaister, of all people! He was such a quiet, meek little man. And although she and Peggy might laugh, there really wasn't anything funny about it. War meant people getting killed. That could mean George Glaister, her Colin and Peggy Shaw's Bob. And Derek Harker and Graham, and all the other men she knew who had joined up or would get their papers soon.

And not only them. She looked up at the sky, with the

mannerism that so many people had developed in the past few weeks. Death had not yet come raining down from the stars, but there was really no reason to suppose that it wasn't going to. Perhaps in six months' time, perhaps tonight. It was going to come.

And not a thing we can do about it, she thought with sudden helpless anger. Not a single, bloody thing we can do about it.

She let herself in the back door. Ted was already home and she dropped her paper on the table and put the kettle on. The girls would be here soon, and then Frank, all of them hungry, and she liked to have a cup of tea ready for them when they came in.

'Ted,' she said, 'you won't go on at our Betty again when she comes in, will you?'

He looked up and saw his mouth set. 'Not if she apologises proper for what she said.'

'But what did she say that was so bad? She was upset – '

'She said she hated me. Isn't that bad enough? What does she have to say, for God's sake – ?'

'Oh, Ted.' She took cups out of the cupboard and set them on the table. One of the saucers had got broken a few days ago and she pursed her lips and found an odd one. Ted wouldn't care, but Annie liked to have things nice and it irritated her. 'You know she didn't mean that. And you were a bit sharp with her. I mean, all she wants to do is help her country – '

'She can do that just as well by stopping at home and giving you a hand. And if that's not enough for her, there's plenty of other things she could be doing. They want people to knit things, don't they? And aren't they asking for women to sew sailors' collars and that sort of thing? She'd be better off doing that than slaving away on some farm.'

'Ted, a girl of eighteen isn't going to be satisfied with sitting by the fire knitting. She wants to be doing something more active.' Annie laid her hand on his arm. 'She only wants to do her bit. You know she's never been one for sitting at home, she likes being out in the fresh air and she's always been interested in nature and that. I think we ought to let her find out a bit more about it.'

'You mean give in to her? Let her have her own way?'

'We've got to sometime, Ted. They've all got to live their own lives eventually.'

He was silent for a few moments and Annie saw that he was coming round. She sighed with relief. She hated rows in the family. She squeezed his arm and he looked at her and gave a reluctant grin.

'Well, all right, she can find out about it. Mind, that doesn't mean to say I'm giving in to her. But there's no harm in asking, I'll grant you that.' He grinned again. 'It might even put her off!'

'That's it,' Annie said with relief, 'that's the best way.' She paused, then took the bull by the horns and broached the other subject on her mind. 'Ted – while we're talking about the girls –you know our Livvy's getting serious about young Derek Harker?'

'I know they've been running round together a lot. I don't know about serious.'

'Well, she is.' Annie paused again. 'And it looks as if he'll be getting his call-up soon. I wouldn't be surprised if they didn't want to get married before he goes off.'

'Get married? But they're not even engaged!'

'Ted, you know we've talked about this before. It's the same as in the last war. Young people aren't going to want to wait – they're going to want to get married, and there's not much we can do to stop—'

'Until they're of age,' Ted said, 'there's everything we can do. They need my name on that consent form, and if I don't sign it—'

'If you don't sign it,' Annie broke in, 'there'll be more rows, and if Derek goes off and gets killed our Olive will never forgive you. Or me.'

'I'd rather that than have her tied up to a man she doesn't love for the next fifty years or so. I've seen it all before, Annie. And if you don't believe me, ask Frank. He'll tell you.'

'He won't. He never talks about it.'

'No, but he's told your Jess and Jess told you. And I knew Frank when we were boys, you know that. I knew his mum and dad and I knew what went on in that house. His dad coming home drunk every Friday night, taking a strap to poor Mrs Budd, and belting the daylights out of young Frank if he dared speak up. And all because they'd got married in a hurry and then found they hated the sight of each other.'

'But that wasn't because of the war.'

'It doesn't matter why it was,' Ted said. 'Ivy Budd was only nineteen when she got married and it ruined her life. I won't have the same thing happen to my girls.' He gave her a determined glare. 'All right, I might give in to Betty over the Land Army but she can always come home if it don't suit her. But getting married – that's another thing and I won't be responsible for it. That's something they've got to decide for themselves when they're of age, and not before.'

The kettle boiled and Annie got up to make the tea. She sighed. She knew that when Ted looked like that and spoke in that tone of voice, there was no shifting him. The world could be coming to an end next Saturday and he still wouldn't budge. If Olive wanted to marry Derek, she could do it on her twenty-first birthday, but she wouldn't be able to do it a moment before.

When Frank came in, Ted was sitting at the kitchen table, the *Evening News* spread out in front of him, reading a report that had come through that day.

'Dachau, they call it,' he said. 'It's full of Jews. Nearly twenty thousand of them. They arrested them and took them there in trains, all squashed in together. They made them look up at the light the whole way and if they couldn't, they shot them. They threw cold water over them in the night and made them stand ten hours in sleet and snow on the parade ground. Anyone they didn't like, they executed.'

'Anyone they didn't like? What does that mean?' Annie asked, shocked by the story.

Frank answered. He had read the story in his own paper.

'Anyone without blue eyes, I should think, wouldn't you?'

'But they were Jews,' Annie said. 'None of them would have – ' She caught her husband's ironic glance and fell silent. 'Ted, that's terrible. People shouldn't be killed for the colour of their eyes.'

'That's why we're at war,' Ted said heavily. 'Remember? We heard all about this before, only no one believed it. And it's not the only place they've got. There's others at – ' he looked down at the newspaper again ' – places called Ravensbruck, Buchenwald and Sach – Sach-sen-hausen. And they reckon they're going to set up more in Poland.'

'Poland,' Annie said. 'We were supposed to be helping Poland.'

'I know. That's why we're in it.' Ted got up suddenly and screwed the newspaper up in both hands. He flung the crumpled ball down on the floor. 'And a fat lot of bloody use we are to them! What are we doing? Sitting around on our backsides while Hitler marches roughshod over the whole of Europe. What was Chamberlain playing at, sending him ultimatums, declaring war? Did he think we'd frighten him? Nothing frightens that man – he's just impervious. He's laughing at us, that's what he's doing. Cocking a snook. He needs a good, sharp lesson, and I reckon that's what we thought we were going to give him. And instead – what?'

'He's just going on, doing what he likes,' Frank said. 'He's started labour camps in Poland now. The Jews are having to build them themselves before they've even got huts to sleep in. And the people aren't even allowed to walk on the pavements – they've got to be left for German soldiers to strut along like peacocks. They're turning them into slaves.'

'And it's what they'd do here,' Ted agreed. 'We had to go to war, Annie. I just wish we could get on and do something.'

'We will,' she said. 'We will, as soon as the time's right. Our boys aren't going to sit around for ever. They'll do something, if nobody else does. You see.'

'Well, I hope you're right.' Ted bent down and picked up the crumpled newspaper. He smoothed it out and looked again at the report of the German concentration camps. 'I just have a feeling it's going to take something big to pull people together now. But I don't reckon it's going to happen here. They're too busy over in Poland and Czechoslovakia. I don't think we're going to get the bombs after all.'

I don't think we're going to get the bombs after all.

The words were on many people's lips as autumn slipped into winter and still no aeroplanes came over with their dreaded load. And, inevitably, those with children in the country began to think of bringing them home.

'I've missed you so much,' Jess said to her husband when he came out on his first visit to her and the children. A new scheme had been started, allowing parents to buy cheap railway tickets to travel on one Sunday a month. 'It's very nice here – the

Greenberrys have been very kind and Reg and Edna Corner have looked after Tim and Keith like they were their own – but I'd rather be at home.'

'I'd like to have you home too,' he said. He didn't mention Ethel Glaister, who had offered her services again – 'anything you want, Frank, anything, you just say the word' – but he suspected that he didn't need to. Jess had never liked their next-door neighbour much and probably had a very good idea of what Ethel might be up to. 'The house is like a morgue without you. And Henry's getting thin.'

'Oh, poor Henry.' Jess thought of the big tabby cat, sitting outside on the windowsill all day wondering where they all were. 'He won't even know who we are when we come back.'

'He won't forget.' *When we come back.* When would that be? he wondered. He knew a lot of the evacuated children had already begun to drift back. Their parents had decided there was no danger, or just couldn't bear to be without their kids. Or thought they weren't being treated right in their foster-homes.

It was better for the Budd children. They had their mother with them. But it wasn't better for him and Jess.

We need each other, he thought. I need to have Jess in the house. I need to know she's there when I go to work in the morning, and I need her there when I come home. And I reckon she needs me too. She's looking thin. I reckon that's why she's lost her milk.

'How's the baby?' he asked. Maureen had been asleep ever since he arrived and he was half afraid she'd still be asleep when he left. A few hours of a Sunday wasn't enough. The Greenberrys had gone off for a walk, leaving the family alone, but even so . . . He wanted to do so much with these few hours. He wanted to play with his sons and talk to them, he wanted to take Rose on his knee, he wanted to hold the baby and see her smile. Most of all, he wanted to be alone with his wife.

No chance of that, he thought wryly, and tightened his fingers over her hand.

'The baby's all right now. She smiles a lot.' But Jess didn't seem to want to discuss Maureen's progress. She looked at Frank's hand on hers, then lifted her eyes to his face and said again, 'Oh, Frank, I've missed you so much.'

'I know, love. I know.' But he didn't know what to do about it. I ought to be able to hold her and kiss her and love her properly, he thought with helpless anger. That's what we both need. But we can't. Not here in someone else's house, with the children all around. And in an hour or so the Greenberrys will be back and then we'll all have supper together, and at seven o'clock I'm going to have to go back. And it'll be another month before we see each other again . . .'

'Let's go for a walk,' he suggested. 'It's a nice afternoon and I haven't been out this way before. Show me the sights.'

Jess looked at him with understanding. Sitting in here was doing nobody any good. Rose was standing stiff and awkward, acting as if she'd never seen her father before, and the boys were showing off. She knew it was because they all felt uneasy in this strange situation, with their father a visitor, but it would be better outside. The boys could scamper about and let out some of their silliness and Rose wouldn't feel so shy. And maybe Maureen would wake up soon and create a bit of interest.

'Come on, then,' she said. 'Tim, Keith, get your coats on. Rose, bring the baby's blanket down from upstairs, will you? And you'll need your coat too.'

The children scrambled into their outdoor clothes, as thankful as their parents to have something positive to do. They ran outside and Frank and Jess looked at each other.

'Give us a kiss, love,' he said, pulling her into his arms. 'Give us a kiss, for God's sake. Oh, you don't know how I've been missing you.'

'I do,' she said, and pressed her mouth against his. She felt his lips move against hers, felt the hunger in them, felt the need in his arms that were like steel bands about her, in his body that was so hard against her. 'Oh, Frank, I do . . .'

Ethel Glaister also understood that Frank was missing Jess.

'It's the same for me,' she confided as she came out into the back garden the next Saturday afternoon to find him clearing out tomato plants. 'I mean, with my George away. Joe and Carol do their best, but they can't do everything, can they? I mean, there's some things a son just can't do for his mother.'

206

Frank straightened his back. If he'd known Ethel was in the house he wouldn't have come out in the garden. He'd made sure he'd heard the whole family go out only half an hour earlier. Ethel must have just walked up the street with them, perhaps to the shops, and then come back.

'We all have to make sacrifices,' he said. 'At least you've got your kids at home.'

'Oh, I know.' She touched her hair. It was even brighter these days and he wondered why she bothered. It wasn't as if George was here to appreciate it – not that Frank thought he appreciated it anyway. As Jess would say, there was no love lost between those two. So perhaps the trouble Ethel took with her appearance wasn't for her husband's benefit at all, but just to satisfy her own vanity.

'Mind, it's not easy, being a woman on your own,' she said. 'Not when there's kids to bring up. They need a father's hand, don't you agree, Frank? A man's hand.' Her voice lingered over the words and she gave him a coy look. 'I could say the same for myself sometimes!'

Frank felt his face grow hot. He wasn't used to this sort of talk. At work he was with men all day and at home he was with Jess and the kids, or relatives like Annie and friends they'd known for years. Nobody ever spoke to him like this, each word invested with double meanings.

He said, 'I'm sure your kids know how to behave, Ethel. You don't need to worry about them.'

'Well, I don't, most of the time. But just now and then – I need someone to advise me, Frank. Someone to talk to – you know?'

'Our Annie'd be glad to help, I'm sure. Or Peggy next door.'

'Oh, Peggy Shaw and me don't get on. And your Annie looks down her nose a bit, us being in a terraced house. Besides, it's a man's advice I need. And it's not just the kids – it's things about the house. There's something wrong with the kitchen tap, it won't turn off properly and I don't know what to do.' She looked up at him appealingly. 'You couldn't spare a minute to look at it, could you? I'd appreciate it ever so much.'

Frank hesitated. He could hardly refuse to help the woman with her kitchen tap.

'I'll just fetch my tools,' he said, and Ethel gave him a brilliant smile and turned to go indoors.

Frank had only been in the Glaisters' house a couple of times. He came up the garden path, feeling rather strange to see his own garden on the other side of the fence, and went in through the conservatory door. George hadn't made a bad job of it at all, he thought, looking at the neat workmanship of the wood and glass roof. It certainly must be a boon, having it all dry outside the back door and being able to get to the lavatory without going in the rain. When the war was over, he'd do the same at number 14.

Ethel was waiting for him in the scullery. The kettle was on the gas stove and, just as she had said, the tap was dripping.

Frank set to work. It didn't take long, changing the washer, and when he'd finished the kettle was boiling and Ethel made a pot of tea.

'I can't really stop,' he began, but she was already getting out the cups and saucers and putting a few biscuits on a plate.

'Oh, you've got time for a cup of tea, I'm sure. It'll do you good. You don't look after yourself properly, Frank, and you work too hard – oh yes, I know, I've seen you coming home tired from work, going straight off to that allotment of yours. You need a bit of relaxation and comfort.'

'I'm all right.' He followed her through to the back room. It was the same size as his own but looked different with Ethel's furniture. The armchairs were small and fussy, with lacy things on their backs, not nearly so comfortable-looking as his own and Jess's. On the walls were pictures made of some glittery material. There was no piano, which made it look bigger – Jess's piano took up nearly all of one wall, but he couldn't ask her to get rid of it and there was no space in the front room now that Rose had to sleep there. Instead, Ethel had a sideboard and, in the space under the stairs, a smart gramophone.

'Sit down, Frank. Make yourself at home. Milk and sugar?' She poured his tea and sat opposite him. Her skirt was up to her knees, showing legs that must surely be clad in silk, not the lisle that Jess wore most of the time. She saw him looking and crossed them, smiling, and Frank looked away, angry with himself.

'Is Annie feeding you well, then? I know you go up there for your supper every night.'

'Oh yes. Yes, she looks after me very well.'

'That's good. Mind, if you ever need a change or she can't manage for any reason, you know you're always welcome here, don't you? Always a chair at our table for you, Frank. The children would be pleased too. They think a lot of you, you know.'

Frank could think of nothing to say. He picked up his cup. It was a thin china one with roses all over the outside and a frilly little handle he couldn't get his big fingers around properly. He clutched it, hoping he wasn't going to drop it, and sipped cautiously.

'Still, I daresay I'm not the only one that's offered,' Ethel went on. 'I saw that Nancy Baxter down this end of the street again a few days ago. I hope Jess doesn't get to hear about it and put the wrong construction on it. I mean, she and Nancy Baxter have never been what you might call pally, have they?'

'Jess always used to stop and pass the time of day with them.'

'Oh, well, that's only common politeness, isn't it.' Ethel got up and came over the room. There was a dining chair next to his armchair and she sat in that, leaning down towards him. 'I've told you before, you don't need to go to Nancy Baxter for anything you want, Frank. Cake – a cup of tea now and then – any other home comforts. You've only got to say the word.'

Frank put his cup back in its saucer. His hand threatened to tremble but he kept it steady. It was difficult to stand up without brushing against Ethel, but he did so anyway. He heard her give a little gasp and she put her hand on his arm, as if to support herself. For a moment they stayed like that, both half standing, leaning close.

'Frank . . .' Ethel whispered, and lifted her face towards him.

Frank drew back. His sudden movement knocked against the little table on which Ethel had placed the cups, and he heard a rattle and then a small crash. He turned in dismay.

'Oh, my cups!' Ethel cried. 'My best cups!' She went down on her knees, scrabbling amongst the china and spilt milk. 'One of them's broken.'

'I'm sorry.' Frank watched as she gathered up the pieces. 'I'll mend it for you, Ethel. Give me the bits, I'll stick them together again.'

'Stick them together?' She glared at him from the carpet. 'How

209

can I offer my friends tea in cups that have been *stuck together*? The whole set's spoilt now.'

'I'll get you a new cup then,' he promised desperately. He was at the door by now, anxious only to be out of there. 'Better still, you get one and I'll give you the money. I'm sorry, Ethel, but that's all I can do. I didn't mean to do it, you know that – it was an accident. But I'll pay for a new one.'

He escaped at last and went into his own house. Sinking down in his own armchair, he stared at Jess's empty place. He thought of last weekend and his longing for her, thought of the empty bed upstairs, the emptiness in his heart.

How could Ethel Glaister ever hope to fill any one of those places? How did she even dare to offer?

By December, most of the evacuees had received at least one visit from their parents and knew that home was still there, that it had not been swallowed up as some of them had feared. But for little Alan and Wendy Atkinson there had been no such relief.

Molly Atkinson wanted desperately to visit her children. But she was needed in the shop and when the first chance came she was in bed, suffering a bad attack of pleurisy.

'You go,' she begged her husband. 'Go and see that they're all right. I'm worried about them. Wendy's letters seem so queer and Alan can't write at all.'

'You're worrying too much,' he said. 'There's nothing wrong with Wendy's letters. You can't expect much from a child of eight. And if they weren't all right, their teacher would let us know.'

'Go anyway,' she said, but he shook his head.

'I can't, love. You know Dad's heart's bad. The doctor's told him he's got to rest, so he can't take over the shop. They're all right. In fact, they're probably better off left alone. Mrs Parish down October Street said some of the children are more upset when they've had a visit from their parents than they were when they first went away. It unsettles them.'

'But they need their mother.' Molly turned her head and wept tears of weakness into her pillow. 'They must wonder why I haven't come to see them. They must miss me so much.'

'Of course they miss you,' he said, cradling her in his arms. 'But children don't suffer long, love. They soon bounce back. I daresay they're having the time of their lives now, out there in the country. They won't even want to come home when this is all over.'

But that had been the wrong thing to say. Molly wept all the more and gave herself a relapse. The doctor said she must stay in bed for another two weeks at least, and even then must not go out in the cold. So the Atkinson children remained unvisited.

'Their parents obviously don't care a jot about them,' Miss Eleanor Woddis remarked to her sister. 'They're only too thankful to have them off their hands. And really, one can't blame them.'

'I blame them for not bringing their children up properly,' Miss Millicent retorted. 'I don't care what people say, a boy of almost five years old should be able to use the lavatory. I don't see why we should pay Mrs Cherry to clean up after him. And he's begun to steal now, you know. I found four biscuits gone out of the tin yesterday.'

Miss Eleanor clicked her tongue.

'I hope you gave him a good spanking. It's the only thing he understands.'

'I did something better than that. I shut him in the cupboard under the stairs for half an hour. I don't think he'll steal biscuits again.'

To Alan, the half-hour he had spent in the cupboard had seemed much longer. At first, he had been unable to believe it when Miss Millicent thrust him in and slammed the door shut. He had pushed back, trying to open it again, but already he could hear the key turning in the lock. And his hands, feeling the wood in the darkness, could find no knob to turn or rattle.

In panic, he began to scream and thump on the door with his fists, and then to kick. But nothing happened. And then, as he drew breath for another yell, he heard Miss Millicent's voice.

'Stop making that noise, Alan. And stop kicking. You'll only make it worse for yourself. I'm going out now, to the shop, so no one's going to hear you. You'll be let out when I come back – if you've been quiet.'

He heard her heels tap across the parquet floor to the front door, heard it open and close. The house was silent.

Alan took a deep breath. He wanted desperately to scream again, but he knew it would be useless. Wendy had been invited to another child's house for tea and Miss Eleanor was at something called a bridge club. The house was empty.

Suppose no one ever came back? Suppose something happened to them out there, and they never came back to the house? Nobody would know he was there.

Suppose something happened to Miss Millicent while she was out? He pictured her falling down in the street, like an old lady who used to live in September Street, and being taken to hospital. The old lady had died without ever speaking again. Suppose that happened to Miss Millicent.

Would anyone think to look in the cupboard? It was hardly ever used. Would anyone think that Miss Millicent had locked him in there before she went out?

He could be dead before anyone opened the door again. A skeleton, all bones, like pictures he'd seen in one of Dad's books.

That picture had given him nightmares for a week. Now he was in the middle of a nightmare.

Alan felt around him in the darkness. A few old brooms lived in here, their bristles like those of some long-dead animal. Perhaps some of them were dead animals. He crept down to the end of the cupboard, where the stairs met the floor. There were all sorts of queer things here, things that felt soft to the touch. He shuddered and scrambled back again.

There was no way out. Only the locked door.

Now that his eyes were used to the dark, Alan could see a thin rim of light around the edge of the door. He traced it with his finger and tried hopelessly to push the door open. It remained firm.

Alan sat down on the floor of the cupboard. It was cold and dusty. He wished he could see better, so that he could see if the brooms really were brooms. How did anyone know that what went into cupboards stayed the same once the cupboard was shut? The broom-handles were like thin, strong legs and the bristles like stiff, dead hair. Like very old giant spiders.

Spiders! He stood up suddenly and cracked his head on the stair above. The pain brought tears to his eyes but he dared not make a sound in case Miss Millicent had come back. If she heard him crying, she'd keep him there even longer. He rubbed his head, sobbing and hiccuping in his efforts to keep the tears back, and leaned against the door.

The cupboard must be full of spiders. And not only spiders – there might be all kinds of horrible, nameless things crawling on the floor and walls. Beetles, woodlice, earwigs – they all lived in cupboards. Perhaps even centipedes like the one he'd seen once in Dad's shop, a horrible, bendy thing with a hundred legs.

Alan imagined a hundred legs walking on his skin, and shuddered so violently that he banged his shoulder on something hard. He felt it cautiously and realised it was a step-ladder. As he touched it, something squirmed under his finger and he leapt back and cracked his head again.

It was too much. Miss Millicent's orders were forgotten. Fear and pain swept over him and he began to cry again, bitter sobs that welled up from deep inside and overflowed with tears that were for his mother as much as for himself; for his home, his family, for all things familiar. Would he ever see them again? Would he ever, ever be able to go back?

Too far gone in his grief to worry about spiders, dead or alive, Alan sank down on the floor. He huddled against the door and wept until his eyes and throat and head ached. And when at last he fell into an unhappy sleep, it was no better than slipping from one nightmare into another.

Betty Chapman volunteered for the Land Army, much against her parents' wishes, and found to her surprise that Graham was against it too.

'I wish you hadn't done that, Bet,' he said, sitting in the front room the first time he came to see her after his training on Whale Island. They had spent the first quarter of an hour kissing rapturously and were now taking time to exchange news. Graham had plenty, it seemed, and talked almost non-stop of the training he had received, of the way one of his mates had been sent halfway round the barracks for a pot of distemper to paint the Last Post white, of the way the 'lads' had to 'double' everywhere on the island in pairs. 'It's good for morale,' he told Betty when she raised her eyebrows, but was apparently unable to explain just why. And his conversation was peppered with naval jargon. The sea was no longer the sea, it had become the 'oggin', Portsmouth's rival dockyard Plymouth had become 'Guz' and the Navy itself was now the 'Andrew', while friends were suddenly 'oppos'.

He had also developed a casual arrogance that Betty had noticed in other sailors, which seemed to go with a rolling, swaggering gait that implied long hours at sea on a heaving deck. Graham had not yet been to sea; even Whale Island was reached by a bridge. But he talked of shore leave and liberty boats as if he had been arriving in foreign ports all his life. And Betty listened admiringly and thought how handsome he looked in his uniform.

'So what about you, Bet?' he asked at last. 'Have you managed to talk your old man round to us getting engaged yet?'

Betty shook her head.

'It's no good me mentioning it, Graham. He thinks the man should ask. Anyway, Mum doesn't think he'll let us. Maybe when I've been in the WLA a while – '

'The what?'

'The Women's Land Army. I've volunteered.' She grinned at him. 'I'll be in uniform next, Graham – what d'you think of that?'

He stared at her. 'You've volunteered? What did you want to do that for?'

'Why shouldn't I? I'm fed up, working in that stupid dairy. And I've always liked helping Dad in the garden. I thought it'd be a good idea.' She saw the expression on his face. 'What's wrong with it?'

'Nothing, I suppose.' He frowned at the fireplace. The Chapmans only had a fire in the front room on Sundays or at Christmas, but Annie had put the little electric fire in there for them and its bar glowed red against the reflector. 'I just – well, I wish you hadn't done it, that's all.'

'Why not?'

He scowled again and said nothing for a few minutes. His freckled face was sulky. Then he muttered, 'I thought you wanted to get engaged.'

'So I do. What's that got to do with it?'

'Well, you ought to stay here then,' he said. 'How d'you think I'll feel, going off to sea and not knowing where you are? And you might meet anyone, working on a farm. If we're engaged, you should stay at home and wait for me.'

Betty stared at him.

'Oh, should I? And what about you, going off to sea? I won't know where you are, will I? Or who you're meeting? If you don't trust me, Graham Philpotts, why don't you come right out and say so? Then we'll all know where we stand.'

'I never said I didn't trust you – '

'So it won't matter who I meet, will it?'

'I just don't want you working yourself to death on a farm, that's all,' he said. 'You don't know what it'll be like – '

'You don't know what it'll be like at sea, for all your big talk!'

'That's different. Men have to go away. Women should stay at home.'

'Not in this war,' Betty said. 'Women have to do the jobs men leave behind, or the country'll fall to bits. It was the same in the last war. Women had to take over and run the country. You want to listen to some of the older people, Graham.'

'Older people don't know it all.'

'And nor do you.' Betty sat up straight, moving out of reach of his arms. 'Listen, I'm not going to sit around on my backside when I could be doing something more interesting. Do you know what it's like, working in the dairy? Having to listen to customers complaining about the price of eggs as if it's all *my* fault? Standing about all day because I'm not allowed to sit down, not even when there's no one in the shop? What sort of a life do you think that is?'

'I should think it's a lot better than sloshing about in mud all day picking up potatoes,' he retorted. 'You don't know when you're well off, Bet, that's your trouble.'

'Maybe not. But I'm willing to give it a try. I'd rather work hard all day and know I was doing some good than stay warm and dry in a dairy, bored to tears. And it's a chance – a chance to get away from home, live my own life a bit and do something different.' She looked at him and her face softened. 'Graham, you look just like our Keith does when he can't have his own way. Come on.' She moved a little closer and put her arm round him. 'Stop pushing your lip out like that and give me a kiss instead,' she whispered coaxingly. 'It's not going to make any difference to us, me working on the land. I'll write to you just the same – and I'll have a lot more interesting things to tell you.'

'Oh yeah?' he sneered. 'All about picking potatoes and digging swedes and onions? I can't wait!'

'Well, it'll be better than measuring milk and patting butter,' she giggled, and shook his arm gently. 'Come on, Graham. Don't let's quarrel, the first night you're out. Give us a kiss.' She nuzzled against his neck while he stared woodenly ahead. 'Anyway, I don't know who you think I'm going to meet on the farm. There'll only be old men or boys too young to join up. I'm more likely to meet someone staying here in Pompey, with all you handsome sailors looking for girls!'

Graham grinned unwillingly. He turned his face and allowed himself to be kissed. Then he put his arms round Betty and held her close, the rough serge of his tunic rubbing against her thin blouse.

'Well, maybe there's something in that. But you mind you're here when I come on leave, Bet. I don't want to get engaged and then find my fiancée away whenever I come back to port.'

'I won't be,' she promised. 'And there won't be anyone else, Graham. You can bank on that.' She sighed and rested her head on his shoulder. 'There won't be anyone else for you either, will there?'

'No. But – I wish you'd talk to your old man, Bet. Or let me. I don't know how long I've got before I get a ship, you see. It could be any time. I'd like to get a ring on your finger before I go.'

'Oh, Graham, so would I.' She lifted her head and looked at him. 'But we can still be secretly engaged, can't we? I could have a ring and wear it on a chain, like we said before. And I could put it on at night or when I go out.' Her eyes sparkled suddenly. 'I could wear it all the time if I was away on a farm!'

A knock on the door announced that it was supper-time. If they didn't go at once, the door would be opened and Annie would poke her head round it. She believed in letting the young ones have their privacy, but not enough to feel they could take liberties. And she didn't want young Graham getting ideas about himself and Betty. She'd seen the look in his eyes, before he went off for his training and again when he came in tonight.

They'll be the next ones wanting to get engaged or married, she

216

thought with a sigh. Like Olive, pestering them to let her marry Derek Harker. It was understandable enough, but they didn't realise what it meant. Getting tied down so young, perhaps a baby on the way almost at once, and nowhere to live. Most of the girls would simply stay on with their parents, but it wouldn't be the same. As married women, they'd expect more independence. If they had babies the house would be even more full, and if they didn't they'd as likely as not want to start going out . . . Either way, there'd be trouble of one sort or another.

No, on the whole it was better if they stayed single. After all, it wasn't going to be for long, was it? The war might not be over by Christmas, like they'd said at first, but it didn't look like getting any worse. It would surely be all finished with by Easter, and then everyone could settle down to a normal life again.

And there'd be no more silly talk of kids like her Betty and Gladys Shaw getting married, no more putting boys who'd hardly started to shave into uniform and sending them off to kill other boys who just happened to have been born in a different place. No more lads choking away their lives in the freezing depths of the Atlantic or catching their death of cold in trenches in France.

She pulled herself together. There had been no sound from the other room. What were those two up to in there? She'd heard their voices just now, sounded almost as if they were having a bit of a row. And then it had all gone quiet.

Annie knew perfectly well what might be happening if everything went quiet after two young sweethearts had a row. She gave the door another loud knock and opened it, rattling the doorknob hard as she did so.

Mrs Hutchins would have commiserated with the Woddis sisters if they had ever spoken to her, but the widow did not come within their social sphere. However, she knew them by sight, saw them at church and about the village, and talked to their cleaner Mrs Cherry.

'Sly, that's what I call them,' Mrs Cherry said, referring to the Woddises' evacuees. 'Specially the boy. Looks at you as if butter wouldn't melt in his mouth, then goes and does something dirty in a corner. The times I've washed his clothes out, you wouldn't credit.'

'Oh, I would,' Mrs Hutchins said. 'I have the same trouble with mine. Dirty little pigs, the lot of 'em. And give themselves such airs too, just because they come from Portsmouth. Portsmouth! I never did go much on the place, but if that's the way they live there they can keep it.'

She went indoors. Martin was at school but she had plenty of jobs for him to do when he came in, to keep him out of mischief. Six wasn't too young to give a hand around the place, and besides he ought to earn his keep. Eight shillings and sixpence wasn't much to feed and look after a growing boy, especially with all the washing she had to do. And she'd never be able to use that mattress of his again, not for respectable people.

Martin was late home. Some of the village boys had taken to lying in wait for the smaller evacuees and tormenting and chasing them on the way home. Martin had found a longer way, through the woods. Tim and Keith Budd went that way to their house and let him walk along with them for part of the way. When they arrived at the edge of the big field he stopped and looked at them.

'Go on,' Tim said, giving him a friendly nudge. 'That's the way you've got to go. We go across the field. See you tomorrow.'

They ran off across the stubble, obviously happy to be going back, and Martin stared after them. He felt very small and lonely, standing there on the edge of the meadow, watching as the two brothers zig-zagged away, their arms spread, making aeroplane noises. He wished he could have gone with them. Just to have tea, to see what it was like in another of the village houses. He wanted to reassure himself that they weren't all like Mrs Hutchins.

'There he is!'

Martin jumped violently and turned to see a small gang of boys approaching from the other end of the field. With a lurch of fear, he realised that they were the bullies who had been waiting for him on his normal way home, and he turned and ran into the woods.

'After him! Don't let him get away!' The boys were bigger than he and could run faster. They came to the trees and dived between them, racing between the big grey trunks, shouting and whooping like Indians. 'Catch him and we'll have a bit of fun.'

Martin's heart thumped and he felt sick. He often felt sick these days, but it was no good telling anyone. Mrs Hutchins would simply scold him and his teacher didn't have time to listen. Too many children were complaining about their food, and when the billeting office lady had gone to see them she'd found there was nothing wrong with it.

He ran blindly, his hands held out in front of him to ward off branches, but they whipped back across his arms, caught at his sleeves and slashed across his face. Sobbing with fright, he stumbled, righted himself, cast a wild glance behind him and stumbled again. This time he fell, grazing his knees, but he was up again, cannoning into a tree-trunk before throwing himself into a tangle of bushes and crouching there, breathing hard and peering wide-eyed through the undergrowth at his tormentors.

There were six of them. They were headed by Neil Miller, the biggest boy in the school, and Martin saw that Brian Collins, one of the evacuees, was another. Brian had quickly seen which side his bread was buttered and joined forces with the village boys. He and Neil Miller had recognised each other instantly as kindred spirits and now had the entire village school subject to their own reign of terror.

'Slimy little git,' Neil said as he passed within a couple of feet of Martin. 'He's got away. But we'll catch him tomorrow – now we know which way he comes.'

'That's right,' Brian agreed, standing on Martin's hand, which he'd burrowed under some dead leaves. 'We'll catch him. And then we'll have some fun.' He proceeded to describe in minute detail what they would do to Martin, and Martin lay shuddering under the bushes. His cheeks were wet with tears and he stuffed his other hand into his mouth and bit the knuckles hard to prevent himself from crying out at the pain of Brian's boot on his hand.

It seemed a long time before the two boys moved away. His eyes tight shut, he felt the pressure lift from his hand and then heard their laughter as they ran off through the trees. His blood was thumping hard in his ears but he could hear clearly enough what they were shouting, and he realised, sickeningly, that they had known all along where he was hiding, and were merely using their knowledge as just another form of torture.

'That had him scared!' 'I bet the little bugger just about shitted himself with fright!' 'He won't know which way to go home

219

tomorrow . . .' Their voices faded and with them their raucous laughter, and after a long while Martin dragged himself up.

His hand was red and swollen, pain pounding through the fingers. His clothes were torn and covered in mud and his arms and face were scratched and bleeding. He felt sick and shaky, and his knuckles were sore and bruised where he had bitten them.

Slowly, he made his way through the woods. From the far side, he had to go down a long, grass-covered lane with hedges on either side. Anybody could be hiding there, he thought, glancing fearfully at the trees with their huge boles and creeping claw-like roots that stretched down the banks. Once or twice he heard a sudden rustle and jumped to press himself against the other bank, but it was only a blackbird fossicking amongst the dead leaves, or a squirrel gathering nuts. The third time, however, his courage failed him utterly and he took to panic-stricken flight and ran the rest of the way home.

'Well!' Mrs Hutchins exclaimed, opening the door. 'And what in God's name do you think you've been doing? Look at you! Covered in filth and your clothes ruined. No – you're not coming in here. Not until you're clean. Wait there.'

She disappeared indoors. Martin, by now crying bitterly, stood on the doorstep in the gathering dusk of a foggy December afternoon. How was he to clean himself out here? Would he ever be allowed indoors again, or would he be fed outside like the dog, perhaps even made to sleep in the kennel? He turned to see if there was room for him but before he could move, Mrs Hutchins was back.

'There.' To his dismay, he saw that she was holding a hosepipe. She fixed it to the garden tap and turned it on. 'That'll sluice you off like the dirty pig you are.'

The water hit Martin full in the chest, a icy jet that knocked him off his feet. He lay gasping and spluttering on the path then rose shakily to his feet as Mrs Hutchins turned off the tap.

'Now take off your clothes,' she ordered. 'All of them. You're as dirty underneath as you are on top, I'll be bound.'

With trembling fingers, Martin undid his buttons and laces and took off his clothes. She was right, he discovered, and so was Neil Miller. He dropped the stinking mass on the path and stood naked and shivering in the foggy air.

The jet of water hit him again. This time he stayed on his feet, his arms wrapped about his thin body, shuddering as Mrs Hutchins circled slowly around him, directing the hose at every part of his body. His skin was almost numb with cold, the water like spikes of ice stabbing at every pore. His sobbing had changed to a raw, hopeless retching that threatened to tear his heart and stomach from his body, and he felt the blackness of total despair as he stood at last, his head hanging down in utter subjection, waiting for Mrs Hutchins to tell him what to do next.

'All right, you dirty little Arab,' she said, as if disgruntled that she could not torture him further. 'Get inside and go to bed. I don't want to see you again today. And don't expect any supper – it's going to take me the rest of the evening clearing up after you, you and your filth.'

Martin moved stiffly, his legs blue with cold. He went indoors and up the stairs. At the top he hesitated, wondering if he dared ask for a towel, and then went into the tiny boxroom where he slept. He rolled himself about a bit on his blanket and then crept into bed and lay curled up, hugging himself, and tried to get warm.

But it was a long time before he could sleep. As a little warmth finally crept through his aching bones, his stomach began to make its own protest. Mrs Hutchins never gave him more than a cup of water and a bowl of lumpy porridge for breakfast. He'd been feeling sick all morning, and had eaten little dinner at school. Now his stomach was beginning to ache and he moved a bit and groaned.

When Mrs Hutchins came to wake him in the morning, thrusting a pile of damp clothes on to the bed for him to wear, she found him huddled in a corner, whimpering with pain and white as a sheet.

'I suppose you've wet the bed again,' she said furiously. 'Well, you can just do what Miss Woddis makes her boy do – wash the sheets yourself. I told you yesterday, I'm fed up with cleaning up after you, you filthy little shit!'

Martin looked up at her. His stomach hurt and he knew that if he ate anything at all he would be sick again. He dragged himself up and pulled on his clothes. There was no school in the morning, but he would go out anyway. Out in the damp, chilly lanes, where there were other children about, he might find some mean comfort. There was none to be had there.

Susan Cullen was also out in the lanes that morning. Her foster-mother had tired at last of trying to console her and sent her out for a walk. 'You've got to pull yourself together,' she said, helping the white-faced five-year-old into her coat. 'Think how lucky you are. There's plenty worse off than you.'

Her words had passed over Susan's head. She had no imagination to spare for those who might be worse off, nor the experience to understand it. All she knew was her own small world in the streets of Copnor, where she and her parents had lived in a small house together, and Daddy had got up at four o'clock every morning to deliver milk, and been home in the afternoon in time for the three of them to have tea together and play games.

It had been a warm, cosy world, a world that she had thought would go on for ever. And then it had fallen apart. Her mother had been ill, so ill that she'd had to be taken away from them, to hospital where Susan was not allowed to go and visit her. And then one day her father had come home with a strange, stiff face and told her that Mummy would never be coming back.

His face had screwed up as he told her this, and turned red, and she'd seen the tears drip from his eyes. Susan had been panic-stricken. Daddy crying! Mummy never coming home! Her world had crumbled and fallen away from her, leaving her swinging wildly in a dark, deep vacuum, and she'd clutched him in terror and screamed.

And then, only a few days later, she'd been sent away on the train, sent to live with the Longs. She didn't know why. She didn't know if she would ever go home. She didn't even know whether she would see her father again.

Perhaps, now that her mother was dead, he no longer wanted her.

Susan could not stop crying. She cried herself to sleep at night and in the first moment of waking in the morning, she remembered it all over again, the pain fresh in her mind, and began to cry again.

She was crying as she walked along the dripping lanes and met Martin Baker.

Susan and Martin knew each other well. They had been in the same class at school in Copnor, and sat near each other in the crowded village school. They had started on the same day and shared the same fears and pleasures.

They stopped and looked at each other, recognising the streak of tears on each other's faces. There was no need for questions.

'My tummy aches,' Martin said. 'I've been sick. I want to go home.'

'So do I.'

They stood a moment longer. Then they reached out their hands towards each other.

'Let's go now,' Martin said, and Susan nodded.

Feeling better than they had since the evacuation they turned and began to walk along the lane, towards the main road that they believed led back to Portsmouth.

CHAPTER EIGHT

LIKE ALL the other mothers in Bridge End, Jess was horrified to hear what had happened to little Susan Cullen and Martin Baker.

'Found on the Southampton road they were,' Mrs Greenberry told her. 'Trudging along hand in hand, worn out, crying their poor little hearts out. Lucky it was the rector that found them.'

Jess felt the tears in her eyes. 'What did he do with them?'

'Took them to the hospital in Southampton. He could see the little boy was poorly. Turned out he had appendicitis, so they kept him in and the rector brought little Susan back. But she's in such a state they've had to send for her father.'

'Oh dear. Poor Mr Cullen. And poor little Susan.' Jess thought of the tragic little face, pressed to the bars of the school playground the morning the children had been evacuated. And Martin Baker, stumbling along the village street behind Widow Hutchins. Jess had known neither of them was happy – but what could she have done? Mrs Hutchins seemed a respectable sort of person, and the young woman Susan had been billeted with just had too much to do to take care of the motherless little girl.

'Nobody seems to have thought about whether people were fit to look after children,' she said. 'It was all just done on spare rooms. If you had a spare room, you had to take an evacuee. But not everyone's as kind as you and Edna Corner.'

'And not everyone's as unkind as Widow Hutchins,' Mrs Greenberry consoled her. 'Most of the others have shaken down all right. And it's not your responsibility, Jess.'

It might not be Jess's responsibility, but she felt it just the same. She went out, pushing Maureen in the pram, thinking of the two children, trudging along the main road. It was a mercy they hadn't been run over. Or picked up by someone less kind than the rector. She shuddered at the thought of what might have happened.

How were the little Atkinsons getting along? she wondered. It was some time since she had called at the Woddises' house, though she had seen the children about the village and often looked out for them at the school gates. They looked subdued and quiet, but then they always had been. Molly herself was pale, with mouse-coloured hair, so you couldn't expect Alan and Wendy to be much different. As far as Jess could see, they were clean and tidy enough, and they were at school every day, where their teachers would soon see if anything was wrong.

Well, they'll be going home for Christmas soon, she thought. Almost all the evacuated children at Bridge End were. And then Molly and her children would be together, just as she and Frank and their family would, and perhaps Hitler and the war would be forgotten for a while in happy celebration.

Christmas approached with a blast of bitterly cold weather. The hospitals reported an inundation of people with broken arms, collar-bones and ankles caused by slipping on icy pavements. Molly Atkinson, newly out of bed and determined to visit her children for Christmas, was one of the first. She slipped on ice only a few yards from the door of the shop and cracked two ribs, as well as twisting her knee so badly that she could not walk for a week and even after that could only hobble for short distances.

'Please go and fetch them home for Christmas,' she implored her husband. 'I can't bear to think of them there, wondering why we don't come. I know the shop's busy – but we could get someone in for a day or two. And I can serve if I sit in a chair.'

He hesitated and then gave in. Molly had been worrying herself almost out of her mind about the children, and since little Martin Baker had come home she'd been even worse. It was no use telling her that Frank Budd had been to the village and seen his own children, happy and healthy. She kept all Wendy's letters in her bag or her pocket and carried them about with her, taking them out half a dozen times a day to pore over them.

'She doesn't sound happy,' she said, but Dave read the letters and shook his head. 'You can't expect much more than this from a kiddy of eight. She tells you what she's done at school and what they had for their supper and that. What d'you expect, *Gone With the Wind*?'

Molly smiled but looked unconvinced.

'There's something wrong. I'm sure there is. It looks almost as if the envelope's been opened before.'

Dave turned the letter over in his hand.

'I don't think so, love. Look, you've been ill. Things have preyed on your mind. I know how much you've missed the kids but they're better off where they are, honestly. Why, I bet they're living the life of Riley, being spoilt to death by those two old sisters.'

'That's just it. Two old ladies. They're not used to children.'

Dave laughed. 'They might not have been when the war started – I bet they are now, after a few weeks with our two scallywags!' He put his arm round her and gave her a comforting squeeze. 'Don't worry, love – I'll go and fetch them back for Christmas, provided the bombing hasn't started by then. OK?'

'Oh, they won't start bombing over Christmas, surely,' she said, and gave him the happiest smile he'd seen for months. 'Give me a pencil, Dave. I've got to make a list. We'll need all sorts of special treats if they're going to be home. And we must think what presents to get them.'

'Presents!' he said. 'You've got a stack of toys and things in the wardrobe already, I've seen them.' But his face was soft as he handed her a piece of paper and a pencil. It was good to see Molly cheering up at last. Maybe he hadn't realised just how much she was missing the children.

Perhaps they ought to think about having them back permanently. It really didn't look as if there were going to be any bombs after all. And although he'd been firmly in favour of evacuation, he'd heard about little Martin Baker too and felt uneasy. You thought of children going to the country and being fed like fighting-cocks with eggs and fresh milk and cream. But Martin, from all accounts, looked as if he'd lived on bread and water. All country people, it seemed, weren't so hospitable as they'd been cracked up to be.

Frank Budd had said his seemed happy enough and were well looked after. He hadn't seemed to know much about any others. But he'd only managed to get to see Jess once or twice, and Dave didn't suppose they'd spent much time talking about other people.

He wondered if the Budds would be coming home for Christmas. Perhaps Frank would bring his Alan and Wendy along with theirs. That would save him a trip and save getting someone in for the shop, or having Molly sit in a chair to serve. If he knew her, she'd be working all the hours there were anyway, getting things nice for the kids. He made up his mind to talk to Frank next time he saw him.

Frank was getting ready to visit Jess and the children again. He made a pot of tea for his breakfast and sat with Henry purring on his knee, listening to the wireless, thinking of all the news he'd heard that week. So many things were going on now. So many countries had joined the war. It was difficult to keep track of it all, but he kept trying. If you knew what was happening, you could feel, if only slightly, that there was still some hope of control. Without knowledge, there was nothing.

The whole country was talking about the German pocket battleship, the *Admiral Graf Spee*. It seemed as if a worldwide hunt was on, to try to put a stop to her antics. She was like a firefly, darting round the ocean picking off merchant ships which were bringing essential goods to Britain. Now, everyone believed her to be on her way to South America.

'And if she is, we'll catch her,' Ted had told him with grim satisfaction. 'The *Ajax* convoy is down there, and our Colin's on the *Exeter*. She won't get away again.'

That wasn't the only thing happening, of course. The Russians were attacking Finland. They had bombed Helsinki and columns of soldiers were advancing along the frozen roads. But the Finns were fighting back. On skis, clad in fur-lined boots and reindeer-skin coats, they moved at night about the Russian camps, sniping, laying mines and tossing Molotov cocktails into tanks. Winter was on their side; when spring came, it might be a different story but until then they were putting up a magnificent battle.

Frank spread a piece of toast with margarine and some of Jess's marmalade. The house was bitterly cold. He hadn't lit a fire for a fortnight. Now that he was eating his supper most nights with his sister-in-law, there didn't seem much point in it. Without Jess here, it didn't seem like home anyway.

He thought of the last time he'd gone to see her. Their pleasure at being together again as a family was matched by their frustration at not having any time alone. He sensed the Greenberrys' embarrassment and knew that they realised this and just didn't know what to do about it. They can hardly offer us their bed for the afternoon, he thought with wry amusement, and anyway what would the kids think? As it was, he'd spent the entire afternoon being shown round the farm where Reg Corner worked, Rose clinging to his arm like a limpet the whole way, while Jess walked silently on his other side.

It would be the same today, he knew. And yet what else could they do? Families needed to be together, he couldn't tell the kids to get lost for an hour or so, and there was nowhere to go anyway. He thought of Jess, of her warm body in the bed, the way they would lie for an hour or more of a Sunday morning, just holding each other close. Just thinking like that made him ache with longing. And seeing her would make it worse. He almost wished he wasn't going.

'Can't we come home for Christmas?' she said that afternoon, as they walked through the lanes. 'We've been away all this time and there's not been a single bomb. Surely we could come back, just for the holidays.'

Frank sighed. He wanted her back – wanted them all back – badly, but when he thought of the map on the wall he knew that the battle had hardly begun. As yet, it was mostly a war of the sea, with thousands of tons of shipping lost already, but soon enough, surely, it would become a war of land and air as well. Soldiers were massing in France, aircraft were being built, munitions factories crying out for workers . . . And Hitler meant business too, you could see that. Strutting about in front of his troops, making speeches about what he meant to do with the 'new Europe' when he'd finally won. And threatening to bring Britain to her knees by the summer with his magnetic mines, which Mr Churchill had called 'the lowest form of warfare ever'.

228

No, Hitler wasn't on the point of giving in. And until he did, the country was the safest place for his children to be. But still – Christmas . . . What would Christmas be, without his family around him?

'You can always come and stay here, of course,' Jess said wistfully. 'Mrs Greenberry said we could make up a bed on the parlour floor. It'd be better than nothing. But – oh, Frank,' she turned and put her arms around him, laying her head on his broad chest, 'I really would like to come home. I want to see everyone else – Mum and Dad, our Annie and Ted and the neighbours. I'd even be pleased to see Ethel Glaister!'

Frank had to laugh at that. Jess had never had much time for Ethel, nor Ethel for her. They got along well enough as neighbours, helping out over the odd cup of sugar or taking in each other's washing when it rained, but they weren't friends, not like she was with Peggy Shaw on the other side. And she'd be even less friendly if she knew what Ethel was up to now.

Ethel hadn't given up her pursuit of Frank. A day or two after the teacup episode, she had called to him over the garden fence and handed him the pieces of broken china.

'I was a bit rude to you when we had that little accident,' she told him, all arch coyness and permed hair again. 'I'd be ever so grateful if you'd do whatever you can, Frank. And then we'll have another cup of tea together again, eh? Carry on from where we left off, like.'

Frank had mended the cup. But he'd made sure Ethel was out before he went to her door with it, and he'd left it on the step, wrapped in newspaper. Since then he'd managed to avoid her.

'I want us to be all together for Christmas,' Jess went on. 'Even if you come and stay, the boys will still be over with Reg and Edna. And I know they're looking forward to it – Reg and Edna, I mean – but they're our boys, not theirs. They should be with us.'

'Jess, there's a war on,' he reminded her gently. 'We can't have just what we want. We've all got to make sacrifices.'

Jess stopped and faced him. They were standing under a large beech tree, its trunk smooth and grey, its branches a mass of tracery against the grey sky.

'And you're making more than most,' she said. 'Look, I've been saying how much I'd like to come back – but what about you? I know what you're doing at home, Frank.' He stared at her, wondering if anyone had said anything about Ethel Glaister. Surely not. Not that there was anything to say, but some people had spiteful tongues and would make something out of nothing just for the hell of it.

'You're sitting there with no fire,' Jess continued. 'You're making do with tea and a bit of bread for your breakfast and you're not eating a proper dinner. Oh, I know Annie's giving you a meal in the evenings, and I know what sort of meal it is, too. No wonder Ted looks as thin as a rake! You need more than rice and stuff to keep you going, with the work you do. And you need a bit of warmth and home comfort to come back to of an evening.'

'We were talking about Christmas,' he began, but she stopped him with a finger against his lips.

'I know that. But now I'm talking about something else. I'm talking about coming back permanent, Frank, to look after you.'

He stared at her. 'But you can't do that.'

'Who says I can't?' She lifted her chin. 'Look, if it wasn't for the baby I'd never have been evacuated in the first place. Our Rose and the boys would have been, but I'd have stayed at home, where I belong, to look after you. Well, I think that's what I ought to be doing anyway.' She looked at him with serious brown eyes. 'Frank, it's not doing us any good being parted like this, and what doesn't do me any good doesn't help Maureen. I've already lost my milk through it. I'll be happier back with you, and she'll get on better too.'

'And what about when we're bombed? We're going to be, Jess. Don't make any mistake about that.'

'Then we'll be together.' She moved closer and slid her arms around his neck. 'Isn't that why we got married? Didn't we promise to stick by each other for better or worse? Then what am I doing out here, when you need me at home?' He shook his head. He was sorely tempted, but he looked at the children, who had run on ahead, shouting and laughing.

'They're better here.'

'They are, yes. They've got their lives in front of them. But we –' her voice shook suddenly '– we've only got each other, Frank. And being parted like this – it's wrong. Don't you see that?'

'But – what about the baby?'

'She'll have to come too. She has to be with me.' Jess looked at the borrowed pram. 'I don't want to put her in danger,' she said in a low voice. 'God knows, I don't want anything to happen to her. But I want to be with you more than anything else.'

The children had stopped and were walking back, puzzled and uneasy. Frank put his hands on Jess's shoulders and bent to kiss her.

'Come home for Christmas,' he said. 'And we'll think about it then.'

Annie was polishing a brass bell Colin had given her and listening to the News when Ted came in. Her face was white and he came over to her at once.

'What's the matter, girl?'

'They've just been talking about our Colin's ship,' she said. 'It's been in a battle.'

'A battle? The *Exeter*?'

'That's right. And two others – the *Ajax* and the *Achilles*.' She stared at him, her eyes frightened. 'Ted, I thought they were out of the way down there off South America. I didn't think they'd get caught up in any fighting.'

Ted sighed. He'd known Annie was hiding her head in the sand over this. There'd been news enough of Hitler's pocket battleships sneaking about all over the oceans, picking off British merchant-men. The *Graf Spee* was the most notorious, though the captain seemed a decent sort of chap for a German, taking their crews prisoner before sinking the ships. All the same, he couldn't be allowed to go on doing it, and that was why the three cruisers were off the east coast of South America – to protect the merchant ships and destroy the enemy marauder.

'The Battle of the River Plate, they're calling it,' she said, twisting the polishing rag between her fingers. 'It's been going on for days but they've only just started talking about it. Ted, our Colin's down there. He could be hurt, even killed, and us not know a thing about it.' She picked up the bell and stared at it. Colin had brought it home from his first trip abroad and it had pride of place on top of the sideboard.

He squeezed her shoulders. 'Don't talk like that, love. We'd know soon enough if anything had happened to him. No news is good news, remember.'

'No,' she said. 'No news just means they haven't got around to telling us yet. Or they don't know. There's no good news in this war, Ted.'

'Yes, there is. We've had no bombs here yet – '

'D'you think I care about bombs here, when our Colin's getting torpedoed on the other side of the world?' she cried. 'I wish we were getting bombs here. At least I'd know what was happening then. But this – hearing it on the News and then just having to wait and wonder . . .' She put her hands up to her face and began to cry.

The back door opened, letting in a blast of cold air. Olive burst in and dropped her bag on the table. She stood pulling off her gloves, one finger at a time, and stared with wild eyes at her parents.

'Have you heard the news?'

'About the *Exeter*? Yes, we have. But your dad says we're not to worry – '

'Not to worry? She's been sunk!'

'Sunk?' They came to their feet, staring at her. 'That wasn't on the News,' Annie said, her hand touching her throat.

'Granny Kinch told me.'

'Granny Kinch? What does she know about it?'

Olive looked embarrassed. 'She said her Nancy knows one of the sailors who used to be on the *Exeter* – '

'Only one?' Ted said ironically, and Annie gave him a sharp nudge with her elbow.

'He's over in Gosport now, at the *Dolphin*, working on submarines. He said there'd been a special signal through, saying the *Exeter* had been sunk with all hands.' Olive burst into tears. 'All hands, Mum! That means everyone. Our Colin – everyone.'

'Oh, Ted,' Annie whispered, putting out her hand blindly. Ted put his arm round her shoulders again and held her tight. His face was drained of colour, a dirty grey, the stubble like black pinpoints on his chin. His lower lip was trembling slightly.

'You sure about this, Olive?'

Olive slumped into a chair. The tears were streaming down her face. 'I only know what Granny Kinch told me.'

'It might not be true,' Annie said, her voice shaking. 'They'd have said on the News if it had been, surely. Her Nancy could have got it wrong. Who is this bloke she got it from, anyway?'

'I don't know. A sailor.' Olive buried her face in her hands. 'If our Colin's been killed – '

'Well, I wouldn't put too much credit on that,' Ted said. He was recovering a little now. 'Nancy Baxter knows plenty of sailors but I don't reckon they know any more about the war than you or me. I'd wait till we hear official. Or from the BBC.'

'It would have been on the News,' Annie repeated. 'They'd have said – wouldn't they?' She stared up at her husband's face, willing him to say yes, willing it to be true.

'I reckon so. They wouldn't keep us in the dark, not over a thing like that.'

'Maybe they didn't want Hitler to know,' Olive said through her sobs. 'Maybe the signal's only just come through – '

'And Nancy Baxter came home with it before they got it at the BBC?' Ted asked scathingly. 'Be your age, Olive. It's just a rumour, that's all, and Granny Kinch ought to know better than to go repeating it, specially when she knows our Colin's on that ship. Your mother's right. It would have been on the News if it was true. And I'm not going to believe it until I hear it from them.' He looked at his wife. 'How about a cup of tea? I'll put the kettle on.'

He went over to the sink and mother and daughter looked at each other in amazement. Ted seldom did anything so domestic as making tea. It was a measure of how serious he felt the situation was, in spite of what he said.

Annie saw the tears on her daughter's face and moved round the table. She put her arms around Olive's shoulders and held the girl's head against her body. The tears were hot in her eyes. She knew that Ted was right, whatever Nancy Baxter had got from some sailor wasn't likely to be the truth. All the same, the ship had been in a battle, the BBC had said so, and you just didn't know what that might mean. Perhaps the battle wasn't even over yet. She imagined the ships lined up at sea, firing their guns at one another. And torpedoes . . . They were terrible weapons, torpedoes. How could she be sure that Colin would survive?

Men had come home from the last war horribly maimed.

There'd been one down Commercial Road for years, selling matches. He'd had no legs and had sat on a little cart on the pavement outside Woolworths. Ted had always bought matches from him and been quite sharp with Colin once when the boy had reminded him there were plenty of matches at home.

'He's one of the heroes of the Great War,' he'd said. 'One of the boys who went out to make Britain a land fit for heroes to live in and then found you had to be a hero to live in it. I'm ashamed to walk past that man on my two good legs, and know I've got a job and a home and family, and if all I can do is buy matches from him then I'll fill the house with 'em and be glad to do it.'

After that, Colin had bought matches from the man too, as soon as he was old enough. But the little cart hadn't been outside Woolworths for a long time now, and no one seemed to know what had happened to the legless man. Suppose Colin came home like that? Burned or disfigured, his arms or legs blown off? He was only twenty-five, so tall and strong, so full of life. Suppose he never came home again?

I couldn't bear it, Annie thought, still holding Olive. If he got killed – if any one of them got killed – I just couldn't bear it.

The whole street knew that Colin was on the *Exeter*. They followed the News with anxious interest, switching on the wireless for every bulletin. Frank stopped sticking pins in his big map of Europe and found an atlas with South America in it. He laid it open on top of the piano and looked at it as he listened to the News, tracing the place names with his finger.

Montevideo. It was thousands of miles away. The war was spreading everywhere. What did a little country like Uruguay have to do with Hitler's invasion of Poland? Why did Argentina and Brazil have to get dragged in? Weren't they neutral? Why were British ships having to patrol those faraway seas, when our own shores needed protection?

The *Graf Spee* had been a thorn in the British side for weeks, storming around the oceans and pouncing on vital merchant ships. Disguised as a French warship, she'd eluded the fleet sent to intercept and destroy her, and had slipped away, no doubt cocking a snook at the frustrated British battleships, cruisers and aircraft carriers that pursued her. She had stridden the world, swooping down the Atlantic to terrorise the seas of West Africa and darting around the Cape of Good Hope ('cape of some hope' cynical sailors called it) before sliding away towards South America.

It was here that she had been caught at last and, in the Battle of the River Plate, damaged and forced into the harbour of Montevideo.

'She's trapped now,' Frank said to Ted when his brother-in-law came in to bring a cake Annie had made. 'She's run into Montevideo for safety and our ships are waiting outside. They'll get her the minute she pokes her dirty little nose through the harbour entrance.'

'There's a three-mile limit of neutrality,' Ted said, studying the map. 'They can't do anything inside that. If she came out at night she could slip away before they knew she was there.'

'They'll catch her.' Frank spoke positively, convinced he was right. 'They won't let her get away this time.'

The two men were silent, thinking of what was going on out there, so far away. They had both seen war before, knew what exploding shells were like, could remember the screams of injured and dying men, the stench of fresh blood and festering wounds, gangrene and trench-rot. They could remember men who were brave and men who were not; men who did silently what had to be done, and others who panicked, who screamed and clawed the air and had to be shot by their own officers because they might infect the other men with their terror.

Was that what it had been like on the *Exeter* during the Battle of the River Plate?

Ted's own son must now have witnessed scenes such as those, and perhaps worse. Had he survived to tell the tale? Would he, one day, sit in this room and smile his merry smile, gently pull Rose's hair as he used to do and regale the wide-eyed Tim and Keith with stories of life at sea?

Or was he already dead – rolled over the side for a sea burial, drifting downwards through the waves to be eaten by crabs and end as a clutter of anonymous bones, wafted apart by the turbulence?

'If only we knew,' Ted said, breaking their silence. 'That's the worst of it – not knowing. Poor Annie's in a bad way, I don't mind

235

telling you. She can't sit still, can't rest a minute. And if she's looked out of the front door once she's looked out a hundred times, hoping to see him come down the street.'

'But he'd never get back as quick as this,' Frank said. 'Even if he was sent home – and he wouldn't be.'

'She knows that. She just can't seem to help it.' Ted nodded towards the cake. 'That's why she made that. She's cooking for him to come home. I've told her, we can't afford it, what with shortages the way they are, but it seems to give her some comfort so I've given up. I don't know what she'll do if we don't hear soon, though.'

Frank was silent for a moment.

'It's harder on the women than it is on us, Ted. They still see the lads as their babies. They had to carry them and give birth to them – they take it hard when something happens to them.'

'I know. And our Olive is fretting her heart out now about that young man of hers – Derek Harker. He's expecting to be called up any time now and they're pestering to get married before he goes. Well, you know what I think about that, Frank – same as you do. Twenty-one's time enough for that, when they're old enough to take their own responsibility. We've seen plenty of people marry in haste and repent at leisure, and there's nothing like war for making them hasty.'

'Your Olive'll be twenty-one soon though, won't she?'

'Next October. And there won't be much I can do to stop her then. But I've told her, till then she's under my authority and does what I tell her. Mind, she's got a sensible head on her shoulders. It's young Betty I worry about. She's got proper headstrong just lately.'

He went home and Frank cut himself a slice of cake to take over to the allotment. Not that there was much he could do over there. The ground was frozen hard and he'd done all the digging anyway and sown what he could sow. The carrots he'd sown were wasted now, spoiled by the frost. But with the house empty and himself the only one at the table, there wouldn't have been any point in digging them anyway.

He'd stopped going to Annie's on Sundays. It didn't seem right to be taking up a place at her table every day, and he knew she liked to have Arthur and Mary along then. It gave him a chance to do things about the house and have his dinner when he liked. But it meant he didn't get a proper Sunday dinner – just whatever he could put together. And sitting there alone, he felt lonelier than at any time during the week.

Sunday dinner had always been his favourite meal. Jess always put on a roast, with plenty of vegetables. Her roast potatoes were crisp and golden, her Yorkshire pudding light and fluffy and when she cooked pork the crackling was as crisp as thin toffee. Frank would sit at the table, looking at the feast, most of it grown by himself, and then look at the three children – the two boys on one side of the long table, Rose on the other – and finally at his wife, and feel a warm glow spread through him. This was what life was all about. This was why he went to work in the Yard, slaving hour after hour in the sweltering clamour of the boiler-shop. This was why he went to the allotment in the evenings and at weekends. So that his family could eat food he'd grown and live in a house he'd worked for. And all he needed in return was to see their faces, clean and glowing, around the table, and see them grow into fine citizens who would do the same for their own families.

But now there was no family at the table, and the house was silent. And Frank was taking no pleasure in the work he did, not even in his allotment. There seemed to be little point in it now.

Frank moved impatiently, annoyed with himself for his misery. He had a lot to be thankful for, he reminded himself. His children weren't going off to war like Colin or Bob Shaw, nor likely to. And they were safer in the country than here. Wasn't that enough for him?

What's more, they would be home next weekend, for Christmas, all four of them and Jess too. They'd be together for the first time in three months. And the baby would be sitting up, taking an interest in all that went on.

Frank looked out of the window. There had been another hard frost following a bitter night. Perhaps he wouldn't go over to the allotment today after all. He'd look out the Christmas decorations instead and start getting things ready for next weekend.

By Tuesday, the world knew of the end of the *Graf Spee*, and those who had sons or husbands on the *Exeter* were waiting to know if they should grieve.

'Sixty-one dead,' Annie said, sitting with dry, aching eyes at the kitchen table. 'Sixty-one. And no one to tell us if our Colin's one.'

Ted sat beside her, his arm about her shoulders. He could think of nothing to say. His own thoughts were too painful to be expressed and he had no comfort for either his wife or his daughter.

'Remember when we first come here?' Annie said, still in that dry, painful voice. 'Remember how he thought we were coming to live in a castle? I could see then that blessed turret was going to be a devil to clean and the furniture would never fit in them round rooms, but Colin was so excited I couldn't bring myself to tell him we didn't want the house. He made up his mind right from the start, that upstairs room was going to be his, didn't matter how awkward or small it might be. And so it always has been.'

'I remember him playing the fool up on top,' Ted said. 'Him and his bows and arrows! I thought he'd killed old Mrs Henderson's Tibby, you know.'

'And I thought you'd almost killed him, you gave him such a hiding.' Annie realised what she had said and turned, clinging to her husband and weeping. 'Oh, Ted – Ted! If anything's happened to our Colin – '

He held her tightly. His own throat ached with tears, the first time he had wanted to cry since he was a small boy in his own mother's arms. But he could remember men in the Great War, men who had been injured, crying out in their pain, crying for their own mothers. Was Colin doing the same thing now?

'Put the kettle on, our Olive,' he said, and his daughter rose and went, red-eyed, to the kitchen.

Annie had stopped crying as suddenly as she had begun. She sat watching dully as Olive made the tea and poured out the first cup. When it was placed in front of her, she stared at it as if she did not know what it was.

'I've never let him down before,' she said at last in a dry aching voice. 'When he grazed his knees when he was a baby, he came running to me. When he fell off the wall and broke his arm, I took him to the hospital. When he had measles and mumps and chicken-pox I sat up with him at night. I've always been there, whenever he's needed me.'

'He's a man now, Annie,' Ted said. 'He has to manage without his mum.'

She turned her eyes in his direction but it was as if she did not see him, as if she were blind.

'Yes. That's it. They all do, don't they? All the mothers' sons out there, fighting each other for the sake of one nasty little German –they're all having to manage without their mums. And all the children like our Jess's boys and Molly Atkinson's little Alan and Wendy, and that poor little Martin Baker. All of them, sent away from home, having to manage on their own.' Her face crumpled suddenly. 'It's not right, Ted, it's not right. It shouldn't be happening. There must be better ways than this – there must.'

Once again, the tears poured down her cheeks. She pushed her teacup out of the way and laid her arms on the table. She put her head down on them and wept.

Ted put his arm around her shoulders again. But there was nothing he could say. The tears were on his cheeks too and all he could do was lean his head on his other hand and suffer with his daughter and his wife.

Alan and Wendy Atkinson did not come home for Christmas. Just as Dave was preparing to go and fetch them – for Frank, with some apologies, had told him that he wasn't going to fetch Jess and the kids himself, he couldn't get the time off, and she wouldn't be able to manage Wendy and Alan as well as their four – his father had an accident and was killed.

'He only went down to the Harvest Home for a pint and a game of darts,' Molly told Annie. Molly's knee was still sore and her ribs caught her whenever she laughed or coughed, but with this latest disaster she was forced to come and help in the shop. 'He was crossing the road by the railway. You know what it's like there, with all those trees, you can't see even if there's a moon. And this car came along – and he must have just walked out in front of it. The driver swears he never saw him and I don't suppose he did. And you know Dad was hard of hearing, he probably didn't hear the engine.' Her eyes filled with tears. They were already red, as if she'd spent most of the past few days

239

weeping. 'The doctor said he must have died at once, he couldn't have known anything about it, that's our only comfort.'

'I'm really sorry,' Annie said. Old Arnold Atkinson had been a bit cantankerous sometimes, which was why the shop wasn't as popular as Shepherds', with its genial proprietor who always had a joke and a laugh. But he'd been a good enough neighbour all the same, and part of the community for seventy years. He'd built the business up himself and handed it over to his sons a few years ago, but he was still very much a part of it, serving in the shop while they fetched the produce from the ships down at Camber Dock, or from market gardens round about.

'We'll miss him,' she said sincerely. 'It won't seem the same round here without him. And I reckon you'll miss him too.'

Molly nodded. 'We will. He wasn't always easy but his heart was in the right place. He'd never see anyone go in want if he could help it. And he loved the kids.' Her tears overflowed and ran down her cheeks. 'He missed them nearly as much as Dave and me these past few months,' she said shakily. 'He was just living to see them again at Christmas.'

'Oh, Molly,' Annie said helplessly. 'I'm really sorry. When are they coming home?'

To her dismay, Molly sat down suddenly in the chair that had been brought into the shop for her use. She covered her face with her hands and began to sob. Annie looked round. There was no one else in; it was almost closing time. Quickly, she went to the door and turned round the 'Closed' sign, put the bolt across and then went back to Molly. She laid her hand on the other woman's shoulder and waited for the storm to subside a little.

'That's it, girl,' she said after a moment. 'You cry it out. It'll do you good.' And then, after a further pause, 'Aren't they coming?'

Molly shook her head and felt in her apron pocket for a handkerchief. She blew her nose, wiped her eyes and said shakily, 'We decided it was best to leave them there after all. It's the funeral on Christmas Eve, see – we can't have them here for that. And the shop's so busy – with not having Dad here – Dave can't go, and the doctor says I can't, so – ' She shook her head, the tears beginning again. 'I wanted them so bad,' she wept, 'and it just isn't fair. He was just walking down to the pub for a drink with his mates . . . Why did it have to happen? Why should he get run over like that?'

'It's this awful blackout,' Annie said. 'There's been more accidents these past four months . . . They won't let people shine any lights at all. And I know cars are supposed to go only twenty miles an hour, but how are they supposed to know how fast they're going when they can't see their speedometers?'

'There was a woman over in Gosport,' Molly said, 'put on the dashboard light, just for a quick look, and she got fined. Anyway, you can get killed by a car doing twenty miles an hour.'

They were silent for a few minutes. Molly slowly recovered herself and even gave Annie a watery smile. Annie squeezed her shoulder again and picked up her basket.

'Well, I'd better be getting back. I really am sorry about Dave's dad, Molly. And about the children. You let me know if there's anything we can do, won't you?'

'Yes. Yes, I will.' Molly opened the door for her, watched her go round the corner and then closed and bolted it again. She stood for a moment in the empty shop, looking at the sacks of potatoes, the bins of carrots and turnips and sprouts, the empty shelves where once they had stacked fruits like bananas and coconuts and pineapples, none of them available now.

It seemed very empty without Dad. And the flat upstairs seemed empty too, without the children. She thought of the presents she had bought, the decorations ready to be hung up, the little tree that Dave had managed to acquire.

All useless.

Oh, my babies, she thought, putting her fist to her mouth and biting the knuckles. What are you doing now?

When am I going to see you again?

A list of those killed in the battle with the *Graf Spee* was published at last in the *Evening News*, and Annie and Ted and the girls crowded round the table to read it, their fingers tracing down the columns of names. Once or twice, someone caught back a gasp as a similar name sprang to their eyes, but at last, having read the list at least three times, they drew back and gazed at each other.

'He's not on it,' Annie whispered. 'Our Colin's not on the list.'

241

'That means he's still alive,' Olive said. 'Oh, *Mum*!'

They flung their arms around each other. Once again, the tears flowed, but this time they were smiling and needed no comfort. Even Ted wiped his eyes a couple of times and blew his nose loudly, and then grinned rather self-consciously as Annie hugged him.

'Don't pretend you're not as pleased as we are, Ted Chapman!'

'Well, of course I'm pleased. He's my son, too, isn't he? Or so you've always led me to believe.'

'Ted!' Annie slapped his arm, glancing at the two girls and blushing. But Betty laughed and said, 'Go on, Mum, I bet you had your moments. And why not – it's human nature. And you don't have to look like that, we're not kids any more.'

'So you may not be, but I'll still thank you to keep a decent tongue in your head,' Annie said, but her accustomed sharpness had softened and she gave her daughter a hug too. 'Come on, Olive – give us a kiss. We're celebrating!'

Olive did so. But as she stepped away again, she glanced first at her father and then her mother, and said, 'Why not have something else to celebrate as well? Why not let me and Derek get married at Christmas?'

'Oh, Olive!' Annie sighed and looked at her husband. 'She's not going to let it rest, you know.'

'And I'm not going to give in,' Ted said grimly. 'Just because our Colin's safe doesn't alter my mind about that.' He looked at his daughter's face. 'But I'll tell you what. You can get engaged. How about that?'

Olive bit her lip. It was better than nothing, she thought. At least it showed that her father was willing to accept Derek into the family. But it wasn't what she really wanted.

I want to be *married*, she thought mutinously. I want to be able to let Derek love me without having to say 'no' all the time. I want to be able to have his baby with nobody pointing their finger at me.

And I will. Somehow or other, I *will*.

Jess came home for Christmas late one afternoon, bringing the boys, Rose and baby Maureen with her. She came down October Street with Maureen cradled in her arms, and felt close to tears.

It all seemed so cramped and narrow after the space of the countryside, the terraced houses crowded together and the tiny front gardens of March and October Street, which she had once thought so smart, meagre and useless. A snowstorm a week or so ago had left slush, frozen and dirty, in the gutters and the pavement was lumpy with ice. It had been scraped away from in front of some houses, while other people had thrown down ashes to make it less slippery. The afternoon was already growing dark, with thick, acrid smoke filling the streets as women lit fires to welcome men home from work. It was very different from the open fields and woods of Bridge End. But it was home, and Jess was overwhelmingly thankful to be back.

Granny Kinch came to the door of number 10 as she approached and threw up her hands.

'Mrs Budd! Well, this takes me back, it does really. It's just like the day I first saw you comin' down October Street, with two kiddies and another one on the way. Mrs Seddon was out 'ere too and we said to each other, that poor woman, 'owever's she going to manage? And 'ere you are with another one – let's 'ave a look at the little dear. My, ain't she grown!' She put out a grubby finger and pulled the shawl away from the baby's face. Maureen, who had fallen asleep in the bus, stirred and whimpered a little as the cold air touched her skin. 'Why, she's twice the size of our Vera, and two months younger, ain't she?'

'She's six months old now,' Jess said proudly. 'Sitting up by herself. And weighs a ton!'

'You'd better get her inside,' the old lady advised. 'It's comin' in nasty. We've 'ad this fog now for the past three days, enough to choke a body to death. I've wondered once or twice whether to wear my gas mask, I 'ave really. And 'ow are the boys and Rose? 'Ow d'yer like the country, then?'

The children had been straggling behind, laden with bags and cases. They hadn't been able to bring much luggage and most of it was the baby's, but a lot of their clothes were still at home so it didn't matter. Tim and Keith came level and grinned at the old woman in her brown coat and curlers.

'It's smashing. We can milk cows.'

'Milk cows! Well, I never. You must be a real 'elp to the farmer, then.'

'Yes, we are,' Keith said. 'He didn't really want us to come home. He said we're too useful. But it's all right, we can go back.'

'Well, they seem to be 'aving a good time,' Granny Kinch said to Jess. 'And 'ow about Rose? D'you like being evacuated, love?'

Rose looked at her mother. 'Only if Mum's there too.'

The old woman laughed. 'A proper little mother's girl you are. I daresay you do a lot for your baby sister, don't you? You'll 'ave to pop in and see our Vera one day. 'Ow long are you staying, then?' she asked Jess.

'I don't know. We haven't decided yet. Over Christmas anyway.' Jess shifted her feet. 'I'll have to go now, Mrs Kinch, this baby's getting heavier every minute. I daresay I'll be seeing you in the next few days.' Try not to, she thought with a little smile as she walked along the street. As Tommy Vickers would say, you'd need to be the Invisible Man to get past number 10 without being spotted. But the old woman had a good heart and Jess hadn't forgotten her kindness on the morning that the children had been evacuated.

Number 14 looked much as she'd left it, its windows dark and forbidding with the blackout curtains up. She rested the baby on one hip and felt for her key. But before she could fit it into the lock, the door of number 16 opened and Ethel Glaister came out with a shopping basket hung over her arm.

She gave a start of surprise at seeing Jess, and Jess knew immediately that she was 'putting it on'. Probably the woman had been looking out of the window and seen her talking to Granny Kinch, and now she wanted to get her oar in. She sighed. At this moment, all she wanted was to get indoors in her own home, lay Maureen down somewhere and have a cup of tea. But you had to be polite.

'Jess!' Ethel said with exaggerated astonishment. 'Well! So you decided to come home, then?'

She was looking as smart as ever, Jess thought, conscious all at once of her own shabby tweed coat and hair that had never seen a perm. How she managed to dress so well on George Glaister's money was a mystery.

'What d'you mean?' she asked sharply. 'Of course I've come home. Couldn't leave Frank on his own all over Christmas, could I?'

244

'Oh no, of course not.' Ethel gave a little laugh. 'Mind, I don't think he'd have lacked company. He's a very popular man, is your Frank. And how does life in the country suit you? You're looking well – cheeks like apples, you've got! But the natural look always did suit you best.'

Jess looked at Ethel, her hair waved and shining, her face carefully made up, and decided this wasn't intended as a compliment. But there was no sense in having words with Ethel Glaister the minute she got home, and anyway it was Christmas.

'The country's nice. I'd sooner be home with Frank, though.'

Ethel smiled. 'Course you would. He's a fine man, your Frank. I reckon there's a good many women'd like to be in your shoes. And some of 'em not a million miles from here either.'

'What d'you mean?' It was clear from Ethel's manner, her sideways glance and suggestive tone of voice, that she meant *something*. But then she always did like to pretend she knew more than other people.

'Oh, I don't mean nothing.' Ethel's gaze slid past Jess. Jess was suddenly aware of Rose, standing close beside her, of the boys fidgeting restlessly on the pavement, and of Maureen's weight bearing down on her arms. 'It's just that I don't think *I'd* be too pleased to find that a certain person had been in and out of my house while I'd been away, not if I was in your position.'

Jess sighed. 'Come on, Ethel. You might as well tell me what you're getting at. Otherwise I'll just have to go indoors, I can't keep the baby out in the cold much longer.'

Ethel turned pained eyes on her. 'I'm not getting at anything! I'm just saying, that's all – if I was away and my George here on his own, I wouldn't want Nancy Baxter in and out every five minutes. But each to his own, and if you don't mind – '

Jess felt a sudden fury. She forgot Maureen's weight, forgot the sighs and scuffles of the boys, forgot her good resolutions about Christmas. She lifted her chin and looked Ethel Glaister straight in the eye.

'I know all about Nancy Baxter coming down here. She told me before I went away that she'd be glad to do anything she could to give Frank a hand. She offered to do a bit of cleaning for him when our Annie didn't have time, and she's brought him a bit of cake now and then. *And that's all*. Anything else you might have heard is just spiteful gossip.' She paused and then added deliberately, 'And so is anything you might say, if it's about my Frank, so I'll thank you not to go talking like that to other people. And while we're on the subject, I might as well tell you that there's a few other people I wouldn't want in my house but anyone Frank invites is all right by me, because I happen to trust him. And now if you don't mind, I'll go indoors, I've got my husband's tea to get ready.'

Ethel tossed her head. 'Well! Pardon me for breathing! I'm sure I only wanted to be neighbourly, but if you're going to take it like that – '

Jess was no longer listening. Her key in her hand, she had turned once again to her own front door. But before she could open it, it was flung open and her sister Annie stood on the doorstep, arms held wide and a beaming smile stretched across her face.

'Jess! Our Jess! Come in, love, and have a cup of tea by your own fire. I bet that's what you've been looking forward to all day. Come in, all of you, out of the cold. My, you two boys have grown. And Rose – you've had your hair cut – I wouldn't have recognised you. Oh, it *is* good to see you again!'

Half laughing, half crying, Jess allowed herself to be led into her own house, her baby removed from her arms and her coat unbuttoned as if she were a little girl again. Aware only of the warmth of the room, she sank into her own armchair and smiled up at her sister.

'Oh, Annie, I've missed you all so much.'

'We've missed you too, Jess.' Annie poured cups of tea for them all. 'It hasn't seemed right, not having you down the end of the road. And poor Frank – well, he kept cheerful as best he could, but I could tell it's been a strain. Been right off his food, he has, this past week.'

Jess hid a smile. Frank had told her last week he'd begun to pop a few potatoes on the stove as soon as he came in of an evening, ready to fill up on when he got back from Annie's. But the smile was a tearful one. Her sister had been good to Frank and Jess hated to think of him sitting here on his own, cold and lonely.

Not that it was cold now. Annie had built up a really good fire and the room was warm and cosy. She had laid tea, with plenty of bread and marge, a pot of jam and home-made cake. And a plate of doughnuts too, Jess noticed, and felt tears in her eyes again. That was Annie all over, remembering how much the children liked doughnuts.

'Here!' she said. 'You've put up the Christmas decorations.'

Annie laughed. 'That was Frank. He spent all last Sunday doing it. Went out and got the holly and everything. I must say, he's made a nice job of it, and the fairy-lights look quite pretty strung around the walls like that, better than a tree really.'

'I suppose you can't get trees,' Jess said. 'They managed all right at Bridge End. You wouldn't know there was a war on there, Annie. I wish I'd been able to bring some more stuff back with me. Eggs, butter, cream – there's no shortages out there. Mrs Greenberry's put any amount of eggs into waterglass and they get milk from the house cow – you wouldn't believe it.'

'You'll see a difference here, then,' her sister said. 'We're all expecting the rationing to start soon. Most of the shops are half empty now, especially with Christmas coming – everyone's decided they're going to make it a good one in case it's the last chance.'

'It'll probably be a good thing when they do bring rationing in,' Jess observed. 'Some people are getting more than their share and others have to go without. It's the same even in the village, with things that aren't local. I haven't seen a tin of fruit in weeks.' She looked at Annie, suddenly remembering. 'Here! What about your Colin? Have you heard anything?'

Annie nodded and smiled. 'There was a list of the men killed in the paper. Colin wasn't one of them. And the ship's down in the Falklands now getting repaired, so they're safe enough there for the time being. Ted says they're learning to live posh, even the penguins wear evening dress!'

The two women laughed. Jess felt a wave of thankfulness wash over her. She'd heard little news, knowing only that the *Exeter* had been damaged, but she'd known that Annie and Ted must be worried.

She finished her tea and put the cup back on the table. The boys had dashed upstairs and could be heard thumping about in the bedroom. Rose was cuddling Maureen and giving her a bottle.

Henry, who had been fast asleep on the rug in front of the fire, suddenly woke to the fact that his mistress was home, and stood up to put his front paws on her knee.

'It's so good to be home,' she said, and leaned back in her chair. 'You know, you don't really realise how badly you miss it all till you're back. I mean, I knew I was missing it – but not how much. I don't reckon I'll be able to bear to go away again, Annie.'

'I'm not sure your Frank'll be able to bear to let you,' her sister said shrewdly. 'He's been a different man this past week, getting things ready. And I reckon he'll be glad to have good reason to keep Ethel Glaister at arm's length.'

'Ethel Glaister!' Jess sat up straight. 'You don't mean she's been setting her cap at him!'

'Oh, I'm sure there's nothing in it,' Annie assured her hastily. 'Not on his side, anyway. But you know what she's like – and now George has gone away – '

'I know there wouldn't be anything in it as far as Frank's concerned,' Jess said grimly. 'He doesn't like her any more than I do. But if she thinks she's going to pester my husband while I'm away – '

'Well, I don't know that she has been. It's only one or two little things Frank's let drop – and knowing what she's like. She won't try anything now you're home, anyway.'

'She'd better not.' Jess remembered Ethel's malicious hints and repressed a small smile. So that was what was the matter with her! She'd tried it on with Frank and he'd given her the cold shoulder. Well, what else did she expect – she wasn't his type at all. And even if she was . . .

Jess got up out of her chair. Suddenly she was no longer the little sister, to be looked after, but a woman in charge of her own home.

'Well, thanks for coming round and doing everything, Annie. I'll get my pinafore and start Frank's tea. He told me he'd try to get home early tonight, if they'd let him off the overtime. And there's a lot to be done, with Christmas only a few days away.'

Annie recognised that Jess wanted to be alone with her family when Frank came in. She got up, leaving her own cup of tea half finished, and gave her sister a kiss.

'I'll be getting back too. I'll see you tomorrow, Jess – pop up whenever you like. And don't forget you're all coming to us for Christmas dinner.'

'I won't forget. Thanks, Annie.' But Jess's smile was absent-minded and she was already thinking of something else as she saw Annie out into the dark, foggy street.

Frank would be home soon. They'd be a proper family again, clustered around the table, warmed by their own fire. And then the children would go to bed. First the boys, in the iron bunks up in the back bedroom, then Rose in the Put-u-Up in the front room downstairs. And then she and Frank would be alone together, for the first time in three long months. She heard his key in the front door, then the tramp of his boots along the passage. Her heart thumping suddenly, she stood by the dining-table, facing the door. And then he was in the room, dirty in his working clothes, his lunch box in his hand and, held clumsily in the other, a straggly bunch of flowers from the corner shop.

Jess moved forward and found herself in his arms, pressed once more against that firm, broad chest, feeling his big, strong hands on her shoulders and back.

'Oh Frank,' she said, 'I've missed you so much!'

CHAPTER NINE

BOB SHAW was home for Christmas, proud to wear his rough new khaki uniform in the streets, but glad to take it off indoors and sit in his old grey flannels and the Fair Isle pullover Gladys had knitted him. He was still waiting to go to France – twice he had been expecting to go within twenty-four hours, only to be kept back at the last minute. He basked in the adulation of his sister Diane, who was getting on for sixteen now and missing the blue-eyed young delivery man at the laundry who used to stop and flirt with her. He had been called up and posted in November.

But it wasn't Diane's admiration Bob craved. All the time he'd been away, he'd been thinking about Betty Chapman. He still carried the photo of her in her bathing costume and looked at it every night before he fell on his camp bed in the hut and slept an exhausted sleep. At the first opportunity, he asked Gladys if Betty was still going out with Graham Philpotts.

Gladys snorted. 'Going out with him? She says they're "secretly engaged" – whatever that might mean! Far as I can see, it just means she don't get a ring and her dad doesn't know. I mean, how can you be engaged if you don't have a ring? It doesn't make sense.'

'I suppose if you say you'll marry someone, you're engaged,' Bob said, feeling depressed. 'But they can't get married without her dad knowing, can they.'

'Well, of course not. I don't think they're even thinking about it. If you ask me, Betty doesn't even care about being engaged, not properly, except that she'd like a ring to flash about. She just wants to be able to tell people she's got a boy in the Navy. But she's got no more idea of settling down than flying to the moon. You know she's going off to work on a farm, don't you?'

Bob stared. 'On a *farm*?'

'That's right. Land girl. Fancies herself in trousers, driving a tractor. I don't know what her "secret fiancé" thinks about that!'

Bob looked at his sister. 'I thought you liked Betty.'

'I do really.' Gladys grinned at him. 'But it riles me a bit to see her messing about. I mean, she could find she's bitten off more than she can chew, leading Graham on, letting him think she's serious when all she wants is someone to show off. I wouldn't like to see her in trouble.'

Bob said no more. But when he met Betty in the street next morning, he remembered all that Gladys had said and wondered if it was really true.

'Bob!' Betty exclaimed. 'My, you do look smart. And I reckon you've put on weight too. You look bigger. How d'you like being a soldier?'

'It's all right. I still wish I'd gone in the Navy though. I'd have liked to go to sea.'

'You ought to have joined the Marines, then.' She put out a hand and stroked the rough khaki. 'I bet that's nice and warm. Have you heard when you're going to France?'

'Pretty soon, I think. I've been on standby to go twice and kept back at the last minute.' He grinned self-consciously. 'They're saving the best for the last.'

'That's it,' Betty said. 'Our Olive's boyfriend, Derek Harker, he's waiting for a posting too. They're getting engaged at Christmas. They wanted to get married but Dad won't let them till she's twenty-one. Daft, I call it.'

They stood awkwardly for a moment and then Betty moved her feet as if preparing to go. Bob tried frantically to think of something to say, to keep her there, talking to him. He looked at her brown hair, shining in the wintry sun, at her clear skin and sparkling hazel eyes. If only she was my girl, he thought miserably, and wondered what it was she saw in Ginger Philpotts.

'Our Gladys says you're going in the Land Army,' he said, and Betty nodded vigorously.

'That's right – soon as they'll have me. Mum and Dad don't like it much but I told them, this is something you *can't* stop me doing. Not when there's a war on. I'm looking forward to it –being in the open air, working with the animals and that.'

'Well, I think it's a good idea,' Bob said, and she looked at him in surprise.

'Do you? Graham doesn't! He thinks I'll get off with some handsome young farmer.'

'He ought to trust you,' Bob said warmly. 'He ought to be *glad* you're doing something for the war. He ought to be pleased you're doing something you'll enjoy.'

Betty looked at him again. Her face softened and she put out a hand and touched his arm.

'Thanks, Bob. Thanks for saying that.' She hesitated and then said quietly, 'You know, if you'd asked me to go out with you before we'd met Graham that day – I would've done. I've always liked you, Bob.'

He stared at her, remembering the day he and Graham had walked down Queen Street and met Betty eating fish and chips from newspaper. He'd seen her then as if for the first time – bright-eyed, laughing, attractive, a girl he'd be proud to be seen out with. Before that, she'd just been good old Bet, a sport who didn't mind being wicket-keeper or goalie in the street games, who'd climb trees and fish for crabs without fussing about her clothes, who could use her fists as well as any boy and wouldn't go crying home to her mother if she got hurt.

Trust me to leave it too late, he thought bitterly.

'I wish I had asked you out,' he said. 'I think a lot of you too, Bet. And if – well, if things don't work out – you know, with you and Graham – well, I'm always here. At least, I s'pose I *won't* be here, not once I've gone away, but – oh, you know what I mean.' He floundered to a stop and Betty laughed and squeezed his arm.

'I know what you mean, Bob. Thanks. I'll remember.' She tilted her head to one side and gave him a saucy grin that turned his heart over. 'And there's no reason why you shouldn't write to me once in a while, is there? Let me know how you are and all that. After all, we're friends, aren't we? There's no reason why we shouldn't.'

Bob thought Graham Philpotts would think there was every

252

reason why they shouldn't, but he didn't say so. That was for Betty to decide. He nodded eagerly.

'I'll write to you every week. And you'll write back?'

She smiled. 'Course I will. That's what friends are for.' Then she flicked back her curls, gave him another heart-stopping smile and dropped her hand from his arm. 'Well, I've got to be going now, Bob. Have a smashing Christmas. And don't go away without saying goodbye.'

'I won't.' He watched her flit away up the street. His arm burned from the touch of her fingers. His mind went over everything she had just said, every expression of her face, every movement of her body.

I've always liked you, Bob . . . If you'd asked me to go out with you, I would've done . . . I've always liked you, Bob . . . Write to me . . . Don't go away without saying goodbye . . . I've always liked you . . .'

He went back into number 13, forgetting why he had gone out in the first place, and sat for half an hour in his father's armchair, gazing at the photograph he always carried of Betty Chapman.

The Budds and Chapmans were in celebratory mood. Jess and Frank were thankful to be together again, the whole family under one roof. And although Colin was still down in the South Atlantic on the *Exeter*, he was safe and had written long letters home. Not about the Battle of the River Plate, or the *Graf Spee*, for that would have been crossed out by the censor, but about the unexpected summer holiday he was having on the islands, about soft blue skies, rolling moorland and penguins.

'To absent friends,' Ted said, holding up his glass of sherry at Christmas dinner. 'To absent friends, and especially our Colin.'

Everyone joined in. The whole family was there, including Arthur and Mary, Jess and Annie's parents, and all raised their glasses – even Frank was willing to break his rule and have a glass of sherry at Christmas – and responded to Ted's toast of 'absent friends'. And Frank thought gratefully how good it was to have Jess and the children at home again, and the house turned back into a home.

'And the toast to the engaged couple,' Ted said.

All eyes turned to Olive and Derek. Olive went pink and giggled, looking at the ring with its tiny diamond that flashed on her finger. Derek cleared his throat and grinned sheepishly. It wasn't really what they'd wanted – he'd have liked to be married to Olive by now – but it was all Ted would agree to, so they had to make the best of it. And surely he'd let them get married at Easter, if Derek was home again then.

Betty glanced down at her own hands. Graham had given her a ring too, a little gold one with her initial engraved on it, which she was wearing on her right hand. She'd swap it to her left hand as soon as she was on her own with him. But he wasn't even here at the moment – he was over in Gosport with his own family. Unless you were properly engaged, that was what you were expected to do.

Ted hadn't approved of Graham giving Betty a ring, but as Annie had pointed out, there wasn't much you could do about it. It wasn't a proper engagement ring – though she had a pretty good idea what Betty meant to do with it – and if Graham went away the whole thing would probably blow over and no harm done.

'Anyway, our Betty will be off on her own before long,' she said. 'We're not going to be able to keep an eye on her once she's on that farm.'

'I should hope the farmer would do that,' Ted said. 'He'll be responsible for her, after all. She's under age.'

'I daresay they'll look after her,' Annie said, hoping it was true. 'Anyway, that'd be one good thing about letting her get engaged – she wouldn't be wanting to go off with anyone else. Like our Olive.'

Watching the pair of them now, she decided that they'd done the right thing. Olive certainly had no eyes for anyone but Derek, and he was like a dog with two tails, sitting back in his chair with his arm possessively along the back of hers. And there was no chance of their getting married too soon – he'd be off before long and Ted had made it clear there was to be no talk of weddings until the war was over. And not then, if it was very quick.

'Twenty-one's old enough for that,' he'd said firmly, and with that Olive and Derek had to be satisfied.

Annie looked around the big table. It almost filled the room. They'd had to carry Frank and Jess's extending table up the road and put it at the end of Annie's. She sat at one end and Ted at the other. Jess sat near Annie, to be handy for the kitchen, with Olive beside her. Frank was opposite and had Rose on one side of him and Tim on the other. Derek was next to Olive, with Keith on his left and Betty sat on the other side of Keith, with her grandparents opposite.

'Twelve,' Annie said, dishing out the turkey. 'That's a good number for Christmas dinner. What d'you want, Mum, white meat or dark?'

'White, please.' At seventy-five, Mary still had a healthy appetite but her husband Arthur ate like a bird. He was a thin, fragile man of eighty who seemed to have shrunk over the past few months. He had spent his life in the Army, too old to fight in the last war but had seen action in Africa during the Boer War, and he spent most of his days reading the newspaper and trying to relate his own experiences to what was happening now. He was shaky and walked with two sticks, and he said little but turned his cloudy eyes from one to the other as the family chattered.

'You've got a good table,' Mary said appreciatively, cutting up Arthur's meat for him. 'You'd never think there was shortages, looking at this lot.'

'I was lucky, getting a turkey. I thought I'd have to do with two chickens but I got the last one. And I made my puddings early on, before the shortages really started.'

'The vegetables are all from the garden,' Ted said. 'It's a good thing I lifted them early. It's been so cold, you can't get them out of the ground now. We're going to lose a lot if it doesn't ease up soon.'

'I don't reckon it's going to ease up,' Frank said. 'I don't think we've seen the worst of it yet.'

'It's a nuisance not getting any weather forecasts.' Annie finished dishing out the turkey and took the big meat plate back to the kitchen. 'I don't really see what harm there'd have been in it, do you? I mean, the Germans must have their own weather forecasters. They don't rely on ours.'

'It might help them to know what we're expecting, though,' Derek said. 'And where the bad weather is. I mean, if they know we've got bad power cuts or the telephone lines are down, they'd know where to hit us. That's why it's not allowed to be reported.'

'Well, they haven't started hitting us at all yet,' Jess remarked.

255

'All this time and nothing's happened. Not here, anyway.' She looked at Frank.

They were still discussing whether or not she should return to the country after Christmas. Jess badly wanted to stay at home and Frank just as badly wanted her there, but he was still afraid of the threatened air raids. Just because they hadn't happened yet, didn't mean they weren't going to. We were making aircraft as fast as we could, weren't we, at Airspeed and the Spitfire factory near Southampton? Well, so were the Germans. It stood to reason. And one day – one day soon, if he was any judge – all hell was going to break loose.

But he wasn't going to start that argument again, not at Christmas dinner with all the kids listening in.

'Let's forget the war for a day or two,' he said, helping himself to roast potatoes. 'It's Christmas. After dinner I want a walk out to the shore.'

'Can we play some games?' Tim asked. 'We always play games at Christmas.'

'We'll play games after tea.' Traditionally, Christmas Day tea was salad and tinned salmon with trifle and fruit salad and small fancy cakes made by Olive, who was turning into what Annie called a 'handy little cook'. Rose had spent Christmas Eve helping her ice them. There was a large Christmas cake too, but nobody ever wanted it on Christmas Day, they were all too full.

A rather newer tradition was the King's Christmas broadcast on the wireless. George VI had been King for only a couple of years, after his brother's abdication, and had broadcast his message for the first time a year ago. His voice was slow and hesitant, for as everyone knew he suffered from a bad stammer, but in spite of that – perhaps, in a way, because of it – his short talk was moving, and brought tears to the eyes of most of his listeners.

'That was lovely,' Annie said, wiping her eyes. 'And I liked that bit of poetry he read out. The man who stood at the gate of the year – it's just right for now, isn't it?'

'Yes,' Ted said. 'He's a good man, King George, and he's been handed a packet of trouble by that brother of his. At least he knows what his duty is, and he'll do it.'

'I 'ad a lot of time for the Duke of Windsor,' Arthur said, in his piping voice, speaking up suddenly so that they all stopped and looked at him. 'He 'ad the common touch. Look 'ow 'e went round the mines that time and said something 'ad got to be done about the way working people lived. None of the others ever did that.'

'And did he ever do anything?' Ted demanded. 'No – he was too busy running around with that Mrs Simpson, who was no better than she should be. If you want my opinion—'

'We don't,' Annie cut in. 'We just want to enjoy Christmas.' She softened her tone a little. 'Don't get into politics now, Ted. Let's just forget all that and have a nice day with the family all together.'

The whole family, except for Arthur and Mary, went out in the afternoon. Rose pushed the pram with Maureen now sitting up inside, her face almost obliterated by a woolly bonnet that Annie had made. Her eyes turned solemnly from one face to another.

'She doesn't know us now,' Annie said. 'We're all strangers to her – her own family.' She took her sister's arm. 'I'm glad you came home for Christmas, Jess.'

'So am I. They're very nice at Bridge End, but it's not the same as being with your own, is it? Specially not at Christmas. And they needed the room too, they've got their own families coming.'

Tim and Keith ran on ahead, wearing the new scarves Jess had knitted them. They were chattering about the games that would be played later in the evening.

'Family Coach,' Keith said. 'Dad'll tell the story and we'll all be different parts. I'll be the lamps.'

'Yes, and I'll be the whip. And whenever he says our bit we have to stand up and turn round. I bet our Rose will want to be the horse, she always does.'

'Land, Sea and Air,' Keith said. 'We'll play that too. I can think of lots of things for land and air but there's only fish or whales in the sea.'

'You have to think of different fish. Cod. Herrings. Sprats.'

'Crabs,' Keith said. 'Lobsters, shrimps, sticklebacks.'

'Sticklebacks aren't in the sea. They're in the rivers.'

'It's the same thing. It's water.'

'It has to be sea, dopey.'

'It doesn't. Does it, Mum?' he appealed as the others caught up with them. 'If someone throws the ball of paper at you and shouts 'sea' you can say things that live in rivers, can't you?'

257

'So long as you get it in before they get to ten, yes.'

'But it's not sea,' Tim expostulated. 'Sticklebacks live in rivers. Reg showed us some.'

'Well, we'll say "water" then,' Jess said. They had arrived at the shore and she stood gazing out across Langstone Harbour. Rose had joined her brothers now and they were poking about amongst some rocks. Olive and Derek were lagging behind and Annie knew they were hoping to find some corner out of sight for a while. Betty was walking alone, her hands in her coat pockets, brooding about Graham.

'It looks just the same as always,' Jess remarked. 'So peaceful. You can't believe there's a war on, can you, Annie?'

'You can if you go down to Portsmouth Harbour,' her sister replied. 'There's plenty of activity there. Ships going in and out. The Yard working at full stretch. Ted says the ferry's loaded with men, from six in the morning till nine at night.'

'I know. Frank's worn out with overtime.' Jess stood silent for a moment. The air was bitterly cold and the shore, left muddy on an outgoing tide, was already covered with a thin film of ice. The sky was lowering, with heavy, yellow-bellied clouds like bruises. 'I don't want to go back to the country, Annie.'

Annie turned and looked at her. 'What does Frank say?'

'Oh, we've talked about it – but he thinks I ought to go.' Jess turned and spoke passionately. 'Annie, I hate thinking of him all by himself. It's not right, us being apart. I'm his wife – I ought to be here with him.'

'But what about the children?'

'Oh, I agree with him there. We've got to keep them as safe as we can.' She looked at the pram. Maureen had slipped down now and fallen asleep, and she bent forwards to tuck the covers in more securely about her. 'The baby'd have to stay with me, of course. But my place is with Frank.'

Annie nodded. She agreed with her sister that a woman's place was in her own home, by her man's side. It had never seemed right, Jess being away. But it would be hard to make up her mind to being away from the rest of the children.

'This war,' she said, looking out over the gleaming mud, at the little boats that lay keeled over waiting for the next tide, at the

258

sullen, threatening clouds. 'This war . . . It's getting us all down, Jess. And it hasn't even got started yet – not here.' She shivered suddenly. 'It's too cold to stand about, Jess. Let's get home and have a cup of tea.'

They called the children and then turned and walked back along the path. After a few minutes, Jess said quietly, 'Frank was right. We shouldn't be thinking about the war today. It's Christmas. We ought to be making it a really good one. The best we can.'

Annie nodded. There was no need to say why. Everyone she knew had the same idea in mind. To make the Christmas of 1939 the best they could, for who knew what the next year might bring . . . ?

The Woddis sisters were regular churchgoers, and Christmas Day was no exception. Holy Communion at eight, matins at eleven. They would be at both services, sitting upright in their pew, dressed in their best navy-blue coats and hats, with gloves on and their own prayer-books.

They did not take Alan and Wendy with them. They did not take Alan and Wendy anywhere. That was not, as they saw it, their job. They had been compelled to take in two evacuees, to give them beds and feed them, but they were under no obligation to do any more than that. They would have been startled and indignant to be told anything different.

Their main concern, having done their duty by their country, was to ensure that their lives were disrupted as little as possible and that their home remained undamaged by the two children. At seven forty-five, therefore, they donned their navy-blue coats and hats and left Wendy and Alan in bed, with strict instructions that they were not to get up until the sisters returned.

For a short while, there was silence. Then Alan said in a small voice, 'Didn't Father Christmas know we were here?'

'I don't think he did,' Wendy said miserably.

'We didn't write any notes.' They had asked a week ago if they could write their letters to Father Christmas and put them up the chimney but had been refused outright. That was the way fires started! In any case, it was all nonsense, there was no such person as Father Christmas and they were old enough to stop believing in

259

such fairy-tales. Any presents that might come would arrive through the post, just like any other parcel.

Alan did not believe this. Since hearing Miss Eleanor tell a friend that he was a wicked little fiend and not even house-trained, he had not believed a word either of them said. He knew perfectly well that they had told him these lies because they didn't want him to have any presents. Perhaps they had even written their own note, telling Father Christmas that the children weren't here.

'Let's go down and see if he's been,' he suggested. 'He might have done. They haven't been in the sitting-room yet.'

Wendy considered this. She didn't want to disobey the sisters' instructions, since she too, by now, had experienced the cupboard, but on the other hand, if Alan was right . . . There could be presents down there now. Would the sisters give them their presents if they came home and found them first? Or would they keep them for themselves? Wendy couldn't believe that they would really want the Rupert Bear annual she always received, or the two new aprons, or the car that Alan was hoping for, but you never knew.

'All right,' she said, getting out of bed. 'But we'd better be quick.'

They crept downstairs, half afraid that the sisters had not gone out after all but were lying in wait in case their instructions were disobeyed, but the house was empty. They went into the sitting-room and looked at the fireplace.

It had been laid yesterday morning by Mrs Cherry and left unlit, so that it did not need to be cleaned and relit this morning. It was undisturbed, each piece of wood and coal still in place. Clearly, no one had come down there during the night.

They went into the dining-room. It was icily cold and again the fireplace was undisturbed.

'He didn't come,' Alan said sadly.

Wendy stood thoughtful for a moment. She was remembering past Christmases, when she had been given presents by her parents and had always done some little task in return, as her gift to them. Perhaps she and Alan should do something now for Miss Eleanor and Miss Millicent. You couldn't expect presents if you didn't do something for other people first, her mother had always said.

'I'll go and lay the breakfast table.' She looked around for something Alan could do. 'You could polish the sideboard.' At least it was something they'd done before, something he knew how to do. And there had been so much fuss about it last time, surely they couldn't help being pleased.

They went into the kitchen. It was warmer in here, for there was a stove that burned wood and coal, which the Woddis sisters were keeping alight most of the time in the cold weather. Wendy started to get things out of the cupboards and Alan looked around for the polish.

He found the cloth but no tin of polish. He went into the pantry and looked on the shelf where it was normally kept. There was a mixture of tins, for the sisters had a brother in America who had started to send parcels of food and anything else he thought might be useful. Alan had been there when the last one was opened and thought he could remember a tin of polish being amongst the items unpacked.

Perhaps this was it. It was quite a struggle to open it but he managed it and looked inside. It was yellow and waxy so he carried it into the dining-room and began work.

When the sisters came home, half an hour later, Wendy had the table laid and the kettle almost boiling. She waited nervously, hoping she had done everything right. She wondered how Alan was getting on; she had heard no sound from the dining-room.

The front door opened and a blast of bitter air blew through the passage to the kitchen. Wendy heard the two sisters come in discussing the service.

'. . . and did you see her hat, Millicent? Quite unsuitable for Holy Communion, in my opinion. Why, she looked as if she were going to a wedding. But then she never has had any sense of what's correct.'

'And can you be surprised, with a mother like hers? They say she was nothing but a common housemaid.'

'Common is the word!' Miss Eleanor paused by the hallstand. Wendy, peeping through the kitchen door, saw her give her navy hat with its little veil one last admiring glance before removing it. She turned her head and gasped.

'What is it, Eleanor?' Miss Millicent, also in the middle of taking off her hat and coat, stopped and gave her sister an enquiring glance. 'Is something the matter?'

'Something the matter?' Miss Eleanor was looking through the half-open door of the dining-room. She walked through, and Wendy heard an exclamation.

'What on earth do you think you're doing? Oh – you naughty, *naughty* little boy!'

'What is it? What have they done now?' Miss Millicent followed her quickly and Wendy, trembling with fear and dismay, came behind.

'Look at him. Just *look* at him.' Miss Eleanor was standing in the middle of the dining-room, her hands on her hips, quivering with anger. Her face was white, her cheekbones burning red. 'Oh, whatever will they do next? What will they do next?'

'What? What's he done?' There was a greedy note in Miss Millicent's voice as she pushed into the room, almost as if she gained some twisted kind of pleasure out of Alan's misdoings. Or perhaps out of what followed them. 'Let me see . . . Oh-h-h. You little *beast* . . .' She sounded almost awed.

Wendy peered through the door. The sisters were standing just inside and she had to hold Miss Millicent's skirt back to see past. For a moment or two she stared, puzzled. What was it that Alan was doing? Why were they so angry?

Alan was kneeling by the sideboard. He had a cloth in one hand and a flat, round tin in the other. He seemed to be frozen in the act of rubbing yellow grease from the tin into the ornate carving of the sideboard drawers. Much of the wood was already smeared and the tin was half empty. He was looking up at Miss Eleanor with large, frightened eyes.

'You . . . horrible . . . little . . . boy,' Miss Eleanor said, speaking very slowly. 'You . . . nasty . . . little . . . wretch. You little demon.'

'*Butter!*' Miss Millicent said, snatching the tin out of his hand. 'Our best butter, that Howard sent us. Nearly all gone – '

'Never mind that,' Miss Eleanor snapped. 'Look what he's done with it!! Oh, the sideboard will never be the same again. We'll never get it all out, never.'

Alan's terrified eyes went to his sister and Wendy stepped forward, trembling.

'It's not his fault,' she said. 'He thought it was polish. He wanted to – '

'Thought it was polish? Don't talk nonsense! Look on the lid, it says *Butter*, as plain as plain.'

'But he can't read – '

'Then it's time he learned to. And it's time he learned to keep his hands off other people's property.' Miss Eleanor lunged forward and grabbed Alan by the arm, jerking him roughly to his feet. 'And if his own parents won't teach him, I will! You'll spend the rest of the morning in the cupboard, my lad, and maybe that will give you time to think things over.'

'But that's not fair!' Wendy exclaimed. 'He didn't mean to do any harm. He was only trying to help. He wanted to do it for Christmas – '

'Stop it at once!' Both sisters turned on her. 'Don't you dare answer back. Trying to help, indeed! Trying to make a mess, that's what he was doing, it's the only thing he knows how to do. He's a naughty little boy and he has to be taught a lesson.'

'But he's not a naughty boy, he's *not*!' Wendy felt rage well up inside her. She stared at the two women. 'He's always been a good boy – everyone says so. It's only since we've been here – he doesn't know what you want – he tries his best – and we wanted to do something for you for Christmas, so I laid the table and Alan polished the sideboard, how was he to know it was butter and not polish, he can't read, it was on the same shelf in the pantry, it's not his fault!' She ran out of breath. The sisters stood staring at her. 'It's *your* fault he gets into trouble, *yours*!' she continued, her voice rising to a shout. 'He wets the bed because he's frightened of you and he's frightened of that horrible cupboard and the spiders in it, and he's frightened of the dark. And you're horrible to him. You're horrible to both of us, you don't give us any nice food or let us sit by the fire or anything and now we haven't even got any Christmas presents.' She burst into tears and stamped her foot.

'Well!' Miss Eleanor gasped. She stared at the furious little girl for a full minute. 'Well! You insolent little hussy. I think you'd better go into the cupboard too, along with your brother.'

Wendy glowered at her.

'I won't!'

'You certainly will.'

'I won't!' Overcome with her fury, she pushed Miss Millicent aside and marched into the room. She grabbed Alan's arm and pulled him towards the door. 'Come on, Alan. We won't stay here any longer. We'll run away. We'll go home – we can walk all the way, even if it takes us weeks – and we'll tell Mummy and Daddy what these horrible people have done to us.'

The Woddis sisters were transfixed. They stared as the two children ran through the door. And then they came to life, gave each other a swift glance and made for the passage, where Wendy was already turning the knob on the front door.

'Don't let her! Don't let her get out.' Miss Eleanor thrust past her sister and rushed to grab them. 'How dare you! How *dare* you try to run away. Showing us up like that – what would people think?' She hustled the crying children back along the passage. Miss Millicent had already opened the cupboard door. Together, they thrust the squirming, fighting bodies in and slammed the door against them. Miss Eleanor locked it and then stood with a hand to her side, breathing hard.

'Well!' she said. 'And I think that's the best place for them today, don't you, Millicent? Now let's go and have our breakfast. And by the time that's over it will be almost time for matins. Really! Such behaviour! On Christmas Day too, of all days.'

The two children, crouching in the dark and stuffy space amongst the coats and brooms and step-ladders, heard their voices fade as they went towards the kitchen. The last they heard, before the door closed, was Miss Millicent remarking on the kitchen table, laid for breakfast.

'Look at this, Eleanor. As if we'd eat breakfast in the kitchen on Christmas Day. Can you believe that they didn't even notice the dining-table was already laid?'

'It's just another piece of insolence,' came Miss Eleanor's voice. And then the door closed and they heard no more.

Alan and Wendy sank down, trying to find a space to sit on the cluttered floor. They knew from bitter experience that it was no use making a noise. They would be left here for hours, perhaps most of the day. And when they were let out, it would be only to go to the lavatory and then back to their bedroom, with a plate of scraps for their Christmas dinner.

Father Christmas had indeed forgotten them. And so, it seemed, had their mother and father. And as they clung together in that dark and foetid little space under the stairs, it was as if the whole world had forgotten that it contained two children called Alan and Wendy.

The Budds and Chapmans kept their party going until two in the morning. They always did this, staying up until they could barely keep their eyelids propped open. After their hearty tea they washed up and then played games. Some of these were noisy, hilarious ones, such as the Jelly Race, in which Annie provided a plate of jelly, kept back from supper, and a knife and fork. With the plate was a large pair of thick fur gloves, donated by Grandma, Grandpa's cap and Tim's new scarf. The racers had to pass a dice to each other and the first one to throw a six ran forwards, donned gloves, scarf and cap and proceeded to try to cut and eat the jelly with the knife and fork. As often as not, they had barely got the clothes on when another six had been thrown and the scarf was being unceremoniously unwound and the gloves and cap dragged off. Sometimes there were three or even four people milling about by the plate of jelly, tugging at each other's clothes and howling with laughter while the rest screamed, 'Two! Four! Five! One! *Si-i-ix!*'

Other games were more restful. Pencil and paper games, such as Consequences or Telegrams. For 'Alibis', two people were sent out to fabricate some story of how they had spent a day together and then brought in one at a time to be interrogated. 'Scissors' involved the whole group lounging back in chairs passing a pair of scissors to each other and saying 'I pass these scissors to you closed' or 'I pass these scissors to you open'. This was a game that could only be played once, or with people who had not come across it before, for once you knew the secret there was no fun in it any more.

To the boys' delight, they were allowed a game of Murder, with the lights switched off and a bloodcurdling scream from the victim, and then it was time for Family Coach, with Frank telling the story of a disastrous family picnic and everyone else taking the part of some accessory. And then Annie and Jess went out to 'get a bit of supper ready', returning with trays laden with sausage rolls, cheese and biscuits and Marmite sandwiches, and everyone fell to once more.

After that, refreshed, they were all supplied with drinks of lemonade or squash, with beer for the men (except Frank), and settled down for a sing-song. The room resounded to the strains of 'Tavern in the Town', 'Roaming in the Gloaming', and 'Hello, Hello, Who's your Lady Friend?' They went from old songs – 'Daisy, Daisy', 'Two Little Girls in Blue' – to the more modern songs from shows by Noel Coward or Ivor Novello, and finished up with songs that had been popular during the Great War – 'Tipperary', 'Pack Up Your Troubles in Your Old Kitbag', and 'There's a Long, Long Trail A-winding'.

There was a sadness in their voices as they sang these. Jess and Annie, who could remember when men had been forced to leave their homes then as soldiers and sailors, found tears in their eyes. And they both noticed Olive's face as Derek sang 'If You Were the Only Girl in the World', looking at her as if she were indeed the only girl in his world, and her sudden movement to cover her eyes when they began on 'Keep the Home Fires Burning'.

'I reckon that girl's had just about enough,' Jess murmured under cover of the words. 'Let's find something more cheerful, Annie.'

'. . . till the boys come home,' they sang, and there was a muffled sob from the corner where Olive was sitting.

Jess jumped to her feet. 'Let's have something a bit more jolly. *Old Macdonald had a farm* – '

'*Ee-I-ee-I-oh,*' they roared back.

'*And on that farm he had some pigs* – '

'*Eei-ee-i-oh!*'

'*With an oink-oink here* – '

'*An oink-oink there* – '

'*Here an oink* – '

'*There an oink* – '

'*Everywhere an oink-oink* – '

'*Old Macdonald had a farm* – '

'*Ee-i-ee-i-oh!*'

They went through the entire farmyard, including chickens, ducks, turkeys, cows, sheep and (Tim's contribution) elephants, by which time Olive had dried her tears and was smiling again, though a little tremulously. The last verse finished with a trumpeting that could surely have been heard at the top of September Street, if every other house in the row hadn't been making exactly the same kind of noise.

'All right,' Annie said, 'and now let's have some nice carols to finish off with.'

Jess sat down again, breathless, and Keith, who had been recently discovered to possess a soprano voice, began to sing 'Once in Royal David's City'. His voice rose above the others and one by one they fell silent, listening to the sweet young tones. Faces grew abstracted and eyes looked at the carpet or into the fire. Olive's eyes filled with tears again and Jess felt for Frank's hand. He squeezed her fingers.

'I'm not going back,' she whispered to him as the carol came to an end and the others applauded Keith. 'I'm not leaving you again.'

'We'll talk about it tomorrow,' he said. 'Tomorrow. That'll be the best time.'

After that, nobody seemed to want to sing any more. They lolled in chairs or on the floor, leaning back against people's knees. Keith's eyes were closing and Rose was asleep with her head on Ted's knee. Olive and Derek were on the sofa, their hands entwined. Frank and Ted had the two big armchairs and Annie and Jess the smaller ones. Arthur and Mary had gone home soon after supper.

'Well, I think we'd better be getting off home,' Jess said with a yawn. 'It's been a good Christmas, Annie.'

'Well, we had to make it as good as we could, didn't we?' Annie said. 'We don't know where we'll all be this time next year. Our Colin still at sea, likely as not – Betty down on the farm, if she can stand the hard work. And the rest of us – '

'Still here holding the fort,' Frank said stoutly. 'It'll take more than a few bombs to bring us to our knees, Annie. We're not going to let old Hitler beat us, are we?'

'No!' they all shouted, and broke into laughter. And with that and several reminders that next day they would all gather again for tea at number 14, the Budds found their coats and wrapped themselves up for the short walk home.

Jess looked up at the sky. The surly clouds had drifted apart a little and stars were visible between them. With no city lights to dim them they looked large and bright, and so close that she felt she needed only to reach out her fingertips to be able to touch them.

'It's freezing cold,' she said, holding the baby close against her. She was wrapped in blankets and fast asleep. Jess looked down from the stars at her small, sleeping face.

'Your first Christmas,' she said softly. 'Well, my love, it was as good as we could make it. But what'll the next one be like? And what will you remember about Christmas when you grow up?'

Two days after Boxing Day there was a slight lessening of the bitter temperatures. And as if they had been waiting for it, the great clouds sighed and opened their bruised bellies to let the snow fall.

It came softly at first, then gathered power as the rising wind whipped the whirling snowflakes into a maelstrom of icy shards, their feathery softness sharpened like needles by the storm. All day they swirled through the air, coming to rest at last in great pillowy mounds, piled up against walls and fences and turning gardens and allotments into mysterious fairylands. By next morning, the streets were ankle-deep and few vehicles were moving.

Olive was at Derek Harker's house. His parents had gone to Southampton to visit his married sister, and Derek had invited Olive to tea. She went, knowing that her mother and father would have disapproved had they known Derek was alone in the house. But Derek would be going away soon and they had had so little time together lately. What with the blackout and the bitter cold, it was impossible to go out at night, and indoors there just wasn't the chance of any privacy.

'Mind, I'll have to be home by ten,' she said. 'And – you know what we agreed, Derek.'

He nodded. He knew, but there was no harm in hoping, was there? Girls were famous for changing their minds, after all. And in an empty house, with just the two of them and a cosy fire – well, who knew what might happen?

The truth was that both he and Olive were tired of waiting to get married. They knew he was likely to be going away soon, and both were dreading the separation. Each time they parted, it was more difficult to say goodnight, more difficult to give each other that last kiss. They clung together, achingly aware of each other's bodies, miserably conscious that this might be the last time, that Derek could be called up at a moment's notice. And each time, Olive felt her resolution ebb a little more. Why not? she thought recklessly. Why shouldn't we love each other properly? It'd be Dad's fault if anything happened – he should've let us get married.

But she had never quite dared to say such things to Derek. Instead, she buried her face against his shoulder and held him tightly, unaware of the almost intolerable frustration this was causing him.

Derek, facing not only separation but a total disruption of his life, was almost desperate. To him, the future was like a deep black abyss, an almost unimaginable chaos of tumult, of fear, of killing and being killed. He thought of all he had ever heard about war and especially about the Great War of 1914–18. The war to end all wars, they had called it – yet here they were, only twenty years later, starting the whole thing over again, with worse to come. And he and all the other young men like him were expected to throw up their whole lives, toss aside all they'd planned and give themselves up for a cause they barely understood. All right, so Hitler was marching across Europe, trampling over everyone and everything in his path, but who had allowed him to get into that position to start with? Politicians, that was who – old men who'd had their day. Wasn't it up to them to put right the wrongs that had been done, without involving people like him and Olive – people who were just starting their lives and had a right to live them as they chose?

Derek's thoughts were bitter. If he had known it was possible, he would have refused to serve. But he had heard about the 'conchies' of the Great War, and knew what had been done to them. Strapped to the wheels of gun carriages, forced into labour, even shot . . . He knew he did not have the courage to face such things and he dared not ask whether it would be the same again. They wanted people to fight. There would be no sympathy for those who thought it was no way to run the world.

His frustration, his bitterness and his fears found their outlet in his feelings for Olive. He lived now for the times when they would be together, when he could hold her in his arms and feel safe. He lived for her touch, her kisses, and he yearned for her loving. He knew that he could not go away without having at least once known what it was to lie in her arms, to feel the ecstasy of making her his. And he knew that Olive longed for it too.

Tonight, with his parents out for the evening and unlikely to return unexpectedly, might be their only chance.

He made his preparations carefully. Plenty of coal and wood in, and the fire alight early so as to warm the room. The Christmas decorations were still up and a few cards stood on the mantelpiece. There was a plate of sandwiches and some Christmas cake for tea and, for later on, some sherry or port and an unopened bottle of cider. He wondered if Olive had ever drunk gin, and put that out too with some orange squash. He brought down his mother's bedside lamp and set it on a low table, then turned out the main light. It made the room look quite different. Then he moved the settee in front of the fire, found some Glenn Miller records to put on the gramophone and checked that there was a packet of fresh needles.

Olive arrived, rather shy and nervous at finding herself alone with Derek in his parents' house. She stamped snow off her boots and came in, taking off her headscarf and shaking out her hair. They looked at each other, remembering the last time they had been alone here, remembering how close they'd come to losing control. What was going to happen tonight?

Olive closed the front door.

'My, it's wild out there!' Her eyes took in the room and she giggled. 'Goodness, you have made it look cosy!'

'Well, we don't often get the chance of an evening on our own.' He helped her off with her coat and kept his hands on her shoulders. 'I thought we'd make the most of it.' He dropped his head and nuzzled the back of her neck.

Olive quivered a little, then moved away. 'And just what d'you mean by that, Derek Harker? You know what you promised.'

'I meant it, Livvy. I won't do anything you don't want me to.' He pulled her into his arms again, hard enough to squeeze the breath out of her. 'But I'm sure you want me to give you a kiss!'

'Derek! *Derek!*' Laughing and protesting, she allowed herself to be kissed and then slid her arms round his neck, winding her fingers in his hair. 'Oh, Derek, it *is* nice to be on our own.'

'So let's enjoy it.' He led her to the settee. The fire was blazing. 'You sit there and I'll pour you a cup of tea. There's plenty to eat, look – I made the sandwiches myself. Well, I couldn't ask Mum to do it, could I? She'd have started to ask awkward questions.'

'Doesn't she know I'm coming then?'

'Does your mum know you're here with me, on our own?'

Olive blushed. 'No. Well, actually she doesn't know I'm here. She thinks I'm over at Iris Bentley's. I thought – well, I thought she might hear your mum and dad weren't here, and since she never actually asked – '

'You didn't tell her. And mine never asked either.' He sat down beside her. 'Don't let's waste time talking about them, Livvy. Let's just think about ourselves tonight. Pretend – let's pretend we're married.'

'Derek – '

'I don't mean that. I mean, just sitting here, looking at the fire and having our tea. Pretend it's our house and we've been married – oh, two or three years. Pretend we've got kids asleep upstairs.' He grinned and Olive blushed again.

'Derek! The things you say.'

'Well, what's wrong with that?' He took a sandwich. 'People do have kids when they get married. We will.'

'Yes, but not yet.' Olive sipped her tea. 'We're not married yet.'

'Nor don't know when we will be,' he said. 'Livvy, can't we get round your dad? I'll be going away soon. We don't know when we're going to be together again.'

'I know.' She looked miserably down at her hands, at the little engagement ring. 'But when I said I'd heard of lots of girls getting married before their boys went off, he said it was just a craze and they'd be sorry for it later. Like he did before. So I knew it'd be no use keeping on about it.'

'But we can't just leave it like that!' Derek took her empty plate and put it on the table. He put his arm round her and cuddled her against him. 'Livvy, it takes time to get married. You can't just walk in and out like buying a pound of sausages. You have to – to

271

give notice of some sort. It takes nearly a month.' He stared at her. 'We've probably left it too late already.'

Olive began to cry.

'Oh, Derek'! What are we going to do?'

Derek drew her head down on to his shoulder. He rested his cheek on her hair. If only Olive would agree to let him love her properly. It wouldn't be so bad, not being married, if she'd do that. After all, what difference would marriage actually make to them just now? They wouldn't have anywhere to live, they'd have to stay with either her parents or his – hers, he supposed, since she was the one being left behind. He'd be able to stay with her when he was on leave, all open and above board, that was true – but if she'd just let him love her as he wanted to, it wouldn't really matter that they had to wait. They'd belong to each other and that was what he really wanted. To go away knowing that his love for Olive was safe, that they'd been everything to each other if only for a little while.

It would be something to remember in the long, dark days that lay ahead.

'Don't worry,' he said. 'We'll think of something.'

They sat by the fire, watching the flames and listening to Glenn Miller. After a while, Derek got up and they cleared away the tea things together. They came back to the fire with a glass of gin and orange each, Olive giggling because she had never drunk it before, and Derek began to kiss her.

'I love you, Livvy,' he murmured, his hands moving gently over her body. They had evolved a pattern of permitted caresses. Derek was now allowed to touch Olive's breasts – even, sometimes, to undo her brassière and slip his hands inside. He could caress her anywhere above the waist, but was not allowed to go below it nor to touch her legs. He could kiss her as much as he liked, though Olive was nervous of him kissing her neck in case he left love bites which her father might see.

'Oh, Livvy,' Derek whispered. He had got her brassière off now, as well as her blouse, and she could feel the warmth of the fire on her skin. She shivered and clung to him, not wanting him to see her breasts, but Derek pulled his head down and kissed them, burying his face in their softness.

Olive gasped. Her arms tightened involuntarily about his

272

shoulders. He was half lying over her now and she felt suddenly frightened and tried to push him away, but her efforts were feeble and she knew she didn't really want him to move. It was nice, feeling him there, feeling his body so hard against hers, feeling his lips on her breasts. She looked down at his head and stroked his hair.

Derek moved his head. He kissed her bare shoulders, then trailed his mouth all the way down to her waist. He nuzzled at the waistband of her skirt and Olive shivered again and tried to pull up his head. It was suddenly heavy, immovable and she glanced frantically at the clock.

'Derek – you mum and dad, they'll be back soon. Derek, please – '

'Not yet,' he murmured, lifting himself to kiss her mouth again. 'They won't be back for a long time yet. Oh, Livvy – '

'They will. It's half-past nine. And I've got to be in by ten, you know I have. Derek – please – you promised – ' She pulled his head, trying to lift it away from her body, but again her arms were treacherously weak. 'Oh, Derek – Derek . . .'

He looked at her. His eyes were dark, the lids heavy. 'Olive, I love you. You know I do. I can't go away without loving you – I can't. And you feel the same, I know, I can tell. Olive, we'll never get another chance – ' But his words were drowned by the sudden shrilling of the telephone.

Derek's house was the only one Olive knew with a telephone. It was needed for business, which was run from the house, but there was an extension indoors as well as in the office. It sounded loud and intrusive in the quiet room and Olive jumped. Derek, more accustomed to it, cursed briefly and went to pick it up.

'Hullo. Yes. Oh, hullo, Dad. What's happened?' He listened for a moment and Olive saw his eyebrows go up. He looked across at her and winked. 'Is it really? Gosh. No, much better not, specially with the blackout. It'd be lethal . . . No, everything's all right here. Yes, I can manage.' He smiled. 'Yes, I'm sure. Don't worry. See you tomorrow then.' He hung up the receiver and his face almost split in a wide, excited grin.

Olive gazed at him. 'Derek? What was that all about?'

'It was Dad,' he said. 'They're stuck over in Southampton. The trains have stopped because of the snow and they can't get home

273

tonight. They're stopping there till morning.' He bounded across to the settee and leapt over the back of it, catching her up in his arms. 'Till *morning*!'

Olive stared at him. She tried to draw away. Panic fluttered like a trapped bird in her breasts. 'Till morning? But – that doesn't make any difference to us.'

'Doesn't it?' He snatched up her jacket and flung it round her shoulders, drawing her into the passage where it was dark. With a quick glance to be sure no light was showing, he pulled open the front door. The wind immediately gusted in their faces, half choking them with snow as if someone had thrown a bucketful directly over them. It caught the door, almost tearing it from its hinges, and ripped through Olive's hair. She felt it lift her skirt and swirl like icy water around her thighs. It struck her naked breasts and she pulled the jacket more tightly about her.

Derek slammed the door again and they stood in the darkness, breathing quickly. Olive could feel him very close. He slid his arms around her, pushing the jacket from her shoulders, and pulled her face round until his lips found hers. She gasped as he ground his body against hers, and felt her own excitement rise and with it, inevitably, her panic.

'Derek! No! I've got to go home – '

'Why? You told me, they don't know you're here.'

'No, but – ' His hands were moving over her body, searching and insistent. 'Derek, please – '

'Please what?' he murmured against her ear. 'Pleast stop? Or please don't stop?' He cradled her breasts in both hands, leaning over to kiss her. 'Olive, this is the only chance we'll ever get – we can't let it go. You can't say no – not now. You can't.'

'They'll expect me back. I've got to be in by ten, you know that.'

'But you can't go out in this weather. You've seen what it's like. They won't expect you to – not in the blackout and everything.' He was holding her close again, moving his body against hers, and she moaned at the feel of it. One hand strayed down her buttocks, slid down her thigh and pulled up her skirt. She felt his fingertips on the bare strip of thigh between stocking-top and knickers. 'They'll think you've stayed with this – what's her name? Iris? Won't they think that? Wouldn't anyone, on a night like this?'

274

Olive was almost past speaking. Her head on Derek's shoulder, she whimpered as his fingers explored further, inserting themselves delicately into her knickers and stroking with the utmost gentleness along the deepest crease of her thigh. Her legs weak, she clung and leaned against him, squirming as he found a sensitivity she had not known existed. When he kissed her, her mouth was slack under his, her lips parted, and she felt her heart jerk and begin to pound rapidly in her breast.

'Stay with me, Livvy,' he muttered against her throat. 'Stay with me tonight. We'll never get another chance like this.'

'Derek – ' She must, she knew, make one last effort. And if this one failed, as she already knew it must, she could make no more. 'Derek – you promised – '

'I promised not to do anything you didn't want me to.' He moved slightly away, but his arm was still about her and his fingers were still stroking, gently, firmly and insistently. 'Tell me you don't want me to, Livvy, and I'll stop.' He kissed her again. 'Tell me you don't want to – and mean it – and I'll stop straight away.'

There was a breathless pause. And Olive knew that it was too late. It had been too late from the moment she had stepped through the door.

'Oh, Derek,' she breathed, and turned her face for his kiss. 'Oh, Derek, love me. Please, please love me . . .'

The year ended almost without comment. Portsmouth was swathed in a blanket of snow, its traffic stilled, its lights dimmed. The New Year celebrations that normally filled the Guildhall Square with revellers were forbidden, the sirens of vessels in the harbour, which would normally have sounded at midnight, were silenced.

'It's as if we're all glad to say goodbye to 1939 but no better pleased to see 1940 instead,' Jess said, getting ready for bed. She and Frank had thought about stopping up and toasting the new year, as they usually did, but it seemed like a bad joke. 'The only good thing that happened to us in 1939 was Maureen,' she said, bending over the cot.

Frank looked at her. She was wearing a nightdress she'd made herself, white with some bits of lace at the neck. It had always been his favourite. He felt his heartbeat quicken.

He slid into bed beside her and slipped his arms around her, cradling her against his shoulder, thinking of the months she had been away, when he had come lonely night after night to this empty bed, cold without Jess's warm body. The past week had been like a honeymoon again, rediscovering each other after their parting.

A honeymoon, he thought with amusement, and us married for thirteen, fourteen years!

'What are you laughing at?' Jess asked, and he turned and smiled at her.

'Us. No, not us – I'm just laughing for happiness. I'm happy that you're staying an extra week. I'm happy that you're going to be here while I'm at work and every evening when I come home. And I'm happy you're going to be in bed at night.'

Jess laughed softly. 'Oh, you! You're like all the other men. You never think of anything else.'

'So I'm normal.' He squeezed her against him. 'And so are you, Jess – thank the Lord. So – why don't we prove it, eh?' He kissed her and his hands and body began the pattern of love-making that was so familiar to them both. Each knew all the places to touch, to caress, to linger over and to savour. Each knew the other's response and when to proceed, when to hold back. And, at the end, each knew just how to bring the other to that soaring, satisfying climax that had reinforced their love so regularly for the past fourteen years.

Afterwards, Frank fell asleep at once. But Jess, in the few moments before she too closed her eyes, lay for a few moments listening to the house breathe.

It seemed so long since her family had been all together under the same roof. In the next room, Tim and Keith lay curled up in the old iron bunks, a web of cotton stretched across the ceiling where they had fixed up the small wooden aeroplanes they had carved with Reg Corner. In the room beneath, Rose lay sleeping in the Put-u-Up. Beside her, baby Maureen slumbered peacefully, one fist crumpled under her chin.

Soon they would be parted again and there would be fresh tears to shed. But for tonight, number 14 April Grove was a family house once more and she felt as though it had wrapped its arms about them all and was keeping them safe.

God keep them safe, she thought as she drifted into her dreams. God keep them all safe, wherever they might be.

CHAPTER TEN

THE WEATHER grew steadily worse. The day after the boys and Rose went back to Bridge End for the start of school, there was a blizzard. The snow blocked roads, stopped traffic and brought down telephone lines. The water in Langstone Harbour froze and people skated on the ice. For three days, no electric trains ran between Portsmouth, London and Brighton. Twice rain fell and froze immediately, coating ground, walls and trees with a glittering layer of ice. The city was in chaos, with almost all services no longer functioning and the roads turning rapidly to ice-rinks.

'It's as bad as 1881,' Arthur told Jess when she went round to make sure her parents were all right. 'My, that was a winter and no mistake! Railways blocked – the trains were just running into mountains of snow and getting stuck in it. There was seven foot of snow in Stubbington Lane, down North End, and a huge drift out at Portscreek. And Hilsea Pond was buried and gone.'

'Well, let's hope this one isn't going to be so bad,' Jess said, looking out of the window, but the sullen clouds seemed to snarl at her and she shivered and turned back. 'How are you managing for coal?'

'Oh, we've got enough so long as we're careful,' her mother said. 'Mind, there's not much about, is there? Some people have run out already, having to use the electric. But that's not much good when there's a power-cut!'

'I hope there's not one tonight,' Arthur observed. 'I want to listen to *ITMA*.'

Jess went back home, pushing Maureen's pram with difficulty

along the slippery streets. She'd been planning to go to the sales at the Landport Drapery Bazaar and McIlroys today with Annie but the snow had stopped the buses and Jess didn't think many people would have managed to get down to Commercial Road anyway. That meant that those who did make it would have got all the best bargains, she reflected.

Well, it couldn't be helped. And it was time now to start Frank's supper. With only the two of them there she'd started cooking in the evening, like Annie did. It meant he came in to a good hot meal and she could pack up his box afterwards so he could take another helping for dinner tomorrow.

Tonight she was making stew with dumplings. She'd managed to get a nice piece of shin and some kidney at the butcher's at the top of the street and it had been simmering on top of the stove all afternoon, along with some onions, carrots and turnips out of the garden. She'd made a bread-and-butter pudding to go with it – not that it had seen much butter, but it would be hot and sweet and filling, and that was what Frank needed.

She was more than ever thankful that she'd decided to stay home for a few extra days and even glad of the bitter weather which was keeping her for longer. Annie had been good to him, but there was no getting away from it, he'd lost weight and he looked tired. Annie's meals weren't enough for a man doing heavy work. Jess didn't think they were enough for Ted either, standing up in all weathers on the bridge of the *Ferry King*, and she knew he sometimes got one of the lads to fetch him a penn'orth of chips or a pasty from the kiosk on the Hard.

Ted looked tired too. He hadn't said much, but he'd let drop a few things and Jess had gathered that he hated taking the ferryboat across the harbour in the blackout. She wasn't surprised. It must be nerve-racking, trying to feel your way across the water with buoys and moored boats floating about, more or less invisible, not to mention other ships going in and out.

'They're telling people to take cod-liver oil to help them see at night,' she said to Frank, reading the *Evenings News* after supper. 'Does it really help, d'you think?'

He shrugged. 'I suppose it might do. Can't do any harm, anyway. It's good for you, isn't it? Prevents colds, so they say.'

278

'Oh yes. I've always given it to the children when they were babies. I heard carrots were good too.'

'What, for babies?'

'No, silly – for helping you to see at night. Oh, look – Anna Neagle's on at the Odeon. In *Nurse Edith Cavell*.'

'My God,' Frank said, 'isn't there enough war without going to see it at the pictures?'

'I suppose so. I just like Anna Neagle.' Jess put down the newspaper and sighed. 'How long d'you think this is going to go on for, Frank?'

'How long's what going on for?' He was engrossed in the *Daily Express*.

'This war. I mean, it's so queer. We were told there'd be bombing right from the start and there hasn't been any at all. What's he waiting for? And there's more and more soldiers going over to France and nothing much seems to be happening there either. The Navy seems to be getting the worst of it so far.'

'They are.' Frank spent his days making or mending for ships. The boiler-shop was like an inferno, with furnaces going full blast day and night, and a never-ceasing racket of metal being hammered, drilled and welded. 'But I'll tell you why there's nothing happening on the ground or in the air, Jess, and you've only got to look out of the window to see it for yourself. It's too bloody cold. I mean, if it's like this here it must be like it over there, mustn't it? Stands to reason. They're just waiting for a thaw, that's all.'

Jess pursed her lips and nodded. It made sense. She remembered another piece of news. 'Derek Harker's gone.'

'Gone? Called up, d'you mean?'

'That's right. He came round to say goodbye to Annie and Ted last night. Olive is in a right old state about it, crying and going on like he's been killed already.' Jess stopped and bit her lip. 'He thinks he's going to France. And Peggy Shaw's in a panic about their Bob now, she thinks he'll be off any minute too.'

'Well,' Frank said, 'I think he probably will. They're getting themselves into position, see. Once the weather starts to get a bit better they'll start. And then we'd all better keep our heads down. And you'd better get back to Bridge End before it starts.'

Jess said nothing. The thought of bombs dropping on

Portsmouth – perhaps on April Grove, on number 14 itself – made her feel sick with fear. But she still wished she could stay with Frank. We ought to be together, she thought miserably. It's not right, being apart like this, for months, perhaps even for years.

Upstairs, the baby began to cry and she got up to go to her. If it wasn't for you, I'd never have gone away at all, she thought, gathering the damp little bundle up in her arms. But you can't be blamed, can you? It's not your fault you were born at such a time. And we wouldn't be without you now.

Sighing, she went back downstairs. Perhaps it had never been easy for women, trying to be all things to all people, keeping the family going, to be both mother and wife. And in war, it was easy for nobody.

As Frank would say, everyone had to make sacrifices.

Olive was crying into her pillow and feeling a different kind of fear.

She had said goodbye to Derek this morning at the builder's yard. He'd come in, wearing his stiff new uniform, and shaken hands all round with the men, and then walked out with her and his father to the gate. They'd stood, the three of them, looking awkwardly at each other.

'You've seen your mother?' John Harker said at last, though it was difficult to see how Derek could have got out of the house without seeing her.

'Yes. She's a bit upset.'

John nodded. 'I'll go in for a bit. Make her a cup of tea.' He glanced at Olive. 'Or maybe you could do that. Women are better together at times like this.'

Olive was biting her lip, fighting back her own tears. She blinked hard and nodded. She would be quite glad not to have to go straight back into the office.

'Well, cheerio then,' Derek said at last, and shook hands with his father. He turned to Olive, 'Bye, love.'

Olive looked up at him. Her mouth was trembling uncontrollably. She wanted to fling her arms around him, hold him tightly against her as she'd done last night, keep him with her by force. She could not believe that he was standing in front of her now, still within touching distance, and that in a few minutes he would turn and walk away. When would she be able to touch him again? When would she see him again? What would she do if he never came back . . . ?

Derek dropped his case and put his arms round her and she clung to him, the tears flowing. For a long moment he held her close, and then he turned her face to his and kissed her on the mouth.

'Keep your pecker up, girl,' he said softly. 'I'll be back.'

'Oh, Derek,' was all she could say. 'Oh, Derek, Derek . . .'

Gently, he unwound her arms from about his neck and bent to give her a last brief kiss. Then he let her go, picked up his case and turned. She reached out both hands but he was already marching firmly away, and she stood there, leaning forward slightly, her hands held out towards him as if begging him to return while the tears streamed unchecked, unnoticed, down her cheeks.

'Go inside, girl,' John Harker said. 'Go and have a cup of tea with the wife. I reckon she'll appreciate it just now.'

That had been their final goodbye, taken in public with most of the men looking on. But as Olive lay in her bed that night, fresh tears soaking her pillow, she was thinking of their real goodbye – the one they had shared last night. And with her grief there mingled a terror that had nothing to do with war.

Since the night of the snowstorm, two days after Christmas, Derek and Olive had taken every opportunity to make love. As Derek said, once they'd started it seemed daft to stop – and he didn't want to stop. Olive didn't either. She spent her days dreaming of the night before and looking forward to the next one. Whenever she remembered the way he'd touched her, the way he'd kissed and caressed her, the way he'd finally come inside her, she felt her stomach tingle, as if someone had passed a tiny, fizzing electrical current through her body. It was a feeling she liked. She called it up as often as she could, by thinking and remembering.

They were never again able to enjoy the luxury of that first night. Olive remembered the warmth of the room, the flickering firelight, the softness of the big settee. Still shaking with nerves, she had allowed Derek to undress her and lain naked before him, the fire casting an apricot glow over her smooth skin. She had watched as he began to pull off his own clothes, then turned her eyes away in embarrassment.

281

'No need to be shy, Livvy,' he said. 'Look. See what an effect you have on me.'

She looked and blushed scarlet as she saw what he meant. 'But surely it's too big!' she said. 'It'll never – '

'Oh yes, it will,' he said with a grin, and stretched himself beside her on the sofa. She gasped as their bodies touched, his chest rough and hairy against her tender breasts, his flat stomach hard against the soft cushion of hers. His thighs were hard too, long and muscular as he twined his legs about hers, and his hands trembled a little as they moved almost reverently over her smooth skin.

He hadn't hurried her. He had taken his time, bringing every part of her to life with his kisses and with his touch. Here, the brush of his fingertips was as gentle as the brush of a feather; there, it was firm and decisive, leaving no doubt as to his confidence. As Olive's fears fell away his touch became more intimate, more demanding, until the pressure of his fingers had her twisting and crying out in his arms. Almost, she wanted him to stop. It was unbearable, it was too much, she couldn't go on feeling like this, she would be driven crazy . . . But Derek continued, his own breathing quickening as he murmured against her ear and held her close with his other arm.

'Livvy . . . Livvy, my sweet girl, you're lovely, you're beautiful . . . oh, Livvy, I've wanted you so much. I want you to be mine, mine . . . I want to go away knowing you're mine. Mine. Mine.' He was rearing above her now, thrusting into her with an urgency he could not hold back. Olive lay flat, staring up at him, but his head was flung back and he saw her no longer. What did he see? What did he feel? Her wild thoughts careered and tumbled through her mind as she held his shoulders and braced herself. He was pushing hard now, hard . . . it was hurting, hurting, hurting . . . and then there was a small tearing sensation, a sudden pain and a feeling of being given something she had wanted, needed always, and never ever understood the wanting.

Derek quivered and seemed to regain control. He looked down at her and she saw the darkness of his eyes. His face was almost stern, taut with emotion, and she reached up tentatively to touch his cheek. He leaned down and kissed her, and with the touch passion flared again, leaping through them so that they both gasped and clung to each other. Olive felt his tongue on her lips and in her

282

mouth, and her mind reeled. She clutched his shoulders, lifted herself towards him and twined her legs about his body. And she felt Derek's stillness break in a fury of desire, a desire that pounded through him, a desire he had no choice but to fulfil, a desire that sliced through the last vestige of her fear and defeated it for ever.

Derek cried out and held himself above her, tense as a steel rod. And then he collapsed on to her body, moaning and breathing hard, and Olive put her arms around his shoulders and held him, moving her hands on his back almost as if she comforted him in some desperate extremity.

Later, they went upstairs and there, holding her close in his narrow bed, Derek made love to her again, differently this time, more slowly, luxuriating in each small sensation, savouring the steady rise of passion, until they were once more caught up in its tumult and strained together as if endeavouring to merge their bodies, to become one being, one world, one total universe.

'When we're married and this war is over,' Derek said, in the moment before he fell asleep, 'we'll be able to do that whenever we feel like it.'

He would have felt like it again in the morning, but Olive woke in a panic, imagining his parents at the door, and hers wondering all night where she was. Would they believe she'd stayed with Iris? Were they on their way there now, to find her? She ran naked down the stairs to collect her clothes, saw the chaos they had left last night – the settee pulled up before the fire, plates and glasses on the floor. Derek would have to see to that. She scrambled into her clothes and he appeared at the door and came over to take her in his arms.

'Don't worry, Livvy. It's early yet. I'll clear this lot up.'

Olive looked up at him, trembling. A new fear had struck her now and she wondered how she could possibly have forgotten. 'Derek – suppose there's a baby?'

'There won't be,' he assured her easily. 'It hardly ever happens the first time.'

'But it might – '

'No. It just doesn't. It'll be all right, Livvy. And I'll get something for next time – a french letter. You'll be all right.' He kissed her lingeringly. 'It was marvellous,' he murmured. 'You're marvellous, Livvy. And you're mine now.'

She leaned against him. 'I was anyway.' But she couldn't regret what had happened. 'I love you, Derek.'

'I love you. And now – you'd better go.' He pulled down the blackout curtain and looked out at the garden. 'Wow, it certainly did snow! You're going to leave your footprints all the way.' He laughed at her look of alarm. 'Don't worry – no one's going to trace them back here. Why should they?'

Olive had walked home through the snow in a dream. And she had stayed in that dream ever since. But now Derek was gone and the dream ended, and she feared that it could be all too easily replaced with a nightmare.

Was it true? she wondered as she lay weeping into her pillow after Derek had left in his khaki uniform.

Was it really true that you couldn't get pregnant the first time?

Food rationing began on 8 January and everyone got out the ration books they had been issued with and stared at them, trying to make sense of the little squares and the numbers on them.

'It's just butter, sugar and bacon so far,' Jess said. 'Four ounces of butter and bacon, and twelve ounces of sugar! Where's that going to go? And it surely won't be long before meat's rationed. You can hardly get any now, but I bet some people aren't going without. I saw Mrs Carter getting a big parcel from Hines's yesterday, he had it under the counter for her. She said it was some sewing his wife had done for her, but Mrs Hines can't be much of a needlewoman if she pricks her fingers that badly!'

Most of the young men were away now. Bob had gone off the same day as Derek and both were in the same unit. The wireless, which was the country's mainstay for information, was now broadcasting messages from someone called Lord Haw-Haw, who could be heard by switching to Hamburg radio after the Nine o'clock News. Lord Haw-Haw, whose real name wasn't known, would introduce himself with a plummy 'Jairmany calling, Jairmany calling' and spent a quarter of an hour giving more detailed news and sneering at the British. 'Where is your *Ark Royal* today?' he would demand. 'Ask your government. She has been sunk, along with many more of your ships.'

'I hate that man,' Jess said to Annie. 'I won't listen to him. If he's really a lord he's a traitor.'

'I don't believe he's a lord – he just talks that way. Ted says he's a traitor anyway, and ought to be shot. But he does seem to know what's going on, and he tells us more than our own people do.'

'That's if it's all true. The trouble is, you don't know what is and what isn't. That stuff about the *Ark* – I mean, we know that's nonsense. He's just trying to frighten us.'

'Well, he's taken on a big job, then,' Annie said staunchly. 'He's not going to frighten us in a hurry.'

These days, she was being determinedly cheerful, though she was worried about Olive. The girl was pale and had lost weight. She picked at her food and sat about looking miserable in the evenings. She spent most of her time writing long letters to Derek and refused to go out dancing or to the pictures.

'You ought to have a bit of fun,' Annie told her. 'It doesn't do you any good, moping about the way you do. And it's not helping Derek.'

'Don't keep on at me, Mum,' Olive said snappily. 'I don't feel like going out. I don't have to, do I?'

Annie looked at her closely. 'Are you all right, Livvy?'

'All right? Of course I'm all right. I've just had to send my feller off to war, that's all, and don't know if I'll ever see him again, but that's nothing to worry about, is it?'

'There's a lot of girls in the same boat,' Annie said quietly. 'And young wives with children – '

'And I could have been Derek's wife if you and Dad had let me!' Olive burst out. 'It wouldn't be so bad, if you'd just let us get married first.'

Annie stared at her. 'I hope there's no reason why you should have got married, our Olive.'

Olive blushed scarlet. 'No, of course there isn't. What reason could there be?' Her eyes, red from nights of weeping, mocked her mother. 'Only that we love each other and want to be married, that's all. But you and Dad wouldn't care about that, would you?'

She turned and flung herself out of the room and Annie heard her footsteps stumbling upstairs and then the creak of the bed as she threw herself down on it. She'd be up there crying till supper-time now, and then only come down to collect a cup of cocoa and take it back up with her. No wonder she was getting thin.

Annie sighed and went out to the kitchen to start peeling potatoes. She was still nagged by the thought of that night just after Christmas, when Olive hadn't come home. She'd said she was round at Iris Bentley's and had stayed the night when the snow came on, but was that true? She'd done it before, and Annie could have found out easily enough by mentioning it – just casually – to Mrs Bentley, but she didn't want to to that. To tell the truth, she thought, she didn't want to know.

She remembered the argument she'd had with Ted over Olive wearing make-up. She'd said then, if we don't let her do things she'll do them anyway, behind our backs. And told him how she'd done just the same when her father had forbidden her to go dancing with Ted himself. She'd smuggled her dancing shoes out in a bag, pretending she was going round to a friend's for the evening – just like Olive saying she was going to Iris's – and her dad had never known.

Nor had Ted until she'd told him, but it made him realise that he had to let Olive grow up. It hadn't been enough to persuade him to let her marry Derek, though.

Annie sliced the potatoes into thin, neat lengths for chips. Olive had wanted badly to get married and they'd said no. They'd wanted her to wait. But in times like these, no one wanted to wait. Life was too uncertain. They wanted happiness when it was within reach, not postponed to a time that might never come.

Would she and Ted have wanted to wait?

Tim and Keith woke on the first morning back at Bridge End to find the countryside swathed in a heavy white blanket of snow. They stared out of their bedroom window, marvelling at the shape of the trees and bushes, and then dragged on their clothes and rushed downstairs.

'It's snowed! It's snowed!'

'You don't say.' Reg grinned at them. The kitchen was warm and cosy and they could smell bacon frying. The shortages in the towns and cities had not yet reached the country. Edna was stirring a saucepan full of porridge and she smiled at them. She and Reg had missed the boys over Christmas.

'I suppose you want to go out and play in it. Sit up to the table, then. You're not going out without something hot inside you.'

The boys watched as she ladled porridge into four bowls and then dug a spoon into the golden syrup tin. She poured a gleaming pool of syrup on top of three bowls and handed them round. The fourth she gave to Keith, who took his own syrup and trailed it round the top of the porridge in circles.

'Don't forget you've got something to do before you start building snowmen and getting into snowball fights,' she said. 'You've got to go round and see Alan and Wendy Atkinson.'

Tim made a face. Mrs Atkinson had come down to number 14 the day before he and Keith had come back, bringing a parcel for them to give her children. She had already posted their Christmas presents but wanted to send them something else, to make up for not having had them home for Christmas. The parcel contained fruit and sweets, with a few groceries for the ladies who were looking after them.

'Do they live near you?' Edna asked. 'I thought they'd gone home for Christmas.'

'They live up the top of our street,' Keith said. 'In a green-grocer's shop.'

'They don't live in the shop, silly,' Tim corrected him. 'They live over the top of it. In a flat.'

'Well, Wendy's in my class at school,' Keith retorted, as if that clinched it.

'Never mind that,' Edna said. 'Did Wendy and Alan go home for Christmas or did they go somewhere else?'

'They stayed here,' Tim told her. 'Their grandad died just before we went home. Their mum's been ill too. That's why they couldn't go back.'

Edna glanced at her husband. 'I don't know what to do. You know what the Woddises are like. They'd be so annoyed if they thought I was interfering.'

'But if you're worried about the kids . . .' Reg said. 'I mean, if they're all right there's no harm done. But if they're not . . .'

'That's right,' she said. 'I'd never forgive myself if . . .'

There was a short silence, then Reg said, 'Kids come first, before offending old ladies.'

287

Tim and Keith listened, only half understanding the conversation. The Corners were worried about Alan and Wendy, they could see that, but why?

'D'you think they've been kidnapped?' Tim enquired at length.

The Corners gave him a startled glance.

'Kidnapped? Why should we think that?'

Tim shrugged. To him, it seemed obvious. Edna had asked him if the Atkinsons had gone home for Christmas, so they couldn't be in the village. What other conclusion was there?

Edna seemed to understand what he was thinking and smiled. 'No, Tim, I don't think they've been kidnapped. But I'm a bit worried about them all the same. They didn't go to church all over Christmas and they didn't go to the evacuees' party in the church hall. And nobody seems to have seen them since school finished. I just wondered if they were ill.' She hesitated, then said, 'Ask to see them when you take the parcel round. Ask them over to tea.'

Tim frowned, remembering the time he had gone to the Woddis sisters' house with his mother. The old lady with the mole frightened him and he didn't much like her sister either. He didn't want to go there again, especially on his own. But he knew this would be difficult to explain to the Corners.

'All right,' he said unenthusiastically. 'So long as Keith comes too. And then can we make a snowman and have a snowball fight?'

Edna smiled. 'Of course you can.'

The two boys set out half an hour later, wrapped up in coats and scarves, their wellingtons packed with as many pairs of socks as could be squeezed in and hats made from the tops of a pair of old socks of Reg's, cut down and sewn up at one end.

'We're soldiers,' Tim said, 'spying round the enemies' camp. Our leader's held hostage and we've got to get essential supplies to him or he'll die.'

'What's essential supplies?' Keith asked, clutching Mrs Atkinson's parcel against his chest.

'Food and gold and stuff like that. A rope ladder to escape with.' Tim had a parcel too. 'Anyway, we must make sure nobody sees us approaching the enemy camp.'

Keith looked doubtfully at their footprints. The snow was almost up to the tops of their wellingtons and they were making

288

deep pits in its smooth, sparkling surface. They seemed to be the first people to make their way down the lane leading to the Victorian house this morning.

'Will we have to run away?' he asked a little fearfully. 'They won't shoot at us, will they?'

'They might.' Tim always threw himself wholeheartedly into such play, forgetting that Keith could not always sort out imagination from reality. 'I expect they've got guns trained on us at this very moment.'

The lane was silent. Even the birds seemed to have stopped moving and the snow muffled all sound from the village. Cattle had been taken in from the fields and all around the boys was an expanse of white. It was as if nobody else existed.

Tim was struck by the idea. Half abandoning his earlier scenario, he announced that they were in an unknown world completely covered in snow.

'Nobody knows what kinds of creatures live here,' he said. 'Probably monsters. We've got to rescue our leader before they freeze our world too.'

'What'll happen if we're caught?'

'We'll be frozen too. Like statues made of ice.'

They were almost at the house now. They stopped and stared at it. It looked dark and forbidding, its roof frowning over the windows.

'D'you think there's ghosts there?' Keith asked in a whisper. 'D'you think it's haunted?'

'Bound to be.' Tim crouched and then sprang up with a weird howl. He spread his arms and capered round his brother. 'Whoo-oo! I'm a ghost – I've come to hau-aunt you!'

Keith squealed and ducked away. 'Don't! It's horrible!'

Tim giggled, but there was a note of hysteria in his giggle. He was uneasily aware that he was almost as nervous as Keith at the idea of going right up to the house, summoning one of the sisters to the door and demanding to see Alan and Wendy. They hadn't let his mother see them, after all – why should they let him and Keith? And whatever Reg and Edna said, he still thought it possible that something had happened to the two Atkinsons. If not kidnapped, they might be kept in the house by force. Or worse . . .

Stories of children being eaten came into his mind and he felt sick.

They were almost at the house now and Keith stopped at the gate, looking nervously up at the dark hedge surrounding the house and garden. Anything might lurk behind there, he thought, and looked at his brother.

Tim returned his look. His stories had been intended to boost his own courage but now he felt it ebb away from him. He stared at the gate again and it looked forbiddingly back. The thought of opening it, entering the cold shadowed world beyond and then actually pulling on that stiff, old-fashioned bellpull brought a tremble to his lips. He wished he hadn't started to talk about enemy soldiers and monsters. He wished Keith hadn't talked about ghosts and most of all he wished he'd never thought about children being eaten.

'Go on,' he said to Keith. 'Open the gate.'

'You,' Keith said, shrinking back.

'You open the gate and I'll ring the bell.' Let's just get it over with, he thought. Let's get out of here and back to Reg and Edna.

Keith pushed the gate and it swung open slowly, creaking loudly.

It was the creak that did it. That and the sight of a pale face pressed against the window. It was Alan, his nose squashed flat as a pig's, but neither boy recognised him. For, worse still, there was someone behind him – a tall, indistinct figure, draped with dark, flowing clothes, that loomed waveringly like a shadow in water: a more realistically supernatural figure than any Tim could mimic.

With squeals of pure terror, they dropped the parcels on the path and turned to run. With the snow tugging at their boots and hampering every step, they lurched panic-stricken from the garden and along the lane. Slithering and sliding, occasionally falling full length in the snow, they ran along the lane and scrambled across the stile to cross the fields, not stopping until they were well out of sight of the lonely Victorian house and its cold, unhappy occupants and could see the first comforting glimpse of smoke from the Corners' chimneys.

By this time they were slightly ashamed of their panic. They glanced sideways at each other and grinned a little, then began to giggle. The sight of Alan's face, pressed piglike against the glass, struck them as hilariously funny and the glimpse of Miss Eleanor, towering behind him like a wavering shadow, as deliciously spooky. Pushing each other, snorting and holding their stomachs in exaggerated laughter, they staggered up the garden path, which Reg had by now cleared of snow, and tumbled breathless into the kitchen.

'And are Alan and Wendy all right, then?' Edna asked. 'Did they like their presents? When are they coming to tea?'

The two boys looked at each other guiltily.

'We didn't actually see them,' Tim admitted. 'But we left the presents.'

'Weren't they in?' Edna looked surprised. 'They must have gone out very early, then. We'll have to ask them another day.' She handed the boys a mug of cocoa each. 'Drink that and then you can go out and help Reg chop some wood. And then you can make a start on the snowman.'

The bitter winter continued and, with it, the war. The Navy were still in the forefront; on 19 January, three British submarines, the *Seahorse*, the *Starfish* and the *Undine*, were reported lost. The local weekly paper, the *Hampshire Telegraph and Post*, described them as having been engaged in 'particularly hazardous service' and published a list of the men still missing. Others were claimed to have been rescued by the Germans and would be kept as prisoners – bringing comfort to their families that they were still alive but fresh anxiety about their treatment and welfare.

'Cliff Barker from round June Close was on one of those subs,' Peggy Shaw told Annie when they met in the street. She and Bert had just had a letter from Bob, who was 'somewhere in France' with Derek. The two families kept each other in touch, sharing news and letters as they arrived.

Still talking about Cliff Barker, Peggy went on, 'His mother doesn't know whether to be thankful he's saved or worried sick about what they're doing to him. You hear such stories! Someone told me they're torturing the prisoners and using them in experiments.'

'They wouldn't do that, surely,' Annie said. 'I mean, they're not allowed to. They'd be in trouble when the war's over.'

'Not if they win the war,' Bert said with grim cynicism. 'Who's to take them to court then?'

'They're not going to win, Bert Shaw,' Peggy said sharply, 'and don't let me hear you say so.'

Graham had gone to sea and Betty was still waiting for her call-up papers from the WLA and looking forward to becoming a farmer's girl.

'Mind, I don't know how she'll stand up to the work,' Annie remarked. 'She turns dizzy if Ted asks her to hold a trowel. But she's set on it and it's war work, so what can you do?'

'It's better than going in the Services, anyway,' Peggy said. 'You wouldn't credit what those ATS girls get up to, in and out of pubs after the soldiers. And I don't suppose the Wrens are much better. Well, the temptation's there all the time, isn't it, with all those sailors about. No, I think your Betty's better off on the land.'

Annie nodded, but she was more worried about Olive. The girl was no better but it was difficult to tell whether she was just moping over her Derek or whether there was some other reason for her pale, miserable face.

There were more children in the city now. Tired of life in the country and believing that Hitler did not, after all, intend to bomb Britain, the evacuees were drifting back home. With only a few schools to go to and nobody to ensure they attended, they formed gangs and roamed the streets. Micky Baxter, from number 10, was leader of one of the gangs and the rest of the community looked on him with disfavour.

'They're up to no good, that lot,' Frank said darkly. 'I reckon it's them been over the allotments, trampling about all over the gardens. Just because there's snow on the ground don't mean there's nothing to worry about underneath. Half my cabbages have been broken down and two blackcurrant bushes knocked about. I'll knock them about, if I catch them at it!'

'They've got nothing to do, that's their trouble,' Jess commented. 'The authorities ought to open more schools.'

More and more people were demanding that the schools be reopened, as they brought their children home from the country. When their own school at Copnor Road reopened, Jess suggested once again that Rose and the boys should come back, but Frank firmly vetoed the idea.

'I still think we're going to be bombed. This winter's holding everything up – even Hitler seems to have decided against any invasion. But as soon as spring comes – mark my words, there'll be action on all fronts. Anyway, the boys and Rose are getting some schooling at least, where they are. I don't want 'em coming home and getting mixed up with Micky Baxter and his lot.'

Jess had to admit that he was right, especially when they heard that Micky and a gang of other boys, none of them aged over twelve, had marched into a jeweller's shop one day brandishing a gun. It was a pistol left over from the 1914–18 war, kept carelessly lying about by the father of one of the boys, but it was Micky who carried it and waved it in the face of the terrified girl behind the counter. Fortunately, at that moment, the manager came out of the inner room, grabbed Micky by the wrist so that he dropped the gun, and held him while his assistant rang the police. The other boys had fled, but were soon caught and the whole gang brought before the juvenile court.

'Probation!' Frank exclaimed in disgust when he read the report in the *Evening News*. 'They ought to be sent away to an approved school and taught a lesson.'

'There aren't any approved schools now,' Jess said. 'They've all been requisitioned too.'

Frank snorted. 'What sort of world are we building up? We're sending decent young men like Bob Shaw and our Colin off to fight and be killed, and meanwhile the likes of Micky Baxter run wild and turn into criminals. It's crazy.'

'I've always thought so,' she said. 'The whole world's gone crazy.'

By the end of January, everyone was caught up in a new fever. The national waste campaign was under way and as well as exhorting people to 'dig for victory' and reminding them that 'careless talk costs lives' there were posters appealing for all kinds of household waste. Paper and rags were wanted for pulping, bones were needed for fertilizer and kitchen waste for pigswill. One afternoon, Annie came down October Street to find men cutting off the iron railings from the low walls in front of the houses, and was

293

told they were wanted for ships and tanks. Even old saucepans, fire-irons and bedsteads were needed, nothing was too small.

And still there were no bombs. The barrage balloons still floated in quiet skies. And more children came back from the countryside.

Molly Atkinson, who had not seen her children since they went away, was almost at her wits' end.

'I've got to see them,' she said to Dave. 'It's February – they've been away since the beginning of September. Six months! They'll have forgotten us!'

'They won't. Children don't forget their parents.'

'But they'll be missing us so much,' she said, her eyes filling with the tears that came so readily these days. 'They must wonder why we've never been to see them.'

Dave sighed. 'I know. I miss them as much as you do, Molly. But you know how impossible it's been. First you were ill, then you had that fall, then Dad died . . . And the weather's been too bad for travelling. You've never pulled up since the pleurisy you had. You can't go off on a train that might take hours to get there and be freezing cold as well. You know what the railway's been like these past few weeks.'

Molly nodded. There had been numerous complaints to the Railway Executive about train delays, most of which had been excused on the grounds that the blackout had made the loading of goods slow and difficult. There were also frequent unexpected arrivals of fresh food at ports, which must be distributed as quickly as possible, and constant troop movements.

'If only I knew the children were all right,' she said miserably. 'I know we get letters from Wendy, and Miss Woddis wrote thanking us for the groceries and saying the children were well – but I want to see for myself.'

'And so you will,' Dave said. 'As soon as the weather gets better. We'll make a special trip out there, and maybe bring them home for a few days if it's still quiet.'

Molly knew that once the children were home she would never be able to let them go again, but she didn't say so. She stared out of the window at the snow which lay about the streets, piled up in the gutters in huge frozen mounds. It was grey and dirty now, whitened every now and then by a fresh snowfall. Once it did begin to thaw the streets would be running with water.

I wish I'd never sent them away, she thought. There was no need for them to go. They could have been here all the time, perfectly safe. It's not right for little children to be taken away from their mothers.

If only she knew for certain that they were all right . . .

Before the end of February, however, there was cause for celebration in April Grove when the *Exeter* finally arrived home from the South Atlantic. With her sister ship the *Ajax*, she steamed into a harbour still half frozen over, with grey skies threatening yet more snow, but the men aboard her cared nothing for the weather, and neither did the families who thronged the beaches to watch the ships appear and cheered them in. The sailors were fêted again when they marched through the streets of London, smart and proud as the Navy always was, to be given lunch at the Guildhall by the Lord Mayor himself. Headed by a band playing tunes of victory, they strode through crowds of cheering people and as Colin said when he was eventually back in Portsmouth and could toast his toes in front of a roaring fire, it was all a far cry from the Falkland Islands and the River Plate.

'Seems a long time ago now,' Colin said, accepting a cup of tea from his mother. Annie was waiting on him hand and foot, almost unable to let him out of her sight. 'But I'll never forget seeing that ship blow up. I mean, we knew by then what was going to happen – but it was a tremendous sight all the same. And a bit sad, somehow.'

'But what happened?' Jess asked. 'Why did it blow up?'

Colin shrugged. 'What he did, see, he took her out of the main channel into shallow water and just opened the sea-cocks. That's what people usually do when they scuttle their own ships. But that would've meant we'd raise her and get a good look at her, so he had to destroy her. Blow her up. So he hung torpedoes over the ammunition hatches. They led straight down to the magazines, of course. The last men to leave the ship sloshed petrol all over the decks to set light to it.'

'So the ropes burned through,' Ted said thoughtfully, 'and

295

the torpedoes fell, exploded and blew up the magazines. Just like that.'

Colin nodded. 'That's right. Only the torpedo at the fore end went first and as the ship went nose down, a colossal wave of sea-water flooded up over the aft part and put out the flames! So that torpedo never dropped and never blew up.' He chuckled. 'The first man aboard afterwards was a bloke called Kilroy – a lieutenant-commander. He found the torpedo still hanging there and wrote his name on it – "Kilroy was here". Since then, it's turned into a sort of gag, people have been writing it in all sorts of places.'

'I've seen it!' Frank exclaimed. 'Last week, someone wrote it on one of our boilers. I didn't know what it meant.'

'Probably someone who knew a bloke off the *Exeter* or the *Ajax*,' Colin said. 'Heard the story and thought it would be funny.'

'Wasn't he brave, though?' Betty said admiringly, and Colin nodded. 'He certainly had a nerve, writing his name on a live torpedo hanging over a magazine full of ammo. That rope was pretty charred – it could have gone through at any minute.'

Annie shuddered. 'I hate thinking about it. You could have been blown up, if that ship hadn't been sunk. We thought for a while you had been. Granny Kinch told us the *Exeter* had been sunk.'

'Not us. Takes more than a German battleship to get rid of Colin Chapman.'

'You don't want to listen to rumours,' Frank said. 'There's too many of them about. Someone said German soldiers had landed on the beach over at Gosport the other day – Stokes Bay. Three hundred of them killed, I was told! Absolute rubbish.'

'It might have been true, though,' Betty said, wide-eyed, but Frank shook his head.

'It was just a rumour. I reckon there's a lot of people just putting rumours about to scare us. It's all part of Hitler's propaganda.'

'Well, I don't care about any of that,' Annie said, looking at her son. 'I'm just thankful you're home.'

February drew into March and Jess went back at last to Bridge End, reluctant to leave Frank but anxious to see the children again. She saw Molly Atkinson before she left and promised to go and see Alan and Wendy and take them another parcel.

'The boys have been round, I know,' she comforted the unhappy woman. 'I'm sure your two are all right. They're very respectable ladies.' She thought uneasily of the way she had been rebuffed by the sisters, and made up her mind to do more for the little Atkinsons this time. I should have done more before Christmas, she thought remorsefully, I was just too wrapped up in my own worries about Frank and the baby.

Meat was rationed, not by weight but by price – one shilling and tenpence worth a week. A family of four could buy a six-pound joint of lamb at one and four a pound, an announcement that made Annie laugh. Find one first, she said to Ted – in Hines's shop that morning she had seen lambs that weighed only nine pounds whole. Not much bigger than rabbits, and that's what she'd have taken them for if it hadn't been for their hooves.

'At least our Jess and the children will be getting fed better, out in the country,' she said.

For many of the children, that was true. Rose, who had gone back to the Greenberrys, was learning to cook and although they were subject to rationing like everyone else, there were eggs in plenty and milk with which Mrs Greenberry made her own butter. Bacon too was there at every breakfast-time. All the same, she and Mrs Greenberry experimented with some of the recipes that were being given out over the wireless or in the papers, and were constantly surprising Mr Greenberry with such dishes as passion dock pudding, made with boiled dock leaves and oatmeal, Portman pudding which, with its combination of carrot, potato, sugar and dried fruit, could have been either a vegetable dish or a sweet, and Lord Woolton Pie, which everyone tried.

'A pound each of diced potatoes, cauliflower, carrots and swede, three or four spring onions, or an ordinary one if you haven't got them, a teaspoonful of vegetable extract – what's that?'

'Marmite'll do,' Mrs Greenberry said, getting the jar out of the cupboard.

' – and a tablespoonful of oatmeal.' They gathered the ingredients together and looked at the mound of chopped vegetables. 'Cover with water and cook for ten minutes. Put into a pie dish, sprinkle with chopped parsley – what's parsley?'

'It's that crinkly green plant just outside the kitchen door.'

Rose went to fetch some. 'And cover with a crust of potatoes or wholemeal pastry. Why wholemeal?'

'I suppose it's better for you. We'll just have to make do with ordinary.'

'Bake in a moderate oven until the pastry is brown and serve hot with gravy.'

It was very good, and filling too. The Greenberrys ate it often; so did the Shaws, back in Portsmouth, and even the Chapmans. The Minister of Food was credited with good sense and his recipes and advice regularly followed. There was even a song about him.

> *Those who have the will to win*
> *Cook potatoes in their skin*
> *Knowing that the sight of peelings*
> *Deeply hurts Lord Woolton's feelings.*

Woolton Pie was not made in the thin Victorian house where the Woddis sisters lived. They were still doing their best to ignore the war, taking each new deprivation as a personal affront, and behaved as if rationing were an impertinence of the local shopkeeper. They snatched the children's ration books as soon as Molly sent them, complaining that as Alan was under six he was allowed only half the meat ration, and gave the children sausages and offal, which were off ration. They liked the sausages but hated the liver, which Miss Millicent cooked to the texture of shoe leather, and never knew that the sisters were sitting down to meat stew or roast after they had gone to bed.

'Children don't appreciate good meat,' Miss Eleanor observed. 'It's not good for them anyway – it makes them aggressive.'

Miss Millicent sniffed. 'The boy's quite aggressive enough already. Do you know, he actually tried to bite my hand yesterday!'

'I hope you smacked him for that, Millicent!'

'Oh, I did. Quite hard. But I don't suppose it will make any difference. There's bad blood there, in my opinion.'

'They obviously had no discipline at home. And we're the ones who have to suffer for it.'

'It's this dreadul war,' Miss Millicent said. 'It's always the innocent who have to suffer.'

298

Mostly, however, they kept the war at bay. Except for church and shopping, they rarely left the house and Mrs Cherry's visits were cut to twice a week. Wendy and Alan found themselves being given a list of jobs to do each day, and went to bed each night worn out with sweeping and scrubbing, polishing and washing. The episode of the butter had not been forgotten and they were strictly supervised all the time. In fact, a curious change had come about in the sisters' attitude towards them. From finding their presence a nuisance and an intrusion in the house, they now seemed to look forward to their return from school each day and find positive enjoyment in harrying them about their tasks.

'Why doesn't Mummy come to see us?' Alan asked as they struggled through the snow to school. 'I want her to take us home.'

'She's too poorly.' Wendy too lay awake at night, longing for her mother. She had watched, her heart breaking with misery and yearning, as other children went home for Christmas, and hung around them when they returned, avid for any news of her own family.

Tim and Keith Budd had come to the house again one day, shortly after the snowy morning when they had left her mother's parcel on the step, and she'd stood behind Miss Millicent in the hall and heard them invite her and Alan to the Corners' house, to play snowballs and have tea. But Miss Millicent had refused the invitation. Wendy and Alan both had heavy colds, she said, had stayed in bed all over Christmas and couldn't possibly come out in the snow. And Tim and Keith had gone off down the path, giving Wendy a cheerful wave, and scampered off across the fields, up to their knees in snow, shouting and laughing as they went.

'Why is Mummy poorly?' Alan asked. 'Doesn't she need us to make her better?'

'Daddy says she needs a rest.' Wendy knew that Grandad had died just before Christmas. She had cried for him at night but when Alan asked what was the matter she shook her head. He did not yet understand about death.

'She could have a rest if we went home,' he said now. 'We could do the work and she could sit down.'

They were back at school, sitting like mice at the back of the classroom. The teachers were struggling to teach large groups of

299

children at different stages, all in the same room, and only noticed the noisy ones. Miss Langrish did occasionally glance at Wendy's pale, pinched face and Alan's bruised legs – for Miss Millicent used the strap quite liberally now – but she was too tired and anxious herself to do anything. Her fiancé was in the RAF, flying over Germany most nights, and she slept little as she lay imagining him shot down, his plane spinning in flames and out of control. Besides, her job was teaching, she was not supposed to interfere with the children's home life.

Edna Corner stopped and spoke to them a few times after school. She asked them to tea again, but they shook their heads, knowing that there would be jobs for them back at the house. She looked at them doubtfully and asked if they were all right and Wendy, conscious of Miss Millicent's warnings, said yes thank you, they were quite all right, but they had to go now please as they'd promised to be home early. And with that Edna had had to be satisfied.

It was now a regular occurrence for the children to be shut in the cupboard. Whenever Miss Eleanor and Miss Millicent left the house, for church or shopping, and often when they were indoors, the two children were bundled into the dark space under the stairs and left there. They grew accustomed to it and accustomed to the fear and sick loathing that they experienced inside. Together, unprotesting, they would huddle on the floor, their tears flowing silently, and they would remain silent for a long time after they came out.

In fact, Alan spoke very little these days. His eyes, large and dark, looked out in mute appeal from his white face and if he could not be close to his sister he would find a corner and crouch there, pressing his shoulders against the walls.

'There's something very odd about that boy,' Miss Eleanor said, watching him as he cowered like a frightened animal in a corner of the kitchen. 'I think he's mentally retarded. No, Wendy, leave him alone. If he can't come to the table and eat like a human being he must have his food on the floor like the animal he seems to want to be.' She dropped a few scraps into an old bowl. 'Give him those.'

'He doesn't like liver,' Wendy said timidly, looking at the

unappetising collection, and Miss Eleanor snorted with exasperation.

'He'll eat if he's hungry. Here's some bread to go with it – quite enough for a child of his age. If he doesn't like it, all he has to do is sit up at the table and behave like a human being.'

'But he *is* a human being,' Wendy said, and was sent to the cupboard for half an hour for insolence.

'If we're going to be forced to take care of these children for the duration of the war, simply because their own parents are too feckless,' Miss Eleanor said to her sister, 'they must learn to behave as we want them to.' And she carried a tureen of steaming soup, made that morning by Mrs Cherry, into the dining-room, leaving Alan with his bowl of scraps.

Meanwhile, Jess was in Edna Corner's kitchen, also eating soup and catching up on the news. She had been surprised to find herself quite pleased to be renewing acquaintance with the friends she had made at Bridge End, and there was a good deal of gossip to exchange before she came to the subject of the little Atkinsons.

'It's funny you should mention them,' Edna said. 'There's a few of us been wondering just what's going on in that house. I mean, the little ones go to school and that, but they're never out to play with the rest of the children. And I've invited them over to tea a couple of times but there's always been some reason why they can't come.'

'That sounds queer.' Jess wiped the last few drops of soup from the bowl with a piece of Edna's home-made bread. 'It's not as if they're all that fond of children – at least, it didn't strike me that way when I went there. You'd think they'd be glad to let the children out to play so they could get a bit of peace.'

'That's right. I mean, it doesn't matter how much you like children, you're always glad of an hour or two without them.' Edna went to the stove and took out a rice pudding. 'I've been meaning to go round again myself, but you know how time goes by.'

Jess nodded. It had been the same for her before Christmas. She'd really intended to visit the children but somehow there had always been something else that needed doing. But now she was determined not to waste any more time.

'Well, I've got another parcel for them in my pram,' she said. 'I'll go in this afternoon, on my way back to Mrs Greenberry's.'

'And I'll come with you,' Edna said. 'We'll find out just what's going on and maybe I'll bring them back to tea this afternoon. I don't care what those two old tabbies say, it's not good for children to be kept away from their friends.'

'I suppose they think ordinary boys like my Tim and Keith aren't good enough,' Jess said with a sniff. 'Well, they may be little ruffians at times but they're as good as any other child, and a lot better than some.' She told Edna about Micky Baxter and the jeweller's shop. 'And the Atkinsons are little dears. Alan's sweet and Wendy's always ready to help anyone.'

They finished their lunch and Jess fed the baby while Edna put a casserole of brisket and vegetables in the oven for supper. Then, with Maureen once again wrapped up in the white velvet coat and leggings Annie had given her for Christmas, the two women set off along the twisting country lanes for the house at the other side of the village.

On Wednesday afternoons, the two sisters went out to have tea with their old friends Colonel and Mrs Lovel, who lived near the church. If the weather was bad, Colonel Lovel would send his car to collect them, but today, although cold, the sky was clear and they elected to walk.

'Really, we haven't been able to get out much at all this winter,' Miss Eleanor remarked as they put on their galoshes. 'It's been so cold and the paths are so slippery. But now it's thawing we should have some pleasant spring weather.'

As a matter of course, they shut both children in the cupboard. Wendy had been allowed out to go to the lavatory, but pushed back in immediately. She went sulkily but without protest, for by now they both knew that protests were futile. The sisters were adept at turning deaf ears to anything they did not wish to hear and if they became really annoyed were capable of leaving the children shut up for the rest of the day.

Alan and Wendy sat huddled in the darkness. By now it was familiar, but it was no less frightening for all that. There were still spiders and probably worse, the brooms were still half suspected of coming to life when the door was closed, and who knew what other monstrosities might have taken possession since they were last shut in here?

Wendy, more angry than afraid, was less inclined to these imaginings than Alan, but she still hated and feared the long hours of incarceration and spent much of her time planning dreadful revenge on the sisters once she had grown up. But to Alan, the darkness was worse every time, and he crouched in his corner, sobbing with quiet, hopeless despair.

They heard the sisters talking as they put on their coats. Their voices faded as they went down the passage to the front door. The door opened and closed. The house was silent.

'Suppose they never come back?' Alan said, voicing his greatest fear. 'Suppose nobody ever finds us?'

Wendy could not answer. Alan always asked this and she knew that no words of comfort could reassure him. And her own heart echoed his terror. Suppose something *did* happen to the sisters while they were out . . .

It was cold in the cupboard. The only heating in the house came from the solid fuel stove in the kitchen and the fire in the living-room. The passage, which never got any sun, was particularly cold and nobody lingered there. The children huddled close, trying to keep themselves warm, but as the afternoon dragged on their fingers and toes began first to throb and then grow numb.

There was a knock on the door. The children jumped and then sat still, listening.

The bell rang, pealing through the empty house. There was a short silence, then it rang again. Wendy, straining her ears, could just hear faint voices.

'Alan!' she said. 'Bang on the door. Shout. Scream. Come on – we've got to make them hear us. They mustn't go away.'

Together, they began to hammer on the door, yelling at the tops of their voices. 'Help! Help! We're locked in – let us out! Help Help! *Help!*'

The bell rang once more, drowning their cries. They waited until the jangling stopped and then began again. 'Help! *Help!*'

'Stop,' Wendy said after a few minutes when both were hoarse and breathless. 'Listen.'

They held their breath. Then they heard the rattle of the letter-box.

'I can't see anyone,' someone murmured faintly. 'The house

seems to be empty. But I'm sure I heard . . .' There was a brief
silence and then the voice called through more loudly. 'Wendy?
Alan? Are you there?'

'We're here!' Wendy screamed. She knew the voice. It was Mrs
Budd, who lived in April Grove, Tim and Keith's mum. 'We're
locked in the cupboard under the stairs. Let us out! Please, *please*
let us out!'

There was another silence. Wendy leaned against the rim of light
that showed round the edges of the door. Could she hear voices
whispering, or was it her imagination? Perhaps Mrs Budd hadn't
heard her at all. Perhaps she had given up and gone away.

'Please,' she shouted again, her voice liquid with tears, 'please
don't go away. Please, please help us.'

The letter-box rattled again.

'Wendy,' Mrs Budd's voice said. 'We heard what you said. We're
going to try to get in and help you. Don't worry. It might take a
little while but we're not going away. We'll be as quick as we can.'

The letter-box rattled once more and there was silence. Wendy
sank back, leaning her head on the cobwebby wall. For once, she
hardly cared about spiders. She peered through the darkness to
where Alan was sitting, silent except for the occasional sobbing
breath.

'Alan, it's all right!' she said. 'Mrs Budd's going to save us. She'll
get a policeman, I expect, and he'll break down the door and get us
out.'

Jess and Edna straightened up and stared at each other.

'Did you hear that? Those two poor little children, locked in a
cupboard!'

'And where are the old ladies?' Edna asked. 'Where have they
gone?'

'Out to tea, I expect,' Jess said grimly. 'But don't let's waste time
worrying about them. We've got to get those children out.' She
stepped back, staring up at the house. It stared forbiddingly back,
its windows like blind eyes. 'How can we get in?'

'I don't know.' But it was clear Edna was as determined as Jess to
rescue the Atkinsons. 'Round the back, perhaps? The door's sure
to be unlocked.'

The two women hurried along the narrow, mossy path that led along the side of the house. But the back door was firmly locked. There were two windows in the side wall and they tried them both, but it was probably years since either was open and they stayed firm. They went back round the corner.

'I blame myself,' Jess said. 'I told Molly Atkinson I'd look out for her two and I kept meaning to come round and see how they were and never did. If anything's happened to them – '

'I meant to as well,' Edna said. 'I was a bit worried about them over Christmas. I sent the boys round a couple of times – I ought to have come myself. But you know what it is – I saw them coming out of school, and you don't like to interfere, do you?'

'Maybe we should.' Jess was looking for something to prise a window open with. 'Maybe we should always interfere, just in case – ah!'

'What is it? What've you found?'

'A key,' Jess said triumphantly, holding it up. 'The back-door key – hidden under a flowerpot. Well, if they leave it lying around they can't be surprised if anyone uses it, can they!'

'Hardly anyone round here locks their doors anyway,' Edna observed. 'Trust the Woddises . . . Does it fit?'

For answer, Jess pushed the back door open and they marched inside. The afternoon was growing dark and it was difficult to see across the kitchen, but they found the door to the passage and went quickly to the cupboard. Jess felt for the knob and wrenched the door open, and the two children tumbled out.

'You poor little mites!' Jess and Edna sank to their knees and gathered the crying children into their arms. 'You poor, poor little mites.'

Alan and Wendy leaned against them, sobbing. All the tears they had shed in the past six months, all the other tears they had held back, poured out a hundredfold as they felt, for the first time since leaving home, arms that were warm and comforting. Soft breasts that had become no more than a memory were once again real, and bodies that could wrap around you and keep you safe no longer a dream.

'The bitches,' Jess said in a shaking voice. 'The cruel, disgusting bitches!'

'Let's get them out of here,' Edna said. 'We'll take them back to my house. They can sleep in our bed tonight. They need cuddles – lots of them. And then we'll decide what to do.'

'I've already decided. I'm taking them back to their mother. She's the person they need, and she needs them too. She's been driving herself frantic with worrying about these two. If she had any idea what they've been going through – '

Edna began to straighten up. Alan was clinging to her, his little fingers curled tightly in her clothes, and she lifted him in her arms. Jess gave Wendy a hug and stood up too. They paused for a moment, looking at the dark cavern of the cupboard and the chilly length of the passage.

'Someone's coming,' Edna breathed, and they saw the shape of a person outlined against the stained glass of the front door. 'Let's get out, Jess!'

'No.' Jess stood firm. Her anger was still running high and she wanted to face the Woddis sisters with it, to see their guilt. She took a firm grip of Wendy's hand and stood watching the front door open. 'Let's see what you've got to say about this, you hypocrites,' she muttered.

The sisters entered and stopped dead, staring at the little group in the passage.

'What's this?' Miss Eleanor's voice was high with fear and indignation. 'What are you doing here? And the children – what naughtiness have they been about now?'

'*Naughtiness?*' Jess exclaimed. 'Naughtiness? Why, the poor little scraps hardly know what naughtiness is. What have *you* been about, that's what I want to know, locking them in a cupboard and then going off out and leaving them?'

Miss Eleanor advanced. She was terrifyingly tall in the half light and Jess felt Wendy cringe back against her skirt. She squeezed her hand reassuringly.

'I don't know what nonsense they've been telling you,' Miss Woddis said coldly. 'Of course we didn't lock them in the cupboard. It's one of their games. They're always playing it.'

'It doesn't seem like a game to me. Look at them – filthy dirty and sobbing their poor little hearts out. They were terrified!'

'They frighten themselves with silly stories.' She stared at Jess. 'You're an evacuee woman, aren't you?'

'Yes.' She made it sound like something that had crawled out from under a stone, Jess thought. 'I know these children. I know their mother. They're not naughty and they don't lock themselves into cupboards.'

'I tell you, they were not locked in – '

'And *I* tell *you*, they were.'

'We heard them crying when we knocked at the door,' Edna put in. 'When we came in, it was shut fast.'

Miss Eleanor transferred her gaze to Edna. 'You're not an evacuee. You're one of the village women.'

'Yes, I am,' Edna said boldly. 'And I think the village is going to be very upset to find how you've been treating these poor little children.'

Miss Eleanor brushed that aside. 'How did you get in? What made you think you had the right to walk into my house uninvited?' She glanced round and said to her sister, 'Go and look in the dining-room, Millicent, and see that the silver's all there. And then check the drawing-room.'

Jess gasped. She drew herself up and said angrily, 'We're not thieves. We came in because we heard these children crying. We had every right to come and help them. They could have been hurt – injured. Anybody else would have done the same. And now – '

'And now that you can see they're not, you may leave. Millicent and I will deal with the children.'

Jess felt Wendy press closer. Behind her, she heard Alan begin to cry again, and Edna bent to comfort him.

'We're not going without the children. We couldn't possibly leave them here.' Jess's anger was rising rapidly. How dared these women treat little children so cruelly and then behave as if she and Edna were common criminals? Didn't they have any shame? Didn't they even realise that what they had done was wrong?

'Not hurt?' she said. 'Not injured? Of course they're hurt and injured! They've been away from their mother for months, brought to live in a strange place with strange people – they needed comfort and love, not neglect and cruelty. Look at their little faces! Look at Alan's legs! You've been hitting them, tormenting them, terrifying them and God knows what else. You're not fit to have charge of children for five minutes and I'll not leave them in this house with you a moment longer. Why, you're not even human!'

307

Millicent gasped and Miss Eleanor took a step forward. Her face was white save for the scarlet patches on her cheeks, and her pale eyes blazed. She put out a hand and grasped Wendy's collar.

'You will not take them away! They're our responsibility – '

'Not any more,' Jess said. 'They're coming with us.'

'They most certainly are *not*. They were brought here to be under our care and – '

'*Your care?* You call this *care*?' Jess stared at the elderly lady. 'Do you know what the police would do if they knew what you'd done to these poor little mites? Do you – ?'

'The police!' Eleanor gave a high laugh. 'I wonder you dare to threaten me with the police! After breaking into my house – '

'We did not break in. We used the key you left lying about in the garden. It's still in the door. And any normal person would have done the same.' Jess lifted her chin. 'But if you're not satisfied, why not call them? I'll be happy to tell them what we found here and so will Edna, won't you, Edna?'

'Yes, I will.'

'They'd never believe you,' Miss Eleanor said haughtily, but her voice shook a little. 'Millicent and I have lived here all our lives, and we've known Constable Jenner since he was a child. Why should he take your word against mine?'

'Because we'd be telling him the truth,' Jess said steadily. 'And you know it. And now we're going. Let go of Wendy's collar, please. Wendy, find your coats, it's cold outside.' She watched as the little girl ran into the kitchen, coming back with the coats Molly had sent them at Christmas. 'If you want to send for the police you can do so,' she told Miss Eleanor. 'I'll be happy to tell them whatever they want to know. But they'll have to come and find us, we're not keeping these children in this house a minute longer. Are you ready, Wendy?'

'Yes,' the child whispered.

'Is there anything you need to take at this moment?'

'No.'

'Then let's go.' She half turned, then hesitated and said, 'We may as well use the front door. Excuse me, please,' and stalked past the two speechless ladies. Edna, with Alan once again in her arms, followed her. At the front door, Jess turned.

308

'I'll call for the children's things tomorrow morning. Please have them ready.'

There was a moment's silence as the four women faced each other. Jess, her anger still high, allowed all her contempt, all her disgust, all her fury, show to its full in her raking gaze. And then she turned away as if the Woddises were worthy of no further consideration and marched down the garden path.

'You were marvellous!' Edna said. 'They won't dare do a thing. But what are we going to do now?'

'We're going to take them to your house,' Jess said. 'There isn't room at the Greenberrys. And then I'm going to take them home to their mother. They need to be at home. After that, it's for her to decide what to do about it.' She looked at the children, at Alan in Edna's arms, his face still stained with dust and tears, his body still heaving with sobs. She looked down at Wendy, at a face that looked too old for eight years, at eyes that had seen depths of misery she could barely comprehend. What had the past few months done to these children? What scars would they bear from this experience?

She stopped in the cold, frozen lane and crouched down beside the little girl, taking her into her arms and holding her close. She felt the too-thin body, the fragile bones, heard the ragged breathing and thought of her own children, so sturdy and cheerful, so well cared for and loved.

'It's all right, Wendy,' she murmured. 'It's all over. You're never going back there again. You're going home.'

CHAPTER ELEVEN

AS THE SPRING WEATHER brought a thaw to frozen Europe, Frank's prediction proved correct and the phoney war came to an end. The map on the wall at number 14 was now covered in pins showing the march of war across the world, and nobody could doubt now that it was real, in all its ruthless brutality.

'They're spreading everywhere,' Jess said as Frank stuck a pin in Holland, where the Germans were now carrying out one of their terrifying *blitzkrieg*, or lightning wars. 'It's like some horrible disease. A cancer.'

'I know. Look at it – Denmark occupied with barely a squeak. Our forces brought out of Norway when we'd only been there a fortnight. Tanks and paratroops all over Holland. Belgium and France expecting to be attacked at any moment.' He shook his head. 'It's a mess.'

Jess stood up, baby Maureen on her hip. Maureen was ten months old now and already walking. She was a smiling, contented child who would sit on the floor for hours playing with a set of old wooden bricks belonging to Tim. She had few other toys – those belonging to the other children had been mostly broken or discarded years ago, and there were none in the shops. A battered teddy-bear that had once been Rose's was her constant companion, and Jess had knitted an elephant from an old cardigan, but apart from these she had to be content with makeshift toys.

'Not that she seems to miss them,' Jess would remark. 'She's happy enough with a cardboard box and a few clothes-pegs, or a couple of saucepan lids to bang together.'

After bringing the Atkinson children home, Jess had stayed at number 14. She'd told Frank firmly that being away from him was bad for her and therefore bad for the baby, and she wouldn't go away again until the bombing started. 'And maybe not then,' she added under her breath. The children were settled and happy in the country – though Rose would have liked to come home too – and she agreed to leave them there, but she'd had enough.

'Mind, Mrs Greenberry couldn't have been kinder and I'm quite happy for Rose to be with her. But my place is here with you, Frank, and I'm not going off and leaving you again, so there's not a bit of use you arguing about it.'

Frank looked at her curiously. 'Something's happened to you out in the country, Jess. You've never spoken like that before. As if – well, as if you'd made up your mind – '

'So I have.'

' – and nothing I can say is going to make any difference.'

'It isn't.' She smiled. 'Perhaps it's standing up to those two old ladies – I've never been one to talk back, as you know. But when I looked at those two poor little children and thought what those two old cats had put them through – well, I saw red.'

'I'm glad you did, Jess. You were right to do what you did. There's times when we have to get up on our hind legs and say what we think, yes and put our own selves at risk for what we think's right, too.' He looked at the map again. 'That's why we're fighting this war. What those two old ladies were doing to Alan and Wendy is what Hitler was doing to the Jews. And we can't let it happen, any more than you could let it go on happening to those children.'

Jess listened thoughtfully. More than once she had railed against this war, bitterly angry with those who had dragged Britain into it. For every young man who went off to fight, for every mother who had to watch him go, her heart had ached anew. The sight of the children in the school playgrounds, waiting for evacuation, of their mothers and fathers who stood outside the railings, had haunted her for months and she had raged inwardly at the injustice of it, at the disruption of so many lives.

It was that rage which had enabled her to stand up to the Woddis sisters on behalf of two helpless children. And it was the same rage, she saw now, that had made Britain go to war on behalf of a helpless nation.

But how long could this terrible destruction last? She looked now at Frank's map, at the pins that represented the German forces, and her heart was cold.

'They're winning,' she said in a low voice. 'Look at it, Frank. They're everywhere. They're driving us back and we don't seem to be able to do a thing about it. They're going to win.'

'It looks bad,' he agreed heavily. 'But they haven't beaten us yet, Jess. We may have pulled out of Norway and we might not have been much help to Denmark or the Low Countries, but we've got plenty of troops in France and it's there that the big battle's going to be fought. The British Expeditionary Force is there now – thousands of soldiers just waiting for the chance to have a go. We're not beaten yet, not by a long way. And now that fool Chamberlain's gone and Churchill's taken over at last . . .'

Jess nodded. Frank had never liked Neville Chamberlain, calling him weak and spineless. It was a view shared by many others, including apparently most of his own government. Only a few days ago, at the end of a debate on the tragic abandonment of Norway, he had been denounced by some of the leading MPs of his own party, and others had chanted at him to resign while the rebellious young Harold Macmillan led a chorus of 'Rule, Britannia!' to jeer him from the House of Commons.

Now Winston Churchill was Prime Minister. As First Lord of the Admiralty, he had claimed his own share of responsibility for what had happened in Norway, but had been told not to allow himself to be 'converted into an air-raid shelter' to 'keep the splinters from his colleagues'. All the same, he had kept Chamberlain on in his War Cabinet and that evening Jess and Frank listened to Chamberlain's final broadcast.

With tears in his voice, he told the nation how he had striven with all his might to maintain peace 'as long as it could be preserved honourably'. And Jess, sensing his emotion, felt a great pity wash over her.

'Poor man,' she said when Frank switched off the wireless. 'He did his best, after all. He never wanted the war.'

'Well, there's plenty more to be sorry for now,' Fank

commented. 'And the next time we hear Winnie's voice he'll be Prime Minister. I bet he'll have something to say, and it'll be worth listening to.'

Portsmouth was doing its best for the war effort. As well as collecting kitchen waste for pigswill, the city had been thrown into chaos by the removal of two thousand tons of disused tram rails, half buried under the roads. And at the end of April, the Lord Mayor had inaugurated a National Savings Week, which brought in over twelve hundred pounds and ended with a grand parade in the Guildhall Square by bands of the Royal Navy, the Marines and the Royal Army Service Corps. 'An impressive start to our campaign,' he said from the Guildhall steps, and exhorted the citizens to save even harder.

There was other news too, in the little community around September Street. In March, Heinrich Brunner had been interned, just as he had feared would happen. He had been taken away by the police early one morning while marking up the newspapers.

'They took him to prison,' Alice told Jess when she went into the shop. 'Prison! My Heinrich! Just for being born in the wrong place.' Her red-rimmed eyes stared at Jess and her mouth trembled. 'What did he ever do to deserve that?'

'I don't know, Alice. It's all part of this terrible war. Nobody's safe any more. How long are they going to keep him there?'

Alice shook her head. 'Who knows? As long as the war lasts, I suppose. For the duration. They treated him like a criminal, Jess. Prison! My Heinrich!'

She was struggling now to keep the shop going by herself, with some help from Joy. But a newsagent's shop wasn't easy for a woman on her own to run. It meant early mornings and late evenings, with all the stock of sweets and stationery to keep going as well as the daily papers and the *Evening News*. She also had a small flock of paper-boys to keep in order, though by the end of the first week several of them had stopped work because of her connection with a 'German spy'.

It wasn't fair. But nothing was fair these days, as Olive Chapman, torn with anxiety over Derek, never lost an opportunity of reminding her parents.

'If only we'd been able to get married. D'you realise, he's out there in France and I may never see him again? And if anything happens to him, it won't be me they'll tell, it'll be his mother. I've got to wait for her to tell me.'

'Well, she will,' Annie said, thinking that if anything happened to her son she would want to be first to know, whether he was married or not. 'You work there, after all. She's only got to walk across the yard.'

'It's not the same,' Olive said. 'If I was his wife, it'd be me that'd get the telegram.'

'For goodness sake!' Annie exclaimed. 'You talk as if you *want* a telegram! I should think you'd be thankful there hasn't been one.'

Olive gave her mother a scathing look and flounced out of the room. Of course she didn't want a telegram saying that Derek had been killed or injured. But if there *was* going to be one . . . But it was no use talking to Mum. She didn't understand. All she did was look suspicious and ask if there was any 'reason' why Olive was so upset that they hadn't got married before Derek had gone away.

Well, she must know by now that there wasn't. After a bit of a scare the first month after Derek had gone, Olive's periods had returned to normal and the bag of stained sanitary towels had been in the cupboard waiting to be burnt each month just as usual. It seemed that he'd been right, you didn't get pregnant the first time.

But the days and weeks seemed very long without him. She missed the little red car standing in the road, and she missed his cheerful rat-a-tat knock on the door. She missed his smile and the dark gold of his hair, she missed his voice and his laugh, and most of all she missed his touch and his kisses. At night, she lay in bed remembering the love-making they had shared, the way he would caress her breasts and bury his face in their softness, the way he would straddle her, clasping her tightly in his arms so that she felt completely enclosed by his warmth. She shaped her mouth for his kisses and tried to pretend he was there; she hugged herself with her arms crossed and tried to believe his body was pressed against hers.

But none of her imaginings could convince her and eventually she would drift into sleep, hoping to meet him in her dreams, hoping that in that mysterious country where anything could happen and anything seem real, she would once again lie in his arms and share the love that had grown between them; even though in the morning she must wake again to the cold greyness of reality.

But her dreams refused to co-operate. If she dreamed of Derek at all, it was of some strange, bleak landscape scored with trenches and pitted with deep craters of mud. Barbed wire lay tangled across the stony ground and the roar of gunfire echoed across the monotonous fields, while overhead she could hear the drone of unseen aircraft and the thud and thunder of a rain of bombs. There were people in this landscape, people in grey and brown with hidden faces, who lurked and crouched and skulked. None of them could be trusted; there were no familiar faces, no friendly grins. There was only an air of hatred and menace that glowered down from the sullen clouds and spread like a canker across the grim countryside of nightmare.

I can't bear it, she thought. I can't bear not knowing what's happening to him. And if he gets killed out there, if he's taken away from me . . . what use will it be to stay alive? How will I go on without him?

If only we could have got married . . .

'It wouldn't have made any difference to how bad you feel now,' Betty said when Olive tried to explain these feelings, taking it for granted that Betty felt the same without Graham. 'You'd still be worrying yourself sick. And it doesn't do any good. It doesn't help Derek and it certainly doesn't help us, seeing you moon about with your face down to your knees.'

Olive stared at her. 'You're callous, that's what you are, Betty Chapman. Your boy's at sea, liable to be torpedoed or blown up by a mine at any minute, and you don't even care! It doesn't even keep you awake at night.'

'Why should it? There's nothing any of us can do.' Betty picked up one of her father's socks and began to darn it. 'We're better off doing something that really does help. There's plenty of war work crying out to be done – learning first aid, helping out with warden work. You could learn to drive – they'll be wanting ambulance drivers once the bombing starts. If you just did some work like that, you'd have other things else to think about and something to make you sleep at night instead of grizzling.'

'Like you and your Land Army work, I suppose,' Olive said sarcastically.

Betty flushed. 'It isn't my fault they haven't called me yet. I volunteered.' In fact, she had been to the office several times to ask when she would be going, but had been told that for the moment they were taking no more girls. Bitterly disappointed, she was now looking for something else to do and, without telling her family, had sent for details of the women's Services. But she still hankered after the Land Army.

When Olive had left to take some magazines down to Jess, she thought about Graham. Was Olive right to say that she didn't care? Of course I care, she thought indignantly. But . . . do I feel like Olive seems to feel about Derek?

She wasn't even sure that she *wanted* to feel like that. It was more sensible, surely, to take things calmly, not get in a state over something you couldn't alter. Did she really want to feel that her life would be ruined, just because a certain man wasn't around any more? Was it really possible that the next fifty or sixty years would be miserable because of someone she'd met at eighteen and lost six months later?

And did all this mean she wasn't really in love with Graham?

Of course I'd be upset if anything happened to him, she thought. But I'd be upset if Bob Shaw was killed too. She glanced up at the mantelpiece. A letter from Bob had been waiting there for her this afternoon when she had come in from work. She'd torn it open eagerly, knowing it would be filled with interesting and amusing anecdotes. She looked forward to Graham's letters as well, but he wasn't so good at putting himself on paper as Bob was – all his jokes and mischief seemed to rely on his being there in person. But Bob's personality leapt out of the page as she read, and she laughed, her eyes bright.

That had been wrong too, according to Olive.

'You shouldn't be writing to another boy. It's not fair.'

'Oh, shut up.' Betty had had enough of her sister lately. 'You're always nagging. I'll be glad when I do go into the Land Army, just to get away from you!'

Now, as she sat darning her father's socks, she felt ashamed. She

316

and Olive never used to quarrel like this. It's this war, she thought, this bloody war. It's getting everyone down.

On the day that Winston Churchill became Prime Minister, an order came through that all motor vessels must be officially registered.

Ted told Annie about it when he came home from morning shift. 'Right down to the smallest. I mean, what are we supposed to make of that? What use is some creaky little dinghy with an outboard to the government? They must be in a right panic if they think little tubs like that are going to help win the war.'

Annie listened in dismay. 'Even the ferryboats?'

'Well, of course!' Ted's voice was irritable. Although the hours of darkness were shorter now, he still hated taking the boat across the harbour in the pitch-black of night. 'They're not small, are they. Not by these standards, anyway.' He thought of his own boat, the *Ferry King*. She weighed in at fifty-seven tons and was about twenty years old – a fine, sturdy little vessel with another forty or fifty years ahead of her. Like the rest of the boats that plied between Portsmouth and Gosport she was driven by steam and carried her own coal. She needed only three men to run her – himself, the engineer Sam Hardy and the young apprentice Ben. 'What do they want with them all, that's what I want to know?'

A good many other people were wondering the same thing. The latest measures did indeed look like panic. The stormy arguments in Parliament, culminating in the resignation of Mr Chamberlain – the terrible events in Holland, Belgium and Luxembourg – it seemed that every day brought fresh bad news. And in comparison with Hitler's might, the efforts made at fighting back seemed puny.

The registering of the small boats was not the only new measure. A new army was being formed – Dad's Army, some people were calling it, for it was to comprise mostly men too old to be called up, some of them in their seventies. As Local Defence Volunteers, its members had already started parading with broomsticks to simulate guns, provoking almost as much mirth as poor Fred Stokes with his home-made bomb. But the laughter was bitter now. Too many men were dying, at sea, in the air and on the battlefields of Europe, and nobody seriously believed that the coasts could be defended from invasion by a few old men with broomsticks or what Ted scornfully called 'rubber ducks'.

Frank tuned in eagerly to the wireless on 13 May to hear the first broadcast by Winston Churchill as Prime Minister. He had already, as First Lord of the Admiralty, made several broadcasts to the nation and everyone was familiar with his rolling, mellifluous tones. But now he spoke with new authority.

His message was no more cheering. But he had a unique way of making bad news sound like inspiration, and the grim reality of the war that was only just beginning, an opportunity at last to come to grips with the enemy.

'*I have nothing to offer but blood, toil, tears and sweat,*' he declaimed. '*We have before us an ordeal of the most grievous kind . . . our policy is to wage war against a monstrous tyranny, never surpassed in the dark, lamentable catalogue of human crime . . . our aim is victory – victory at all costs, in spite of all terror . . . for without victory there is no survival . . . But I take up my task with buoyancy and hope and I say: Let us go forward together, with our united strength.*'

Frank switched off again. He and Jess looked at each other soberly.

'It sounds bad. But I'll say this for Winnie, he doesn't mince words. He tells you straight. You know just what you're in for with him.'

Jess nodded. 'He's got a way with words. He makes you feel that however bad it is, we're all in it together – and nobody can beat us. If we can win this war at all, he's the man who'll lead us to it. But – oh, Frank – ' She reached out her hand. 'How many people are going to die before we're done with it?'

Four days later they heard that Brussels was now occupied by the Germans. The next day Antwerp also capitulated. On the following Wednesday the Emergency Powers Act was passed in Parliament, giving the government full power over almost everybody and everything in the country. Attlee, the new deputy prime minister, urged everyone to keep calm. 'Continue at your jobs until ordered otherwise,' he said, and people realised that their lives could no longer be considered their own. The liberty of the Briton was a thing of the past.

'And the future,' Frank said, 'when we win this war.'

But were the Allies going to win? Grave faces in the streets proclaimed their doubts. News from Europe worsened. German forces were spreading across France, driving the Allies before them. How could the tide be turned? It seemed hopeless, impossible.

Thursday morning brought news closer to home, when Woolworths store in Commercial Road was burned down. There was talk of spies and arson, scornfully discounted by some who declared that Jerry had better things to do than rob the city of its stock of cheap screwdrivers and paper bags. But the thought of treachery in the heart of the city brought a new kind of fear, and with it a suspicion and distrust that were worse.

'At least nobody can say it was Heinrich Brunner,' Jess said as a group of women stood in September Street, discussing the fire. 'He might not like being in prison but it does stop people throwing mud at him.'

She looked at Ethel Glaister as she spoke. The two women had maintained a barbed neutrality since Jess had returned home. Jess had more than a suspicion that Ethel had been setting her cap at Frank while she was away, and Ethel was disgruntled at having been baulked of her prey. Now she tossed her head and looked scornful.

'*He* might be in prison but that doesn't mean he can't give orders to those left outside. Everyone knows about the Fifth Column. Who's to say he doesn't pass messages to his associates?'

'Oh, for goodness sake!' Jess turned away in disgust. 'I've never heard such rubbish. Heinrich Brunner organising a Fifth Column, indeed! You want your head looking at, Ethel Glaister.'

Ethel gasped with indignation but Jess was already walking away. I don't want to be seen talking to her again, she thought. She's mean, spiteful and not worth wasting my breath on.

Granny Kinch was standing at her door as usual. She'd recovered from the shame of having Micky brought up before the Juvenile Court, which had kept her indoors for a whole fortnight, and gave Jess her usual gap-toothed smile.

'They're saying 'Itler's starting his air raids soon.'

'Air raids?' Jess stopped, her heart growing cold. 'How do you know that?'

'My Nancy 'eard it from a friend of 'ers.' She looked over her shoulder. 'Come and tell Mrs Budd what you told me, Nance.'

Nancy Baxter came to the door. As usual, she had a cigarette hanging from her lip but her hair had been set and she looked smarter than usual. She must be making good money these days, Jess thought, and was immediately ashamed of her cynicism. All the same, it was probably true.

'That's right,' Nancy said. 'He's going to start bombing any day. Then we can all look out. If you ask me, this war's all but over. He's going to hammer us into the ground.'

Jess gazed at her. Nancy spoke with a kind of dreary resignation. As if she had lost hope. And perhaps she was right. Everywhere you turned, you met bad news. Britain and her allies were being driven back from Europe, where they had marched so full of hope and determination. Scandinavia and the Low Countries gone – France about to fall. What was happening to the troops that had been sent there, to the thousands of young men who had been torn from their homes to fight what was beginning to seem a useless fight? And what would happen here, once they had been beaten?

As Ted said, how could a few old men with broomsticks and an unruly rabble of small boats prevent invasion from such powerful attack?

'We mustn't think like that,' she said to Nancy. 'We've got to do what Mr Churchill said – we've got to pull together and aim for victory. We can't lose heart now.'

But Nancy just shrugged and turned away.

Granny Kinch looked at Jess and made a rueful face. 'She's worn out. Life's never bin easy for her. And now she's 'aving to watch all 'er friends go off to be mashed to pulp by some ugly Jerry – well, you can't blame 'er for getting a bit low, can you?'

Perhaps you couldn't, Jess thought, making her way back home. It had never occurred to her before that Nancy might actually be fond of her 'friends'. Or even if she had never met them before and would probably never meet them again, that she might still feel pity at knowing what they were going to when when they left her arms. A sudden dim realisation came to her of what life must be like for someone like Nancy: a succession of encounters, empty of love, yet still with enough humanity about

320

them to feel sad that the body you had known so intimately was soon to be no more than dead flesh.

Jess shuddered and went indoors to light the fire and get Frank's supper ready. He was working overtime again, coming home late in the evening worn out from a day's hard toil, with time and strength only to eat his meal, read the newspaper and then go to bed. He was up again at five-thirty and away soon after six, bringing Jess a cup of tea before he left. Yet he still managed to work the allotment at weekends.

'Dig for Victory,' he said to Jess, quoting one of the government exhortations to be seen on posters everywhere. 'It's something I can do. And we're going to need food, Jess. The rationing and shortages are going to get worse.'

Everything was getting worse. In this third week of May 1940, it seemed that the world was holding its breath, waiting for something. The sun shone down from a serene blue sky. The sea rippled gently on the shingle beach of Southsea. Birds who knew nothing of war sang oblivious from their trees, and Henry the cat slumbered contentedly on top of the Anderson shelter, too idle even to stalk the mice who lived behind the shed.

It made the truth of what was happening seem all the more ugly.

Frank stuck pins in his map every day, marking the advance of the German troops through France. It was clear that the Allies were being driven into a trap. The BEF was moving back towards the beaches of Dunkirk. Calais was still held but must surely fall at any moment. And the call came for the motor vessels, registered only a fortnight ago, to make their way to Dover.

'What are they going to do?' Jess asked, and Frank stared at his map and then turned to look at her.

'It's my guess they're going to evacuate,' he said, and the word was like a knell. 'They're bringing them back. We're on the run, Jess.'

'You're going to France?' Annie stared at her husband. 'You're going to France in the *Ferry King*?'

He nodded. 'That's what they tell us.'

'But – you've never been outside the harbour. You've only ever gone to Gosport and back.'

'Think I'll get lost?' He was pacing the room nervously, pausing to look out of the window. 'Think I can't do it?'

Annie lifted her hands helplessly. 'What can I think? I mean, just going over with the ferry in the dark – you hate it. How're you going to manage – '

He turned on her. 'The same way we're all going to manage, Annie. By just getting on and doing it. And not whingeing and whining about it.' He jabbed his finger at the map that he, like Frank, had stuck up on the wall. 'There's men over there, Annie, thousands of them like rats in a trap. If we don't go and fetch 'em, they're going to get killed. Some of them are being killed already. Think of it, Annie – *at this very moment*, men are getting killed on those beaches. We've *got* to get them out. We can't just leave 'em to be massacred because we're scared of the dark!' He paused for a moment, then added quietly, 'I owe it to our Olive, Annie. Her Derek's over there somewhere. I've got to go for her sake. It was me wouldn't let them get married, remember?'

Annie gazed at him, then crossed the room and laid her hands on his arms. She looked up into his face and smiled, her eyes tender.

'I'm proud of you, Ted, you know that? All right, you go. But don't go doing anything foolhardy, will you? I want you back here, safe and sound and all in one piece.'

He grinned at her, but his mouth twisted a little as he took her in his arms and held her close. 'I'll be back, Annie. You don't have to worry about me. The old *Ferry King* will look after us.'

They called it Operation Dynamo, after the generator room deep in the cliffs beneath Dover Castle where it was planned. It was a mission that should never have succeeded – this desperate mobilisation of pleasure steamers, ferries, fishing boats and motor yachts. There were over a thousand of them, requisitioned, voluntarily offered, or in some cases simply taken from their moorings. They came down the Thames, round the coasts and through the Solent to mass at Dover for the crossing to Dunkirk. They were manned by naval reservists and volunteers, often by their owners or skippers like Ted Chapman. But most of them were commanded by Navy personnel, and for this Ted was grateful. As Annie said, crossing the Channel was a far cry from shuttling back and forth across Portsmouth Harbour.

'I hope he'll be all right,' she said to Jess as they sat at the kitchen table with a pot of tea between them. 'I know how it's been preying on his mind, having to take the boat across the harbour in the blackout. And this is going to be a thousand times worse. They're gunning them down from the air.' She twisted her hands in front of her. Her eyes were swollen and tired, and her hair untidy. The normally immaculate kitchen was littered with washing-up from the last meal. 'Jess, I never thought we'd have to face anything like this. I thought this was a young man's war.'

'It's everyone's war,' Jess returned gravely. How could she comfort her sister, how could she tell her that of course Ted would return? The *Ferry King* was a small boat, never intended to cross the Channel, though she had no doubt it was capable of the trip. Small dinghies made it, after all. But under fire, being strafed by enemy warplanes, fired on from the beaches? She shook her head. The whole enterprise seemed crazy. It was like sending mice into the jaws of a tiger. 'We're all going to have to do our bit, Annie, even if it's not what we thought. Like Mr Churchill said, we've got to pull together.'

Annie nodded. She sniffed and blew her nose. 'I know, Jess. And it's not just Ted. It's all the others, all those young men . . . Our Olive is nearly out of her mind over Derek.'

'There's not been any news, then?'

'Not a word. "Somewhere in France",' that's all we know. He could be anywhere. He might even be a prisoner now. Or he might be – '

'He might be dead.'

Both women jumped and turned to see Olive standing in the doorway. She was wearing a summer frock, blue with small white spots and a white collar. She looked fresh and pretty, her dark hair brushed into a long bob, almost touching her shoulders, but her eyes were pools of tragedy.

'That's what you were going to say, wasn't it? He might be dead. He might be lying in some field, forgotten. I might never know what's happened to him.' She came slowly into the kitchen and sank down in the chair Ted normally used. She laid her arms on the table and dropped her head down on them as if she had no more strength to hold it up. 'I'll have nothing to remember him by. No wedding, no baby . . . not even his name.'

'Oh, Olive.' Anne reached out and touched her daughter's shoulder. 'Olive, I'm sorry.'

The girl's head came up at that and there was a flash of the old rebellion in her eyes. 'Sorry? Sorry for what? For not letting us get married?' Then the flame died and her eyes were dull again. 'Oh, it doesn't matter. It wouldn't have made any difference now.' She laid her head once again on her arms. 'If he's dead, it's all over. And if he's not, we'll get married, whatever you and Dad say.'

'I know,' Annie said gently. 'I know. And we won't stand in your way any longer.' She paused and then added very quietly, 'If Dad comes back . . .'

Jess felt the tears burn her own eyes. Already, she thought, there had been too much tragedy in this war, too many tears. Tears for Colin, when they had thought him lost on the *Exeter*. Tears for the children who had been wrenched from their homes and families and sent, bewildered, into the care of strangers – or, like the Atkinsons and Martin Baker, to neglect and cruelty. Tears for Heinrich Brunner, so unfairly torn from his wife and child, and now tears for Derek and Ted.

And if they came home safe, when and for whom would the next tears be shed? For Colin again, back on his ship? For Graham, also at sea? Or for those nearer home, killed in their own beds when the threatened air raids started at last?

Jess had no doubt now that the bombing was going to come. Hitler's success had been too absolute for him to ease off now. Even though he seemed to have paused long enough to enable the evacuation of the BEF to get under way, he could be only drawing breath before launching the next offensive. And with no more troops to be fought on land, he must turn his attention to the air and his final invasion.

By June or July there could be German troops marching the streets of Portsmouth. The streets could ring to the stamp of jackboots and the guttural shouts of *'Heil Hitler!'* The harbour could be filled with the stark shapes of Germans warships and the air throb with the drone of German aircraft.

What will they do with us? she thought. What will they do *to* us? Will we be able to live our normal lives or will we all be turned into slaves? And what about the children?

She raised her eyes and looked around the kitchen. It looked normal enough, though untidy by Annie's standards. She saw the wireless Ted had made in the varnished wooden cabinet he had made for it.

Only a fortnight ago, she and Frank had listened to Winston Churchill's broadcast. And she remembered again the grim message he had passed on – and the inspiration of his final words.

'I have nothing to offer but blood, toil, tears and sweat . . . Our aim is victory at all costs . . . I take up my task with buoyancy and hope . . . Let us go forward together, with our united strength.'

Buoyancy and hope. Victory at all costs. Let us go forward together.

Jess got up from her chair. She went to the sink and refilled the kettle. She looked at the bowed heads of her sister and niece and went to lay her hands upon them.

'I'm making another cup of tea,' she said. 'And then we're going over to Ted's allotment. We'll give your Betty a hand and we'll dig for victory, like Frank says. We've got to pull together in this, and sitting here worrying's not going to help anyone.'

Annie smiled ruefully. 'I've been telling our Olive that. And here I am, doing the same thing!'

'We all do it,' Jess said quietly. 'And we all need someone to remind us not to. Of course we can't help worrying – it's human nature. But somehow or other we've got to get over it and carry on, or the whole country's going to fall apart. It's up to us as well, Annie – not just the men, going out to fight and not just those who're bringing them back from France at this moment. It's us women, left at home, who've got to keep things going. Otherwise there's going to be nothing worth bringing them back for.'

It was strange to be on your own ship and yet not in command.

Not that the *Ferry King* was strictly a ship, Ted thought wryly as he stood on the bridge beside the naval reservist who had taken over. But Lieutenant Horner clearly saw it as such and behaved as if he had the wheel of a battleship in his hands. He stared ahead, giving Ted orders in a clipped voice and obviously expecting to be obeyed.

'You're under military authority now,' he said as they steamed out through the harbour mouth on the evening of 26 May. 'I hope that's clearly understood. As far as you and your men are concerned, you're Navy personnel.'

Ted nodded. He'd already accepted this and was glad to do so. He knew that although his expertise in handling the boat was essential, his experience wasn't enough to take the ferryboat across the Channel, and that of his 'men' – Sam Hardy and young Ben! – was even less. It wasn't that they were incapable of handling the boat in rougher waters, it was the navigation involved that might be their undoing. He and Sam had taken their exams of course, but without practical experience and plenty of it, they were sure to have become rusty.

In fact, they were unlikely to get lost, for once out in the Solent they found themselves part of a fleet of assorted ships on their way to Dover to answer the call. From Portsmouth, they recognised the Isle of Wight paddle steamers, *Whippingham* and *Portsdown*, and their own sister ship *Fawley*. The *Bee*, a seventy-five-foot powered barge which normally took cargo between Portsmouth and the Isle of Wight, was in company with four others, and there was a number of ships and small boats from Southampton, Poole, Weymouth and Plymouth. It seemed that the whole of the south coast was involved in the exercise.

If Ted had disliked the journeys across the harbour, that night's steaming east along the coast of England showed him that he had experienced nothing yet. The darkness was absolute. The only relief was from the stars massed above, a brilliant shimmer of needlepoint lights, blotted out to the north by the bulk of the South Downs. Around the boat, the sea lay black and menacing, heaving gently as they pushed their way across it.

Thank God it's not rough, Ted thought, but he did not say so. Everyone was keeping quiet; you never knew who or what might be about this night, and voices carried far over water. The engine ran as softly as Sam Hardy and Ben knew how to make it. Around them, the other ships glided like black-shrouded ghosts, a strange, bizarre navy called to the aid of a country in extremity.

By five they were nearing Dover and daylight was breaking over the harbour. Ben came up from the engine-room with mugs of cocoa for Ted and Lieutenant Horner, and stared.

'Whew! Look at all them boats, Skip!'

The three of them gazed at the scene. With the famous white cliffs as a backdrop, it was difficult to see the water for the craft that covered it. Ships and boats of all sizes, from large ferry steamers from the Isle of Man to small sailing dinghies, rocked gently on the calm blue sea. It looked like the largest regatta ever held, but there was no air of carnival about this flotilla. Instead, there was a grim, determined purpose in the preparations that were going on, and barely had they anchored when the lieutenant ordered Ben to drop overboard the small dinghy intended for use as a lifeboat, should the *Ferry King* ever meet with an accident, and rowed himself ashore.

'We might as well make ourselves useful while he's gone,' Ted remarked, and they cooked breakfast with the stores that had been brought aboard the previous afternoon and set themselves to checking the engine and making sure all was ready for the crossing. But they had not done much before Lieutenant Horner was back.

'We're going to Dunkirk,' he said, confirming the guess they had all made. 'Now look – it's going to be no picnic over there. There's getting on for half a million men stranded and we've got to get them out and bring them back before the Germans shell them all to pieces.'

Ted gaped. 'Half a million? But – ' He stared at the fleet of small boats. 'Even this lot'll never get all them out.'

'We're not meant to. Our job's to act as ferries – getting the soldiers from the beach to the ships that are already there, waiting to bring them back. They can't get in close enough, y'see. Now it's not going to be easy. The Germans are strafing them, gunning them and bombing them. They're doing everything bar hold their hands and tell them bedtime stories. And if you don't fancy it, you've only got to say. We can put a couple of sailors on board the vessel and you can go back home, and no hard feelings.' He looked at them hard. 'What do you say?'

There was a small silence. Ted looked at Sam Hardy, nearly sixty years old and a grandfather. He looked at Ben, only sixteen and too young yet for active service. He thought of Annie, sitting at home worrying about him and of Olive, almost frantic about Derek.

'You two can do as you like,' he said. 'I'm staying with the *King*.'

Sam grinned and rubbed his chin, grey with the morning's bristly growth.

'Me too. You don't get rid of me that easy.'

They looked at Ben. He'd been with them for two years now and they'd watched him grow from a skinny boy to a youth in the final stage of his growth towards manhood. His voice was breaking, he had a downy growth where Sam had bristles, he was tall and promised to be well-built. But he was still, Ted thought, really a child.

'You don't have to come,' he said gently. 'Nobody'll think any the worse of you if you leave now. You've done a good job, coming this far.'

'Leave?' Ben said. His voice shook with excitement. 'Leave now? You'll have to tie me up and throw me over the side!'

Sam laughed but Ted felt an unaccustomed ache in his throat. What in God's name am I going to say to his mother if anything happens to him? he thought. He doesn't know what he's saying. He looked at Lieutenant Horner.

The reservist sighed. He wasn't here to play nursemaid, nor make other people's decisions for them. The boy had done well enough to come this far and a sailor could be found to take his place, but the more civilians that were ready to help the better it was. And he was willing enough. The trouble was, he had no idea what he was facing.

'Listen, son,' he said. 'This isn't a pleasure cruise. It's going to be hell over there, and I only use that word because I can't think of a worse one. There's going to be bodies floating in the sea —and bits of bodies. You'll see blood and guts and brains spattered on the decks of your own boat. You'll see men killed in front of your eyes and you might be killed yourself. You could be blown up or shot or drowned, or a bit of all three. You could come home minus an arm or a leg. You'll see sights you'll never forget; sights that will haunt your dreams till your dying day. Do you understand what I'm saying?'

Ben stared at him. His face whitened and green shadows appeared around his mouth and eyes. He bit his lips and swallowed once or twice and Ted thought he was going to vomit, perhaps even faint. He put out a hand to steady the boy, but Ben blinked hard and shook him off. He lifted his chin and looked the officer in the eye.

'Yes, sir,' he said. 'I understand. And I still want to come.' He paused for a moment, then added quietly, 'My brother's over there somewhere.'

They slept the rest of the day, on makeshift bunks in the passengers' cabin below decks. While the sun shone warmly on the idyllic scene, men who had been awake all night rested and small boats shuttled to and fro with supplies. Food and water were brought to craft that normally carried no more than a jug of tea, heated up on the engine. Many of them needed coal, and this must be bagged from dumps ashore and heaved aboard. And blankets and first-aid supplies were stowed in every corner.

'There'll be hospital ships waiting for these,' Lieutenant Horner said, 'but we may have to use them too. Know anything about first aid, Skipper?'

Ted nodded. He had done a course, and so had Sam, but he doubted whether they were up to dealing with the kind of injuries the lieutenant had described to Ben. What did you do with a man who had had a leg blown off? Or a hole punched in his side, or his eyes shot through?

'We'll do our best,' he said, and the naval man nodded.

'Nobody can do more.'

By 7.30 in the evening the fleet was beginning to move. Small boats were wired to larger ones and towed, to give them speed, larger ones went under their own steam. Following the glimmering golden pathway flung down by a setting sun, they left Dover behind and set out for what Lieutenant Horner had described as a 'place worse than hell'.

It was dark when they arrived but there had been no doubt that they were approaching war itself as they steamed slowly towards the glow of the burning city. Dunkirk, the last refuge for half a million soldiers, was being bombarded, its docks on fire and a huge blanket of smoke pouring from a blazing oil container. The acrid sky was spattered with the bitter yellow of flames and burning debris and sliced by the beams of searchlights while overhead could be heard the nasal snarl of German aircraft. Once it became light, the bombardment would increase, and it would not be confined to the town.

We're not going to get out of here, Ted thought, listening to the roar of guns somewhere inland. None of us is going to get out. It's a crazy, mad farce, a last-ditch effort to salvage some of the wreckage of this insane war. And we're all going to die for it. Young or old, soldier, sailor or civilian, we're going to die here in fire and water and the sickening stench of our own blood.

And then he saw the grey light of dawn creep up from the east. He saw the apricot glow of the sun colouring the fringe of the sky, saw it throw its warm, glowing dome of hope above his head. And when he looked at the beaches he knew that they must get back, and that there must be no more thought of defeat.

'Bugger me,' Sam Hardy said quietly. 'Look at 'em. They look as if they've bin standing there for hours.'

The beach was packed with soldiers. Grim and silent, standing as if waiting to witness some great and spectacular event, they stood shoulder to shoulder, their tin hats their only protection from the planes that patrolled overhead. Behind them, the town stood half demolished, hardly a building left undamaged and many of them on fire. A clutter of abandoned vehicles – cars, trucks, tanks – stood at random, as if they were toys thrown down by some petulant giant baby. And the whole scene was darkened, even on this bright spring morning, by the spreading black shadow of filthy, stinking smoke from the burning oil containers.

But most tragic, most pitiful of all, was not the scene on the land, but what was in the sea. Lines of soldiers, queuing up as if waiting at a bus stop, stretching out until they were neck-deep in the water, their packs still on their backs, their rifles held in their arms. Though the sea that swirled about their legs and bodies must be numbingly cold, though their uniforms must be dragging with the weight of the salt water that saturated them, though they were under merciless threat from the planes that droned above their heads, they stood still and patient, waiting for rescue because, in this final extremity, there was nothing else for them to do.

How many hours had they stood there? Ted wondered. Had they been there all night, shuffling in the chilly water, their legs tangled with seaweed and slimy, unseen rocks beneath their feet?

330

He gazed down at them, trying to imagine what had brought them to this point, what battles they had fought, what retreat they had endured to arrive here on the beach at Dunkirk, waiting for rescue.

He looked down at them and the men looked up at the little ships that had come to rescue them, they looked up at the men on the *Ferry King*, and Ted knew that inside they must be feeling the relief of men rescued from the jaws of hell. But their faces were without expression, for even those who were trying to grin had faces too stiff, lips too cold, for the muscles to obey. And perhaps they could not have succeeded anyway, for in their eyes was the dullness of suffering, of fatigue and lost hope.

'Get them up,' Lieutenant Horner snapped. 'Get as many on board as you can. We've got to start getting them away.' He glanced around. The patrolling aircraft were beginning to attack, machine-gunning the beaches and the ships that had come to the rescue, and even as he watched Ted saw men begin to fall. The air that had been quiet, save for the drone of patrolling planes, was now curdled with screams.

And there were other things in the sea too; the dead bodies that Lieutenant Horner had told Ben they would see, some face down, sinking beneath the weight of the packs still strapped to their backs, some floating like corks in life-jackets, with faces that were bloated, burned or mutilated turned up to the sky. And there were the arms and legs that had been blown away, and other parts less readily identifiable, lumps of torn and bloody flesh that had once been human.

Ted heard Ben gag and knew that there was no time to waste. If the boy was to be any use, he must be given something to do. And there was only one task before them now – that of getting the living on board and back to safety. The dead must be left to themselves.

Within five minutes they had the first men aboard. The *Ferry King* had not been built for boarding from a beach and her sides were too high and steep for easy climbing but there were two rope ladders aboard and the mooring ropes at the bow and stern, and the soldiers scrambled up these and fell on the deck, gasping and streaming with water. With rough haste, the crew shoved them aside to make way for the next ones. Their sodden clothes were heavy, their packs and rifles weighing them down, and many of them were too weak with fatigue to lift themselves from the water. It needed the strength of two men, sometimes three, to get them up over the railing and then to move them away. And some were injured and screamed with pain at their rough handling, and the water that ran from their clothes was reddened and thick.

One died in Ben's arms as he lifted him aboard. He stared down at the face so abruptly stilled, at the upturned eyes, and then looked horrified at Ted. But Sam saw the look and pulled the body from his arms, shoving it back over the side.

'It's the living we've got to take, we ain't got time to bother with them as is past help. Give that bloke a hand, Ben, get 'em up as fast as you can and let's have 'em out on the ships quick.'

Ben took one last look at the body that had been cast into the sea and then did as he was told. There was no more time for talk. Together, the four of them worked to heave men out of the water and on the deck, but the ferry was still too high for most of them to scramble aboard and Ted began to rip up the slatted benches where passengers would sit. With the help of Lieutenant Horner, he roped them together to form ladders and dropped them over the side and immediately soldiers began to clamber up.

The planes were directly overheard now, the roar of their engines an almost solid menace, sending a rumble of vibration through the whole boat. The water was spattered with machine-gun bullets. Every time they heard the burst of rattling fire the four men ducked and at first Ted wondered if they ought to take cover. But how could they settle down below, leaving these poor devils on deck and in the sea, at the mercy of the Germans who flew inexorably above? And if they did, how would they ever get their job done?

Ted and Sam had both served in the Great War and had been under fire then. They had seen men break up under the strain and shot by their own officers for cowardice. Others had been sent home, unfit for further service; shuddering, gibbering wrecks unable to string more than two or three words together without stuttering, cowering under the table at the slightest loud noise, shambling about the streets without hope of working or making their own lives again. They were as maimed as the match-seller outside Woolworths, and often became as destitute but were given even less sympathy.

332

Ted often thought that he could have been one of these wrecks himself. His dislike, amounting to fear, of crossing the harbour in the blackout stemmed from those nights in the trenches with only the stars above for light, when danger lurked in every corner. Now he was reminded even more sharply by the rattle of machine-gun fire and the drone of planes. For a moment, as he stared at the splattered water, he wanted to turn and dive for cover, to hide his head. Why had he come on this crazy mission? Why had any of them come? How could anyone survive this hell, this holocaust? Wasn't it going to mean an even greater waste of lives?

The thoughts ran through his mind like ants whose nest had been suddenly uncovered. And then he turned his head and saw Ben staring at him. The boy looked as if he had been suddenly struck with paralysis. His eyes were wide with fear, his lip trembled and he lifted his hands towards Ted as if begging for help.

With an almost audible snap, Ted's mind came back into focus. He thrust his memories and his fears to the back of his mind and gave Ben the only help possible.

'Come on!' he snapped. 'Don't stand there gawping. There's work to be done – we're not here on our holidays. *Get those men aboard, damn you!*'

His voice was like the harsh scrape of galvanised iron on stone, and it released Ben from his paralysis. He shook his head briefly, then turned and jerked a man bodily into the boat, lifting him by one shoulder. Dropping him on the deck he turned for the next and suddenly soldiers seemed to be almost flying into the boat, pulled up from the makeshift ladders as if they were little more than babies and pushed aside at once to make room for the next.

Within half an hour the *Ferry King* was fully laden. The cabin below was packed with exhausted soldiers, the decks solid with their sprawling bodies. Most of them were too weary to sit up, but as Lieutenant Horner went up on the bridge and signalled to Sam to get the engines going, Ted and Ben went around with bottles of water. The men gulped it down thankfully and began to revive a little.

'Cor, that's better.' They wiped wet hands over grimy faces, leaving streaks of mud and often blood across unshaven skin. 'Now all we needs is a pint o' booze and a packet o' fish an' chips, an' a stroll dahn Lambeth way an' we'll know we're 'ome again.'

'Lambeth! You Cockneys seem tae think that's the centre of the bliddy universe. It's Glasgae Ah'm headin' for, right enough.' The speaker glanced up at Ted. 'Where's your home port, Jimmy?'

'I'm not Jimmy,' Ted began, unravelling the unfamiliar dialect, but the soldier was already leaning back, exhausted, and he passed the water on to the next man. By then the planes were overhead again and machine-guns once more spraying the boat with their deadly rain.

Lieutenant Horner handed the wheel to Ted and he reversed the boat away from the beach. The queue of men looked even longer than when they had begun loading. He took the *Ferry King* well out of her depth before turning to head for the ships that lay outside the harbour. The sky had now lightened to full daylight and although it was still darkened by the pall of smoke from the burning oil containers he could see that the shore was almost black with a solid army of men. They were marching into the water as if intent on some lemming-like mass suicide, and at the head of the beach he could see that the promenade was crowded with more, hundreds of them, thousands . . . How many had Lieutenant Horner said? Half a million?

We'll never do it, he thought. And then: We bloody *will* . . .

The water was thick with boats of all kinds, each of them loading soldiers like some new and valuable cargo. And that's just what they are, he thought. Cannon-fodder one day, ballast the next. But what else could we have done?

Again, there was no time for thought. The men on the beach, the men in the water, were looking to them for hope, for life. Already their faces were blurred as the *King* headed away from the shore and out beyond the ravaged harbour to the ships in deep water.

'Head for that one,' Lieutenant Horner said. 'The destroyer.'

Like all the other ships, it was surrounded by small boats, jostling for places to transfer their cargoes of humanity as quickly as possible. The *Ferry King* joined the crowd and a sailor took the rope Ben threw him and made it fast. A rope ladder was slung down to them and the soldiers began scrambling aboard.

'Thanks, mate. You bin a real toff.' There was no time for more than a word or two, and most of the men were too weary anyway. They clambered aboard the destroyer as if in a dream, their eyes still dark with the horror of all they had seen. And Ted and the lieutenant were anxious only to get away, to get back to the beach and bring off another cargo, to make another small contribution to the gargantuan task that the small boats of a civilian navy had been given in this strange and terrible war.

Oblivious now of time or fatigue, they worked on all day. The stream of soldiers seemed never-ending. One after another, they scrambled or were dragged aboard, one after another they were given water and some food, one after another they were taken to the ships that would carry them home. The destroyer departed, loaded with men, and its place was taken by another, and then another. Nearby, Ted saw the *Gracie Fields*, one of the Isle of Wight boats which had run from Southampton to Cowes before the war had begun. He and Annie and the girls had gone to the Thornycroft shipyard at Woolston to see her launched by the singer herself, warbling 'Sing as We Go' as the ship slid into the River Itchen.

The vessel had been taken off the Isle of Wight run and converted to a minesweeper soon after the war began, but she was still under the command of Captain Larkin, her old master. It was strange and oddly comforting, seeing her here, and Ted gave her a private salute.

The aeroplanes were still overhead but now they had been joined by heavier craft with full bellies who had their own cargo to disgorge. As well as the spray of machine-gun bullets, there were bombs to deal with, and as Ted watched he saw a company of men, grouped on the beach, vanish from sight in a devastating explosion. Sickened, he saw sand and gravel burst in a thunderous detonation, the roar of it obliterating even the cacophony of aircraft, gunfire, engines and shouts and screams that had been the background accompaniment ever since dawn broke. And when the dirt and dust subsided there was only rubble left where, just a few moments before, there had been living men.

Had Derek been one of them? he thought. At every moment, as he worked to save whosoever came first to hand, the thought of his daughter's sweetheart had been at the back of his mind and he had looked briefly into each face in the hope that he might be there. It was foolish, he knew, with so many men waiting for rescue – and who knew that Derek had lived to come this far anyway? – but he could not help it, any more than he could banish from his mind the memory of his daughter's face as she accused him of ruining her life.

'*All we wanted was to be married, and you wouldn't let us. You wouldn't let us!*'

I'll let you now, he promised her silently. If he gets out of this, I'll let you marry the first minute you can . . .

Night fell and still they went on. They were operating on another part of the shore now, in deeper water where the beach shelved suddenly, working with smaller boats which could run further inshore. Some of them were no more than family pleasure cruisers and Ted wondered how they had managed to get across the Channel so quickly. They worked swiftly, running their noses against the shelving shingle so that the soldiers could scramble aboard without risking the deep water. Then they made the short journey back to the larger boats like the *Ferry King*, transferring their loads as the larger boats would transfer them to the ships taking them back across the Channel.

The sea was still calm and although the darkness of the sky was made deeper by the pall of smoke still issuing from the burning oil containers, it was lightened by the fires on shore. Ted and the lieutenant used them as markers as they plied between the larger ships and the shore.

'I hoped the bastards would go home to bed,' Ted said as they listened to the aircraft snarling above them and ducked involuntarily at the sound of each explosion. 'What are they using as targets, for God's sake?'

It was almost impossible to locate the ships in the dark and he knew that they must stop soon to wait for daylight and snatch a few hours' rest. None of them had eaten since morning, nor even realised how time was passing until the sun began to go down. Now he was aware of a gnawing hunger, but there were still thousands of men out there on the beach and he was driven by their own desperate need.

All the same, common sense told him that they could not work on for ever without food or rest, and Horner echoed his thoughts.

'Whether they leave us alone or not, we'll have to heave to after this lot. That lad of yours is almost dead on his feet. You've worked well, all of you, but there'll be more to do tomorrow.'

336

Ted looked towards the darkened beach. It could have been empty and silent, but he knew that hidden beneath the shroud of night a murmuring mass of defeated and weary soldiers lay huddled on the shore, waiting for rescue. Another trip and they could bring off a hundred or two more. And another . . . and another . . .

But the lieutenant was right. They must rest, to be ready to work even harder when dawn came. For dawn would bring the Messerschmitts again, in greater strength than ever. The last few were flying above them now, dropping their remaining bombs apparently at random but, with so many boats in the sea, almost unable to help scoring hits. And each detonation was accompanied by a searing flash of light that revealed every ship in the vicinity, and each direct hit followed by a blazing fire as yet another ship lurched and wallowed and sank to the bottom.

'They might as well just floodlight the whole bloody place and 'ave done with it,' Sam said as he cooked up a mess of eggs and bacon and fried bread on the fire. ' 'Ere, Ben, you look just about done in. Wrap yerself round this.'

The boy took the plate of food and looked at it as if seeing something else. His face was white, his eyes dark with fatigue. He shook his head slightly but Sam put a knife and fork into his hands, folded his trembling fingers around them and told him to eat.

'You need yer strength. You'll feel more the mark after a coupla bites. And then doss down on one of the benches down below for a bit. The toff's right, there's going to be plenty more where this lot come from.' A nearby explosion deafened them all and rocked the boat violently. They heard debris rain down on the deck above. 'That's another poor bugger hit,' Sam said, and went up the gangway to poke his head out. 'It's that – whatchercallit? That Dutch fisherman, one of them what towed the little 'uns over – '

'*Schuit*,' Lieutenant Horner said.

'That's it, skoot – well, it's just copped a big 'un by the look of it.' He watched for a moment, the flames of the burning ship illuminating his face. 'Ain't nothin' we can do,' he said after a moment. 'There's a coupla boats over there but they're not pickin' anyone up.'

Silent and sober, they finished their meal and found corners to sleep in. Ted and the lieutenant tossed for the first watch and Ted mounted to the bridge and settled himself there with a blanket wrapped about him.

It would be a short night but it would seem long enough, no doubt, with bombs falling about them and the occasional burst of gunfire to splatter the beach. Inland, he could hear the rumble of heavier guns and the thud of shells. Once again, the searchlights were active, sending spears of brilliant light to the stars. What are they looking for? he wondered. Our aircraft? But so far, few British planes had been seen and Horner said they were all inland, fighting off the planes making for the coast. 'It'd be a hell of a sight worse if they weren't,' he said.

After only a few hours' sleep, the four men were up again and back at work, running close into the shore, taking men off from the smallest boats, ferrying them out to the ships. Back and forth they went, back and forth, heaving aboard an endless stream of bodies, almost kicking them aside in their endeavours to rescue yet more, always with one eye on the sky above, always with an ear cocked ready for explosion, always with the knowledge that they might in the next second be blasted from the sea to become nothing more than part of the human flotsam that drifted torn and mangled in the rippling blue water.

'Thanks, mate. Lovely weather for it.' A soldier, unshaven, wet and filthy but still able to manage a twisted grin clambered over the side. 'Don't suppose you got a dry fag, 'ave yer? Mine's a bit damp.'

He had probably been standing in water all night, Ted thought, for the edge of the sea was crowded once again with queues of men. He felt in his pocket and dragged out a crumpled packet of Woodbines. 'Here. There's only a couple left, but you're welcome.' And before the man could thank him, he had turned to help the next aboard.

The sun shone down from a serene blue sky on the calm water. Over and over again, the *Ferry King* chugged out to the waiting ships and back again to the crowded beach for a fresh load. It was the kind of day that should have been set aside for holiday-making, the boats filled with carefree revellers; the waiting passengers could have been any swarm of holiday-makers, eager for a trip round the bay. But they had been waiting too long. Enemy planes droned

338

ceaselessly above. Gunfire crackled and spat about their heads. And bombs fell from the blue sky, blowing sea and ships and men to a cocktail of salt water, blood, debris and mangled flesh that settled at last to become a part of the terrible illusion of calm, sunlit serenity.

The *Ferry King* plied stolidly through the chaos, seemingly immune from attack. Several times she went to supply ships for more fuel, as if in exchange for her human cargo; once the four men went aboard a 'skoot' for a quick meal. The Dutchmen told them of the invasion of Holland only a week or so earlier, of how they had escaped in their boats and fled to England and now found themselves helping with the rescue of their allies.

'We cannot allow this man to take over Europe,' they said in their guttural English. 'He is a terrible man. He is cruel and vicious and if he wins it will be the end of the world.'

Ted listened and agreed, but in his heart there were doubts. This was no victory they were engaged in, but a full-scale retreat. Half a million soldiers were being driven back by the might of an army which had marched unresisted into country after country. How could anyone beat him now? How could anyone think he could be defeated?

But thoughts like that could not – must not – be allowed. His task now was to get as many men off as he could, and he wouldn't do that by sitting in a Dutch fishing-boat quaffing schnapps.

'Come on,' he said, getting to his feet. 'There's blokes out there'd rather be home, and they won't get there if we don't take 'em. Come on, Ben, up off your backside and let's see a smile on your face. Sam? Lieutenant?'

They drained their glasses and went on deck, feeling better. The *Ferry King* cast off from the skoot and chugged away, back towards the beach. Around them, the scene was just as before; the surface of the sea covered with small boats filled with khaki-clad men, the sky loud with enemy aircraft, the air split by the rattle of machine-guns and the roar of exploding bombs.

They were only fifty feet away from the skoot when a German bomber swooped down on her and she was blown out of the water in an explosion that all but sank the *King* as well.

They watched in appalled silence.

'Oh God,' Ben said in a strangled voice. 'Oh *God* . . .'

'Look out,' Sam said, 'he's going!'

The boy was swaying on his feet. His face was green, his eyes wild and unfocused. He reached out both hands, clawing at the air, and sank to his knees. His voice babbled incoherently and he sobbed heart-broken sobs. He covered his face with both hands and wept into them, like a woman mourning.

'Get him on his feet!' Lieutenant Horner ordered harshly. 'We can't afford any backsliding now.'

'He's not backsliding,' Ted retorted angrily, but he knew the lieutenant was right and he bent and grabbed Ben under the arms. 'Come on, Ben, on your feet. We can't give in now. There's men on that beach depending on us. Your own brother's there somewhere, remember? He could be in the next lot.'

The boy stared at him. 'The skoot – those Dutchmen . . .'

'They're out of it now,' Ted said firmly. 'They didn't know a thing about it. It's over for them. But it ain't over for the blokes on the beach, so stop whining and put your back in it, right?'

Night fell again and a third day dawned. It was difficult to remember that there had ever been a different life. Portsmouth, September Street, Annie and the kids, were all but a dream. There had never been anything but this incessant ferrying of broken and exhausted soldiers from shore to ship. Never anything but the rattle of gunfire, the thunder of bombs and the screams and groans of wounded men; never anything but the stench of burning oil and cordite, of blood and guts and shit and fear.

But they must be real, Ted thought, dragging yet another waterlogged body aboard, for when have we had time to dream?

Some of the bigger ships, easier targets, had been sunk. Ted had seen two destroyers go down, one on her way out with a full load of soldiers. The sea was filled with bodies, some alive, others broken and beyond help, and then a different rescue operation was launched by the small boats, and the survivors taken to another ship. It's just one step up and two down, he thought with a wave of hopeless frustration. How many have actually made it to Dover? How many have we really saved?

Sometime on the third day they heard that the *Gracie Fields* had gone. On her way back to Dover, with almost eight hundred soldiers aboard, she had been bombed and hit in the engine room. With her engines impossible to stop and her rudder jammed, the ship had begun to circle, a sitting target for more bombs, until two skoots had managed to come alongside and take off some of the troops. The rest had been transferred to a naval sloop which had then taken the crippled ship in tow. But before the night was over, the slow journey came to an end when the *Gracie Fields* filled with water and sank.

Ted felt a wash of sadness when he heard this. That ship was a part of his life; her launching had been a particularly happy family day. He thought of the jaunt they'd had to Woolston, him and Annie and the girls, and their excitement at seeing the famous singer. And she'd made it a real day out for them, laughing and joking as she cracked a bottle of champagne over the bows and then singing her song. It made you want to follow her anywhere, that song, a real good marching song.

And now, only three years later, her ship was on the bottom. But at least she'd gone heroically, serving a grand cause. And that's what we're all doing, he thought, inspired anew. That's what we're here for. And there's no time for moping – that can come later.

All the same, he couldn't help wondering what had happened to the other ships he knew – his own sister ship, the *Fawley*, the *Whippingham* that had so often towered over him at the Harbour Station jetty, and the *Bee*. Were they still steaming back and forth as he was, or had they too been bombed and sunk? And how many of the little ships, or the big ones either, were going to make it home in the end?

Again, he jerked himself back to the present. But he had been almost four days now with little sleep and erratic meals, working on this never-ending task of dragging men aboard out of the water, ferrying them to one of the big ships, returning to shore for the next load . . . And still they came, and still the beaches were crowded, and still the Messerschmitts flew overhead, battling now with British aircraft but still strafing the waiting soldiers and the ships with gunfire, still hurling death at random, for the whole sea was now one vast and unmissable target. And the planes themselves became bombs as they were shot from the sky by naval guns or by RAF Hurricanes. Ted saw one fall on a motor yacht filled with troops and knew that nobody could survive.

The nightmare went on and on. It was as if they had all died and arrived in hell, a hell that nobody could have imagined. It was as if it would never end, as if they would spend eternity in this blood-soaked chaos, this hopeless yet imperative labour, saving lives only to see them smashed a moment later, throwing dead men back into the water like fish useless in the catch . . . Had someone thrown Derek back like that? Or Bob Shaw, or Ben's older brother?

'Look, Skip,' Ben said suddenly. 'It's the old *Whip*.'

Ted glanced up, startled, at the ship they were approaching with their latest load of soldiers. Its familiar white sides loomed above him, streaked with green, and in gold letters on the bow he read the name *Whippingham*. He grinned, feeling absurdly pleased. It was almost like meeting a member of the family. And once again he felt new heart, and the determination to carry on.

But for both the *Ferry King* and the *Whippingham*, Operation Dynamo was over. As they loaded their last men on to the paddle steamer that was surely already vastly overloaded, they were told that all vessels were being recalled. They could collect one last load from the beach, to take back with them, but then they must return to Dover. The German tanks and troops were at the fringes of Dunkirk and no more men could be saved.

'But what'll happen to them?' Ben asked, staring at the beach. There were fewer men waiting there now, and the still burning town looked empty and deserted compared with the past few days, but it was clear that there must still be many left to face the enemy alone.

'They'll have to do what soldiers always have to do in war,' the lieutenant said tersely. 'Fight or surrender. They'll probably be taken prisoner. But some of them will get away, and then they'll either find some other way home or live wild, fighting on their own account. But they're not our worry. Our job's to get ourselves and as many soldiers as possible back without getting bombed.'

Ted took the boat close in to the shore and the last few men scrambled aboard. There was a subdued air about everyone now, for they knew that when they turned their backs on the beach it was for the last time. Perhaps other boats would come to take those waiting out of danger; perhaps not. And it was no use cursing oneself or the enemy or the fate that had decreed it should be so, for

342

this was war, and war was like a machine that, once started, could not be stopped. Or a disease which must run its course until either it or the body it invaded had been vanquished.

Ted stood on the bridge, watching as the other three hauled the bedraggled soldiers aboard. He felt unutterably weary. Their faces passed before his eyes in a blur, without variation. They could have been one man, passing before him over and over again, for at this stage there was no difference between them, no possibility of recognition.

Except . . . As the last man came aboard, he lifted his eyes for a moment and glanced up at Ted, standing before the funnel. His mouth twitched briefly, then stretched in a travesty of a grin. And Ted saw a lock of hair, still dark gold under the grime and the black, dried blood, and knew that here, at last, was Derek.

There was no time for greetings now. Already there was firing in the town, and the Messerschmitts were renewing their attack. Ted reversed the *King* and took her away from the shore. He turned her for the last time and headed for the open sea.

There would be no towing back to Dover. Only the smallest boats were given that luxury. But the *Whippingham* was still in sight, so heavily laden that the sea was almost on top of her paddles, and he set course to follow her. It felt comfortable and right, and as if they were truly heading for home.

'It's not over yet,' Lieutenant Horner said, coming to his side. 'We're likely to be bombarded still, and there may be minefields. But we're on our way back, Ted, and you and your crew can be proud of yourselves.'

Ted shrugged. 'We've done no more than anyone else. It was a job needed doing, and we did it. But I don't mind admitting I'll be glad enough to be home again.' He glanced at the lieutenant. 'Will you take over now, sir? There's someone I want to see.'

He made his way down from the bridge and through the mass of bodies on deck. Some were sitting up, leaning on each other, some lying exhausted at full length. Many were bandaged, though it was clear that their dressings had not been changed for some time. They looked up at him with dull, hollow eyes that stared from haggard faces, and he was sharply reminded of the man who had sold matches outside Woolworths.

343

Derek was leaning against the roof of the engine-room. He looked up at Ted and again stretched his mouth in a grin.

'Hello, Mr Chapman.' The title sounded strange in these circumstances. 'Bet you thought you'd seen the last of me.'

'Derek,' Ted said. He felt almost as thankful as if it had been his own son sitting there, dirty and unshaven, with blood streaking his face and a bandage round one hand. 'Oh God, Derek . . . Our Olive has been almost out of her mind over you.'

The boy smiled. Like all the other men, he looked tired to death, his face thin and lined below the stubble. But the old glint showed briefly in his eyes and there was a challenge in the way he lifted his chin and looked directly at the man who stood over him.

'Tell her not to worry any more,' he said. 'Tell her I'm on my way home. And tell her mum to buy a new hat, because as soon as I get back Livvy and me are getting married.'

And Ted understood that he was not being asked now, as Derek had asked him a few months ago. He was being told. Because this was no longer the boy from up the road, John Harker's son with his smart job as an accountant and his smart red sports car. That boy had grown up and become a man, and that man would not be put off.

'I'll tell her,' he said. 'I'll tell them both.'

And he bent and shook Derek's hand, and knew that his four days at Dunkirk, saving such men for their families, for their sweethearts and their country, had been time well spent.

By the time Olive and Derek were married, on the sixth of July, France had fallen to the Germans and Mussolini had brought Italy into the war. The Channel Islands had been occupied and the coasts of southern and eastern England were ready for invasion, with a hastily erected barricade of barbed wire, scaffolding and concrete blocks to keep off the might of the invaders. Open ground behind the beaches was littered with old cars, buses, even bedsteads that had escaped the search for scrap-iron. It was now illegal to sound motor-horns or to ring the church bells, for these were the signals of invasion.

'A proper home-made war,' Frank called it, but he was on duty most nights now, watching for the planes that were expected

344

hourly. Air raids had begun in the middle of June though so far there had been no damage. But everyone was on edge, waiting for the devastation they knew must come. Hitler had crushed everything in his path. He had taken almost every country in Europe and he had driven back Britain's own army. There could surely be no stopping him now.

'Well, we'll have a good wedding anyway,' Annie said to Jess as they set the final touches to the long trestle-table in the front room. She stood back, looking at the bowls of salad grown by Frank and Ted, the big plates of tinned salmon and cooked ham. Everyone had helped out with bits from their store-cupboards and it looked as good a spread as they'd had at Christmas. 'They deserve it, the two of them. God knows what they're going to have to face when Derek goes away again.'

'And that could be any day. His unit's on the move again. Peggy Shaw heard from Bob this morning.'

Bob Shaw had escaped from Dunkirk too, so the street had rejoiced for both the young men. But Graham was still away and so was Colin. In almost every house in the street now, there was someone to be anxious for and rejoicing always tempered with fear.

And on the second of July had come the news of the sinking of the *Arandora Star* on her way to Canada. She had been carrying fifteen hundred German and Italian internees, one of them Heinrich Brunner.

'Alice looks terrible,' Jess said sadly. 'It's such a shame. Heinrich was a good man.'

'Well, he might have been saved,' Annie said comfortingly. 'They say there were plenty of survivors. And we can't let it spoil our Olive's day.'

And it seemed that nothing, indeed, could spoil this day. Olive looked radiant in a wedding-dress lent to her by a friend who had got married two years earlier. Derek was handsome in his uniform, his hair gold in the sunshine, his injured hand healed. Rose and Betty were bridesmaids, carrying posies made by Molly Atkinson – for which she refused to charge, in gratitude for what Jess had done for her children. And when they all trooped back from the little church at the top of the street the reception turned into a real party, with singing and laughter late into the night.

345

'You'd think the war was over, from the row they're making,' Jess said to Frank as they walked home with Maureen fast asleep in her pram. She had celebrated her first birthday only two days earlier and seemed convinced that the party had been held in her honour. 'I wish it was.'

'So do we all.' Frank sighed. 'But there's a long road to travel before that happens, Jess. And a lot more pain and misery to suffer too. We've got away with it light so far, hereabouts. I reckon we're going to see a lot more before we're very much older.'

They stopped at the door of number 14. The stars were bright in the night sky. Soon, it would be filled with enemy bombers and they would all get a taste of what Ted and Derek and thousands of others had suffered at Dunkirk.

Frank opened the front door and went inside, lifting Maureen's pram over the step and manoeuvring it through the narrow space. But Jess paused a moment longer, still looking up at the stars and thinking over all that had happened since the baby had been born.

And she remembered the words of Winston Churchill, spoken to the nation after Dunkirk.

'We shall go on to the end . . . we shall fight on the beaches, we shall fight on the landing grounds, we shall fight in the streets, we shall fight in the hills; we shall never surrender.'

And again, after the fall of France:

'The Battle of France is over. The Battle of Britain is about to begin.'